SOULS OF MEN

SOULS OF MEN

An Elaine Hope Novel

A. R. Ashworth

NEW YORK

This is a work of fiction. All of the names, characters, organizations, places, and events portrayed in this novel are either products of the author's imagination or used fictitiously. Any resemblance to real or actual events, locales, or persons, living or dead, is entirely coincidental.

Published in the United States by Crooked Lane Books, an imprint of The Quick Brown Fox & Company LLC.

Crooked Lane Books and its logo are trademarks of The Quick Brown Fox & Company LLC.

Library of Congress Catalog-in-Publication data available upon request.

ISBN (hardcover): 978-1-68331-117-1
ISBN (ePub): 978-1-68331-119-5
ISBN (Kindle): 978-1-68331-120-1
ISBN (ePDF): 978-1-68331-121-8

Cover design by Lori Palmer.
Book design by Jennifer Canzone.

Printed in the United States.

www.crookedlanebooks.com

Crooked Lane Books
34 West 27th St., 10th Floor
New York, NY 10001

First Edition: April 2017

10 9 8 7 6 5 4 3 2 1

To Anna, Ryan, and Hilary, my family,
for their encouragement and patience

ONE

The girl's half-naked body sprawled at the edge of the ditch, face-down. Her deathly white skin seemed to glow against the dark mud, a forlorn beacon signaling, "Here I am. Find me." One arm twisted crookedly at her side while the other angled over her head, obscuring her face. If she had been lying on a beach, a passerby might have thought she had died in a shipwreck. But this was East London, and her death had surely not been an accident.

Detective Inspector Elaine Hope stalked the lifeless form, circling in an arc five meters from the corpse, mud squishing under her wellies with each careful step. She took her time, scanning the scene with her large brown eyes. Hadn't anyone been looking out for this child? She couldn't have been more than fifteen or sixteen years old. Elaine imagined the girl ensconced in an upstairs bedroom with three friends, gorging on chocolate and gossiping about boys. What could she have done to deserve this?

She turned to Liz Barker, the young detective constable who hovered just behind. "Just a teenager. Certainly still in school. She should have been with her mates on a Friday night."

A cluster of purple splotches trailed down the girl's back. "See the bruising? Beaten, stomped most likely." She pointed at a thin stream of crimson that had flowed from under the girl's face. "And that. Dr. Kumar will confirm what killed her."

At last Elaine completed her circuit of the corpse and stood straight, stretching to her six-foot height, gazing up and down the disused railway line that extended several hundred meters in both directions. A week of rain had filled the hollows on each side of the tracks with standing water, which appeared to be knee deep in some places. Jettisoned appliances heaved out of the mud. The charred carcass of a burnt-out automobile provided surreal testament to what passed for juvenile fun in this neighborhood.

Farther down, a line of uniformed police picked and poked its way along the abandoned tracks. Elaine recognized the stocky frame and jug ears of DC Jenkins loitering behind the line.

A dead girl, cold rain, and Jenkins—a poor start for a Saturday.

The temperature had dropped several degrees since her arrival, but at least the rain wasn't pounding down in sheets anymore. Elaine pulled her worn, black donkey jacket tighter around her and turned up its wide collar. The ancient jacket was something of a joke among her colleagues, but it spoke to her of the working-class neighborhood in Glasgow where she grew up. The dense woven wool and old-fashioned leather shoulders denied the cold and shed the misty rain. It had never failed to keep her warm and dry. She plunged her hands deep into its huge pockets and assessed the crime scene yet again.

"What a godforsaken cesspit to die in," she muttered. "Why was she out in this bloody cold rain?"

A discreet cough interrupted Liz before she could answer. Elaine looked up to see a group of white-suited forensic technicians gathered at the edge of the water-filled ditch. One carried a collapsible tent while three others were laden with steel stepping plates and large portable lights. They wanted access to the body, but Elaine shook her head. They could wait another few seconds. She raised her eyebrows at Liz, who hesitated at first, then answered with some conviction.

"A couple of possibilities. If she was on the game. Or a boy. Most likely a boy."

"That's what I'm thinking. And I don't think she was killed here." Elaine swept her hand in an arc. "There's no sign of struggle, no footprints. But it rained overnight, so . . . what do you think about that?"

Liz sloshed to the edge of the gray water. "Not deep enough to float to where she is. Maybe he stood in the water and just dumped her." She made a hunching motion as if she were lifting a heavy sack off her shoulder. "It was a he."

"Oh, yes. I'd bet on a strong male. He had to carry her from somewhere." Where was that somewhere?

"Inspector?" The forensic technicians were eager to get started. Elaine couldn't learn any more right now, so she opened her hands to indicate she was finished. The technicians set out the stepping plates around the girl and began unfolding the tent.

She motioned to Liz, and together they waded to the bottom of a steep bank that rose from the mire. The bank was crowned by a grassy ledge and a red brick wall that separated the wasteland from the modest terraced houses on the other side.

Elaine pointed to a labyrinth gate in the wall. "That gate we came through is the closest access point."

The women scrabbled up the bank to the grass-covered ledge and stood by the wall. From there, Elaine could overlook the entire scene. Across the wasteland, the ground rose to a bedraggled wire fence that served as a screen for blown paper and plastic bags. The fence separated the wasteland from what appeared to be a derelict industrial estate. She couldn't see any breaks or holes in it. Halfway between where Elaine stood and the fence was the railroad embankment with the white forensic tent sheltering the girl's body. She was familiar with the setting, if not the exact details. In her career, she had been to many derelict places like this, both in London and in her native Glasgow.

"Go out to the street and get some uniforms organized for a house-to-house," Elaine told Liz. "I'll be there in a minute."

Elaine couldn't help but smile when Liz's face brightened at the new responsibility. The young woman was eager, no doubt.

Liz had no sooner disappeared through the gate in the wall, than the dark bulk of Detective Chief Inspector Marcus Benford emerged, followed by Dr. Kumar, the police pathologist.

"Good morning, Chief. Dr. Kumar." Elaine stuck to protocol. "It's a girl, fifteen or sixteen at most. Beaten. I can't see much of her face, but it looks like she took a lot of damage."

Kumar acknowledged Elaine's comment with a brief nod and continued down the bank into the water. His business did not lie by the wall.

Elaine heard Benford breathing heavily as they watched Kumar struggle through the muck toward the body. She glanced at the older detective. His face seemed to sag. "Here?" he asked.

Elaine shook her head. "Dumped. It's still too dark to see much. The lights will be on in a minute." Under the tent, two white-suited technicians were busy erecting large battery-powered lights.

Benford didn't look at Elaine. "Any idea where from?"

Five years his partner and not even a hello, Elaine thought. *Typical.* She pointed at the gate in the wall. "That's my first guess," she said. "Maybe he carried her through that gate. There's one at the end of each street. He might have come from the industrial estate, through that wire fence, but I can't see a break in it."

"So he came through here, where we're standing," Benford stated.

"I didn't say that. But I don't think he would have come from very far up or downstream. Why walk farther than he had to in this muck? He could drop her anywhere. Come to think of it, why did he carry her at all? He could have just dropped her here, at the top, and she would have rolled down the bank into the water."

Benford again didn't look at her as he spoke. "A dog walker found her, right? Funny how many bodies are found that way."

Elaine didn't think it was funny at all. "It's a wonder anyone walks their dog anymore. We've gotten his statement. Should we go see what Kumar turns up?"

Under the tent, Kumar was ready to turn the girl's body over. Benford started to frame a question, but Kumar cut him off and launched into his lecture.

"No identification. Do young girls carry purses these days? I don't see one about. Perhaps the uniforms will find something. She has a tattoo of a green butterfly on the back of her neck that may help. The photographer took snaps. Okay, let's roll her over."

Kumar and an assistant gently turned the girl over. A uniformed officer hurried away and Elaine heard the sound of retching. Thick smears of blood covered the girl's face and upper body. Below her swollen eyes and crushed cheekbones, a mass of pulverized flesh and broken teeth marked where her mouth once was. As if that were not enough damage, a deep incision had been slashed from her right temple, down her cheek, and all the way to her jawline. Looking lower, her breasts and abdomen were a mass of crimson and purple contusions. Judging from the shape of the bruising, Elaine had been correct. The attacker had stomped the poor girl.

Benford groaned. "Oh, bloody hell." His voice trailed off into a deep sigh, and he wiped his hand across his face. "What can you tell us about the time of death?"

Kumar didn't hesitate. "Given that it's cold and she's lying in water, body temperature may not tell us much. Cold affects lividity and rigor too, but as a guess, I put her death between one and four this morning. I'll know more once I get her back to the lab. It looks like you'll need the tattoo for identification. Do you want my opinion?" From experience, Elaine knew that their answer to that question did not matter.

Kumar continued. "Whoever did this beat her somewhere else and then dumped her here immediately afterward. From the amount of blood under her face, I'm thinking she was still alive when she got here. She was close to death, but she wasn't dead yet. See the pooling? She bled here."

Kumar's observations were always acute, and his opinions were most often proven correct. Elaine turned to Benford. "If there's nothing else, sir, I'll get started with the house-to-house."

She sloshed back to the wall and through the gate. The light was better now than when she had arrived, so she could take stock of the neighborhood. She was walking down a street like so many others, a lower-middle-class London vignette of tarmac and concrete lined with cars and bordered by waist-high hedges. Gates interrupted the hedges at regular intervals, one gate for each terraced house that marched along the sides of the street in orderly procession. Some of the houses were less tidy than others, but none appeared neglected or derelict. At each house, a small front garden was overlooked by a sitting room window on the ground floor and two bedroom windows on the first floor.

A dozen uniformed officers waited expectantly at the end of the street with Liz.

Elaine nodded at Liz and spoke. "We need to house-to-house this street and each street that borders the wall, in both directions. Ask about a slender girl, fifteen or sixteen, average height, shoulder-length dark hair, with a tattoo of a green butterfly on the back of her neck. Did they notice anything late last night or early this morning—lights, people, vans, noises, talking, screams, splashing, you name it. Focus especially on the houses that overlook the wall. Let DC Barker know if any of the residents act suspicious or uncooperative. Or overcooperative. The girl may have lived in one of these houses. Any questions?" There were none, so she nodded to Liz. "Okay, get to it. Sniff for smoke, boys and girls."

Elaine stood for a moment after the officers dispersed. *Give me strength*, she thought. Who gave her the strength, she really didn't care. All murder investigations took an emotional toll, and she could compartmentalize most of them, as did every detective she had ever worked with. But when a young girl met death on her own, it chewed at Elaine. In those cases, she would take the gnawing mystery home with her. She would sit alone at her kitchen table, pondering what-ifs. What if someone had been watching over the poor girl? What if Dad had been watching over Moira and me? What if.

Now what's he doing over there?

Jenkins was standing at the wall, talking to Liz. His team had moved down the tracks, inspecting the embankment and ditch. As Elaine watched, Liz tried to walk past him, but Jenkins shifted to stand immediately in front of her, trapping her against the wall.

Elaine scowled. She had developed a thick skin in her years with the Met and could work professionally with any bog-standard misogynist. Her maturity and tall height discouraged most of the bullies. But Liz was only twenty-four, slightly built, with red hair and blue eyes. She appeared vulnerable, and Jenkins was malevolent. He relied on his shaved head, perpetual three-day stubble, and foul-mouthed aggression to intimidate anyone who he thought was against him. And that included women. For the life of her, Elaine could not understand how he had ever been accepted into the Metropolitan Police Service, much less how he had stayed employed for as long as he had. He'd survived several professional standards enquiries. Sometimes it seemed as if he didn't care if he got sacked.

Jenkins was talking too fast to notice Elaine approaching. She stopped just to the side of the pair.

"Don't believe his lies, Liz. Pure fantasy. Lust and cheap bravado. He's giving you his standard chat-up." She turned to Jenkins. "Isn't that right?"

Jenkins laughed and looked her up and down. "Well, if it isn't Hopeless. I see you're still spending more on your makeup than you do on your clothes. How would you know what I say to women? I've got too much good taste to chat you up."

"And I give thanks for that every day. What has your team found?"

Jenkins sneered at Elaine and lapsed into a sing-song voice. "Ohhh, this and that but nothing much, luv. To me, it looks like the vic levitated to where she is . . ."

Elaine was furious. "Jenkins, on your best day you're a damned waste of space! What the hell is . . ." She caught herself before she completely exploded at him.

Jenkins smirked and kept silent. Liz was frozen in place, but two other officers who had been eavesdropping suddenly found new duties farther along the wall.

After a few breaths, Elaine stepped up to Jenkins, close enough to cause him to tilt his head back to look her in the face. "You're not some gutter-puking yobbo; you're a police detective, and you need to act like it. Another thing. The girl lying over there is not 'the vic,' and this isn't a half-baked crime show. She's a young girl who was murdered and possibly raped and who spent her last moments in pain and terror. Don't you have a sister? Or a mother? Don't talk about her like she's rubbish washed up on a beach. You disgust me. Now go back to your team and get some real answers." Elaine kept her eyes focused on Jenkins. "Liz, if DC Jenkins tries to chat you up again, please let me know immediately so I can personally requisition his balls on a plate."

She turned and strode away. Behind her she heard a muttered "That dyke needs a good fucking." She ignored it. She'd see to it that Jenkins would get what he deserved. Besides, men only ever said that about a woman they feared.

Elaine met Benford at the morgue van and watched the medical team load the girl's body into the van. "Anything new?"

Benford shrugged. "She had an unopened condom packet, a house key, and an Oyster card in a pocket in the waist of her skirt. So she could have come to this area from anywhere in London. Order CCTV recordings from the stations and buses near here, and call in her description."

"Right, sir. If there's nothing else, I'll go back and get the incident room set up and enlist some more noses for us." Elaine phoned in the girl's description on the way to her car.

As she passed under the police boundary tape, Liz fell into step next to her. The young detective looked a bit red-faced. "He wouldn't let me get away. Thanks for stepping in, guv."

Elaine didn't look at Liz, but her voice was stern. "I don't usually give personal advice, but here's a bit of it. You're not in school anymore. Don't be afraid to hand out a few choice words to bastards like him. Stand up for yourself, and you'll feel better at the end of the day. Jenkins is a knuckle-dragger. Let's call him an unbloke—uncouth, unevolved, and unredeemable. Does that cover it?"

They stopped by Elaine's blue BMW. "By the time you're my age, you'll have a whole menagerie of hominids like him in your scrapbook. I like to think of them as the blokes who had better call me 'ma'am' if they know what's good for them."

Elaine considered the young woman standing in front of her. Liz was a bit wide-eyed, but she had a good brain. She'd be fine as long as she stood up for herself.

"Right, then," Elaine said as she opened the door of her car. "When you're done with the house-to-house, meet me back at the nick and we'll find this killer."

TWO

Elaine watched Detective Sergeant Paula Ford chew the end of her pencil as she read the roster list on the desk between them. Paula's tiny build, sharp face, and tenacity reminded Elaine of a willful rat terrier on a mission—darting from place to place, keeping the lower-ranked members of her pack focused on searching for another rat to kill.

Paula shook her head and ran her fingers through her black pixie-cut hair. "Even with Bull and Barker on board, we'll still be looking at a lot of overtime."

"Can't be helped. Budgets are tight. Simon Costello's putting in for sergeant. Ask him to keep an eye on them."

An officer rapped on the door frame. Paula turned and took a slip of paper from him. She scanned it and immediately handed it to Elaine. A woman had dialed 1-0-1 to report a missing teenage girl, and the description she had given matched their victim. Elaine immediately went to Benford's office.

"Sheila Watson, age fifteen." She glanced at her notebook. "Her mother called in the report. She fits the description. Her home is about eight kilometers from where we found her body."

Benford rose and retrieved his coat from its hanger. "Let's take your car. We'll get there quicker."

"Are you sure you can handle my driving this early in your day?"

"I drive like a fat, old grandfather. You drive like a crazed female Jenson Button. Besides, when I drive, you sit and twitch and mutter under your breath."

Elaine smiled at Benford's routine joke. She had to complete the little ritual. "I always thought it was because you outrank me."

"It's the way of the world, Elaine."

Sheila Watson's home sat at the end of a row of dismal, slab-sided terraced houses. The family liaison officer arrived at the same time as Elaine and Benford. Together the three carefully picked their way past a broken gate, a tangled garden hose, and two rusted bicycles.

The woman who opened the door was dressed in a faded housecoat. The crow's feet at the corners of her eyes and the frown lines at her mouth testified to a hard-earned middle age. She had obviously been crying. Elaine noted the apparent relief in her red-rimmed eyes when the detectives displayed their warrant cards.

"Thank God. I thought you'd never get here. I'm Loretta Watson. Please come in." She led them into a small sitting room, where a nicotine-stained three-piece suite seemed to match perfectly with the heavy fug of stale cigarette smoke and fried sausage.

A spark of hope had flickered, which Loretta fanned as she brought out a picture album.

"I have so many pictures of Sheila. I'm sure your officers can use them to find her." She brushed back a loose strand of graying hair and sorted through several photographs.

"This was at her cousin Sophie's wedding last August." She pointed at a dark-haired teenage girl standing outside a marquee in a line with Loretta and several other women. "That's our Sheila. Isn't she lovely? The loveliest girl there. She was so happy for Sophie."

The length of Sheila's hair and her hairline looked right. Her height and overall build appeared to be a close match to the murdered girl as well. Elaine's stomach clenched. The interview now might well turn into a death call, but they needed as much information as they could get to be sure. Elaine avoided looking at

Benford and concentrated as she took out her notebook and listened to Loretta Watson's account.

"She's a good girl. She got more independent after her father left. Started staying out all hours, any night she chose. Her uncle, that's my brother, talked some sense into her and it worked. Now she goes every Friday night to stay with her friend Leah, Leah Robinson."

No father at home, Elaine thought. *Which was better—no father at home or one who couldn't look at you?* But she didn't comment. She asked, "And was she at Leah's last night?"

"Yes. Like I said. Every Friday."

Elaine jotted a note. "And what do you normally do on Friday nights?"

The lock of hair strayed again and fell in Loretta's eyes. "Friday's the night that Al, my boyfriend, comes by, and he and I go out to a film or maybe dancing. Leah's house is just a few blocks away, on Mayford Close, third on the right from the main road. Sheila goes so she doesn't have to be alone. But Laura, that's the mum, said Sheila left there last night and weren't there this morning, and I didn't know what to do, so I called you lot. Have you found her?"

"We need as much information as we can gather. Were you at home last night?"

"Why do you need to know where I was?"

"I'm just considering where she may have gone. She may have stopped by if she had decided to go somewhere with another friend. If you weren't here at home, you would have missed her. Did you and Al go out?"

Again, Loretta brushed the stray lock of hair back to its place behind her ear and gathered herself. "Ummm, no. Last night we decided to stay in."

"So you would know if Sheila came home at any time, right, Mrs. Watson?"

Loretta sniffed and nodded her head. "Yes, I think we would have done. But I didn't hear nothing."

"Could Al have heard? Is he here, Mrs. Watson?"

"No, he left a bit after dawn. He's driving a lorry to Blackburn today."

Elaine made a note to check Al's whereabouts before she continued. "Did Sheila have any boyfriends? Was there a boy she was very fond of or one that perhaps she might have gone to see?"

Loretta looked aside. "I only know of a couple, from the school. She hasn't been going on dates much since she started going to Leah's. Do you think maybe she ran off with a boy?"

"It's something we must check. Another officer will be here later to get names from you. Do you know if she was having any problems at school?"

"No. I haven't heard of any. Her marks were average, and I haven't heard from the headmaster about any trouble."

Elaine nodded and wrote in her notebook. Now for the tough part. "We'll follow up at the school. There's one last question for right now, Mrs. Watson." Elaine leaned forward and spoke more calmly than she had since their arrival. "Does Sheila have any distinguishing marks? Maybe a tattoo, Mrs. Watson?"

"Yes, a little butterfly, right on the back of her neck." She pointed to her own nape. "Right about there."

Elaine tried not to register a reaction. But perhaps she averted her eyes ever so slightly. It might have been a simple tightening of her mouth. Or perhaps Benford gave it away. Elaine did not know, but at that moment Loretta Watson's face sagged.

"How did you know that? You've found her, haven't you! Why didn't you say? She's dead, isn't she? Oh my God, Sheila!" she wailed.

Elaine looked at Benford, who interjected quietly. "I'm sorry to have to do this, but . . ." He held out the close-up photo of the green butterfly etched on white skin, with two strands of wet hair crossed over it. "Is this her tattoo, Mrs. Watson?"

Loretta Watson shrieked and collapsed on the sofa. Benford signaled for the family liaison officer to take charge of her, then formally told Mrs. Watson about finding the body they thought was Sheila's. A few minutes later, the detectives left after mumbling their inadequate condolences.

★ ★ ★

The door at the Robinson house on Mayford Close was opened by a small teenage girl with mousy brown hair, large gray eyes, a bad case of teen acne, and streams of tears running down her cheeks. Before they could identify themselves, a torrent of words poured from her.

"You've come about Sheila, haven't you? Have you found her? Please say you've found her and she's all right. I didn't know she wasn't coming back. I swear I didn't know. She said she would be back before dawn."

A woman who appeared old enough to be Leah's grandmother came to the door and introduced herself. "I'm Laura Robinson, Leah's mother. We're so worried about Sheila. She's such a nice girl whenever she's here. Leah has told us that she went out the window last night, but I can't believe that she would do such a thing."

"I know it's hard. We're trying to understand too," Elaine said softly. She turned to Leah. "I'm sure there's a lot of useful information you can tell us, but right now, we need to find out where Sheila went and how she got there. Did she take a bus, or did someone pick her up in a car?"

"She said she was taking a bus." The girl glanced nervously at her mother. "I went out the window with her like I usually did and watched her to the end of the street."

"What time was that, Leah?"

"It was around ten thirty. Right after my parents went to bed."

Mrs. Robinson gasped. "Usually? Usually, Leah? If we had known . . ."

"I know, Mum. That's why I promised Sheila that I'd never tell. If you knew, then she couldn't go out and have her adventures."

The older woman's voice rose to a panicked shriek. "Adventures? Is that what the two of you called it? Adventures?"

Elaine intervened. "Do you know what adventure she was going to have last night? Was she going to meet someone?"

"She said she was meeting a bloke named Danny. She said he's older, like maybe twenty-five, and really hot. I think maybe he's a footballer. He has a posh car, and he was going to take her clubbing. Do you know what's happened to her?" She wrung her hands.

Leah was rapidly losing her composure, so Elaine spoke gently. "A posh car? Did she mention what it was?" Leah sniffled and shook her head. "Thank you. Just a bit more information, please, Leah. We need to find the bus that Sheila took. Do you know what number it was?"

"I think she . . . she said she had to catch the 432. Oh, God, Mum." Leah choked back a sob and drooped against her mother, who leaned over and kissed her forehead. "I think she went to the stop by the hospital." The tears and sobs finally overcame her, and she sank her face into her mother's shoulder.

"Fine. Thank you, Leah. You've been extremely helpful. Some other detectives will be over in a while to get some more information and write it all down." She looked at Mrs. Robinson. "Will you be at home?"

"Yes, we'll be here all day. I can't imagine going out until we find out what has happened to Sheila. That poor girl."

★ ★ ★

Elaine slowed the car as they passed the bus stop near the hospital. Sure enough, 432 appeared on the posted schedule. Benford called the station. "Call Transport and tell them we need to see the CCTV disc from the bus that was on the 432 route last night and interview the driver. Also, tell the constables who are on house-to-house to ask about a bloke named Danny who drives a sports car. Might be a footballer. And tell Paula to get two DCs over to Leah Robinson's house on Mayford Close and interview the girl and her mother in depth about what happened there last evening." He turned to Elaine. "That should keep everyone busy for a while. Let's talk over a curry."

They sat in a small restaurant around the corner from their offices near Earl's Court. Benford looked gray and sounded tired. "Every year it seems like the dead get younger and the murderers get colder blooded. My health isn't what it was, and there's no way on God's earth I could pass the next fitness test. I'm ready, Elaine, and I want you to be the first on the team to know. I've given my retirement notice, effective in thirty days."

She had wondered recently if Benford's retirement was in the works. There were sighs, random comments he made about how long he'd been a copper. Over the last few months, his hair had turned almost completely gray. Lately he'd seemed bone-tired and was walking more slowly, lumbering. He'd lost the bulldog vitality she had once so admired. Elaine set down her fork and waited.

Benford chewed a bite of his tikka masala. His slow Jamaican accent made him sound even more tired than he looked. "Mandie and I are going back to Jamaica. My cousins grow coffee outside a town, a village really, in the mountains five miles above Port Antonio. There's a little house there that we fell in love with years ago. They say it's ours if we want it. And we do. I want to wake up every morning and have breakfast with Mandie, look out over Frenchman's Cove, and go fishing off Navy Island. We've told them we're coming. It's time."

Elaine looked through the window into the cold rain that had begun to drum down yet again. She had been to Jamaica once with a former boyfriend, and she was able to picture the Blue Mountains, where the smooth, world-famous coffee was grown. London in winter was no competition. Even if she had to sleep in a hut and live on ackee and grilled goat, with only Red Stripe beer to drink, she'd retire there gladly.

"It sounds wonderful, sir. Will you have a spare room? I don't eat much."

"Well, you won't fit in our bags, so you'll have to get there on your own. Besides, you'll be a DCI soon, just in time to pick up where I leave off."

"That's not official. I think I have a good shot at it, but . . ."

"Don't worry. You impressed them at the interviews, and in a few weeks, I'll be a hemisphere away. Bygones can be bygones once I've left. DCI is in the bag, Elaine. In the bag."

Benford was quiet for a moment. With a shake of his head, he returned to the present. "Right, then. I'm not done yet. I'm getting this result before I leave."

Elaine's mobile rang as they walked to the car. The CCTV disc and the bus driver were on the way to the station.

THREE

Jitendra Singh's face displayed a full beard and a large mustache, all topped by a white turban. He sat at the table in the interview room, looking puzzled and holding out his hands, palms up, to the two detectives, his dark, thin fingers spread in a quizzical gesture. "Why have you called me here? I am a simple bus driver. I have done nothing wrong."

Elaine spoke in a calm voice. "Please don't be alarmed, Mr. Singh. Thank you for coming to speak with us. We need information about someone who may have been on your bus last night." She arranged her notebook and settled in her chair. "Do you remember a girl boarding your bus around eleven at the stop near Saint Stephen's Hospital?"

"Ah. You need my help." Mr. Singh visibly composed himself, placing his hands in his lap and closing his eyes for a few moments. "The hospital stop. That would be stop D. Yes, there was a girl. A teenager about my daughter's age. She had on a yellow raincoat made of plastic. It looked like she was wearing a party dress under it. There was something else . . . ah, yes. I thought it was odd that she had on blue trainers, the kind that runners wear. And she had a backpack. She had a bin bag to keep the rain off, and she shook it to dry and it sprayed me with water drops. I almost asked her to stop, but there was no point."

Elaine's face was a model of friendly interest. "Do you recall if anyone else got on at that stop?"

"Of course I do. A man in a hoodie got on ahead of her. He is a regular, and he always sits at the back of the bus. He is tall, not two meters, but taller than you, and he has long hair, dark brown, much the same color as yours." He nodded toward Elaine before continuing.

"I think he works at the hospital. It was a very rainy night with not many passengers, so I remember most of it very well." Singh sat forward, as if he sensed the next question.

"Why do you think he works at the hospital?"

"Because several nights I have seen him running to the stop from that direction. I have to wait a moment so he can catch the bus." Singh beat them to the next question. "Like I said, he rides my bus often, at least twice a week, sometimes more. It must be for over a year now." His eyes narrowed shrewdly. "He's American. I think he is from Texas."

Elaine looked at Benford, and having no other choice, she took the bait. "Why do you think that, Mr. Singh?"

"Because when he greets me, he says 'howdy' instead of 'hello.'" Again Singh leaned forward.

"Did he seem to be paying any special attention to the girl? Talking with her, maybe?"

"No, he was quiet. He sat in the back of the bus."

"And do you recall where the girl got off?"

He sat back and smiled, triumphant. "Most certainly I do. She got off at stop S on the high street. The man from the hospital did too, right after her. That is funny, though. He usually gets off at stop T." Singh hesitated again. "The answer to your next question is yes. They both walked south on the high street. Which is the opposite direction from stop T." He beamed. "That is helpful?"

"Yes, thank you. We have a recording we would like you to watch." Elaine pressed a button on the DVD player. "What time do you arrive at stop D?"

"Approximately fourteen minutes after eleven—23:14."

"Thank you, Mr. Singh." Elaine forwarded the video to 23:13. In the recording, they saw a man in a hoodie board the bus and take a seat behind a young couple. A split second later, Sheila boarded and moved to the front, to the left of the camera. The time stamp on the screen said 23:14.

Elaine whispered, "Please. Pull back the hood." When Hoodie Bloke finally pulled it back, his face was mostly hidden by the hijab of the woman in the seat in front of him.

"Mr. Singh, what time do you reach stop S?"

"At about 11:29."

Elaine forwarded the video. At 23:29, they saw Sheila stand and bound off the bus as soon as the doors opened. Hoodie Bloke stood and pulled up his hood. As he got off, he looked straight into the camera.

"Got you, dammit!" Benford slapped his hand on the table. "Now who are you?"

Mr. Singh beamed again, blessing Elaine and Benford with his proud, broad grin.

The rich and sexy Danny could wait until tomorrow, Elaine thought. Right now, she wanted to find Hoodie Bloke. After closing the interview with Mr. Singh, she and Benford returned to the incident room. One of the technical boffins printed screen grabs of Hoodie Bloke's face from the bus CCTV. Elaine kept two.

By this time, it was dark outside. She retrieved her car keys from her pocket. "I suppose you'll want me to drive," she said to Benford.

★ ★ ★

The Accident and Emergency entrance of Saint Stephen's Hospital blazed with white fluorescent light. Elaine parked in a nearby space and verified that she had the printed pictures from the CCTV.

She and Benford struck gold at once. The nurse at the admitting desk spoke before they could identify themselves. "Hello, detectives. Welcome to our little paradise. Yes, I can spot you coppers before you're through the door. What are you selling tonight? Road accident with a whisky chaser? A juicy little murder on toast? What is it?"

Elaine pushed the photo across the counter toward the nurse. "Do you know this man?"

The nurse gave Elaine a tired look, as if to say she didn't need the interruption. "Not even a smile, eh? I swear you wouldn't last long in A&E. Let's see, then." Her eyebrows rose when she picked up the photo. "Now what would you be wanting with him?"

"You know him. Who is he?"

"We all know him. That's Dr. Willend, the surgeon. W-I-L-L-E-N-D. But most of the nurses call him Dr. Hunka-Hunka." Seeing Elaine's steady look, she continued. "He's a senior consultant here."

Another nurse in surgical scrubs walked to the desk and took the photo. "That's Peter. He was on duty last night, but he won't be back until Monday."

Elaine took out her notebook and flipped it to the next blank page. "Do you know where he lives?"

"Somewhere up by Crouch End or maybe Highgate. In that direction, anyway. I've heard he shares a house with his sister. I've never been there. I don't think anyone here has. He's very private. Keeps to himself, mostly."

"What does he do here?"

"He does what a consultant does—teaches and advises junior medical staff, helps set policy, provides emergency care. He has regular shifts here in A&E, but he doesn't socialize much."

Elaine scribbled in her notebook. "A bit of a loner, would you say?"

The nurse shrugged. "He's moody, I guess. Some of us . . . some of the nurses have tried him on, but he's never taken anyone up on their offer. He's all right to work with. He doesn't look down on us nurses, if you know what I mean. Just isn't interested in anything after hours."

"I think I know what you're saying. I've heard he's a Yank."

"He's from Texas. He was a surgeon in the American military. In Iraq. They say he got wounded there."

Elaine looked up from her notebook. "We need to speak with him. How can we find his address?"

"Well, we wouldn't have it here. The staffing office is closed for the weekend. You could check back Monday."

"Perhaps we'll do that. Thanks . . ."

"Sally. Sally Springfield."

Elaine handed Sally and the other nurse her card. "If you see Dr. Willend, will you please ask him to get in touch with me?"

★ ★ ★

Given his profession, Elaine doubted that Peter Willend was going anywhere. But just in case, when she was back at the station, she instructed her team to send notifications to airport, rail, and ferry passport control offices to hold his passport and prevent him from leaving the country.

She then called the team's researcher, DC Evan Cromarty. "I need the address of Peter Willend, surgeon, employed at Saint Stephen's Hospital. American, lives in London."

She knew that was all the impetus Cromarty needed. He was one of those invaluable people who got things done a step at a time—meticulous with details, full of quiet insight. Elaine had the impression that he was a man who measured each day by its small victories.

Cromarty would find Willend, and she and Benford would have a place to go in the morning. As she switched off the light on her desk, she realized she didn't know what she had to eat at home. Probably nothing. That meant she had to stop to pick up supper. She didn't know if her stomach could handle another curry.

★ ★ ★

A dog walker found a body. How trite is that?

Liz Barker laid her head back on her pillow and closed her eyes. It had been her first day of her first murder. She'd left her warm bed and cozy flat before dawn to drive through dark, wet streets toward

God knew what. All the way, she'd gripped the wheel with all her strength to keep her hands from shaking.

It hadn't stopped her stomach from clenching. Halfway there, she'd felt bile rising so fast she didn't think there was time to stop, open the car door, and retch into the gutter. She'd made it though, just barely—no mess in the car or on her clothes for DI Hope to smell, thank God. A couple of peppermints and she was right as rain.

Hope had pulled up right after Liz arrived, the blue BMW skidding to a stop next to Liz's dented white Astra. Her first words to Liz had been "Rotten morning, Barker. Let's see what we have." Hope had pulled on her wellies over her blue jeans, then felt around in the huge pockets of that ridiculous donkey jacket. Once she'd verified that whatever it was she was looking for was there, she'd looked at Liz.

"Got everything, Barker?" She then set a pace for the gate in the wall, so fast that Liz had a hard time keeping up. All the way to the gate, Liz had wondered if she had left something back at her flat.

As they circled the corpse, Liz had seen the wheels turning behind the DI's huge brown eyes and had listened to her soft, deep voice describing, questioning, and explaining. Hope hadn't seemed to mind the cold or the fact that rain had plastered her dark hair to her forehead. Liz had felt proud when Hope agreed with her hypothesis on why there were no footprints around the body.

But Liz had felt absolutely tiny and wretched when Hope had rescued her from that damned jackass! Why couldn't she have handled Jenkins better? What must Hope think of her now, despite the pep talk?

Liz couldn't let herself be bullied again. Success favors the bold and all that. She also knew she wouldn't look bold if she yawned during the morning status meeting. She turned out the lamp next to her bed and closed her eyes.

FOUR

Elaine was burrowed deeply in the warmth of her duvet when her mobile rattled. Without peeking, she extended her arm and patted for the phone on the cluttered nightstand, toppling a cup and sending a rivulet of thick, cold cocoa streaming across the cover of her current novel. *Crap.* She blinked and squinted at the phone. *Crap again. It's seven bleeding AM on Sunday morning! Couldn't they have waited another hour?* She listened to the duty sergeant's voice with her eyes closed, mumbling her responses. Cromarty had found Willend's address. "Yes . . . Does Benford know? . . . Uh-huh, right . . . Text me the address, yeah text me, Sergeant, because no, I do not have a pen handy . . . Yes, I'll collect Benford once he's ready." She groaned silently to herself as she ended the call. *Testy bastard.*

She looked down at Scratch the cat, who was draped over her leg and staring at her with typical feline annoyance.

"No need to stare at me like that, boy-o. I can't help the phone calls. And have I ever not fed you?" She lay back on the pillow, staring at the ceiling, willing her eyes open and her mind awake.

At least Scratch's displeasure was easier to deal with than a man's would have been. Not that she'd had to think about that for some time. It would be two years—give or take a week—at two o'clock on a Sunday morning, when Alan Number Two had appeared at her door drunk, wounded, and blustering because she hadn't been home for thirty-six hours. Before they got together, she had warned him about her job's intrusive, unreasonable demands. She had related how exhaustion and constant stress triggered emotional outbursts or drove her to seek some kind of emotional catharsis through frantic sex. One way or the other, she exhausted herself.

Telling Alan about the realities of her life hadn't made any more difference to him than it had to Alan Number One. She had given each a Hobson's choice: endure the solitude and her emotional fluctuations or there's no hope, lads. They had liked the sex part, at first, before they had realized that despite her attentions in the bedroom, her priorities lay elsewhere. She had not kicked any of them out. Each had eventually chosen to leave her.

She laughed to herself. They wouldn't stay even for the sex; she wasn't *that* good at it. Most likely there would be another man in her life, someday. There hadn't been many men over the years; her trail of broken hearts wasn't long. She was open to romance; she wanted warmth and companionship. But next time, she also wanted something that would last.

How many men in this world wanted to spend their lives with a gangly, six-foot-tall female detective? Not bloody many.

Enough of the daydreaming. Elaine shifted her leg to dislodge Scratch, rolled out of bed, and slouched to the bathroom. Her morning routine didn't take long. She slid through a quick shower and into some jeans, a heavy shirt, and a woolly jersey; ran a comb through her thick chocolate-brown hair; and considered applying some makeup. No, it's a murder investigation. Maybe there would be time for that later or perhaps not. She didn't care if anyone she met today minded whether she had on makeup. They could take it or leave it.

Once in the kitchen, she dolloped some food into Scratch's bowl and topped up his water. A glance at the clock told her she was running a bit late, but Benford hadn't called yet, so she dropped two slices of bread into the toaster, filled the electric kettle, and spooned instant coffee into a large travel mug. She was halfway through a second piece of buttered toast when her mobile rattled and the reggae lilt of Jimmy Cliff's "The Harder They Come" told her Benford was finally texting his usual one-word message: "Ready."

She refilled her coffee mug and grabbed her worn gray-and-black donkey jacket as she headed out the door. It may have been shapeless and ugly, but it was warm and waterproof. People could take or leave the donkey jacket along with the makeup. On her way down the stairs, she patted each of the jacket's capacious zip pockets. Her notebook and two pens were in their usual places in the left pocket. In the right pocket, she felt the rectangle of her wallet and the flat square of her warrant card. The old coat could carry everything she needed to meet a murderer.

⋆ ⋆ ⋆

The drizzle had ended, but the previous week's damp, chilling gloom remained. Standing on the pavement with Benford, Elaine took stock of the house in front of them. It was situated in an upscale enclave of large and obviously expensive Edwardian-era detached homes. While its architecture gave a nod to its surroundings, the Willend house was evidently newer than its neighbors. The facade was dominated by a huge three-part bay window, the arc of which must have enclosed an area larger than a standard bedroom. Warm yellow light illuminated the home's interior and shone out through the window. A straight drive ended in a portico at the side of the house. The sound of a piano filtered out to where they stood.

Benford asked, "Is that music?"

Elaine stifled a laugh. Benford was utterly tone deaf. "'I Get a Kick Out of You.' Cole Porter."

"Ah. To me, it might as well be Coal Bucket. Mandie had the girls take music lessons, violin and piano. Nothing but screeching and banging, if you ask me." He looked sidelong at her. "Which you wouldn't, of course."

Elaine didn't turn her head. "I've learned never to question the guv's taste in music, sir."

"And that's exactly as it should be."

As they walked toward the house, their view through the large window revealed a man with a longish mop of dark hair playing a piano.

Benford turned his head to Elaine. "Can you tell if he's any good?"

She listened a moment. The man's fingers were having just a little trouble keeping up with the notes. "Enthusiastic is the word I would use."

The chords of the piano were joined by an even more enthusiastic amateur tenor voice. "Some may fly high on cocay-ee-ayne. I'm sure that if I took even one sniff, it would bore me terrifically tooooo."

Elaine pressed a backlit button on the right side of the door and chimes rang.

"But I get a kick out of yoo-ooo." With a final flourish, the music stopped. A moment later, the man's face appeared briefly at the side window, the lock turned, and the face reappeared around the edge of the partially open door. "Can I help you?"

He was Hoodie Bloke. Both detectives held out their warrant cards. Benford spoke in his gentle Jamaican accent. "I'm Detective Chief Inspector Benford. This is Detective Inspector Hope. May we have a word, Dr. Willend?"

The man's eyes indicated brief surprise. He barely glanced at their identification but spent a few moments assessing his visitors.

"Sure, come in." He swung the door open and led the way toward two large gray leather chairs flanking an ebony-and-glass table. A similar table separated the chairs from a matching leather sofa.

Elaine looked around. The interior of the house was stylish, but not what she would have called flashy or trendy. The light wood floors were covered with rugs, geometrically patterned in deep blues and greens. The gray leather furniture wasn't new but was well kept. It appeared that whoever furnished the place some years ago liked durable leather and clean lines, knew which pieces they needed, and bought quality. Overall the appearance was modern, inviting, and comfortable. She rather liked it. The sole cluttered area was the large window bay at the front of the house, which was nearly filled with a small grand piano, an electronic keyboard, two guitars and the associated amplifiers, loudspeakers, and cables. The top surface of the piano sprouted a forest of framed photographs and trophies. *Clean, organized, but not OCD*, she thought.

"I'd introduce myself, but it seems you already know my name. Would you care for tea? Coffee?" Willend's accent was American, with soft Western vowels.

Benford spoke. "Coffee sounds nice. Thank you."

Willend indicated the chairs. "Please make yourselves comfortable. I'll only be a few minutes."

Benford followed Willend into the kitchen. Elaine ignored the invitation to sit. Instead, she stood quietly near the piano, ingesting Willend's every move. He appeared to be about her age and height—a couple of years past forty and an inch or two over six feet. A shock of shoulder-length dark hair topped deep-set blue eyes and a clean-shaven face. He was dressed in a tight-fitting long-sleeve T-shirt, its front silk-screened with "Hanwell Harriers" above a pair of oddly shaped oars. The shirt accented his broad, athletic shoulders and back. Below the shirt, loose-fitting sweat pants hung from his hips. When he walked across the room, he moved with the balanced grace of an athlete. Willend was attractive. Any woman, young or old, would gravitate to this man.

Elaine's face tensed, as if the skin were pulling back, baring her teeth. She felt as if she were up on her toes, ready to spring. Perhaps she was recalling Sheila.

She inspected her surroundings, trying to get an idea of who this Dr. Peter Willend was. The ground floor of the house was open and full of natural light, even on such a gray day. While standing in the large bay window enclosure, Elaine could see that the sitting room extended past the entry door on her left to a double archway that revealed a dining area. Beyond the dining area, in the large modern kitchen, she could see Willend fussing over coffee preparations while Benford watched.

On her right, an open-tread stairway with a stainless-steel railing ascended to a landing that overlooked the sitting room where she stood. Above her, the ceiling peaked some twenty feet or so above her head. Cream-colored beams, extending from each side wall, framed juxtaposed skylights at the peak.

From where she stood, she could see two motion sensors attached to the beams. There were also vibration sensors on the glass of each skylight and window pane, agreeing with the two alarm control panels she had noticed near the front door. She understood the need for an alarm system in a house like this, but having two systems was quite a lot of security.

Elaine turned and began examining the photographs that crowded the top of the piano. The photos were all of people. A younger Willend and a woman with blazing copper hair flanked a grinning, gap-toothed young girl dressed in a ladybug costume. A tall, raven-haired woman robed in a full-length academic gown, colorful hood, and scholar's mortarboard posed formally in front of a tall limestone building. Over the woman's shoulder, Elaine could make out an inscription on the building: "Ye Shall Know the Truth . . ." *And who decides what that is?* Elaine thought.

A variety of snapshots surrounded the larger photos. The raven-haired woman and Willend cheek-to-cheek with an older woman between them, clearly taken in a pub. Next to it, Willend and another man flanked a short dark-skinned woman, all of them dressed in military camouflage, standing outside a dismal barrack-looking building.

In another, a running athlete in a white helmet held a stick. Elaine could make out "-EXAS" blazoned in orange letters on the athlete's jersey. The silhouette of a cow's head with huge horns adorned the side of the helmet. The athlete's face was obscured by shadow and the helmet's heavy wire frame, so she could only presume this was Willend again.

But the photo that held her attention was one of Willend standing on a dais, clad in red-white-and-blue boxer trunks, gloved hands held high above him as if in triumph. Seated on the step in front of him was the copper-haired woman, dressed in a toga. Her arms were raised toward him as if in adulation, one hand holding a drink glass.

She snorted. *Some people have a vanity wall*, she thought. *This bloke has a vanity piano. Is he a boxer?*

"Rocky and his Acolyte." Elaine whipped her head around to see Willend standing a few feet from her, holding out a cup of black coffee. "A Halloween party. Fancy dress, as you say over here. It was impossible to hold a drink with those gloves. Diana refused to wear a sleazy bikini like the women at boxing matches, so the costumes didn't make much sense as an integrated theme."

He handed her the cup of coffee. "I'll let you adulterate it yourself. Sugar and cream are on the table."

She looked at his hand as she took the cup. No bruising, but if he owned some rubber gloves, he could have avoided harm. He was a surgeon, and he would have taken precautions. Time to swing into action. "Black's fine." She nodded at Willend's shirt. "Odd name for a rowing club. I would have thought haddock or maybe herring."

Willend looked down at his shirt and hmmphed in amusement. "Halibut would work too, if we were a rowing club. Those aren't oars; they're called crosses. We're a lacrosse team." He turned away and took a seat on the gray leather sofa, watching as Benford dropped his usual three lumps of sugar into the coffee. "How can I help you?"

Elaine stood by the piano with her back to the light that filtered in through the large bay windows. She retrieved her notebook from her bag and looked at Willend. "Can you please relate to us your movements this past Friday night?"

Willend took a moment as he studied her. "I was at work most of Friday evening. I got home by midnight, I think. I didn't go out after that."

Elaine's voice was flat. "Be more specific, Dr. Willend." She kept her face expressionless while she looked at him. "If you don't mind."

Willend raised his eyebrows. "Okay. I got off duty at Saint Stephen's Hospital just after eleven. I changed into my street clothes, went outside, and walked to the bus shelter. The bus stopped a few minutes later and I got on. I got off on the high street and walked to Khoury's store to pick up some dinner. While I was there, I talked to Hassan. I was there for about ten or fifteen minutes, then I walked home. That usually takes about fifteen minutes. I can't be more specific. I'm not obsessive about checking the time. Besides, I wasn't aware anyone would care."

"That was a cold rain to walk home in."

"You can't control the weather."

"Do you like keeping things under control, Dr. Willend? Women, for example?"

Elaine knew from his reaction that she had hit a mark.

"Where did that come from? Of course not! I mean, situations, yes. People, no."

"I wonder how you normally control"—she nodded at the photos—"a situation. An athlete. Competitive. A soldier. Accustomed to violence. A surgeon. God complex. Seems to me you're the kind of man who likes to impose his will on others. You're used to getting your way."

Willend's voice remained steady. "Hold on, now. You don't know me well enough to start psychoanalyzing me."

Elaine's mobile rang and she turned away to answer it. Benford continued. "Can anyone confirm the time you got home?"

"I share the house with my sister, Kate. She's abroad, so unless one of the neighbors noticed, no."

Elaine grunted "Thanks" into her phone and muttered something in Benford's ear. He nodded and turned back to Willend. "May I ask what kind of car you own? What color?"

"A black MINI Cooper Clubman."

"Do you often ride the bus?" Elaine asked.

"Yes, I do."

"One might think that a respected surgical consultant at a major teaching hospital would prefer to drive to work."

Willend's mouth curled. "One might not like to drive in London traffic. One might think the bus is more convenient than driving because it gives one a chance to think."

Benford shifted his bulk in the chair and slowly sipped his coffee. When he had finished, he asked, "Where are you from, Dr. Willend?"

"I'm originally from Texas."

"What brought you to London?"

"I was tired of hot, dry places."

Benford tilted his head. "Come now. It was a simple question."

"I moved here seven years ago to be with my sister and mother. My mother is a British subject. My parents met when my father was stationed here with the US Army."

Benford continued to probe. "That's a common story—and a rather unfortunate one, in my mind. Do you have dual citizenship?"

"Yes. Mom insisted."

"Mom. So you grew up there. You don't have what I would call a Texas accent."

"We never say 'Mum' in Texas. Yes, I grew up there. And I have a normal Texas accent, not the exaggerated drawl you hear on TV. Or that you heard from Dubya."

"You're from Texas and you mock the junior Bush?"

Willend smirked. His voice took on an exaggerated twang. "Y'all think they was Texans? Them Bushes was a herd a carpetbaggin' Yanks, hankerin' after our oil. Dubya just liked playin' at bein' a big, bad Texan. Shoulda run 'em clear back to Connecticut afore they bred."

Benford chuckled. "They say all you Texans are tough. Frontier mentality and all that."

Willend's voice reverted to normal. "It depends on what you mean by 'tough.' Many of us are. Nothing wrong with that as long as a person separates myth from reality. Times have changed. We even do heart transplants and build computers in Texas, believe it or not."

"Do you know what this is about, Dr. Willend?"

"No, I don't. But I bet you'll be telling me that it's something serious any minute now."

"Why would you think that?"

"It's obvious." He turned his head toward Elaine. "You and the lovely inspector wouldn't show up on my doorstep on a Sunday morning simply to nose around and enquire about my heritage."

Interesting, Elaine thought. *Curious, not defensive.*

"Good point. My wife cooks an excellent Sunday roast, which I will miss because of you. And Inspector Hope is one of the best detectives I've ever worked with. She's very good with liars. Tenacious. She could suss out liars for England." He leaned forward, his eyes fixed on Willend's face. "Saturday morning a teenage girl was found murdered. A small dark-colored car was seen in the area shortly before her body was discovered."

Willend leaned back in his chair in surprise. After a moment, he looked at the ceiling and exhaled tiredly. It was a few seconds before he spoke. "I'm so sorry to hear that. I didn't know. I wouldn't have been so flippant."

"I wonder." Elaine folded her notebook and replaced it in her handbag before continuing. "Would you mind coming down to the station, Doctor? I think we should continue our discussion there."

"I don't understand why you're interested in me." Willend looked wary now. "Am I under caution?"

"No, we're merely asking for your assistance. We would like you to view a CCTV video. We believe you may have seen something related to a crime. For now, you can agree to assist us or not."

FIVE

Elaine watched Willend through the observation window of the interview room. He sat quietly, his hands in front of him on the table, fingers interlocked, eyes closed. He appeared to be concentrating on his breathing. *Meditating,* she thought. *Calming himself.* Maybe he needed to think and rehearse. He had had the opportunity to kill Sheila. He had been a soldier, had seen death—maybe he was a murderer. Her gut said no. But he was still a suspect, and Benford was still her boss.

She snapped out of her thoughts when Benford, along with their superior, Detective Chief Superintendent Alec Cranwell, walked in. Cranwell was speaking in a dry voice. "You and Hope think this could be the man, do you? I take it you caught him on camera." They ignored Elaine.

Benford nodded. "On the bus, but I have a feeling we'll get more from him . . . maybe enough to take it to the Crown Prosecutor. I know this kind of bloke. He'll be nonchalant early on. Cheeky. But when we turn the screws, he'll crack. Nothing much gets past Elaine. She gets into their heads."

"Perhaps she'll do so this time." Cranwell finally acknowledged Elaine. "What do you have, Hope?"

"Hello, sir." *Keep your opinions to yourself for now, Lainie.* She looked at the autopsy report in her hand. "Whoever beat Sheila knew what he was doing. Kumar is certain, about two hundred percent, that

Sheila's attacker was male. It would require too much power and upper-body strength for a woman to inflict such precise damage. The guy is a boxer or has had martial arts training. It appears the killer didn't use any blunt weapon other than his fists. He placed the blows to cause maximum pain and damage and pounded her repeatedly to the same places, mainly the ribs, liver, and spleen. From the blood and bruising patterns, Kumar is certain he beat her torso first, then her face. Nearly every bone in her face and jaw was shattered, most of her teeth were broken, and she was bleeding in her brain. Kumar thinks the back of her head came into contact with something hard and flat, like a concrete wall, so she has injuries to the rear of her skull too. In her hair, he found some flakes of what he thinks are paint."

"I thought he'd stomped her to death."

"He stomped her several times, once she was down."

"What about the laceration to her face?"

"The slash came last. A large heavy-bladed weapon, perhaps a hunting or commando knife. Sharp, like a Fairbairn. He only cut her with it. He didn't stab her. It took her about an hour to die, bleeding to death internally from her spleen and liver. Kumar said death was inevitable unless she had gotten heroic medical care. He'll try to get DNA results from scrapings off the contusions where she was beaten, but not much hope there."

"Was she raped?"

"That's interesting. There were no signs of rape, thank God. She wasn't a virgin, but there was no sign of recent sex that Kumar could find. We fast-tracked the toxicology, and he got reports back as we talked. Blood alcohol indicates she was drunk, about .12. Tox shows a high level of Xanax and elevated GHB. No telling how high the GHB peaked . . ."

Cranwell looked confused. "I've heard of Xanax. But GHB? Refresh me on that one."

"It's a date-rape drug." She consulted the report. "Gamma-hydroxybutyric acid. The trade name is Xyrem. Doctors use it to treat narcolepsy and alcoholism. Xyrem has a similar effect to Rohypnol.

It occurs naturally in the body, and the concentration in the blood rises for a while after death. But the high level the lab found is indicative of someone drugging her defenseless. So he did that, but he didn't rape her. He drugged her, beat her, and stomped her to death."

Benford was musing. "And afterward he calmly carried her body to the waste area and dumped her."

Elaine continued. "I don't think he cared whether she lived or died. Just a feeling. She was alive when he left her there."

"She was so drugged, she probably wouldn't have remembered much about the attacker, if anything."

"Probably not, but why would he take that chance? Wouldn't he make sure she was dead? And what was the motive? We've ruled out rape, and she had little or no money, so robbery wasn't a motive. There's no indication that she was on the game. I think it's the punishment he did it for, like she was a punching bag in a boxing gym. Or rage, perhaps. I wonder if he suspended her from something while he was hitting her."

"Maybe he had an accomplice?" Cranwell suggested.

"Maybe. Or ropes under her arms or around her wrists, something like that. She was so drugged, something had to hold her up while he hit her. There's no indication of any restraints in Kumar's report, but I'll call and double check."

"Anything else before we go in?" Benford asked.

"Well, yes, sir. While we were at Willend's house, I asked Paula to send someone to check out the Khoury's store. She sent Simon and Liz Barker. They called back a few minutes ago. The store has been closed since last Thursday. The sign in the window says that 'Sam and Leyla will return on Wednesday next.' We need to nail down Willend on that. And request his criminal and military records from our FBI friends at the American Embassy."

Cranwell asked, "So what do you think, Marcus?"

"I'm confident he's our killer. The evidence is circumstantial so far, but it all adds up. The timeline fits. He was on the same bus and got off at the same place. He lied about stopping at the shop. He drives a small dark car. He followed her when they got off the bus. He was the last person to see her alive. Too much for coincidence."

"You sound quite confident. You're sure?"

Benford nodded. "I think he's a good actor. We'll confront him with the Khoury's store being closed and he'll start to waffle and adjust his timeline. He'll crack."

"Elaine, what do you think?"

"Well, with all due respect to the chief, I'm not sure. It's a gut feeling, mostly. He was calm when we first arrived at his house, and he only got ruffled once, when I got personal with him. I watched him throughout, and I never saw any indication that he was hiding anything. He wasn't defensive, even when he got cheeky."

Benford snorted. "Good actor."

Elaine continued. "Could be. From the photos on his piano, he doesn't strike me as a man who dehumanizes women. Women are a big part of his family life. Besides, he's a surgeon. Why would he risk damaging his hands by beating someone?"

Cranwell glanced through the window. Willend's eyes were closed. "Women are a big part of many men's lives, but sometimes they murder them. You said yourself, it's mostly a gut feeling. Women's intuition can be wrong." He continued to stare through the window at Willend. "He's probably stewed long enough, so stay sharp and get to it. He's our only suspect so far."

"Yes, sir," both Benford and Elaine chimed simultaneously.

Once the detectives were seated at the interview table, Elaine inserted a DVD into the recorder and pressed a button.

"Sunday, 27 January, 12:57 PM. Those present are DCI Benford, DS Hope, and Dr. Peter Willend. Dr. Willend, we are going to play a CCTV recording for you. This recording was made on the 432 bus last Friday night."

She slid a disc into a small DVD player and watched Willend closely as he gazed at the fuzzy black-and-white images from the CCTV recording. He registered no reaction, except for focusing on the sections showing pictures of Sheila.

"Why did you not mention this girl to us before, Dr. Willend?" It was Benford.

Willend hesitated only for a moment. "Because you didn't ask me. You asked what I did, not about who else was on the bus."

"Please tell us everything that happened, from the time you left work until you got home. Try not to leave anything out this time."

Willend started his account again, beginning with the hospital. Elaine listened and watched him intently. When he arrived at the bus stop, she asked, "Was the girl already there when you got to the bus stop?" They had no CCTV showing what happened there.

"You don't have that on video?"

"Please answer the question. Was the girl already there when you got to the bus stop?"

"No. She ran up about a minute later." He hesitated. "From across the road."

"Did you speak with her?" Elaine asked.

Willend shook his head. "No. Why would I? I had no reason."

"Oh, come now. A nice-looking young girl sits next to you at the bus stop and you don't chat her up? Even to remark about the weather?"

"She didn't sit next to me. She stood off to the side."

"So you were sitting under the shelter, and she was standing in the cold rain. And you didn't try to communicate with her?"

"Yes. No. I mean, yes, she stood in the rain. And I did motion to her to move under the shelter."

"And did she?"

"She didn't. Perhaps she was being cautious."

Elaine made show of writing a note. "Really. Why would that be?"

"Hell, I don't know. I'm not a young girl. Maybe it's an urban survival skill?"

That got a bit of a rise out of him, she thought. *But not much.* She studied her notebook and spoke without looking up. "You said she ran up to the stop. Did she appear frightened?"

Willend hesitated. Elaine looked up at him with raised eyebrows.

He continued. "No, she was holding a bin bag over her head and running through the rain. She ran across the street. Nearly got killed."

"How is that?" Elaine asked as she wrote in her notebook.

"She ran between some cars. They had to slam on their brakes and swerve to miss her. All the drivers were honking."

Elaine finished the note she was making and held her notebook so Benford could see it. She pointed to a spot on the page, then replaced the notebook on the table, folded her arms, and stared at Willend.

Benford continued the questioning. "Please continue with your statement." When Willend reached the point at which he exited the bus, Benford spoke again. "Which direction did she take when the two of you got off the bus?"

"She went to the left. That would be south, or maybe southeast."

"And which direction did you take?"

"I went to the left too." He paused. "Toward the store."

Benford harrumphed. "You followed the girl, then."

"Well, I went in the same direction as the girl, but I was going to the Khoury's store."

Elaine repeated the statement with emphasis. "You followed the girl."

Willend looked back and forth between Elaine and Benford. "There's a difference in intent between 'going the same direction' and 'following.' It didn't matter to me which way she went. I was going to the store."

Elaine threw up her hands. "Fine. Fine. So you walked to the Khoury's store. Tell me what happened there."

"When I went in, Hassan was cleaning the floor in front of the fridge. We chatted for a minute, then he asked what he could get me, and I told him I wanted a gyro . . ." Willend caught himself. "In America we call them gyros, here you call them kebabs. Anyway, a kebab with lots of tzatziki sauce, plus a quarter-kilo of couscous and cucumber-and-tomato salad. He joked with me that I must have been really hungry because I usually don't buy the couscous. He got the food, and we chatted for a while longer."

"Be specific. You chatted about what?"

Willend put his hands behind his neck and looked at the ceiling. "Hassan's a big supporter of Arsenal, so we talked for a few minutes about their chances this year. Actually, he was the one who did most of the talking. I'm a novice about the game. We talked about his daughter, Sarah. He's very proud of her. She wants to go into medicine, and he told me how she won the science competition at her school. I had given her some advice when she designed her experiment. That's about it."

Elaine consulted some notes. "I thought Sam and Leyla Khoury owned the store."

"They do, but they're in York, visiting Leyla's sister. Hassan is their son. He covers for them when he's not working his regular job."

"And what job is that?"

"He's a school teacher."

"You seem to know a lot about the Khoury family."

"I've known them almost as long as I've been in London. I see them at least once or twice a week, when I go to the store."

Elaine smirked. "It's very convenient for you that this, umm, Hassan, happened to be in the store on that night. When the store owners were away. Very convenient."

Willend looked perplexed. "What do you mean, 'convenient'? What the hell does that mean? You think I arranged for him to be there?"

Elaine made a note. "I said no such thing, Dr. Willend. Was anyone else in the store?"

Willend was visibly agitated. He took a moment to calm himself, then spoke. "Yes, a woman was there when I got there. She bought some milk and some cans of something, I think, and left before I did."

Elaine heard Cranwell's voice in her earpiece. "Let's talk." She turned to Benford. He nodded. "One twenty-one PM. DS Hope and DCI Benford are leaving the room." She punched the button. The constable in the corner shifted in his chair but remained silent.

Benford and Elaine joined Cranwell in the viewing room. He didn't appear pleased. "Well? It doesn't seem like you're getting very far here, Elaine."

"It takes time. He's calm and confident, not cocky or cheeky. He got a bit flustered there, but he's deflecting very little if at all. I don't see any avoidance or deceit in him. It was the same thing when we were at his house. If he's hiding something, I don't know what it might be yet. It may take some time."

Benford snorted. "Bollocks. He followed Sheila when she got off the bus, and he's the last known person to see her alive. He didn't mention her when we first talked to him. He owns a dark car. He made up that cock-and-bull story about that Hassan bloke. I think he's a bloody good actor and he's rehearsed it."

Cranwell turned to Elaine. "What else do we know about him?"

Elaine paused. "DC Costello interviewed the A&E staff this morning, while we were at Willend's house. He's been a senior surgical consultant at the hospital about two years. Specializes in trauma surgery; he fixes accident victims, that kind of thing. Mostly kids, but adults and wounded soldiers as well. He's apparently very good at it, and the house officers and nursing staff seem to like working with him. But . . ." Her voice trailed off.

"But what?"

"His personal reputation at the hospital is that he's quiet and something of a loner. He's good to work with, but he gets very moody at times. Simon said the word 'withdrawn' was used more than once. He said his main assistant got very nervous when he pressed her on that. It seemed like she didn't want to talk about Willend any further and said that we'd have to ask him." Elaine paused.

"There's one other thing. Simon talked with one of the other surgeons. Apparently there's a locker room the male doctors use. This surgeon said Willend always turns to face the room when he's changing clothes. He said Willend is scarred. His back got badly burned in Iraq and he had skin grafts. Spent a bit of time in hospital. Anyway, when he changes clothes, he keeps his back to the wall, perhaps so other people can't see the damage."

Cranwell perked up. "That's interesting. Brilliant but moody and a loner. Iraq. God knows what happened there. Burned! PTSD, you think? A bipolar Jekyll and Hyde?"

Through the window they could see Willend sitting calmly with his eyes closed, his hands folded on his lap.

Benford nodded toward him. "He's rehearsing his story."

Elaine shook her head. "No. He's meditating."

Cranwell looked at them both. "Whatever he's doing, we're not getting any further while we're standing out here. Go back in and shake him up a bit more. See if he fizzes."

"Yes, sir."

After the preliminaries, Benford began. "Dr. Willend. When we spoke at your home—or I should say, your sister's home—you seemed to get upset when we talked politics."

"Not upset, but yes, I was pulling your chain. It sounded like you were making a supposition about me that was off base."

"There was no supposition on my part. I asked a simple question, based on something you said."

"Actually, it was based on the way I said it. Not every Texan—or American, for that matter—satisfies your preconceptions. Suppose I stereotyped you? Maybe you live exclusively on ackee and saltfish and roll yourself a big fat spliff several times a day? Does Inspector Hope live to suck down cheap whisky and start bar fights?"

Elaine's eyes narrowed. He'd picked up on her Scottish accent. *It's time for a little bit of rough, Lainie.* "Only when Celtic loses. I saw the pictures on your piano. You have a lovely family, Dr. Willend. It's a shame they don't live with you. Did you abandon them back in the States, or did they kick you out back to Mommy in London?"

Willend's eyes flared and he sat bolt upright. His hands gripped the edge of the table, knuckles white. With visible effort, he relaxed, and his gaze shifted away from her and into a thousand-yard stare.

There, Elaine thought. *That hit him hard.* "Dr. Willend?"

"They died."

"I'm so sorry to hear that. How did they die?" Elaine's tone indicated she wasn't sorry at all.

"In a car crash, six years ago." Willend was still staring into the distance.

"I'm over here, Mr. Willend. Look at me. Do you still keep in touch with your soldier friends in the photo?"

His stare didn't vary. "No. They're gone too."

She capped her pen and closed her notebook. When she spoke again, her voice had softened. "You're pretty much on your own, then? Alone?"

Willend's eyes refocused and fixed on Elaine's face. "No, I have my sister and mother. And I . . ." He paused and exhaled audibly. "Am I under arrest?"

"No, but we would like your cooperation." She held her eyes steady on Willend's face.

Willend's gaze didn't move from Elaine. "I think I've cooperated so far. Since I'm not under arrest, I would like to leave now."

Benford spoke up. "You have nothing more to tell us?"

"No."

"And everything you have told us is true?"

"Yes. I would like to leave."

Benford looked at Elaine, and she gave an almost imperceptible nod. He continued. "We will need to search your home and your car. Do we have your permission or must we get a search warrant?"

Willend paused for a moment. "I have a few conditions. You do not search Kate's room or office. I don't have the right to speak for her. Besides, her rooms are locked and I have no pass code. Also, I have a computer system in my office that belongs to the hospital and contains very private patient information, so you cannot touch it. For the rest, you have my permission, but only if I am there."

Benford harrumphed. "We aren't going to squabble over this, are we? We need to search your house and car, and we will."

"No, we won't squabble. You said I'm not under arrest, which means that you're asking me for a favor. If you can't accept my conditions, you'll need to get a warrant. Perhaps you can convince a magistrate to give you one based on circumstances and stereotypes. Whichever option you choose, I'm going home now."

Willend started to rise from the table. Benford spoke. "Will you call your sister to see if she will give her permission to search her rooms?"

"I could call her. She may or may not answer. I doubt if she would give permission in a situation like this. She works directly for the Foreign Secretary, and her current assignment is with the United Nations Human Rights Council. Her specialty is 'rule of law,' so she has an extremely healthy respect for legal protocols. Kate Willend is her name. You can Google her or check with the Foreign Secretary. I'm sure he likes being disturbed by the police on Sunday afternoons."

"This is a murder investigation, Dr. Willend. There are serious consequences for hindering an investigation and wasting police time."

"I'm not hindering your investigation, nor am I wasting your time. Searching a high-profile diplomat's home without her express permission or a warrant would create a huge shit-storm, and you know it. You suspect me of killing this girl, but you know you don't have enough to charge me. You're going fishing, and you're afraid that if I'm alone at home, I might destroy evidence while you go get your warrant."

Willend leaned forward over the table. "I'm willing to cooperate up to a point. Wouldn't you rather at least have my permission to look through the house and keep an eye on me at the same time?

Then if you find something, you can get your warrant and arrest me on the spot."

His eyes locked on Elaine's. "Or more likely, you can go away and leave me alone."

Benford exchanged a look with Elaine before he answered. "I'll agree, for now."

"Since you brought me here, may I get a lift home?"

"Certainly. Inspector Hope will take you and wait with you until the crime scene team arrives—CSIs, as some call them now. And before you leave, we'd like to take a DNA sample from you."

Willend looked relieved. "That's not a problem."

SIX

A beefy plainclothes officer joined Elaine and Willend as they were leaving the station. His shaved round head sat atop a thick neck, which, together with his huge hands, indicated massive strength. Elaine introduced him as DC Bull, to which Willend replied, "I imagine so." DC Bull shook his head and frowned.

Willend apologized. "Sorry, that was rude of me. No offense intended. It's rare that someone's physique and name are so well matched." Bull grunted in acknowledgement and took his seat in the car.

Elaine was a fast and decisive driver who understood her engine's power curve and shifted appropriately. She knew the route and planned ahead, her car moving quickly through the traffic.

She glanced in the rearview mirror. Willend sat quietly, looking out the window. Bull's large frame occupied most of the back seat opposite Willend. He rocked to and fro with her fast turns and lane changes.

She felt rotten about interrogating Willend so harshly. It had made her more than a little grouchy, which probably had come through in her tone. She was almost certain Benford was wrong, but orders were orders. If she were in charge, she would not be so aggressive.

Elaine was a good interrogator because she found it easy to empathize. Her empathy helped her find vulnerability in the suspect's protective shell. Once she knew his weakness, she probed it with questions, like a medieval knight used a stiletto. She pressed relentlessly until her insistent point found its mark, and the guilt and confession gushed out for the world to see. Benford had told her she was a good interrogator because she was a woman.

She figured it was because she knew a lot about guilt. She sensed Willend was carrying deep guilt, but she didn't think it had anything to do with Sheila's murder.

Willend spoke.

"How long will it take the forensic team to get there?"

"Probably an hour, perhaps longer, given that it's a Sunday."

"I was wondering if I'd have time to make some lunch. You and the constable are welcome to join me."

"We'll stop for carryout instead." Elaine jabbed the brakes, downshifted into second gear, flew around a corner, and wheeled into a parking spot in front of an Indian restaurant. She heard Bull sigh hugely. He looked vaguely ill, like a nauseated shot-putter. "Nothing for me," he said.

A short while later, they stood at the door of Willend's house. Bull held the food containers while Willend unlocked the door and asked them to wait while he disabled the alarm systems. Apparently Bull's motion sickness had dissipated, because after smelling the curries, he had decided that he really wanted a burger. Or two. They had stopped at a McDonald's for him.

Once they were settled at the table, Elaine began the conversation. "Two alarm systems. That's quite a bit of security."

Willend nodded. "Three, actually. There's another you don't see here. One is the general system for the exterior that sounds an alarm and notifies the police. The second detects motion inside the house. It's silent and it notifies both the police and a security team at the Foreign Office or Special Branch or somewhere. I don't know anything about the third one, except that it guards Kate's study and it notifies people who none of us really want to meet. I think they wear black and shave their heads and strap big knives to their boots and carry H&K machine pistols. It probably would get messy and unpleasant."

"That's positively Bondian. Or SMERSHian, take your pick. Whatever is she protecting?"

"I don't want to know. Apparently the systems were designed specifically for the house and were installed when it was built. There are details about the house that I find a bit odd, but Kate assures me that they are intentional."

"So if we got a warrant and searched your sister's office or bedroom without her knowing it, we would set off a silent alarm and meet those nasty people who we really do not want to meet?"

"I presume so. And start that shit-storm."

He offered Elaine the naan, and she took a piece. "So Kate had the house built to her specifications?"

"Yes. The previous house on the site had burned down and was tangled up in insurance litigation. Kate, or maybe one of her government friends, was able to come up with a solution that pleased both sides. She and Mom bought the site and built this house."

"But your mother doesn't live here?"

"She did for a while, but then she moved to a flat in the Barbican. Kate was here mostly by herself until I moved in two years ago."

"Mostly by herself? Failed marriage? Boyfriend problems?"

Willend laughed. "Something like that. But that's over now. Even with all the traveling she does, she's been in a steady relationship for over a year."

"In the interview, you got upset when I asked about your family. It was like I had entered a forbidden zone."

"Maybe it was the way you entered it." Willend sat back in his chair. "I only talk about Diana and Liza with Kate and Mom and maybe a couple of friends back in the States."

"Why is that? What happened?"

"Like I said, I don't talk about it. They died in a car accident. That should be enough for you."

Elaine kept pressing. "Well, it may not be enough. In a murder investigation, there isn't room for emotional niceties. Everything we police think should be put on the table will be put on the table, and only then do we and the Crown Prosecutor decide what part is evidence and what is not. I can jail you for obstructing a lawful police enquiry."

Willend looked a bit taken aback. "Be that as it may, my family tragedy six years ago is of no concern to your investigation. I have nothing to hide. I'm innocent, and it's only a matter of time before you and Benford realize it. I have every confidence that you will eventually find the killer, and that killer is not me. I'm patient, and more important, I'm well within my rights."

Elaine had finished her curry and needed some time to collect her thoughts. "May I use your toilet?"

Willend paused, then indicated the stairs. "Be my guest. Up, second door on the right."

"Thank you." Bull appeared to be nodding off in the leather chair. The two burgers had been soporific enough to overcome the caffeine from the large Coca-Cola he had used to chase them down. He hadn't had any chips, though—watching his weight.

Elaine nudged Bull as she passed and continued up the stairs, thinking over what she had learned, which was next to nothing, really. Willend was tough. Every time she had tried to crack his shell and crawl inside, he reverted to some version of his smug refrain. "I'm innocent and I know it. One day you will too." No defensiveness, no prevarication. A portrait of an honest man.

She stared into the mirror as she washed her hands. Her talk with him, and her gut, told her again that Peter Willend was innocent. If she was right, they were wasting their time. With any luck, the team would uncover evidence that pointed in a new direction, and she could leave the difficult doctor behind. She hoped so. As she passed the door next to the lavatory, she noticed it had an electronic combination lock. Curious, she tried the door across the hall. It was locked.

When she returned, Willend had moved to the piano and was syncopating his way through the introduction to "Night and Day." "Do you play?" he asked.

Dammit, she thought. "A bit, but I haven't played seriously in years." Which was a lie. She owned a piano, played it well, and practiced a couple of times a week.

Willend pressed. "Would you care to join me? It might be fun."

"That wouldn't . . . ah, the SOCO team is here. That's scene of crime officers. CSIs to you Yanks." She looked out the front window. A white SOCO van had parked in the drive, and several technicians were walking toward the house.

Elaine said, "Turn off the alarms or whatever so we can open the door."

Willend didn't look up. "I'm playing. The front door alarms aren't on."

She rolled her eyes and motioned to Bull, who opened it to admit the SOCO team. One of them, apparently the leader, said to no one in particular, "I understand there are some restrictions on . . ."

The coda to "Night and Day" interrupted him.

Elaine blurted, "Do you mind, Dr. Willend?" The music stopped.

She briefed the SOCO team. "You're doing the garage and the MINI Cooper, the basement, the ground floor, and the second floor. The locked rooms on the first floor and the computer equipment on the second floor are off limits. I'll show you when you're ready. We're looking for hairs, stray fibers, and such. The usual samples."

She turned to Willend, who was still at the piano. "Party time is over, Dr. Willend. You will confine yourself to this room until further notice. You may not enter any room unaccompanied or any room that has not previously been processed. Under no circumstances will you go outside to your car. Do you understand?"

"Certainly. Search away." He plopped down on the sofa.

The teams split up and began their searches. Willend switched on an e-book and began to read. Elaine busied herself with searching through the various magazines and drawers, monitoring the SOCO progress. After a while, Willend stood and asked Elaine if he could use the toilet.

She replied, "The team isn't finished upstairs yet, so you'll need to wait."

Bull spoke up. "They've searched the toilet off the back of the kitchen. He may be able to use that one." One of the technicians overheard and confirmed.

"Okay. You can use that one, but Bull will need to accompany you." Willend shrugged and walked toward the back of the house. Bull fell in behind him.

Elaine was annoyed. She had not known that there was a toilet on this floor. Why had Willend not directed her there earlier? While they were gone, she got the attention of one of the SOCO techs.

"Do you know if the team found anything peculiar about the toilet in the back?"

He shook his head. "I searched it and bagged a few stray hairs, but there was nothing unusual. I took some swabs and sprayed for blood, but I didn't find any. Riffled through the magazines. Lifted prints. Nothing out of order."

"Thanks."

When Willend returned, she turned on him. "What are you playing at? Earlier you directed me to the toilet upstairs. Why didn't you simply point to the back of the kitchen?"

"Perhaps you really needed to pee, but I suspected that you mainly wanted to nose around in private, so I sent you to Kate's floor. Did you jiggle a door handle?" An amused smile curled his lips. "I've watched *Midsomer Murders*. Sergeant Jones must know every loo and medicine cabinet in the entire Midsomer County. If I'm going to be a suspect, I want it to be as briefly as possible."

"Even innocent people are rarely as calm as you've been."

"I believe in picking my battles," Willend said. "You're investigating a murder, and you'll do what you think you need to do regardless of anything I say. Resisting and being stubborn just clutters the mind and the soul, and it makes it hard to see things. I'm not hiding anything from you."

"Not at all? It's a rare person, or psychopath, who doesn't feel guilty about something."

"True, but I haven't broken any laws that I'm aware of, so no guilt about that, at least."

"You won't discuss your family. Did you pick that battle because you feel guilty about that?"

Willend's jaw tensed. He waited a moment before responding. "You agreed not to search my computer, so may I go upstairs? I have some work to do. Someone can come with me, and I'll leave the door open."

She considered the options and turned to Bull. "Let me know if the team finds anything."

She followed Willend up the stairs to the top floor of the house, where he took a seat in front of two very large computer screens. He indicated an office chair. "If you want to look over my shoulder, you can sit there. I need to check my e-mails and also talk to one of my colleagues at the hospital."

Elaine watched as he opened his e-mail program and scrolled through his inbox. The first e-mail he opened was from "Kwillend," which simply said that the trip had been inspirational and successful. She and Nora were coiled around each other like garter snakes in springtime and did not want to come home. Elaine raised her eyebrows. Quite an image. Willend replied simply, "How lovely for you. Don't." There followed an e-mail from a lacrosse teammate about some games planned over the next few weeks. Other than that, he read a few e-mails from colleagues that dealt with hospital business and medical questions. He responded to them all.

He next downloaded some files and displayed them on the large monitor. To Elaine, they looked like X-rays or scans of a person's lower body and legs, but something was odd—the legs were at the wrong angle. Elaine had studied psychology at the university, not anatomy, so she was no expert.

Willend turned to her. "I need to talk to a surgeon on my team at the hospital. Do you mind if I open a video connection?"

"No, go ahead."

Willend clicked a few buttons with his mouse, and a woman's voice emerged from the speakers next to the monitor. "Hello, Peter. I'm here. Just a second." The image of a woman appeared.

"Hi, Sheena. Any news about Hamid?"

"I've been trying to reach you all afternoon. I left messages."

"Sorry about that. It was unavoidable. What did you need?"

Elaine listened while they talked about the condition of a young boy named Hamid. After a lengthy conversation full of medical terminology, Sheena explained that she had talked to Hamid's parents, and they were okay with continuing the screening process. Willend waited for her to finish, and said, "Okay, Sheena. Go ahead and admit Hamid to the hospital and finish all the necessary screening. I probably won't be able to come in to see the boy until tomorrow. Is that it?"

Sheena cleared her throat. "The police were here earlier today. They showed us a picture of you and started asking questions. How well do we know you, how often do you ride the bus, do you often lose your temper, what has your behavior been like lately, things like that. We're all upset about it. What's going on, Peter?"

"I was on a bus at the same time as a girl who was later found murdered. They got my picture off the CCTV on the bus. It's nothing to worry about. Everything they are doing is routine for a murder investigation. They have to follow it up. Sooner or later, they'll strike me off the list and find who really did it."

"Well, I am hoping it is sooner rather than later. We'll soon fall behind without you here."

"Don't worry, it'll be over soon. I know you'll all hang in and do a great job, especially you. You're a rock star, even if you don't realize it. I need to go now. I'll see you tomorrow morning."

"Okay. Thanks, Peter."

Willend closed the connection and turned to the diagnostic images on the large HD screen.

Elaine spoke. "That's a huge computer monitor. What is it you're looking at?"

"Sheena, that's Dr. Farad to you, sent me X-ray and MRI images from an eleven-year-old Bangladeshi boy who broke his pelvis and leg in a nasty accident. His recovery didn't go well. A rural doctor in his home village back in 'Desh tried to help him by lashing him into some ancient braces. I'm sure he did the best he could with what he had to work with. What else could he do? At least it gave the boy some mobility. To the local doctor's credit, when he heard about our foundation, he contacted the local liaison, and they referred him to us for possible admittance into our program. Sheena performed the initial screens, and these are the pics. I'm going to interview him and his parents tomorrow, and we'll run some more tests to make sure they are good candidates for the surgery."

"What foundation is this?"

"It's called Children Walk. Based out of Stockholm."

"The parents are candidates for surgery too? Like donors?"

"Ah. No, not physically. Only in the sense that parents live for their children, and they need to understand all the risks and costs of their decision."

"Risks and costs."

"Yes. There are risks and costs to everything; you know that. They don't pay money for any of these surgeries—the foundation covers it. But there are huge emotional costs that they have to understand and cope with."

"Such as?"

"What is the price the boy pays if we do nothing? Given the family's low status, he would have a rotten future. He couldn't help on the farm, and there's little or no social support. About all he would be allowed to do is beg or work in some sweatshop. What if we begin the process and discover that it won't be successful? We, and they, would need to control the emotional damage and figure out a new strategy. And what if the surgery is successful, which means months of painful rehabilitation here in Britain and even more back in 'Desh? Do they let him stay in a clinic on his own?

If not, who's going to run their farm while they're away? There are truckloads of questions." He watched Elaine quietly absorb what he was saying, then continued, "So are you finished with me?"

At that point, Bull knocked at the door. Elaine rose, and she and Bull moved a few steps down the hallway.

Bull spoke quietly. "The SOCO team found a blood stain in the basement. It looks old, but they were able to get enough of a sample for testing. There were some drops in the carpet of the car as well."

"Thanks. Wait here." She returned to the door of Willend's office. "Has there been an accident in the basement recently?"

Willend looked surprised at the question. "No, not since I've been living here. Why?"

"No one has cut themselves or been injured?"

"Not that I know of. Did they find blood?"

"What about your car?"

Willend thought for a moment. "If they found blood there, it would be mine."

Elaine motioned for Bull to replace her at the door. She walked down to the basement, discussed the find with the SOCO technicians, and dialed Benford.

"Sir, the SOCO team found what looks like blood in the basement of Willend's house. They got an indication with the UV gear, so they checked closely and found some blood under the bottom of a wall baseboard. They think they have enough for DNA comparison. It appears too old to be from Sheila, but you never know for sure. Willend claims there haven't been any accidents in the basement since he's been living here. They also found some more recent blood drops in the boot of his car."

"What's the basement like?" Benford sounded excited.

Elaine scanned the room. "It's clean. Well lit, plastered, and painted. Some boxes full of books and clothes stacked in the corner, with a note taped on them that says 'OxFam.' An old chair and sofa. There's a toolbox and a workbench with a vise attached. A clothes washer and dryer. A door to the outside that looks like it leads to the garage. I don't see anything sinister that would suggest any torture." Elaine cast her eyes around once more. "Wait. There are two eye bolts screwed into a beam on the ceiling. That's all I see right now."

"Excellent. Tell the SOCO guys to go over the basement again, inch by inch, and have them fast-track the blood. Then arrest Willend and bring him in. We'll hold him until the blood results can confirm Sheila was there or in his car."

"Sir, are you sure about arresting him? Even though we have suspicion, it's based on pretty thin circumstance. What does the prosecutor think?"

"It's him. Arrest him, Elaine."

She recognized his tone. There was no point arguing. "Yes, sir. I'll keep you posted."

She turned to the technicians. "All right then. Inch by inch. The floor, every wall, and the ceiling too. We're looking for blood, tissue, hair, fibers, fluids, you name it. Scrutinize anything that doesn't look like it belongs and everything that does. Was anything hung from those bolts? Was something dragged up the steps, out the door, to the garage? Is that toolbox locked?" A technician lifted the lid of the toolbox, tugged its drawers, and shook his head. "Check everything in it, then do the same for the car and the garage. Let me know when you find something."

The technicians looked miffed at being instructed in the obvious, but they turned to their tasks. Elaine started up the stairs but paused with a thought and spoke again. "Is there anything that can tell us if the basement has been cleaned recently?"

The two technicians looked at each other, clearly annoyed that she would ask such a question. One spoke. "It doesn't appear to have been cleaned for a while. Exactly how long, I don't know. There's a slight layer of dust on the top surfaces. The bench and the toolbox, mainly. The floor is painted and has about the same amount of dust. Perfect for footprints. The only shoe marks we found were between the stairs and the washing machine, and those could have been several days old. We took some oblique shots of the footprints. Once we finish here, we'll see if the prints match any shoes in the house. It will be in our report."

"Right. Of course. Thanks." Elaine headed upstairs, motioning to two uniforms to follow her. They went upstairs, where she strode into Willend's study.

"Dr. Willend, can you account for your whereabouts yesterday, January 26?"

Willend looked taken aback. "I was here until nearly two in the afternoon. Until about five, I was at a lacrosse practice. Then I came home. I didn't go out after that."

"Was anyone with you while you were here at home?"

"No."

"When was the last time you went into the basement?"

"Tuesday or Wednesday, I think. Tuesday. I did some laundry."

"And you have not been back down there since?"

"No."

"When did you bleed in the car?"

"After a lacrosse practice. I accidentally got popped in the nose by a stick. It dripped for some time."

Elaine thought that was a reasonable explanation. She doubted the blood in the basement was Sheila's. She didn't know whose blood it was, but they would test it all anyway. Still, given what she knew, arresting Willend didn't make sense. They didn't have enough evidence.

No matter, she had her orders.

"Peter Montgomery Willend. I am arresting you for the murder of Sheila Jane Watson. You do not have to say anything, but it may harm your defense if you do not mention when questioned something which you later rely on in court. Anything you do say may be given in evidence."

"What the hell is this?" Willend looked dumbfounded. Bull took Willend's arm, but he jerked it away and confronted Elaine face-to-face. "Are you nuts? Do you seriously think I murdered that girl?" Another constable grabbed hold of Willend's arm, and he and Bull pulled him away from her.

Elaine took a step forward and looked Willend in the eye. "Dr. Willend, I suggest that you cooperate and come quietly." Willend's angry blue eyes bored into her, his body pulling against Bull's grasp. As Elaine watched, he took a deep breath and relaxed. A uniform handcuffed him, and together they all marched out to her car and drove to the station.

Two hours later, Elaine stood with Benford and Cranwell, watching Willend and his solicitor through the window of the interview room. Elaine turned to Cranwell.

"We've been over his entire story from beginning to end, and he's told us exactly the same thing he did before. He swears he knows nothing about any blood in the basement."

"Did SOCO find anything else?"

"No more blood. There was dust, a bit of grease and oil, a few metal filings on the tools and the vise. Not any other blood in the basement or in the rest of the house. A couple of hairs from the basement have the root bulb attached, so they'll probably get some DNA from them. We've instructed forensics to fast-track it all."

Cranwell nodded. "Good. We can hold him for thirty-six hours. If it's going to take longer, we'll get an extension. Get him to his cell, and schedule a press briefing for noon tomorrow. Then you can call it a day."

★★★

Elaine pulled her thick robe tighter around her body, plumped the pillows behind her back, and settled against them. She had needed that long shower. Steamy water and a soapy loofah always worked wonders. But she had a nagging unease.

Liars always cracked. Always. As pressure was applied from different angles, as new evidence mounted, as the interrogator's speculations shifted focus, circled around, and grew, a liar either changed his story or denied the evidence. Willend hadn't.

The more she thought about it, the more her gut growled out his innocence. Everything they had was circumstantial, and it was weak at best. The CCTV from the bus showed opportunity, perhaps. As far as means, he had two hands, as did several million other men in the city. How many dark cars are there in London? The only evidence they could nail him on was if the blood in the basement or in his car was Sheila's. Without that, the Crown Prosecutor would laugh them all the way back to the station. Benford and Cranwell wanted Willend too badly.

She scowled. Willend. The guy is not a killer. He's a good-looking charmer and a bit of a smart-ass, but what does that matter? Maybe he killed someone in Iraq, and perhaps he could kill in the heat of the moment or in self-defense, but he is not a man who would cold-bloodedly slaughter a young girl. He showed deep emotional resistance when asked about his family. He'd closed up, so he's probably carrying some guilt around about that. Was he driving when they died in the accident? Did it occur in Britain? She'd have Cromarty look for an accident report. It wouldn't get them any closer to the real killer, but no matter. She wanted to know.

Throughout her entire life, Elaine had always wanted to know. Even when she was a young girl, she had made sure to notice things. In public or at family gatherings, she had watched the people around her go about their activities. Then she had asked questions with the candid curiosity of a child, usually to the embarrassment of her parents. She had always felt she needed to understand why people did what they did, and that innate need had never gone away. If her personality had been slightly different, if she had focused on bugs or trees or test tubes, she would have become a scientist. But she became a detective, and every day she donned the job and its necessities like a comfortable coat she could never part with. Some things don't change.

Tomorrow she'd rethink everything they knew and everything they suspected. She needed to find a new line of enquiry fast, before they were forced to release Willend.

Right now she needed sleep. Scratch had taken his usual place with his head on her leg. She reached down and stroked him, listening to his deep purr grow louder. When she was almost purring with him, she turned off the bedside lamp and closed her eyes.

SEVEN

The light in the cell reminded Peter of the noonday sun in Iraq. It illuminated every crack and crevice and brought even tiny details into clear focus. Not that there were many details inside the cell. A toilet, a basin, a ledge with a woefully thin foam mattress, and that was all. No nooks, few crannies. No place to hide.

He sat, knees tucked under his chin. As he softened his focus and assumed a thousand-yard stare, the creamy tan wall eight feet in front of him seemed to become amorphous, roiling, as if he were staring into an approaching sand storm. *I can escape*, he thought. *Three steps into that whirling chaos and I'll never be seen again.*

The dream would probably come back tonight, and he would wake in a panic, soaked with sweat. If he were at home, he would get up, take a hot shower, and then sit in his chair until daybreak. The cell had no shower or chair.

Which one was it? Who had made the decision to arrest him? Did it matter? Yes. He didn't think it was Hope. Even when she was arresting him, she didn't look convinced. It was Benford or perhaps Benford's boss. He didn't know what the British police protocols were.

God, but he was sleepy. He lay down and turned to face the wall. Death in a sandstorm. It would be slow suffocation, the dust and grit piling in a drift against his cheek as he lay on the sand, gradually filling his nostrils, blocking the air, granting peace.

His body jerked as Diana's voice came to him, but the dry wind was wailing, and he could barely make out what she was saying. Desert dust clogged his nose, choked his throat. Diana stood across the operating table, and beside her, between her arm and the curve of her breast, Liza's solemn face gazed at him with her knowing blue eyes. What were they doing here? The wind took on sharp firecracker punctuation, and he felt heat building behind him. A blow-torch blast seared into his back, and Diana and Liza dissolved and vanished into a vortex of ash and dust. When the air cleared, he was kneeling naked on a desolate plain, staring through haze at a horizon of ragged khaki hills.

"Mister Willend!" Diana? *No, that isn't her voice, and she wouldn't say that.*

"Mister Willend!" His name again rang in his ears from a disembodied voice somewhere above him.

Peter's eyes snapped open with his panicked gasp, and his body convulsed in a sudden spasm. Harsh light revealed a young police officer standing over him and another officer, larger and older, standing in the door. Peter bolted to a sitting position, flung the light jail blanket to the floor, and sat, momentarily confused as the panic and sleep cleared from his mind. "I'm okay. I had a nightmare."

"You were shouting. Do you need anything? Do you need any medications? I can call the custody nurse."

"No. No meds. I'll be fine." He placed his hands over his face, then ran his long fingers through his sweat-drenched hair. "I need to be out of this place, though."

The large officer grunted and moved aside as the younger officer retreated through the door and clanked it shut.

★ ★ ★

Monday promised to be a bit sunnier and less damp than the weekend had been. Funny how that happens so often, Elaine thought as she pulled into the car park at Saint Stephen's Hospital. Not that weekends necessarily mattered to a detective.

Owen Clayton, Willend's superior, was a tall Welshman with a rabbity face, small round spectacles, and an unruly shock of black hair. His white lab coat hung on him crookedly, as if it were two sizes too large for him in his shoulders but two sizes too short in the arms. His shirt cuffs extended well past the sleeves of his coat, and below them, his bony wrists flowed into long hands that terminated in long thin fingers that shook slightly. His high-pitched voice contained more than a hint of his Welsh origins.

"I heard that you were here Saturday, Inspector, asking about Peter Willend. Why are you interested in him?"

"On Friday night, Dr. Willend rode on a bus with a girl who later was found murdered. I'd like to get some background information about him."

Clayton's eyes widened. "Surely you don't suspect Peter."

"We have to be thorough. This is a murder investigation. What can you tell me about him?" At her question, Clayton interlocked his fingers on his desk to stop them from trembling. Parkinson's? Nerves?

"Let me see. Peter has been with us for two years. He had excellent references from his previous post at a teaching hospital in Texas. When he applied for a position as an emergency medicine consultant, he also offered us a proposal for a funded program focused on correcting congenital malformations and injuries in children. Apparently he had been working on it for some time and felt that London was the best setting. We had been looking for something like his program to give Saint Stephen's a bit more international visibility, so we contacted the Children Walk Foundation and were able to work out an agreement. It was a good fit."

"And you performed a background check on him at the time?"

"Of course we did. No criminal record. He was in the American military. He served in Iraq and was wounded there, which ended his military career. Tragic story, actually. He had serious burns to the back of his torso and legs. He spent months, a couple of years, in the hospital getting skin grafts. But he received impeccable references from everyone we spoke to. He is researching and testing a new reconstructive procedure."

"Testing? Is it experimental?"

"Hardly experimental. His procedure works well, but success is largely a matter of employing it on the right patient at the right time."

"So he and his team screen their patients extensively."

"Yes, candidates are approved only under strict supervision of a joint committee of the foundation and the hospital. I fail to see what this may have to do with a murder investigation."

"I'm trying to get an idea of who Dr. Willend is. For a respected surgeon, he seems a bit . . . unconventional in his lifestyle. His hair and his music, for example."

"He lives with his sister, who has a post in the Foreign Office. And he's somewhat informal in his grooming and attire. Many people are. Does that make them murderers? I don't know about his music. But then, he keeps his private life very much to himself, and he doesn't socialize much except for professional events—dinners and staff parties and such."

"What about his relations with his team and other hospital staff? Any problems there?"

"None at all that I am aware of. Professional disagreements, yes. He seems to have a bit of a temper . . . he's come to me and vented his displeasure with this or that decision several times—always behind closed doors, you understand. But it's never ad hominem, and he seems to get over it quickly and move on. Most of the staff either like him or at worst don't dislike him. I understand that women tend to like him, not that it matters. It's professional respect that counts around here. Outside the hospital, we simply require that staff do nothing to bring discredit to the institution. I would be deeply shocked if Peter were to be involved with anything remotely disreputable, much less murder. Is this enough information, Inspector? I really must get on with my day. But please keep me informed."

"Thank you, Doctor. I will." Elaine had scarcely reached the office door when she heard Clayton punching the buttons on his telephone.

★ ★ ★

Elaine was in Benford's office when Liz Barker knocked and stuck her head in the door. "Elaine, Chief, you need to see this." A cluster of detectives and uniforms gathered around the large television in the corner. Paula Ford made room for them at the front of the crowd. "Replay it, Simon."

The crowd parted so Elaine and Benford could see the screen, which displayed a grainy head shot of Willend next to a school picture of Sheila Watson. A banner across the bottom blazoned "Sheila's Killer?"

"An anonymous Metropolitan Police source has told our news desk that Dr. Peter Willend, an American surgeon working in London, is assisting the investigation team with their enquiries into the death of schoolgirl Sheila Watson. Sheila's bloody and beaten body was found last Saturday morning next to a disused Leaside railroad track.

"Willend is the chief surgeon for the Children Walk Foundation, whose work focuses on helping disabled children in areas such as Bangladesh and sub-Saharan Africa. He is also well known amongst his colleagues at Saint Stephen's Hospital as a trauma surgeon. Previously, Willend served with the American Army in Iraq, where he reportedly was seriously wounded.

"Pers Sjolin, the chairman of Children Walk, and a spokesperson at Saint Stephen's both declined to comment at this time. Stay tuned for updates."

Benford was livid. "Right. Everyone into the incident room! Now, people!"

Elaine sat on a table at the front of the incident room and grimly scanned the faces of the detectives and uniformed constables as they entered. The only expression she could identify was bewilderment. Benford began speaking before everyone had assembled.

"Quiet! Everyone! I'm only going to say this once. I know you all know this, but apparently I need to say it. Investigations are difficult enough without the press scattering information to the public willy-nilly. No one, not one of you, is to talk to the press or anyone who is not on our team about this or any other ongoing investigation. If any of you leaked any information about the case, you had better come to my office immediately and tell me. I mean immediately. You know I will find out sooner or later. If I find out later who blabbed . . . you'll spend the rest of your days working security at a sausage factory. Understood? Any questions?"

There were none.

★ ★ ★

The reporters were filling the press room when Elaine arrived. Cranwell and Benford had led the way and were already at the table adjusting their microphones. She stood to the side, behind them, near the door. She could make a quick getaway once the briefing finished. From her vantage point, she could register most of the room in one glance, scanning the rows of reporters.

The atmosphere in the room was hostile, probably because the leak had intensified the endemic adversarial relations between the press and the police. Benford started with a statement, describing the crime in general terms and appealing for information. Then the reporters started with their usual evidential questions, which Cranwell and Benford easily parried. Then the tone changed. Several reporters had obviously done some superficial homework. One after the other, they asked blatant questions about whether Benford suspected Willend to be a serial killer, by implying a connection between Sheila's case and several unsolved cases from all around Britain and even in America. Benford answered that it was too early in the investigation to make any statement, which led to aggressive questions impugning the competence of the police.

As she usually did, Elaine remained silent, listening to the tone of Cranwell and Benford's voices and watching their body language.

Cranwell was his typical slick self. Nothing new there. Benford's appearance and behavior were another matter. She detected a harried and defensive tone.

After deflecting the third question concerning the apparent lack of progress in the investigation, Benford pointedly stated he had said all he was going to say on that topic and would respond to no more questions about it. At that point, one of the younger reporters asked an insinuating question about Sheila's sexual habits. Before a wide-eyed Benford could splutter his outrage, Cranwell interjected with his appeal to the public for information and ended the briefing.

Why do we bother with press briefings? Elaine stormed out the door before Cranwell had finished speaking.

EIGHT

Elaine bought a sandwich from the vending machine in the canteen and wolfed it down on her way to the interview room. She had returned from the press briefing to find a note from the forensic lab on her desk. They estimated it might take another twenty-four hours to have the results from the blood and hair they found at Willend's house. The news did not improve her mood. After the debacle of the press briefing, she dreaded the hurricane of media outrage that would happen when, or perhaps if, the results were negative for Sheila's DNA. Her bet was on when.

She checked the "Trace, Interview, and Eliminate" actions, called TIEs, to see if there was anything new to ask Willend or if anyone else had popped up as a potential suspect. There wasn't, and no one had.

When Elaine arrived at the interview room, Benford was glowering in the corridor. His shirt already showed rings of perspiration under the arms. It appeared this interview was going to be unpleasant on several levels. She asked, "Did you see the report?"

Benford snorted. "Bloody boffins. Why is it that sometimes they can give us a report in a day and other times it takes for-bloody-fucking-ever?" He sighed. "Sorry, Elaine."

"No worries, Marcus." Elaine thought Benford's use of profanity was out of character. The old detective was known for being colorful, but he usually used expletives for their effect on others rather than blurting them out to cope with stress. "It will take longer than thirty-six hours. We'll need to apply for a custody extension."

"Not a problem. Cranwell knows and agrees." Benford looked through the observation window at Willend, who was talking quietly with his solicitor in the interview room. "He's been jabbering with his brief for a half-hour now. It's not going to help him. Let's get in there and get started."

Together they entered the room, along with Bull. Benford began after Elaine had recorded the preliminaries. "Dr. Willend. The DNA results for the samples from your basement will take another day. We have applied to keep you in custody an additional forty-eight hours."

The solicitor spoke. "We will protest. It's a serious breach for you to keep Dr. Willend in custody even for this long. All you have is ridiculous circumstance and conjecture. You know the Crown Prosecution Service will laugh you out of the room. I've already filed for Dr. Willend's release. You've made a mistake with this one, Mr. Benford."

Benford pulled a handkerchief from the inner pocket of his jacket and mopped his face. "We'll see who has made the mistakes. Now, Dr. Willend, do you know what I think? I think you have a much higher opinion of yourself than is warranted. And here's what you think. You think you've committed a damn perfect murder. You think you cleaned that blood out of your car and basement and that you'll get away with it. But you won't."

Willend was studying Benford intently.

Benford almost hissed his disdain. "You said you didn't know whose blood it is in the basement. You said the blood in the car is probably yours. I think you're lying. I think that after you left the bus, you lured Sheila to your car and drove to your house. You drugged her, dragged her to the basement, hung her up from those hooks, and beat her to death. That's what I think. Look at you. A posh surgeon with a posh house in a posh neighborhood, and you think you can kill a poor young girl and then lie your way out of it!"

"That's preposterous. I did no such thing, and you damn well know I didn't because you found no trace of her there! Besides, I'm a surgeon. I would never take the chance of breaking my hands. And if I'd beaten the girl, I'd have abrasions and bruises on my knuckles." He paused and inspected Benford's face. "Are you feeling all right?"

Benford raised his voice. "What I'm feeling is outrage. No, you didn't do it there. You took her somewhere else. Some place private. And you wore rubber gloves. We'll find the place, you know, and the gloves. And when we do, you're done for. You are a fucking liar!"

Willend kept his voice level. "I did not lie to you. And I suggest that you calm down a bit. You . . ."

Streams of sweat ran down Benford's temples, and he sounded confused. He was nearly shouting. "I'll calm down when you stop all this lying and tell us the truth! You see, we know you're lying! And you're a doctor. You have access to all kinds of drugs. You're alone in your house, so you can do anything you want and no one will see."

Willend looked at Elaine, imploring her. He extended his arm, his finger pointing past her, toward the alarm button on the wall. "Please, I'm worried about him. He's not well, he may . . ."

Benford lunged to his feet, knocked Willend's hand to the side, then pounded his fist on the table. The solicitor backed his chair away. Elaine had never seen Benford like this. And what was Willend up to? What did he mean, "not well"?

The old detective was shouting and gasping. "You took her to the basement. You beat her, then you . . . you wrapped her in a rug . . . something . . . you can be sure that we'll find it . . . and dragged her to . . . out . . . your garage, put her in the boot of your car, drove away, and dumped her on the tracks." Drops of sweat flew from him as he continued to hammer his fist into the table.

"You did that, didn't you! You're a murderer, Willend. A cold-blooded killer! And before we're finished, we'll find that this isn't the first time. You've killed other girls too!" He stood over the table, wavering on his feet. "Haven't you! How many, Doctor? How many girls have you murdered?"

The solicitor spoke sharply. "Don't reply to that, Dr. Willend! I warn you, Benford, you'll be called on the carpet for this abuse!"

Benford blinked tightly and put his hand up as if to clear his eyes, but it was shaking so hard he placed it back on the table. His raspy breathing sounded labored, coming in short gasps.

Willend again looked at Elaine, making frantic motions for her to push the alarm button on the wall next to her. "You've got to stop him now. I'm afraid he's going to . . ."

But Benford shouted him down. "Afraid of what? Abuse? You call this abuse? What about the . . . on Sheila . . . with his fists . . . fifteen year-old girl . . . drugged . . . beaten and you . . . ?" He leaned over the table, swaying over Willend, who started to rise. Elaine reached out to take Benford's arm, but he swung around, catching her on the shoulder and knocking her to the floor. Bull leapt from his chair as Benford lurched forward over the table, clutching his chest and gasping. Willend blocked Benford's fall and shouted, "Push the goddamn alarm!"

Elaine regained her feet and stabbed her hand at the alarm button. A loud shrieking filled the room as Willend and Bull together lowered Benford's bulk to the floor. Willend opened his collar and felt for a carotid pulse. Immediately, he began CPR. "Call an ambulance! Does he have any medication on him?" Elaine searched Benford's pockets frantically.

The door banged open and two custody officers burst into the room, followed by Cranwell. Seeing Willend bending over Benford's prone body, the constables immediately sprang to pull him off, but Bull prevented them.

Elaine yelled, "Leave him be; he's a doctor. Go get the defibrillator, and call an ambulance." She held up two medicine bottles she had found in Benford's pockets. "Are these the ones?"

Willend glanced at them. "The smaller bottle. Give me one of those." He squeezed open Benford's mouth, shoved the small tablet under Benford's tongue, and went back to CPR.

A constable arrived with the defibrillator, holding it out to Willend, who checked Benford's carotid and held up his hand. "He's got a pulse. But keep it handy."

Benford's breathing finally steadied, and he began to splutter. Elaine, kneeling on the other side of Benford, shushed him softly.

Bull and Cranwell stood to the back, stunned. A second constable pushed his way through a clutch of jail staffers who had gathered around the door and handed Willend a blanket. Willend covered the stricken detective and gestured to Bull. "Can you get those gawkers away from the door? They aren't helping, and they'll block the way for the medics." He looked at Elaine. "I know it's human nature, but I can't tolerate it when people stand around and stare at someone who's having problems. It only adds to the indignity of it all."

Elaine felt her throat tighten, so she swallowed hard. "How's he doing?"

Willend looked at her and his voice took on a gentle, supportive aspect. "You found his heart meds quickly. Now we need to keep him warm and quiet until the medics get here. If he makes it to the hospital, he has a good chance."

He turned his attention back to Benford, opening his shirt and bending over to listen to the heart rhythm. Elaine saw nothing but a pure professional who was concerned for his patient. He had also considered Benford's dignity during the crisis, even though Benford had been hurling foul accusations. He had given her encouragement and support when he noticed her anxiety.

Within a few minutes, the medics arrived, placed Benford on a gurney, and wheeled him away. Cranwell and Elaine took their places opposite Willend and the solicitor.

Cranwell clasped his hands in front of him on the table. "Thank you for your quick action, Dr. Willend. Do you have anything further to add?"

Willend cleared his throat and began to speak. The solicitor touched his shoulder to stop him, but Willend shrugged him off.

His voice was calm and steady as he put his hands on the table and leaned forward.

"Everything I've told you is the truth. I have no idea how that blood came to be in the basement. I don't know whose it is." He turned to Elaine and continued as if he were speaking only to her.

"I have seen enough violent, needless death in my life to know that I never want to see it again. I did not kill Sheila. I could never have harmed Sheila." He gazed intently at Elaine. "I think you know that."

★ ★ ★

An hour later, she knocked on Cranwell's office door. "You wanted to see me, sir?"

"Elaine. Come in." Cranwell indicated the chair in front of his desk. "I talked to the hospital. Marcus is resting and appears out of immediate danger. He'll be there at least for a few days, though. After that, he probably will stay at home. I doubt he'll be back to work before his retirement."

"I'm glad he's doing well. I'll stop by and see him later. I have to ask, sir. Who will be taking over the investigation?"

"You will. That's what I wanted to talk about. I've gotten approval to make you acting DCI, so you'll keep this case. I have it on good authority that your promotion is only a few weeks away, anyway. What's your opinion about Willend?"

Elaine knew she needed to tread carefully. Loyalty was highly valued in any police force, so she shouldn't be too critical of Benford. "I think he's innocent and that we need to find a new line of enquiry as soon as possible."

Cranwell shifted in his chair. "Do you have any plans for finding one?"

"I'm going to look over the scene and interview the dog walker again. DC Costello said he's a retired soldier and that he's very perceptive, so he might be worth another go. Then tomorrow morning, I'll go over everything with the team. I'm sure we'll find a lead to follow."

"After what happened this afternoon, you need to find it fast."

"You know we're stretched thin, sir. We could use another two or three detectives."

"I don't have them to give you. And you've gone and filed a disciplinary action against Jenkins. He asked to be assigned to the case, you kick him out, and then you ask for more people. That's not good for building confidence."

Elaine pressed on. "I understand it doesn't look good, sir. But Jenkins would be worse than nothing. He'd slack off and undermine me at every opportunity."

"You might think twice about testifying against him at the hearing. The tribunal will have all the reports. It's not the first time he's been disciplined."

"I have to have my say, sir. I filed the complaint." She didn't say that she'd be damned if she wasn't the one to kick him off the force.

"Elaine . . ." Cranwell paused. "Fine then, do what you think is right."

She needed to change the subject. "What about this, sir? Bull and Barker have been helping us tremendously. They're very keen on the investigation. Can I have them full time?"

"They're awfully young. I'm not sure they're ready to be part of a murder investigation team."

"I don't see a problem there, sir. Barker was one of the first on the scene when Sheila was found, and she's been helping with canvassing and research. She has a good head on her shoulders. Near the top of her class at police college. Bull's been involved in the search of Willend's house and the interviews. They're already about as up to speed as anyone would be. The investigation will expand. If we're going to crack it, we need more noses."

Cranwell raised his hands in capitulation. "I'm not entirely comfortable with it, but . . . right. I'll see to it. You can tell them to report to your incident room tomorrow."

NINE

The dog walker's house was two doors from the end of the street, directly across the wall from where Sheila's body had lain. A bright light at the front gate pooled its glow in the gathering dusk, revealing an immaculate hedge and front garden. Elaine probably didn't need to worry about tripping over any uncoiled garden hoses.

Retired Regimental Sergeant Major Bernard Alfred Higgins and his aged and friendly looking spaniel, named "Enfield" according to his statement, welcomed her at the door. After Elaine held her hand down to let Enfield have an introductory sniff, they proceeded inside Higgins's orderly home. Higgins was tall, upright, and imposing, especially dressed as he was in his ribbed olive-colored commando jersey and serge pants. She got the impression that he dressed like that every day. A constellation of photos and plaques lining the walls testified that as a young man, Higgins had served His Majesty in North Africa, Europe, and Korea. Later in his career, he had served Her Majesty in the Suez and Malaysia. His military record was apparently as spotless as his home, his clothing, and Enfield.

Sensing Higgins's eagerness, Elaine declined the obligatory offer of tea and got straight to the point. "Thanks for seeing me, Sergeant Major. I'm DI Hope. Can you go over again what happened that morning, when you saw the body?"

"My pleasure, Inspector." It was clear that Higgins had rehearsed his speech. He pulled his frame up to its full height. "At zero-five-thirty hours, I went out to walk Enfield. I took my torch because it was still dark outside." Higgins indicated a large four-cell torch sitting next to a stool by the door. "We proceeded through the wall and turned left. At that time, Enfield began acting agitated, whining and looking toward the rail tracks. I shone the beam of my torch there to see what had gotten his attention. I tracked the beam in a zigzag pattern, beginning at the top of the embankment. I saw nothing along the slope or in the water. However, when I shone the beam at the tracks, I saw what I took to be a bundle lying half out of the water. I could not see it properly, so I moved to the side and down to the bottom of the slope, at the water's edge. From that vantage point, the bundle appeared to me to be a young woman. As I was no more than ten meters from her, I waded across and shone the torch on her. I have seen far too many dead people in my day, so I could tell that she was already gone. Enfield and I did not touch the body, and I saw no one else in the area. I retraced my path through the water, came back to my house, and called nine-nine-nine to report. Once I made the call, I walked back to the embankment and waited for the first officers to arrive. I did not want anyone else to disturb the body."

"Excellent, Sergeant Major. You did exactly as you should have done. I wish more people were as conscientious and observant. Before you took Enfield out, and during the night, did you see any lights or hear any activity from the direction of the tracks?"

"No, I did not. I am very familiar with the area across the wall. Enfield and I walk there twice a day. There is still a bit of light outside. Would it help if I gave you a guided tour?"

"I would appreciate that very much. My wellies are in the car. I'll meet you at the gate."

While she was donning her wellies, Elaine pondered what they knew about the murder up to this point. Given the information they had gathered, they had assumed that Willend had come from the main road in his small dark MINI Cooper and had carried Sheila's body through the wall to the tracks. Then he had turned around and left. But what if the small dark car had nothing to do with the murder? How would the body have gotten there? What if . . .

"Sergeant Major Higgins," Elaine asked as they wove through the labyrinth gate to the grassy embankment, "how many other ways are there to get to this point on the tracks?"

"Many. There is an opening like this for each street, so the murderer could have gained entrance through any of them and walked along the tracks. Or he could have come from the other side, through those buildings." He indicated the industrial park. "I've seen young hooligans do that. There are two openings in the fence along here. There are no lights over there at night, so it's quite dark."

Elaine considered this information. The killer could have driven down any of the streets that abutted the wall. But that meant he—or, unlikely, she—risked being seen from one of the houses while unloading the body from the boot and would have had to carry the body quite a distance before dumping it where it was found. "Can you show me the openings in the fence?"

"Of course. Follow me." Higgins marched straight down the bank, with Elaine scrambling and slipping behind him. Together they sloshed through the water and across the tracks to the overgrown verge along the fence. Higgins shone his light along the fence until it came to rest at a point about three yards to his right. He grunted in satisfaction. It appeared that a section of the fence about three yards long had been removed then patched with a different type of wire.

"Look at this." Higgins indicated the edges of the opening. Pieces of wire had been twisted to hold the patch in place. Elaine shook her head. This had not been in the report of the crime scene. *Who the hell was supposed to have checked this out?* Probably that moron Jenkins. He was notorious for slacking and filing incomplete reports, especially if he felt the job was beneath him. *Sod him to hell.*

"Here's the main spot the hooligans come through. I've watched them unfasten the wire and carry in all sorts of rubbish. That's how most of these washing machines and fridges have gotten here. They can open the fence, dump whatever they have, and be gone inside five minutes. I've tried to contact the company that manages those buildings, to see about mending the fence and installing some lights, but I get only an answering machine. They never return my calls. There are several breaks in the fence along here."

She and Higgins examined the fence for a few minutes, but the deepening darkness made it difficult, so they squished back through the water. When they reached Elaine's car, she opened the boot and began to de-wellie. "Thank you, Sergeant Major. And thank Enfield for me. This has been very illuminating."

Higgins grinned. "It's a good torch. You are quite welcome, Inspector Hope."

Maybe a new line of enquiry was out there in that wasteland. She wanted to visit Benford at the hospital, but there was another thing she needed to check first.

⋆ ⋆ ⋆

Khoury's store was open and brightly lit, so Elaine swung her car into an alley and entered the store. A small man, slightly under middle age and quite below medium height, greeted her from behind the counter.

"Welcome. All of our dairy products are on sale today."

Elaine showed her warrant card and identified herself. "Are you Hassan Khoury?"

The man looked a bit taken aback. "Yes, that's me. How can I help you?"

"I need to know where you were last Friday night, after about eleven PM."

"Where I was? I was here. We close the store at midnight. Why do you want to know?"

"Were any customers here during that time?"

"Yes, let me see." He paused to reflect. "There were at least three." He waited.

Apparently he was going to make her dredge. "And did you know them? Can you describe what happened with them?"

"I know two of them. I had one customer right at eleven. He bought only some cigarettes. I don't know his name. Then Mrs. Connolly came in. She bought some milk and cat food. A few minutes later, Peter came in. He's a regular. He bought his usual kebab, some salad, and some couscous. He was here for about ten or fifteen minutes. There was no one after that."

"The sign says the store is closed."

"My parents are up north for a week. I open the store after I finish at school. Around six o'clock. Our neighborhood regulars all know when to stop by if they need anything."

"Can you describe the man who bought cigarettes? Have you seen him before?"

"Maybe once or twice. He's young. Tall, dark hair, looked very fit. He has an accent. Maybe Russian. That's all."

Elaine considered that Mr. Khoury probably thought most people were tall. "Can you estimate how tall he would be, Mr. Khoury?"

Khoury looked at the door and thought a moment. "He was as tall as the kebab sign. Maybe a little taller."

Elaine studied the sign and concluded the man was just under six feet. She turned back to Khoury. "Tell me about this Peter fellow. Is he a friend?"

"I don't know if he's a friend, but he's more than a customer. He comes in several times a week, probably, and he always talks with us when he is here. If my daughter, Sarah, is here, he asks about her science homework. He's a surgeon."

"What about Mrs. Connolly? How well do you know her?"

"About the same. She is older, and I think she's a widow. My mother would know more. She lives right around the corner, and she comes in every day. Although that night she was later than usual. I think she said she had been at a concert. No, a lecture."

"Thank you, Mr. Khoury. That's all I need for now. Here's my card. Please call me if you can think of anything else that happened that night or if you see the young Russian man again."

She pointed her car in the direction of the hospital. After a few minutes, she found herself humming some song she didn't quite recognize, but she stopped when she thought of Benford. What a day it had been.

TEN

So this is what being a DCI feels like, Elaine thought as she made her way to the incident room for the morning status meeting. *It's not much different, except I can't wear a jersey and jeans to work—most days, anyway. There's a daily mound of paperwork and a raft of meetings. And now I'm in the crosshairs. When I have to release Willend, the press will look for a target, and I'll have one painted on my back.*

And why did I think I wanted this? She knew the answer; she could take her own path to the truth. She was confident that something would turn up in the industrial park.

From the front of the room, she looked out at the sober faces of the investigation team. They were good coppers. Each had individual strengths. For all Marcus's faults and old-fashioned ways, he knew how to assemble a good team. But even the best team needed a strong leader, and transitions can be difficult. It was time for her to step up.

"All right, boys and girls. Listen up. I talked to Mandie at the hospital this morning. She said the chief is doing much better, but he probably won't be back to work before his retirement, so I'll be acting in his place until further notice. Paula will be taking over my duties." She waited a moment for the murmurs to die down and then proceeded. "First item, Barker, start a whip 'round for a get-well card and a gift for Marcus. Remember that he and Mandie are retiring to Jamaica. If anyone has any suggestions for the gift, let Barker know. I'll check with Mandie about a retirement party. I suppose it depends on how Marcus is doing. And beginning today, we've got Bull and Barker on the team full time for the duration. Paula, you interviewed Leah and Sheila's mum again yesterday. Tell us about it."

Paula moved to the front. "Her mum was still stunned. She's a nice enough woman, no drugs or anything sinister going on with her, but she's been living on the edge financially ever since Sheila's dad ran off to Oz with a coworker. She had nothing but good things to say about Sheila, but then mums mostly say that, don't they?"

"What about Friday nights?" Elaine asked.

"Loretta confirmed what she told us earlier. Friday was the regular night for her to go out with her boyfriend. Loretta figured it was better for Sheila to have a regular place to go than to stay home alone. Makes sense in theory but didn't in real life.

"According to Leah, Sheila led quite a romantic existence. The first couple of times Sheila stayed over, she stayed there all night. Then it changed. It sounds like Sheila had begun to dominate Leah, and the house became her base of operations. Sheila would show up early, they'd eat, talk, and listen to music. Then when Leah's parents went to bed, Sheila would pop out the window and be gone, almost until dawn. Sometimes she told Leah where she was going, sometimes not. She talked about a new boy every few weeks. Leah knew some of the boys, so we'll get on to them to see if they know anything."

"What about Danny, last Friday night?"

"She was able to add more details. Sheila had told her that he was older and had his own flat and a flash car . . . an Audi sports job, which she thought was posh. She told Leah that she had met him at a rave a couple of weeks ago. Leah wasn't with her at the time, so she couldn't give us a description, but Sheila had said he was a footballer. We've notified uniform, and we're canvassing the area for Danny and the Audi, preferably as a matched set. We're checking through registrations for an Audi owned by a Daniel. Looking at CCTV. The usual. And that's about it right now. We'll check football clubs tomorrow."

"Try the lower-division clubs first. If he's premier league, he's driving a Ferrari or a Lambo. Search the rosters on the team web-sites. That will save some time."

A voice piped up. "If he's a footballer, he's already crashed his Lambo and the Audi is his backup." This remark prompted a few chuckles.

"Not a bad point. Evan, have someone ask rental agencies about Audis. Anything else before we move on?"

DC Simon Costello stood. He spoke in a crisp BBC accent that was perfectly in harmony with his tailored suits. Elaine sometimes wondered how many he owned and how much he spent on his haircuts. He looked like a successful banker, but he was one of the most intelligent detectives Elaine had ever worked with. "We got a call from a young man this morning who might have been driving the dark car that was seen." He consulted his notes. "Ian Plimpton, seventeen, address in Kentish Town. He had a late night out with friends and was trying to get home before his father needed the car to get to work. He was unfamiliar with the area, and he turned there thinking it was a shortcut. He has no form or arrests. He's coming in after school to give a formal statement."

"Good. Whoever takes his statement, make absolutely sure of the street he turned on, if he can remember. Anything else new?" No one spoke, so she continued.

"Last night, I interviewed the dog walker, and then I traced Sheila's route to have a look at it. The Khoury's store was open, so I went in. As luck would have it, Hassan Khoury was working, and he was able to confirm that Willend was there, along with a couple of other customers. One was a young man he didn't recognize—tall, thin, Eastern European, bought smokes. The other was a Mrs. Connolly, who lives in the area. We'll track her down today, but I have no reason to believe that Khoury was lying. It's starting to look like Willend's story checks out."

"But the sign said it was closed." Simon looked nervous.

"Don't worry. It is, during the day. Hassan opens it after he finishes his day job, just like Willend told us. It's not looking good for those of you who had a tenner on Willend. Metaphorically speaking, of course. Fortunately, we have a new line of enquiry." She related what she had learned from Higgins. "Simon, take Bull and Barker and a couple of uniforms and check out that industrial estate on the east side of the tracks. Evan, find out who owns it and scrape up any more information you can. I've got some other work for you too. Come see me after you get them started.

"All right then, one other thing. I called forensics earlier. The DNA results will be available by the end of today. I don't want to be negative, but I think we need to get moving in a new direction. Let's keep sniffing."

★ ★ ★

By noon, Elaine had moved into Benford's office. She liked having a door she could close. At some point, she would need to box up his mementos, take down his plaques, and eventually, perhaps, have her name put on the door. But not yet.

Evan Cromarty entered and sat across the desk, looking at her expectantly, so she began. "You're our researcher. I need you to put on your research hat. Is that all right with you?"

Evan appeared pleased. "Sure is, guv."

"Excellent. Something tells me our killer's done this before. The beating looked too scientific, and it wasn't spontaneous. If he's done it before, it could be part of a pattern that we need to find. I want to know about any unsolved crimes similar to Sheila's in the UK in the last five years. Severe beating with fists, a signature slash. Grievous bodily harm or murder. Victim dumped, perhaps drugs in her system—although that's not a strict criterion. For victims, we're looking for women between, say, fifteen and thirty-five. Start local and expand out from there. Keep in mind that it doesn't have to be identical. The older the crime, the more leeway there is for variation. Like I said, we're looking for a pattern."

"So not specifically murder. Include GBH?"

"Correct. Murder and GBH. Like I said, start local. Once you've found some, correlate them with each other on the crime scene, method, or other aspects. Look for a pattern."

"If we find a pattern, we might stray into Serial Crime's patch. Will that be a problem?"

"We'll decide what to do about that if the time comes. Any questions?"

"Eventually, but not right now. There's one other thing, though. You asked me to check the traffic accident report for Willend's family." He handed her several sheets of paper. "And the background report from the FBI liaison at the American Embassy came just now. It's there too. Is that all?"

"For now, thanks. Set it up and get started. Shout if you need anything."

Once Evan had left, she turned to the accident report. Diana and Liza Willend were riding in a taxi on the M23, having been picked up at Gatwick earlier. Heavy fog had caused traffic to slow down to a snail's pace, and an articulated lorry had slammed into their taxi from behind, starting a chain reaction that ultimately involved nineteen vehicles. The lorry driver apparently hadn't slowed down despite the low visibility, and toxicology showed he was full of amphetamines. The impact had instantly killed Diana, Liza, and the taxi driver.

The American Embassy had provided Willend's background and military records in record time. Willend had no criminal record in the States. He had graduated cum laude from the University of Texas and then had gone to medical school. His military record was only a summary, but it was impressive. First there was officer's school and assignments at Walter Reed Hospital and the Brooke Army Medical Center in San Antonio, then Iraq. Captain Willend had been wounded halfway through his second tour of duty there.

After that, there was another year in San Antonio. He had left the military for unspecified medical reasons.

All of which was interesting, but not too helpful from any angle. Why had his wife and daughter come from Texas? Perhaps he was scheduled for leave and they were meeting in London. Why hadn't he told her about the tragic accident instead of refusing to talk about it? He hadn't been there. Judging from the dates, he was in Iraq when it happened. Maybe that in itself had something to do with it, but still, why not say that? In her experience, suspects, except for hardened criminals, seek empathy under aggressive interrogation. A guilty conscience causes them to clam up, but Willend hadn't been anywhere near the M23. Why would he feel guilty about it?

She decided to put aside any questions about Willend or his background. He wasn't guilty, so at this point it was only personal interest, right? It was time to take care of an hour or so of administrative work, so she turned to her computer and logged in. She'd grab a quick bite of lunch once that was done.

Elaine's mobile rang as she made her way back from the canteen. It was Simon.

"Hi, guv. When we were searching along the fence line, one of the uniforms spotted a trainer lying several yards on the other side. We drove around to the entrance of the estate. It had no gate or security and was wide open, so we went in and bagged the shoe. It fits the description of the ones Sheila was wearing that night, and Barker's taking it to Sheila's house to see if Mrs. Watson can verify it."

"Excellent! I was thinking maybe she would show up at a rave dressed in trainers, but maybe she had another pair of shoes with her. Have Barker ask Mrs. Watson if any other of Sheila's shoes are missing. I didn't see any mention in the previous action report, but ask again."

She heard Simon giving instructions to Liz, then he was back on the line. "Okay, done. Another thing, most of the warehouse units were locked up tight, but a couple had broken windows and one showed a forced lock. It looked like suspicious entry."

"Do you have any reason to suspect that someone is in there now?"

"One of the uniforms thinks he might have heard a noise."

Elaine rolled her eyes and chuckled. It was tempting, but she didn't want to jeopardize any evidence if the trainer turned out to be Sheila's. "I know you want to, but no. Keep an eye on it and see if anyone loaded down with loot tries to get away. Set up a perimeter while I apply for a warrant. Are there any CCTV cameras covering the entrance?"

"Point made, guv. There's a camera at the corner, about a hundred meters or so from the gate. It might have caught cars driving down the street or turning in. But nothing any closer than that. I'll ask for footage."

"Is there any indication who owns the place?"

"There's a sign, but all it has is the name and phone number of the estate agent, one Geri Harding. I'll text it to you."

"Good job. Keep nosing around, but don't let enthusiasm get in the way of proper procedure. There are times to push the limits, but this isn't one of them."

"Right, guv. I'll keep you posted."

The texts arrived a minute later, and Elaine dialed the estate agent's number. A woman's voice answered after four rings.

"Geri Harding's number. Alicia speaking."

"Hello, Alicia. Is Geri Harding available?"

"No, she's on holiday this week. May I ask your name and what this is in reference to?"

"I'm Acting DCI Hope from the Met. Don't be alarmed. She's not in any trouble. I have a question about the industrial park in Leaside. There's a sign at the entrance with Geri's name on it. Would you have her mobile?"

"This is her mobile number. I'm the receptionist in the offices. She's forwarding her calls to me while she's gone."

"Well then, perhaps you can help me. I was wondering who owns it. Some of the units appear to have been broken into, and we need to contact them. Do you have their number?"

"No, I don't. Geri works alone, and I can't get hold of her. But there's a solicitor she works with, Jackson Greene. Maybe he can help. His office is in Newham. Let's see." Elaine heard a keyboard clicking. "Here's his number."

Elaine repeated the series of digits back to Alicia, thanked her, and rang off. So Harding's a loner. There was no answer at Greene's office when she tried the number, so she sent an action to Cromarty to do a background check on Harding and Greene and returned to her paperwork.

A half hour later, Liz rang. "Hi, Chief. Mrs. Watson said the shoe looks to be one of Sheila's. Sheila wasn't trying to be Imelda Marcos, but she owned three pairs of trainers, two pairs of flats, and about thirty pairs of ridiculous glamour shoes. They mostly look like she bought them in flea markets and thrift shops. I asked Mrs. Watson to look through them closely, and she thinks there's a pair of silver pumps missing, but she's not completely sure. They could be in the backpack we haven't found, I suppose."

"Thanks, Liz. Phone Simon and tell him I said to sit tight and wait for the warrant. Then get back there yourself. And, Liz, please don't suppose."

They had the warrant within an hour.

★ ★ ★

Geri Harding zipped up her roller suitcase and glanced at the clock next to her bed. There was more than enough time to get to the airport, so she retrieved the enameled box from the lower drawer of her nightstand, opened it, and tapped out a pile of powder onto the glass surface. As she chopped and arranged the white crystals, she reflected that her monthly leasing numbers were looking pretty good. She'd exceeded her targets slightly, so she would get her usual bonus. But she hungered, even ached, for the astoundingly generous reward promised to her if she doubled her normal monthly goal. She wanted it desperately.

Of course, she networked like crazy. Her diary was packed with wine schmoozes and seminars, lunch presentations, and breakfast meet-ups. On occasion, she would fuck a hesitant businessman to ensure a deal would close. She planned extravagant promotions that she prophesied would pack the buildings like so many sardine tins, and she knew that with a bit more promo budget, she could have waiting lists for all the office and warehouse spaces in her portfolio. She had worked up dozens of proposals and submitted them to Greene. And not one had ever been approved.

That bloody Jackson Greene. He calls himself a solicitor, but he's nothing but a lecher. He had never approached her for sex, but she was sure it was what he wanted. She never would agree. He was a sweaty pig. *Yech.*

Greene made sure he stayed between her and the real clients—the "cousins," as he called them. When she gave Greene her proposals, he would listen politely, sometimes even enthusiastically, to her plans. Then he would confer with the cousins and either kill her proposal with a "Sorry, maybe next year" or scale down her plan so much that it had no hope of joyous resounding success. "Tight marketing budget," he'd say. Or "There have been unforeseen renovation costs in Birmingham." Or "There's a competing project in Aberdeen." Granted, she only saw her part of the picture, but still . . . she didn't understand.

Maybe Greene never actually showed her work to the cousins. That was a thought. Maybe the cousins were content with what they had. Geri didn't know any businessmen who were content with what they had, and she knew she wasn't. She'd think about it in Ibiza. She picked the gold-plated tube from the box and snorted the line.

ELEVEN

Elaine was walking out of her office to go to the industrial estate when her mobile rang.

"Hi, Nige. What joy have you got for me?"

"We have the DNA results from the Willend house. Sorry it took so long. I hope you're sitting down."

"I'm ready. Please keep the boffin-speak to a minimum, though."

Nigel chuckled. "I'll try, but I can't guarantee it. In a nutshell, the blood that we found at Willend's house does not belong to Sheila."

"Neither sample?"

"Right. The DNA from the car matches Willend. The DNA from the basement is a woman's, but it belongs to either Willend's mother or his sister. Can't tell which, but the mitochondrial DNA is the same as his."

"That's the DNA that's passed from mother to child, right?"

"And I thought you weren't a nerd. Yes. *Seven Daughters of Eve* and all that."

"Okay. Thanks, Nige."

She sat at her desk. The truth will come out, and innocence was as true as guilt. She regretted that an innocent man had been subjected to interrogation and jail, but unfortunately, it was sometimes part of the winnowing process. Still, she needed to inform the police solicitors and the Professional Standards unit. There would be an internal investigation, no doubt watched closely by certain members of the press.

A short while later, she stood outside Willend's cell as the custody sergeant opened the door. Willend sat on the thin mattress, looking drawn and tired. "You got the DNA results back."

"Yes. You're free to go."

"It took a while." Willend studied her. "You don't look disappointed."

It was not the response she had anticipated. She'd expected to feel his wrath, not a comment on her own emotions. "Well, it's important to get a result, but it's more important to get the right result."

"I'm glad someone around here thinks that way. How is Benford?"

"He's getting better. The doctors say he'll be able to go home in a couple of days."

Willend nodded. "He pushed himself over an edge."

The custody clerk handed Willend his possessions. He signed for them, Elaine signed the release order, and they walked to the door.

"Is there a bus stop near here?"

"Yes, there's one at the corner. But I'll arrange for a car to take you home, if you like. In fact, I'll take you home. I'm going out anyway. Wait here and I'll come around."

As soon as she turned to get her car, she thought, *Why did you offer that, Lainie? Guilt? What on earth can you say to him? Ugh. Awkward.*

★ ★ ★

Elaine was silent the first few minutes of the drive to Willend's house. She didn't feel exactly guilty, but it was hard for her not to feel some responsibility. "Dr. Willend, I hope you realize that I was only doing my job. There was nothing personal about it." She turned her head toward him. Their eyes met, and she could see fire in his.

When he spoke, his voice was flat, articulated. "That's a cop-out. Everything you do to a person is personal from their point of view. There's no such thing as 'just business.' Let's start with this. Do you know how hard it is for me to get past the fact that you thought I was a murderer? That the entire country thought, still thinks, I am a murderer?"

She felt like she was on the defensive, and she didn't want to be. She needed to shift the argument. "See, that's what I mean. It's not true. I never thought you were a murderer. I thought you were a suspect. You could have been a murderer, but I didn't know the truth about you then."

"There were moments when you certainly sounded like you thought I was."

"I was doing my job. It's not always pleasant, and it's rarely nice. I had to get at the truth, and the only way to do that is to gather evidence and ask tough questions."

Willend looked out his window, watching the parades of shops and rows of terraced houses scroll past. "And I thought you lot acted on hunches and experience. What you're saying sounds scientific."

It was spoken like a sneer. Elaine had to remind herself not to lose her temper. She continued. "It is, when done properly. We're taught to assume nothing, believe nothing, challenge everything. Experience certainly helps, but sometimes it can get in the way too. You have to learn how to use it. For me to find the truth, I rely on training and discipline, then add the experience."

Willend snorted. "I thought the police's job was to investigate, gather evidence, and then let the courts decide what's true."

"We have to construct a solid case. Else how can a jury get it right?" Elaine checked traffic, downshifted, and turned. "I can't speak for anyone else, but I'm not the kind of copper who fits people up."

Willend turned in his seat and fixed his eyes on her. "So the truth matters to you, then?"

"Beyond anything you can imagine! Why do you think I became a cop? Is there justice without truth?"

Willend laughed. "There was no truth or justice as far as I was concerned, wouldn't you say? Do you want to hear the real, uncomfortable truth?" Willend's voice rose. "The truth is that I've been hounded by you people and jailed for no reason other than I happened to take a particular bus home from work. The truth is that I've been set up as a murderer by you and then had my name blasted across the nation by the sleazy tabloid hacks that masquerade as journalists over here. And the outcome of all of it is that I will very likely be hounded by those hacks until you catch the real killer. And even beyond if they think it will give their readers a thrill by dredging up an old story. I can see it now! 'It's the first anniversary of Sheila's murder, so what's Dr. Death doing these days?' Jesus. I may never fucking get out of the news. Did you ever consider what your actions would do to my reputation? My career? Do you have any idea?"

Elaine pulled the car to the side of the road and turned to Willend. "Our first responsibility is to find justice for the victim, Dr. Willend. And however it shakes out, the evidence, the law, and the jury will ensure justice for the suspect. We were doing our job. I . . ."

Willend interrupted her. "A minute ago you said there's no justice without truth. You're right, there's not. There's been damn little truth in the way I've been dealt with. And because of that, there's been no justice for Sheila either. You're back to square one, aren't you? Admit it."

Despite taking a deep breath, Elaine had trouble keeping her voice steady. "It's not like there's a bloody big flashing sign that points the way to the truth. Like I said, we have to find it. We have to turn over ugly rocks and inspect all the slimy things underneath. We have to pressure people and disrupt their lives. If that means saying provocative things, asking disturbing questions, then, well, we have to do it. It's never pleasant. Murder isn't pleasant. It's never convenient for anyone."

She shifted the car into gear and pulled back into the traffic. "And one more thing, it's because I, because we, searched for the truth that you've been released. Did you think about that?"

Willend stared out the car's window, his eyes tracking the people hurrying along through the rain. He appeared to be gathering himself. When he spoke again, his voice had softened. "All during this, I was trying to read you. It wasn't as easy as reading Benford, but I got the impression you disagreed with him about me. Is that true?"

Elaine considered her answer. They were talking about truth, after all. "I was never convinced he was right about you."

"Why not?"

She plunged ahead. "The way you reacted when we first interviewed you. The pictures on your piano. The ones of you and your wife and daughter. The relationship you appear to have with your mother and sister. You care deeply about the foundation kids and their families. Then you helped Benford when he had the heart attack. You tried to prevent it. All that together, I guess. You respect women and you care about fixing what's wrong. And you seem to try to do the right thing, regardless."

They were both silent until she pulled the car under the portico at Willend's house. "Here you are, Dr. Willend."

Willend opened the door, paused, and looked at her. She sensed a churning behind his eyes and saw him breathe deeply before he continued. "Thank you for that. For what you said just now. And for being honest with me. I'm going to the hospital as soon as I can to try to save my job. Would you please call Owen Clayton? I need him to know you've released me and that I'm no longer under any suspicion." He stopped before he closed the car door. "And call me Peter. I can't help but wish that we'd met under different circumstances." He closed the door and disappeared into his house.

What was that about? "Call me Peter?" She doubted she would ever get the chance. Willend was an interesting man, successful, decent looking and smart, musical and witty, but there was darkness inside him. *Intense sorrow*, she thought. She reversed the car and headed for the industrial estate. She would call his boss as soon as she could.

TWELVE

Owen Clayton put down the phone and looked across his desk at Peter. "It was that police inspector. She confirmed what you've told me. Even with that, I can't promise it will change the board's decision."

"Why not? Nothing can touch the hospital if I'm no longer a suspect. I've been exonerated."

"Have you talked to Sjolin at the foundation?"

"No, I haven't. I didn't see any point until I spoke with you."

"Well, I have talked with him, as has Lindsay. He's upset to say the least."

"Okay, I'll give him a call right away."

Clayton held up his hand. "Peter, there's really no point right now. Sjolin and the other foundation directors have spoken with Lindsay. You know how hospitals are. Rumors have been flying. All the TV and tabloid press coverage stirs the pot. Lindsay can't be seen as complacent, especially where the hospital's image is concerned. Sjolin has to think about the foundation first, philanthropists being what they are and all. He's appointed Sheena as head of the foundation's reconstructive team. For God's sake, Peter, you were a suspect in a murder!"

Peter stood and leaned over the desk, glowering at Clayton. "But I'm not anymore! I've been exonerated! You heard it yourself, from the detective in charge of the investigation. What more do you need? The greedy bastard who owns those tabloids will rule us all as long as we let him. What's the saying? 'All it takes is for good people to do nothing'? My god, don't any of you have the balls to stand up for what's right?"

Clayton shook his head. "Peter, sit down, please. Look, we have to distance the hospital from anything about this investigation, at least until people have moved on to the next scandal. You've got to stay away until this thing is wrapped up, then perhaps we can talk about you coming back."

"Perhaps? I see. I always pegged the board members as gutless ass-kissing sons-of-bitches. But not you, Owen. I thought you had a backbone. Don't you feel the least bit culpable in the destruction of my career?"

"You'd be back in A&E tonight if it were up to me. But I'm just the messenger."

"Yeah, right. How long is this supposed to last?"

"I have no idea. I know only what I've told you."

"Is Lindsay here?"

"There's a conference in Edinburgh this week."

Peter left without another word. Perhaps it was a good thing that Lindsay wasn't there.

⋆ ⋆ ⋆

From the chair in front of his large bedroom window, Peter could see the glittering tower of the Shard in the distance. He remembered how he had thought it was an unfortunate eyesore when it was under construction, but now that it was complete, he realized it was a masterpiece. He enjoyed watching the late afternoon sunlight play on the glass planes of its surface. So he sat, his mind drifting, staring over the rooftops at the lovely jagged glimmer in the distance, until a soft, familiar voice jogged him out of his reverie.

"It's times like these when you really need someone." Diana sat in the smaller chair set at an angle at the base of the window. Her eyes were in shadow, but the glow of the fading sunlight played on her copper hair and caught the straight line of her jaw.

"And you're always here for me, aren't you?"

"I always will be. What happened can't change that."

"Me too, Daddy. We're both here for you," Liza said. Peter felt her take his hand.

"I know, sweetie, and it always helps me to know that."

"Mommy says that we'll always be there with you."

Peter's eyes met Diana's. "She's right. You and Mommy are always with me, no matter what."

"But we're not really there, you know. I mean, like before. I was talking with Mommy about that. I had some questions."

"Like what? What questions did you have?"

"I was wondering like you and Mommy always told me to do. It seems like we don't talk about silly stuff anymore. And we can't go swimming and ride horses at the ranch with you and Romero. Or go shopping with Nana and get ice cream. It's like we only get glimpses of you, and it's always when you're alone."

Memories welled up in his mind. He looked at Liza. "Do you remember that petting zoo we used to go to? The one outside New Braunfels? The one with all the baby goats?"

Liza's face lit up. "Yes! I had a bottle of milk and all the baby kids were mobbing me. And when you bent over to help me feed one, a billy goat butted you in your rear and knocked you over!" She howled with laughter. "And Aunt Kate took your picture. You were sitting on the ground and the billy goat was standing there looking at you."

Peter nodded. "I still have that picture. It's on my desk upstairs."

Liza asked, "How is Aunt Kate?"

"She's fine. She's in Italy with Nora."

"I never met Nora. I would have liked to, but that was after. Is Nana okay?"

"Yep, she is. She went to Antarctica on a cruise ship. Then she's going to Machu Picchu before she comes home. You remember the book you had about Antarctica, right?"

"Yes. There are a lot of penguins there, and it's so cold the male penguins hold the eggs on their feet to keep them from freezing. Nana really gets around, doesn't she?" This prompted chuckles from Peter and Diana. "But I want to know what's going to happen with you. And why every time I see you, it seems like you're sad. Or frightened from what happened. I really don't want you to be sad. I don't think Mommy does either."

"Ah. I see. It helps to know that you both feel that way. I guess you stay with me in my heart until those times when I really need to be with you. Then you come out and we talk."

"Or maybe that's when you let us out? When you're alone and sad? Or scared?"

"Perhaps. It's when I miss you and need you the most. What do you think about that?"

Liza looked at Diana, then back at him. "It feels good to be able to help you. But I wish you didn't need our help. I wish you weren't always so alone. There's nothing we can do about what happened. I think we'd rather stay in your heart, because that's when we know you're busier and happier. I mean, we know we'll always be there. We both love you so much."

"And I love you both, no matter what."

"Well, it would be nice to come out and talk to you when you're happy too."

She had always been a wise child.

Peter looked at Diana, the woman he had instantly fallen in love with years ago, in his second year at the university. On the first day of the term, she sat next to him in Dr. Livingston's parliamentary government class. He was reading the international edition of *The Guardian* when a gentle voice asked him if a subscription was required. When he turned his head to answer, he was confronted by a pair of confident deep-green eyes, and he knew immediately that she was the one. All he could do was stammer an affirmative, clumsily adding that if she wanted, they could share his copy.

With that memory, he looked across the room. Diana gazed back at him with the green eyes that, from the first time they met, had turned all his darkness into light. He felt Liza watching them both.

Peter knew he was seeing and feeling what his heart wanted. He laid his head against the back of the chair and wept himself to sleep.

★ ★ ★

Elaine twisted the valve as far as it would go and levered it fully open. Hot water was what she needed, and lots of it, as she did many nights during an investigation. She tilted her head back and let it filter through her hair, trickle down her spine, cascade over her breasts, flow over her belly, and, with a gurgle, disappear down the drain. She hoped that each rivulet that wound its way over her torso somehow neutralized a sin she had come in contact with that day. Perhaps in doing so, it would wash away the one she carried with her.

Elaine was unsure if it worked, however long she rinsed. This was because the next morning she would rise, wash away the sleep, and begin her daily process of gathering to herself the knowledge of murder, in order to eliminate the evil.

Sometimes the task seemed as futile as her nightly shower, but she had to do it. In a back corner of her psyche, Elaine was still seven years old, still curled on the sitting room floor, bewildered and frozen with fright. And Moira was still in the bedroom, screaming her last breaths through the thin wall of the council flat.

THIRTEEN

Elaine finished tapping in her report and clicked Submit to file the update into the case history. The good news was that a mounting trail of evidence increasingly validated her decision to release Willend. The bad news was that it wasn't pointing to anyone else in particular. For all his good qualities, Benford had succumbed to an obsession with the first suspect in the case, and it had cost him dearly. It was one thing to speculate ahead of the facts but quite another to ignore what the evidence was saying. She didn't know it for a fact, but she suspected that he and Cranwell had been under pressure from higher up to get a good result quickly. Someone up there was looking for a knighthood or an OBE. Nothing new about that.

She turned her chair and gazed at the situation board through the window of the office. Let's get back to the basics: means, opportunity, motive. Fill in the gaps.

They could track Sheila's movements until she got off the bus and disappeared into the night to meet her murderer. The last fix they had on her mobile was near the bus stop, but it had apparently been turned off shortly afterward. Where had she met him? There was no evidence that she had ever actually met Danny that night. He had not picked her up near Leah's house or the bus stop. Why not? Because he had a place they could meet, where she could have a drink or three. And having her come to him reduced the chances that they would be seen together. But that didn't mean that someone hadn't seen her entering a house. Maybe she had passed Mrs. Connolly on the pavement. She wrote an action to do a house-to-house in the blocks around the Khoury's store and e-mailed it to Paula.

Sheila was either assaulted at that house or taken to the industrial park and assaulted there. That was a distance of about twelve kilometers. So that was the next gap. The warrant had come through the day before, and Simon had been there with SOCO. What they found might determine if the derelict warehouse was the site of the assault or not. She would wait and see.

The big gaps in opportunity still pointed at Danny. Who was he? Was he really a footballer? That was a standard pickup lie. If every young stud in London were the footballer he claimed to be, the entire city would be awash with flying soccer balls. How did he live his life, get his money, seduce his women? The meager description they had would fit any number of young London hipsters. The hipster population tended to circulate in fairly regular patterns among the latest hot clubs. Close questioning of bartenders and bouncers at the clubs might turn something up. So they had to ask the questions about Audi-driving footballers and club-hopping hipsters at every football stadium and dance club in East London. It was a daunting, expensive task with little hope of success. Elaine doubted that Sheila had ever made it to a club that night.

Now what about motive? It was the slipperiest of the three. Not all people were motivated to violence in the same way. Money, sex, revenge, love (or for gangs, group acceptance), and power, singly or in some combination, were the motivators for most violent crimes. Almost anything could be a motive for murder, and a grievance that would motivate one person to murder would prompt another to deliver a slap across the chops and a third person to utter only a heartfelt "Fuck you." Gang beatings typically carried a blatant message—what was the point if no one knew why it had happened? There was no gang affiliation in Sheila's profile.

She pressed her fingers into her temples. Kumar had said that Sheila wasn't dead until after her body was dumped. She had so many drugs in her system and had sustained such a beating that it was likely that, had she not died, she would have been comatose for some time and would not remember much if she had ever awakened. She possibly would not have even registered that she was in torment. Now that was a thought. Sadists get satisfaction by registering the discomfort or pain they cause their victims. Would a sadist enjoy destroying a comatose victim? She needed to check with the police shrink. Had the killer done it before? What if the slashed face was a signature? One occurrence does not a signature make, but it surely looked like one.

Or was the killer a spurned boyfriend whose revenge had gone a vicious step too far? It was possible, but she didn't think so. Love, betrayal, and beatings commonly went hand-in-hand, but intentional disfigurement was rare. By all reports, Sheila had never indicated she had any close relationship with anyone.

No, motive wasn't the key to solving Sheila's murder. The real evidence was in the chain of events. Find where and when, and she'd find who. There was nothing new about that.

There was a knock at her office door, and she looked up to see Paula Ford. Without a word, Paula held up a tabloid newspaper with a headline that screamed "Sheila Slashed!"

"We didn't release that! Who the hell . . . ? Get everyone in the room, right now."

★ ★ ★

After five minutes of making sure that everyone knew she could dress them down as well as Benford ever had and that there was no doubt whatsoever about her position on maintaining security, Elaine felt like it was time to move on. "So if you know something, come forward by the end of the day. I don't want to start an internal investigation, but I will if I have to. Is that perfectly clear to everyone?" From the stunned expressions throughout the room, she knew it was. "Simon, please bring everyone up to date on what you found at the Leaside industrial estate."

Simon stood. "In the unit, we found a chair set against a wall, various debris, and what appeared to be small blood smears and splatters. It looked like someone had wiped the place down, but enough was left to suggest that something violent happened. A SOCO team is there now. As soon as we're finished here, I'll go back and have a look through the rest of the estate. We've called a locksmith to get us into the locked units."

"Good work. Be sure to have SOCO get a paint chip from the wall. If it matches the one Kumar found in Sheila's hair, we'll be certain that's where she was killed."

Simon nodded, then Bull spoke. "Wouldn't that be a bit too close for comfort, given where her body was dumped? Usually a killer will dump the body some distance away."

Elaine nodded. "Perhaps there wasn't time, or maybe something interfered. Or maybe the guy got lazy. We don't know. Right now, let's concentrate on finding out where Sheila went after she got off the bus. Follow up with Mrs. Connolly to see if she passed Sheila on her way to the store, and if there's no joy there, organize some uniforms and start a house-to-house. Who saw her walking down the street or go into a house? Who saw a young drunk girl and a slim hipster get into a posh Audi sports car? My hypothesis is that from there, they went to the industrial estate. A sign on the street showed a leasing agent, a Geri Harding. She's on holiday, can't be contacted, but she's due back at the beginning of next week, and she works with a solicitor in Newham named Jackson Greene. Any luck tracking down Jackson Greene? Evan?"

Cromarty stood. "We've done a bit of background. Office is in Newham. He's known to Vice to have some rather dodgy clients . . . strip clubs, massage parlors, and such."

"So he definitely deserves a visit. I'll give him one later. What about the ownership?"

"The property is owned by a company called Cambrian Estates, which is owned by Bitola, a company registered in Macedonia, of all places. Cambrian bought the property a year ago but has done nothing with it. They don't have a website, and the only UK address appears to be a council flat in Cardiff. We're on to our embassy in Skopje to follow up on Bitola and have a call in to the former owners of the property and their agent to see what they can tell us."

Elaine considered. "So we have a dodgy solicitor, a Welsh front, and a Macedonian holding company that may turn out to be nothing more than a postal box. Someone is hiding something. It may or may not have anything to do with Sheila, but if we can find out who had access to the warehouse, we might learn something. Stay on it, and keep the team informed."

At Evan's acknowledgement, she continued. "One more thing. Paula, I need you to dig deeper with Leah to see if you can find out any more about Sheila's habits. Teenagers always withhold information, and if you sense that, push her. Push gently, but push her. And give some uniforms Sheila's picture and send them to clubs in the area to talk to the bouncers and bartenders. Have them ask about Danny. Sheila was underage, so maybe she was turned away at some point."

FOURTEEN

For whatever reason, the next morning Elaine was optimistic enough to wear a light-green silk blouse, her reasonably nice second-best suit, and a complementary-hued scarf. Paula Ford followed her to the office and shut the door.

"Hmmm. Nice choices. I like the scarf. Definitely a step up from your usual. Either you're making progress or you've found a new man."

Elaine laughed. "Wouldn't that be something? If it was a new man, I'd have worn my red satin teddy under all this."

"A red satin teddy? Better and better, girl. You can't fool me . . . let's see . . . the new DI came down from Newcastle. Not too shabby to look at, and he has that boyish Northern charm. I heard he's single."

"Don't you start any rumors."

Paula lifted her eyebrows. "Okay, I'll start an office pool."

"Don't you dare. Remember, I'm the guv now. You do that and you might find yourself partnered with Jenkins." She gave Paula a smile and picked up her notes. Together they walked to the front of the incident room.

"All right, boys and girls. What have we got?"

She looked at Simon, who took the cue. "SOCO should have the final report on the industrial estate by early afternoon. The rain has let up for now, and the water in the drain will have subsided, so we'll finish up looking for anything in the mud and check farther downstream just in case."

"Right. Keep at it." She raised her eyebrows at Evan. "Any luck yet on finding a pattern of some kind? Related cases? What about the company ownership?"

"We're still waiting for our Macedonian Embassy to get back to us. They should have something later today. I'll do some more digging on the shell companies and Greene. And I have some data on similar crimes over the last five years."

"Okay, then. Let's meet in my office in fifteen minutes." She scanned the room. "Fine. Good work, everyone. Keep at it, and be sure to check in with either me or Paula if you have any news or need anything."

Evan's knock came precisely fifteen minutes later. He entered and sat.

"Okay, where are we?"

Evan placed his laptop on Elaine's desk and turned it so she could see the screen. She saw a spreadsheet matrix, a web of rectangles filled with data in tiny print.

Evan pointed at the bottom row of the data. "We've found roughly eighteen hundred cases within the last five years. First we divided them into murder and GBH, then solved and unsolved. We've got sixteen unsolved murders and fifty-seven unsolved GBH. Most of the unsolved cases are categorized as gang related."

Elaine chuckled. "Does this come with a magnifying glass? I can barely read it. I don't see any correlation. We need to extract a pattern if there is one."

Evan grinned. "Well, I can make the type size larger, but you're right. This is the raw data. Any patterns we look for are dependent on our base assumptions and predispositions. So what I'm wondering is . . . patterns in what? Are we looking for victim type? Male or female? Or method? Time frame? Or maybe location? Are we looking for a signature? There's a lot of inconsistency and variation in how the original information was entered. I wanted to run some ideas past you but mostly get your ideas. Sorry I'm not further along, but beyond this, I'm not quite sure what you're thinking."

"Okay, fair enough. First, no need to apologize. You've made progress. I'm a bit uncertain myself on what we're looking for, so let's see if we can narrow this down." Elaine leaned back and looked at the ceiling. "What I'm thinking is that the killer has done this before. The more I think about it, the more I think that the victim was random but the crime was premeditated. I mean, whether it was Sheila or some other young woman, it didn't matter to him, and I'm sure it's a him. Rape wasn't the motive. For whatever reason, he wanted to beat someone up. He didn't even care if he killed them or not. He finished his punching bag routine and dumped her there."

Evan cleared his throat. "I understand what you're saying, but he must have picked her for a reason, even if it wasn't personal. So we're looking for female victims?"

"Let's not worry about female or male victim right now. We'll winnow that down later. Why don't you start sorting by location? Can you overlay the incidents on a map?"

"There's a software app I can use for that."

"Great. Then get started."

"Once I have the locations clustered, I can filter it for time. That can help point out a cycle if there is one. Weekly, monthly, whatever. And also, the more we know about Sheila, especially about what she wasn't, the more we can narrow it down."

"Explain. You lost me."

"Well, if she wasn't on the game, and if she wasn't using or dealing drugs, then why was she chosen? Can we eliminate, or at least discount, victims in our database who were?"

"There's not much in crime that's completely random."

"I know, but saying that she's a somewhat wild teenage girl who wasn't using drugs and who wasn't on the game defines her type."

"I see. That's a point, but I think it's cutting too fine. And it points at motive. Right now, I'm more concerned with means and opportunity. Let's not look too closely at those criteria until we've got it all sorted by location and date."

"Right. There's one thing that's bothering me. You said it yourself. Maybe it didn't matter that Sheila was the victim or not—the only thing he wanted was a victim. And suppose we find a pattern. Suppose we can connect more than three similar murders? What then?"

Elaine had wondered when this would come up. If they strongly linked three or more similar unsolved murders, they would have to inform the Serial Crimes Unit. "Good point, and if that's what we find, we'll decide then. Let's not think about that right now."

Evan rose to leave, but she stopped him. "I'm looking for patterns, Evan. In the crime, in the property where it occurred, in anything. Map the crimes, map the properties. Also, pull together any public records for Greene that show who he represents. We need connections. Do you think that will keep you busy for a while?"

Evan laughed. "There's nothing like being needed."

He had no sooner left than Cranwell entered and closed the door. "A word, Elaine. I've had a call from Commander Hughes. The press is clamoring for progress. He wants to make a statement and also implied that a public appeal might be in order."

"What? We're not at that point yet. We need to re-create Sheila's activities."

"I think we should certainly include that, but he wants more. Perhaps we can ask for anyone who saw her at a club last Friday?"

"We've got uniforms canvassing the nearest dance clubs with her picture, but there's no result yet, and we're not at all sure if she ever made it to a club. It was Friday night in London. There were thousands of girls out on the town who fit Sheila's description. We would be interviewing for a year. If he can give us another week, then perhaps we'll have something more concrete, and we can appeal for more specific information."

Cranwell sighed. "Okay. A week. Go over everything again. If we don't have anything solid by then, we'll do a television appeal. And thanks for taking over so smoothly. Let me know if you need help."

"Thank you, sir. We've got a good team, sir, for the most part."

"Speaking of your team, I've reassigned Jenkins. He's up for a disciplinary review, and he's damn lucky his bollocks are still connected. I suggested that he work on his attitude or consider a change of career, perhaps as a security guard. He put all the blame squarely on you, even though there were complaints from other officers."

"How has he lasted this long, sir? I've never met anyone more insubordinate. How many disciplinary reviews has he had? Three? Four? But he always comes back. It's like he has some dark angel watching over him, protecting him from any consequences."

"That doesn't bear thinking about. Just be wary of him, Elaine."

Did he just call me off? Careful, Lainie. "I can handle Jenkins."

"I've no doubt you can, if you see him coming. Anything else?"

"Not right now, sir. I'll keep you posted."

Cranwell left, and Elaine turned to look out her window. Staring into space helped bring decisions to the surface of her mind. The teams were interviewing bouncers, Sheila's friends, Leah's neighbors, and the houses within two blocks of the Khoury's store, with no luck so far. She needed to start over. She referred to some notes, picked up her mobile, and dialed.

"Peter Willend."

Elaine took a deep breath. "Hello, Dr. Willend. Peter. It's Elaine Hope. Please don't be alarmed, but I'd like to speak with you again about the night Sheila died. May I interview you this afternoon?"

There was a long pause before he replied. "I guess you're not going to arrest me again or you'd already be here. Let me check my diary. Oh, wow, what luck. It turns out that I'm free this afternoon, as I have no job anymore. What time?"

★ ★ ★

Peter set a cup of coffee in front of Elaine. "You take it black, as I recall from the first time I entertained you here. But there's the milk and sugar if you want it."

"Thank you." Elaine sat forward and placed her arms on the kitchen table. *He's different,* she thought. *Subdued and wary.* She couldn't blame him.

"Dr. Willend . . ."

"Peter, please."

Elaine began again. "Dr. Willend, the last time I was here, you were a suspect. We have cleared you. I have no doubt of your innocence. But you are still the last person we know of to see Sheila alive. I thought perhaps there may be something else you recall from that night that may help us."

"If I can. I think I covered it last time, but I wasn't very relaxed. Why don't we walk through it?"

"All right. Anything more you can recall may help. Take it a step at a time."

He did. "Okay, the bus stop. She was wary of me. Maybe it was the hoodie. Wait. She texted someone. Or got a text and answered. I don't know which. I recall seeing her face in the glow of the phone, and she looked like she was keying something."

Elaine noted it. They had not found Sheila's mobile. She continued. "The bus ride?"

"She was at the front. I didn't pay any attention to her. She got off first. Then I went into the store and didn't see her again." This time Peter paused. "No. That's not right. I did see her again."

Elaine leaned forward. "What was she doing?"

Peter sat back, his eyes gazing unfocused, over her shoulder. "The lady was paying Hassan for canned goods. Cat food, whatever it was. She had her hands full, so I held the door open for her. As she walked through the door—the lady, I mean—she dropped her umbrella. I picked it up and opened it for her. When I handed it to her, I saw Sheila turn the corner at the end of the block."

"She turned. You're sure?"

"Yeah. She turned right."

So that's new information, Elaine thought. They didn't need to go house to house on all the surrounding streets because she hadn't gone straight down the high street. "Was there anything else? Any other activity you noticed?"

"Not that I can recall. Cars passing. One turned about the same time she did."

"Did you see what kind?"

"Small, that's about it. I wasn't paying attention."

"Pardon me for a moment," she said to Peter, and she dialed Paula on her mobile.

"Sheila turned right on Crouch Hall. Have the house-to-house concentrate on Crouch Hall and each side street, all the way down to, what is it, Hurst? I think. Pull uniforms off the other streets and focus them there." She listened as Paula repeated the instructions. "Right. Thanks." She rang off.

"You look a bit stressed. Something I said?" Peter's voice was friendly.

Of course I am, Elaine thought. She said, "I'm in the middle of an investigation. There's always stress."

He poured another cup for her from the French press. "But you came back here. It feels like you're starting over, doesn't it?"

"We had to. This is excellent coffee, by the way."

"Hawaiian. It's the same you had last time. You deflected."

"I wasn't deflecting, Dr. Willend," she snapped. She looked away, then back at him. "Yes, I guess I was. ACPO is turning the screws."

"Please. Can't you call me Peter now? Who's ACPO?"

"Chief police officers. It's a term we use for the upper ranks. My bosses need a result; they're watching me."

"You didn't start the investigation. You had to start over."

"Right, but that doesn't matter. It certainly doesn't mean anything to the press or the public."

Peter shook his head. "We do our best, don't we?" At her questioning look, he continued. "Doctors, police, engineers, whoever. Most of us do, anyway. We're human, but we're not supposed to be. The letters behind our names remove that excuse. Or a rank, like yours."

"Maybe our mistakes cost more."

"They surely do. It's obligation. We're in the same boat."

"I guess we are." *And you understand what it's like, don't you?* Elaine thought. She asked, "You can't put it down?"

"Nope. Neither can you. It's seductive, you know. Having a purposeful existence. And you understand what it means. We're alike that way. How do you deal with it?"

"Exercise when I can. Thank God I don't drink much. Yet, anyway."

They sat in silence. Peter spoke first. "Look, I don't want to seem aggressive or anything, but if you ever want to talk . . ."

"You should be careful." She smiled at him. "You don't know what you might get into telling strange women you'll listen to them."

"A man can be too careful for too long. You're interesting, not strange."

"Some would argue."

He persisted. "Perhaps we can meet sometime? To talk. I'd like that."

"Maybe. I need to go now. Thanks again. You've truly been helpful."

He held the door for her. "Peter."

"Peter," she said.

So that's his opening move, Elaine thought after she reversed out of the drive. *I haven't been the objective of a real man's opening move in years. Not of anyone I remotely considered, anyway. Are you considering him, Lainie? And is he really interested?*

She supposed she would find out.

FIFTEEN

Liz Barker liked to categorize people at first sight by assigning them a letter of the alphabet. A portly person might be an *O*. An athletic male might be a *T*, and possibly a *V* if he had a good back and shoulders.

Jackson Greene was a *U*, or rather, a stack of *U*s. His pasty jowls were covered with stubble, and the dark bags under his eyes gave his face the appearance of a letter *U* capped with an umlaut. His underhung physical motif continued downward to his paunch, which overhung a black leather belt that curved a too-thin line beneath it. A pair of red braces extended upward, bending around the bulge of his belly, as if Greene realized how precarious his modesty was with only a belt for support. He looked to be a physical wreck. Given his appearance and socially marginal clientele, Liz was sure that he traded his legal services for his clients' stock in trade, enjoying as many cocaine-fueled threesomes, midnight lap dances, and tequila-blurred sunrises as he could wheedle.

Greene's office wasn't in much better shape than its denizen. Dingy, half-drawn curtains blocked much of the light that slipped through the window. Piles of papers covered and surrounded the desk, rising like clusters of stalagmites from the gray-brown carpet. Liz let Elaine take the relatively clean chair, then removed a takeout container and plastic utensils from another and reluctantly sat. She would have to add another few quid to this week's laundry budget.

"How can I help you?" Greene sounded wary.

Elaine spoke. "We understand that one of your clients is a property company called Cambrian Estates."

"I don't recognize that name."

"Cambrian Estates is the owner of an industrial estate in Leaside. Does that ring any bells?"

"I don't keep track of every bit of property my clients own. I don't represent every client in everything they do. Most of my clients are involved in multiple partnerships and ventures."

Liz leaned forward to brace her notebook on the desk for taking notes. As she did, her elbow knocked a stack of papers to the floor. "Oh, please excuse me!"

Greene looked peeved and began to rise from his chair. Liz raised her hand to stop him. "Please don't get up. I'll take care of it." She carefully gathered the papers together, shuffling them back into order, and then replaced them in their previous spot.

Elaine continued. "We think you may know something about this particular property. The leasing agent is a woman named Geri Harding. We understand that you engage her to represent your clients."

Greene sat back. "Geri Harding? Yes, I know her. Leaside, you say? Ah, yes. Now I recall. Cambrian Estates. They contracted me to find someone to manage it for them. I think they are the UK entity for an offshore investment firm. I don't know who. I've never met them personally, only through the mail and e-mail."

"Is that normal in your practice?"

"I wouldn't say it's normal, but it's not unusual, especially for an offshore business. If we don't need to meet face-to-face, we don't."

"You have never met anyone from Cambrian?"

"No, I act as a go-between. Geri manages the property and sends me leasing contracts, invoices for any repairs, and the like. I review them and forward them on. Rents are usually deposited directly into a bank account, as are my fees. I'm just here to make sure that everything is handled. It doesn't take much of my time."

Liz moved her foot, toppling a paper stalagmite growing next to the desk. Its layers of paper slid across the floor like a slick deck of cards spread by the hand of a con artist. "Oh, I am so sorry again! I am terribly clumsy, aren't I? I'll gather them up."

She slid out of the chair to her knees and began collecting the sheets a few at a time, regrowing the column next to the desk.

"Please. I'll take care of it. Those are my client's papers, and they are confidential, after all."

Liz smiled and kept on gathering. "I'm restacking them. It's only polite to clean up my own mess."

Greene stood and gestured toward the door. "Look, if you don't have any more questions, I would like for you to go. I've been as cooperative as I can be about this. What's all this interest in a run-down Leaside industrial estate that one of my clients may or may not own?"

Elaine remained seated. "Our interest, as you put it, is that we believe it's the place where a young girl was brutally murdered. We have a warrant, and our forensic officers are looking it over as we speak."

The solicitor blanched and sat down. "Murder? I'm sure none of my clients is involved."

"I wouldn't be too sure, judging from what our Vice division has told us about your clients."

Greene's face hardened. "Leave now. I will answer no more questions. You can see yourselves out."

Both detectives stood, and Elaine handed Greene her card. "All right. You have my card. If there's any more you'd like to tell us, give me a call. In any event, I'm positive we'll be speaking again soon."

Back in the car park, Elaine beeped open the door of her BMW, but hesitated before getting in. She looked across the top of the car at Liz. "I feel like I need to shower and change clothes before I get in."

"What a wretched hovel. Do you think he hibernates in there?"

"Among other things. Did you get anything while you were shuffling his papers? Nice moves, by the way."

Liz laughed. "Thanks. There were some interesting company names on those papers I picked up."

"Give them to Cromarty when we get back to the nick. But before that, let's stop somewhere. I need to wash my hands."

★ ★ ★

Geri Harding forced her eyes open and moved her seat to the upright position. She was groggy and cranky. Whoever said she could sleep on the plane was a fucking liar. She didn't even remember who it was. Raul, perhaps? No, she searched her brain for a visual. Pontus, she decided. Yeah. Pontus, that gorgeous Swede with the big pecs and the cock to go with them. Pontus. What a name, like a Roman general with an ego to match his dick. Sleeping sure hadn't been in his plans. She didn't recall if she'd taken the usual precautions. Christ. She'd have to find some time to get tested.

The pile of late notices and unpaid accounts inside her post box did nothing to improve her mood. The bank was on her back for everything she owned. She needed to find some money and find it quickly. Greene and the cousins accounted for about 80 percent of her business. Granted, she only saw her part of the picture, but there were things that didn't add up. First, there was the fact that she had never met the cousins. She hadn't asked too many questions when Greene first approached her, and she didn't even know who they were, although they clearly lived and operated in the UK. Being an estate agent was a profession that relied on personal contact. All her estate agent friends dealt directly with the property owners except in rare cases. Even when the owners lived abroad, they could communicate using e-mail, fax, or the telephone.

Come to think of it, several times she had been told by Greene to not show a property because it was being renovated, but she knew that wasn't the case because she had gone to see for herself. The secretive cousins and Greene had something going on that they didn't want her to know about. And what was happening with that Leaside dump? It shouldn't take a graduate of the London Bloody

School of Economics to tell them that they'd never get a better offer than the one she had lined up for them. She needed to do some digging. Perhaps her files could tell her something that would help her put pressure on Greene. She would start tonight.

★ ★ ★

Peter spent much of Friday morning at the piano, quiet and lost, not buoyant enough for Cole Porter or Fats Waller or even the Count. After an hour playing Satie, he went out for a run to try to clear his head. He had looped around Queen's Wood and was headed north up Wood Vale on his way to Alexandra Palace when his mobile chirped. It was Sheena, so he stopped and answered.

"Hey, what's up?"

"Hi, Peter. I wanted to tell you that we've gotten all of Hamid's imaging back, and it's confirmed what we thought. His parents want us to move ahead, so we've scheduled his surgery for Monday morning."

"That's good news. Let me know how it goes."

"I was wondering. I thought about asking Lindsay if you could attend. Maybe you can watch from the observation gallery. Would you want to do that?"

"I'm not sure." He thought for a moment. "Go ahead and ask, and then I'll decide."

"I'll let you know. It will be the first time we've done this without you there, and . . . well, I'll feel better if you're handy."

"Sheena, you're ready. You know the procedure backward and forward. The team's done it before. You don't need me as a backup."

"I will ask anyway and let you know."

"Right." He pressed the end-call button. *It's over, Sheena*, he thought. *It's yours now and probably will never be mine again.* He resumed the uphill run to Ally Pally. He was seriously out of shape.

Once he had reached the park grounds, he plopped down panting on a bench. What a view. He looked out over the huge, gritty, vibrant city he had begun to call home. To say that he had come here to be with Kate and their mother was an incomplete statement. True, he had needed both his mother's almost whimsical joy of living and Kate's big-sister down-to-earth practicality, and here also was where he felt closest to Diana and Liza. From a professional standpoint, London gave him the location, contacts, and opportunity to do the work he needed to do to rebuild his career. Moving here had been an easy decision.

But in this one rotten week, it had all turned to crap. He certainly hadn't seen it coming. The arrest and the resulting loss of his position had taken away the half of his life that he had been successful in rebuilding. Shortage of funds wasn't the issue. He had more than enough put aside to survive even an extended period without an income, but he needed to work. Experienced emergency room physicians and trauma surgeons were damned hard to come by in Britain, so he was reasonably confident that he could get a hospital job right away. Hell, Clayton would probably call him back in a week or two. They'd better hurry before someone else called.

The loss of the foundation position disturbed him more. He had hoped that he could use it to move away from the high-stress shifts in the A&E. Once he was back to work and the arrest was far behind him, he could begin to resurrect that part of his career.

In the meantime, what about the other half of his life? He knew that Mom and Kate would be solid as they had always been. They would be there for him until death. He wondered if they ever tired of being his crutches; did they think they were? They had never given any indication that was the case.

Then there was Elaine Hope. From the moment she had walked in his door that Sunday morning, his gut had told him there was something special about her. She stood well above average height for a woman, only a couple of inches shorter than he, and moved with a confident, loose-limbed grace, striding rather than walking. Her gold-flecked brown eyes looked into him, not at him. Truth, she had said. She focused on finding the truth. He chuckled to himself. He could picture her striding through the gates of hell in search of it. And he was as certain as he could be that she had never thought he was guilty. Why had he told her to call him Peter? It had been a spur-of-the-moment decision. He had wanted to see her again, as long as it wasn't under the same circumstances.

Then she had shown up at his door. She really did want more information. She must be under a lot of pressure from her bosses. Would they meet again? He wanted to find out more about her. He should give it a little time to see if the fascination faded. And if it didn't, he knew where he could contact her. But he wouldn't give it very long. He needed to know.

A hundred meters down the path, a tall brunette runner moved up the hill toward him, her long legs stretching out in front of her. She was not Elaine. He waited for her to pass, did some stretching, and started the jog home. Judging by the feeling in his legs, it was a good thing the return trip was all downhill.

SIXTEEN

Geri Harding glowered across the desk at Greene. "So are you I clear on what I want?"

"Crystalline. More money."

"Isn't that what we all want? It's not like I'm asking for a handout. What I want is more marketing support and a chance to make my bonuses. Every time I have an opportunity to hit it big, you come up with a reason I can't. I want you to stop lying to me about this cost or that budget. I can make a lot more for you and those cousins you keep talking about if you get out of my way and let me do my job right."

"I assure you that I'm not obstructing you. The cousins run a very tight ship. They don't give me much leeway at all."

"Bollocks. I've been looking back through some of my contracts, and I keep very good notes. A number of strange little companies keep popping up. Little companies that no one has ever heard of. Then there are the renovations and sales that never happened, aren't happening, and never will happen. I never asked any questions before, but that was when I was dumb enough to believe the bullshit you were throwing my way. I think I may do a bit of investigating on my own. A trip to Companies House would likely turn up some interesting information that Revenue and Customs might be interested in."

Greene looked at her and rolled his eyes. "That sounds an awful lot like you're thinking about some kind of extortion. I don't recommend you doing that, given that the cousins and I are pretty much your only clients."

"Really? What about the Leaside estate? I can't believe they would buy it and then do nothing. We've had offer after offer. Good ones. Solid. And they just sat on it, even during the run-up to the Olympics, when they could have sold it for ten times what they paid. How many others like that have there been over the last three years? Don't answer. I can tell you. Seven."

She opened a notebook and began reading. "The industrial estate in Dagenham. Another in Charlton. The office block in Brent Park with the top two floors empty, even though I've brought several offers. Then there's . . ."

"Stop." Greene held up his hand. "You're wasting your time with all this. There's nothing to interest R&C in any of that. Everything is aboveboard."

"You're a lawyer. You know it doesn't matter much if it is or isn't. There's always a detail or two the tax man might want to scrutinize."

This time Greene's eyes narrowed. "Like I said, I don't recommend you pressing on this. It would not be wise. Still, if you have a particular promotion you want them to see, I'll bring it up when I meet with them this afternoon."

Geri opened her briefcase and extracted some papers. "Here's the marketing plan I gave you last month. Don't cock it up, Jackson. I need the money."

"I don't plan to, Geri."

★ ★ ★

The young man sitting in the corner of Anton Srecko's office annoyed Greene immensely. He was young, stylishly dressed, and fidgeted too much. His wide-set brown eyes darted back and forth, from Greene to Anton then back to Greene. He sniffed constantly as he brushed at his trendy clothes, smoothing imaginary wrinkles and picking off invisible pieces of lint.

Cocaine? Greene wondered. *As if I'm not nervous enough sitting here with Anton, I've got his idiot nephew to deal with.* Greene shifted his attention to the papers on the table and tried to concentrate.

Anton didn't lift his gray eyes from the sales contract in front of him. He spoke in a clipped Eastern European monotone. "Nilo, would you please go make coffee for Mr. Greene and me? Strong. And there is a box of tissues in the kitchen. Please use it. Thank you."

Nilo sprang to the side of the table as if the chair had ejected him. "Sure, Anton. Cream and sugar? Would you care for any biscuits?"

Anton looked at Greene, who shook his head. "No, thank you. And please, take your time. Mr. Greene and I have something to discuss."

Greene's nervous gaze followed Nilo out the door and then refocused on Anton. *Shit, what does he know that he needs to discuss in private?* He cleared his throat. "What else did you want to talk about?"

"Nothing." Anton spoke without looking up from the papers on the table. "I tired of the sniffling."

Anton had finished reviewing the contract when Nilo returned with the cafetière, looking even more fidgety, if that were possible. He glanced at Greene. "Anton, there's a woman in the lobby who insists on seeing you. She won't go away and she's creating a fuss, something about Mr. Greene won't listen to her and she needs to talk directly to the cousins. I guess that's you."

Greene sighed. "Spiky bottle-blonde hair, big tits, heavy eye shadow?"

"Yeah, that's about right."

"Geri Harding. I apologize, Anton. She hounded me all morning, and she must have followed me here."

"Ah. Her. What does she want?"

"More money for her promotions and her commissions. She showed up at my office with a list of properties and subsidiaries.

Southwark was one of them. And Brent Park. She implied she'd talk to R&C if she didn't get what she wanted."

"And should she get what she wants?"

"It might not hurt to throw her a bone. Especially if Brent Park is involved." Greene rose from his chair. "I'll go take care of it."

"No, Nilo will take care of it. Nilo, go tell her that I'm sorry, I can't meet with her right now, but I will be happy to talk with her, ummm, at two PM. Monday."

"But you'll be in . . ." The young man glanced at Greene. "You won't be here."

"Tell her what she wants to hear, set an appointment. I'm sure you can charm her. Then see her on her way." He looked up at Greene. "Is there anything else you want to discuss? No? Why don't you avoid a confrontation and leave down the back stairs."

SEVENTEEN

Elaine's Monday started with a status meeting. Paula and Simon were unable to interview Geri Harding, the estate agent. She apparently hadn't been into the office, nor had she called. The receptionist at the business center implied that it wasn't the first time. They had left a request for her to call as soon as she arrived and would check again Tuesday.

Evan Cromarty had done excellent work. He had succeeded in identifying eighteen similar unsolved cases in various cities around England, including three in London. The correlation between the cases was striking, and two of the victims in London had the signature slashed cheek. Elaine set an action to call the investigating officers and track down the London victims, both of whom who had survived the assault.

Cranwell called her to his office after the meeting adjourned. "I have something for you. This came today." He handed her an envelope. "I suggest that you open it now." Elaine took the envelope and ripped it open. "Congratulations, DCI Hope. A little bird told me last week, but I was sworn to secrecy."

"Thank you, sir. It's been one of my goals ever since I began with the force."

"Well, I'm very pleased with you. I think the committee made an excellent choice. Now tell me what's new with Sheila's case."

He listened as she explained the team's progress. When she told him about the similar crimes they had found, he held up his hand.

"That makes three unsolved crimes with a similar signature. Serial Crime won't be happy if we don't report it to them."

"Sir, I think we can hold off doing that until we can investigate further. There's no definite connection between any of the incidents. If we establish one—and if there's a strong indication the attacker is the same person—then let's make that decision."

"You know as well as I do that I can't delay. It's the regulation, and they carry a much bigger political stick than I do."

"I'd like it better if you'd keep what we've found to yourself until we know more."

Cranwell considered. "Look at it this way. Let's suppose you don't have enough evidence to draw a solid connection. That it's speculation, a working hypothesis . . . which it is right now, right?" His voice trailed off and he looked at her askance.

She returned his gaze. "Of course it is, sir. Speculation. Nothing solid at all. And I've heard Serial Crime is stretched even thinner than we are."

"Right. Let's let them make the decision now, while they have a choice. Pull together what you have and I'll notify them."

She nodded. "Right away, sir."

"You seem to already have a good feel for the DCI role, Elaine."

"Thank you, sir." She rose to leave.

Back in her office, Paula, Bull, and Liz stared at Elaine across her desk. Their downcast expressions portrayed the disappointment she knew they each felt about turning the case over to Serial Crime. Perhaps they felt a bit of betrayal as well. She had set the table and then had thrown the meal in the bin as soon as they had sat down. It couldn't be helped. "Pull together what we have. Facts only, though. No interesting conjectures or speculations. Serial Crime will make a quicker decision that way. Now why don't we adjourn and you can start that after lunch. Food's on me."

A noise caused her to look up. Jenkins stood at her office door, his fists clenched at his side, his face contorted with anger.

"You're finally doing it, aren't you, bitch!" Jenkins hissed. "You and the other cunts! Filing disciplinary complaints. You're getting me sacked! Do you want to know what I think of that?"

Elaine rose from her chair and walked around her desk to confront him. "I don't care what you think. It's high time you left. You'll go to your hearing and you'll be sacked. But you did it to yourself. It's all catching up to you."

"I won't be going to any bloody hearing. I'll quit before I let a whore like you run me out." He took a step toward Elaine.

Bull leaped up and moved in front of Elaine. Jenkins appeared unfazed. He looked up at the huge man towering over him. "Right, Bull. You always were a suck-up."

Bull bristled. Elaine put her hand on his arm. "You can sit down, Bull. I can handle him." She leveled her gaze at Jenkins. "If you're going to quit, do it. The sooner the better. Now get out of my office."

Jenkins turned but hesitated at the door. "You think you're rid of me, Hopeless. You're not."

EIGHTEEN

DC Prameela Patel pressed herself against the wall of the entrance foyer to let a hurrying constable pass on his way down the stairs. No sooner had she turned to resume her climb than she heard the sound of retching behind her. *So it's one of those*, she thought, and she readied herself for the inevitable sensory onslaught.

Her partner, DS Andy Stockbridge, stood on the first-floor landing, consulting his notes. "The deceased is Geri Harding, age thirty-two, real estate agent. At least, that's who lives in the flat. We found a purse with ID in it, although it's hard to tell given the state of the body. It's female, anyway."

"Decomposed?"

"More like dissolved. She's been lying in a bathtub full of bleach for at least two days, according to the forensic examiner. You'll need one of these. It won't help much; the flat is full of the fumes." He handed her a filter mask.

She fumbled with the straps of the mask. "Murder or suicide?" she asked and immediately regretted it. "Forget I asked that." Of course it was murder. A person would hardly commit suicide and then jump into a bathtub full of bleach. "I guess that does it for DNA, then. Cause of death?"

"Doc said probably a broken neck. Do you want to see the body?"

Of course I don't, she thought. But if she didn't go look, word would get around that she was weak, probably because she was a woman or Indian. Female, Asian—two strikes, wasn't that the American phrase? Never mind that no person in their right mind would want to look at half-dissolved human remains.

All the windows were open in an effort to vent the chlorine fumes. She forced a breath and looked around the crime scene. Everything in the flat was spotless. No dust. No sign of struggle in the sitting room or adjoining kitchen. It was the same in the bedroom, even to the extent there were no sheets on the bed. She turned the corner to the bathroom and was assaulted by an even more overpowering odor of bleach.

Two SOCOs were trying to stuff what looked like bed sheets into a large plastic evidence bag. Some kind of grayish goo had run down the side of the bag and puddled on the floor. In the tub lay what was left of a woman. Her head was tilted to the side and turned at an impossible angle but not submerged in the liquid. She had been blonde.

Prameela was able to keep her lunch down only with effort. She rushed out past the landing, shoved her way through the front doors, and was gasping on the pavement when Stockbridge caught her up.

"You going to be okay?"

"Yes. Those fumes. Even with the mask, I couldn't breathe. Chlorine and curry don't mix well at all." Prameela told herself to take deep breaths. "Okay. Thanks. Who found her?"

Fortunately, Stockbridge was one of the more evolved detectives she worked with. He studiously consulted his notebook, giving her a few moments to compose herself.

"The call came in from one Alicia O-ku-chuk-we." He pronounced the name slowly, then repeated it. "Okuchukwe. I think that's right. She's the receptionist in the business center where Harding has an office. It's one of those places where you can rent an office and the phone, fax, receptionist, Internet, whatever, all come wrapped up with it. Harding supposedly had gotten back on the weekend from a trip to Ibiza, and things were piling up. She hadn't come to the office, hadn't phoned, and wasn't retrieving her calls from her answering machine. She, that's Alicia, decided to pop 'round at lunch to see if she was okay. On her way over, she walked past Harding's parked car, so she was expecting her to be here. Harding didn't answer, so she let herself in. She's outside in the ambulance, getting some air."

"She has a key?"

"Yes. She said they were friends, and Geri left one with her to get mail and whatnot. Alicia had collected the mail last Wednesday and hadn't noticed anything out of the ordinary. Anyway, when she opened the door, the chlorine smell hit her hard. She apparently never went into the bathroom because the fumes overwhelmed her, and she thought there might be a fire or accident or something, so she went back outside and dialed nine-nine-nine."

"No one went in or out while she was waiting?"

"No. It looks like everyone in the building is out. Probably at work. We're calling who we can."

"What did you say the victim's name was?"

"Harding. Geri Harding, thirty-two, real estate agent."

"That sounds familiar." She took out her notebook and began flipping through pages. "Here it is, last week. Liz Barker at Murder Investigation called asking about a Geri Harding. Liz and I were at Shoreditch together a couple of years back and she knew I was in Richmond now. They wanted to ask her some questions regarding that young girl they found murdered a couple of weeks ago."

"It looks like we found her. Give her a call."

★ ★ ★

Elaine was deeply immersed in a two-inch-thick Neighbourhood Policing report when Liz stuck her head in the door. "How do you like it in here, Inspector? Ooops, I mean, *Chief Inspector.*" She grinned.

"I'm looking at this decorator's catalog. I can't decide if I want marble floors with mahogany and rosewood paneling or minimalist white and Scandinavian pine. What do you think?"

"White and pine. Definitely more you. I thought you'd want to know, they found Geri Harding. Though it might not matter anymore."

Elaine put down the report. "You say they *found* Geri Harding? Tell me more."

"Well, I know it's in Serial's hands now, but I thought you'd be interested anyway. Last week when we were looking for Harding, I rang up Prameela Patel, a DC in Richmond. She called me back a few minutes ago. One of Harding's friends found her in her flat this morning. All signs point to murder."

"Was she beaten like Sheila? Slashed?"

"I asked Prameela the same thing. No beating. The killer broke her neck and dumped her in a bathtub full of bleach. She'd been lying in it a couple of days before they found her, so there's not much hope for DNA. She had the slash, though."

"Raped?"

Liz shook her head. "Don't know."

"Right. Let's pay Patel a visit. Call her and tell her I want to see the crime scene. You come with me. After that, I think it's time to put some pressure on Greene."

"What about Serial Crime? We gave it to them."

"You know me. Ask forgiveness, not permission. Let's keep at it until we're told otherwise." She rang Cranwell on her way out the door.

Elaine's mobile warbled as she and Liz walked up the pavement just off Onslow Road in Richmond. It was Cranwell ringing back. "We're at the Harding crime scene. Good news?"

Cranwell sounded buoyant. "Serial Crime won't take Sheila's case. They said that it didn't appear to involve serial predation, and it wasn't clear to them what the link was between all those crimes Cromarty dug up on the computer, so it didn't fit their remit. I think it's mostly because they are as stretched as we are. So we have it. And you'll get Geri Harding's murder as well."

"That's good news, sir!" Elaine rang off and gave Liz a thumbs-up sign. "Serial didn't want Sheila, and we've got this one as well. Let's see what we can find out."

Prameela Patel looked shaken when she met them at the building entrance and took them to the second-floor landing. She brought them up to speed as they donned their scene suits. "Dr. Kumar is removing Harding's body from the bathtub. It's a hazmat site, and it's taken a while to pump all the liquid into containers."

The odor of chlorine was still strong despite two ventilation fans whirring away near the windows. Several SOCO technicians were at work inspecting furniture and the floor. They stood aside to make way for a stretcher with a body bag on it.

Kumar nodded to Elaine and Liz. "Is this one yours too? If I had known you were coming, I would have left her in the bath until you got here. But here, you can have a look." He unzipped the top of the body bag, revealing Harding's shoulders, face, and head.

Elaine grimaced and looked away. "That's enough for now. Do you have anything yet?"

"Her neck is cleanly broken, and right now, that appears to be the cause of death. The sodium hypochlorite solution most likely destroyed DNA evidence on the body and has obscured obvious indications of violence. Even the fumes are corrosive over time. We'll process as much as we can. Her face and head are mostly intact. And there's the slash on her right cheek. It wasn't submerged in the bleach, so . . ."

"Right. Keep us posted. My suspicion is that this is tied into Sheila Watson's murder."

Kumar looked mildly surprised. "It was my first impression when I saw her, but it doesn't look like there was any beating. Aside from the slash, it's completely different, I'd say."

Elaine nodded assent. "Yes, but she—Harding, here—was the leasing agent for the industrial park near where we found Sheila's body."

Kumar nodded. "Ah. More than coincidence, right?"

"Right." Elaine nodded at Kumar, and he followed the stretcher as the attendants carefully maneuvered it down the stairs. She turned to Prameela. "Have you found anything else?"

Prameela pointed. "The bedroom is this way. When we first looked, it appeared that everything in the apartment had been cleaned. No dust, no smudges, nothing. But whoever cleaned up didn't get everything. We found some blonde head hairs that were most likely from Harding. And beside the bed, we found several dark pubic hairs. There was also a fragment of thin, curved glass on the bathroom floor. Possibly from what he used to cut her with. And we found several grams of what we think is cocaine in the drawer of her nightstand along with the usual paraphernalia. We've bagged it all."

Elaine walked to a corner of the bed and studied it. "Were the sheets on the bed when you got here? Have you bagged them?" She walked to the other corner, then knelt down with her eyes slightly above bed level.

Prameela answered. "No luck there. The sheets were wadded up and in the tub along with Harding and the bleach. We've got them, but . . ."

Elaine pointed at the bed. "Here. What do you see?"

Prameela and Liz knelt at her side and scanned the top of the mattress. Both were silent and only looked at Elaine, who pointed again at several places.

"There are two depressions up near the headboard, two depressions farther down, and then two more near them. What does that tell you?"

Liz and Prameela looked more closely at the mattress. Liz spoke first. "This looks like an old mattress, so it didn't spring back. Someone was having sex the last time it was used. Doggy-style, I'd say."

"That's what I'd say. The knees go deeper." Elaine pointed to the six hollows. She pointed to each set of depressions as she spoke. "Hands, farther apart. Then knees-knees, so it was vaginal sex. Not much chance of DNA given her bleach bath. Kumar will get mouth and throat swabs. Have the photographer grab some shots of these. Make sure he lights them so they are as distinct as possible."

Prameela sighed. "Right, ma'am. Sorry I missed those."

"You won't next time. I have to show off every now and then. And it's not 'ma'am,' Prameela. I answer to mostly anything else; 'guv' or 'chief' or something like that works fine. Ask Kumar to check her hair for touch transfer. You never know."

Prameela turned to go find the SOCO photographer, but Elaine called after her. "Is her friend still here?"

Prameela nodded and pointed toward the street. "She should be, Chief. We told her to stay because we had a few more questions."

"Okay, I want to talk with her. You stick with the photographer and make sure no one touches this bed until he's done."

Alicia Okuchukwe rose from her seat on the bus stop bench as Elaine and Liz approached. She was a tall and statuesque woman, wearing an expensive camel hair coat and shoes that had no doubt cycled through the upscale stalls of Marylebone or a similar street market. "What's happened to Geri? I saw a body bag . . . is she dead? No one will tell me anything."

Elaine identified herself. "I'm sorry to have to tell you, but yes, Geri's dead. I have some questions I'd like to ask you, if you don't mind."

Alicia sat back down and put her face in her hands. "I want to go home. Please."

Elaine sat next to her. "It won't take long, then you can go. How long have you known Geri Harding?"

"A couple of years. Ever since she rented the office in the building."

"When was the last time you talked with her?"

"She called me on her way to Gatwick, right before she left for Ibiza," Alicia said. "Just to chat and say when she'd be back."

"Do you know if she ever used drugs?"

Alicia started and stammered before blurting, "You're the copper who called last week, aren't you? Does this have anything to do with why you called? How did she die?"

Elaine put her hand on Alicia's shoulder and assumed a calm voice. "Yes, that was me. Don't worry. You're not in trouble, but we need to learn everything we can about your friend. It might help to find who did this to her."

The distressed woman took a moment to gather herself. She gazed into the distance for several seconds before answering. "Geri had a cocaine habit. Quite a hungry one. She would stop every now and then, sometimes for a few weeks, but she always went back to it."

"What about men? Did she have a regular boyfriend she was seeing?"

Alicia scoffed. "A regular boyfriend? Not a chance. She had an itch for men, as many and as often as it took to scratch it." She shook her head. "She never talked about anyone in particular. Is this all? I want to leave now."

Elaine nodded. "We'll need a list of names for all her men friends you know of, and we may have some more questions. Do you need any help getting home?"

"She has family in Kent. Near Headcorn, I think. Will you contact them? And I can make it. I'm not far from here."

"Right. We'll contact her family. Thank you. Please let us know if you think of something that might help us."

NINETEEN

Elaine looked around the room at the team. "Listen up, boys and girls. I have two announcements. First, Serial decided that Sheila's case doesn't belong in their basket, so we've got it back. And we've picked up Geri Harding's murder in Richmond. DS Stockbridge and DC Patel from Richmond CID are with us. Please make them welcome. They've been briefed, and they will be investigating the Harding murder, coordinating through Paula. We will share everything we have with them, and they with us. I have a feeling it's the same killer or at least the same mind behind both. It's not a coincidence that Sheila is killed on a property that Harding represented and then Harding is murdered as soon as she's back in town. Two murders connected through a hole in a fence.

"Next, I've been informed we're in a budget squeeze this month, like that makes February any different from January. So until further notice, overtime is curtailed and I have to clear it through the chief super. We'll mostly work alone. If you have any questions, see me or Paula. Liz, tell us all about our favorite solicitor."

Liz moved to the incident board. "Jackson Greene keeps his cave in an office block in Newham. When I say cave, it really is more a cave than an office. I seriously doubt that he ever meets with clients there. He initially lied to us when we asked about Cambrian Estates, and once he admitted knowing the name, he was resistant to giving us any information.

"While we were there, we were able to discover the names of several of his other clients. We're following up on them today, but the one that is most interesting to us right now is called the Imperial and Republic Group, IRG for short. That name appeared at the top of several stacks of documents that were strewn about the place. It's a real estate investment firm that owns properties across the UK. They are primarily active in office and industrial, but they also have housing in each city.

"Evan has done some digging. IRG is owned by two cousins. On the surface, both of them appear squeaky clean. Janko Srecko is the founder and chairman. Their website says he was educated at an unpronounceable university in Serbia and that he's active in several charities, for which he sponsors local fundraising events. He lives in Bucks with his wife and two children plus pets and blah blah blah. The very model of a successful, upright citizen. Anton Srecko is managing director and oversees the day-to-day operations. His bio is thinner. He was educated at some other unpronounceable Serbian university and has vast experience managing real estate. That's all it says, not even a picture."

Elaine took over. "We think that IRG warrants a deeper look for a couple of very good reasons. First, the Vice has told us that Greene tends to represent strip clubs, massage parlors, and the like. Why would a respectable firm like IRG engage a sleazebag like Greene? Especially since IRG press releases indicate that a very well-known firm of solicitors is their mouthpiece. It doesn't make sense unless Greene handles situations that they don't want their regular solicitors to know about.

"Second, when Evan mapped IRG's geographic footprint against his database, something very interesting popped up. It turns out that there is a very high correlation between IRG's offices and property holdings and the unsolved GBH and murder cases."

Bull spoke up. "But wouldn't that be true for many property firms?"

"Yes, except for the fact that we strongly suspect that Sheila was killed in a warehouse belonging to one of Greene's clients and that Geri Harding, who was the leasing agent for that property, was murdered last week. Also, we contacted our friends in Cardiff for some help with Cambrian Estates. The constable they sent to the council flat address reported that the elderly widow who lived there had never heard of Cambrian. It's a shell.

"So we have a string of questions. We can draw a line running from Sheila to the Leaside property to Geri to Greene to IRG. We know very little about the Srecko cousins other than what the website tells us, but we know they showed up here a little while after the Balkan wars quieted down. That in itself is interesting. Put it all together, and it gets very interesting, very quickly. Greene is the hub. And he is such a poor fit for IRG. Evan, I want to have a look at his bank accounts. How much is he pulling in from IRG? I want him watched. See where he goes and who he talks to. We don't have enough overtime in the budget to do it around the clock, but we need to find something and tighten the screws. Bull and Barker, your assignment is to follow him. What does he do, where does he go, who does he see? Go ahead and pair up for the first couple of days. I'll clear it with Cranwell. We should have his finances by then, and if you see something suspicious, we'll have a lot to talk with him about."

Evan spoke up. "Our embassy in Skopje got back to us yesterday. Bitola Holdings apparently exists in name only. It's a dead end."

"Okay. That's something else for the list when we talk to Greene again. Put your research cap on and get to work on IRG. On our crime map, there's a cluster in Leeds. Focus on IRG properties in Leeds and in London. How many, what kind? Relate them to specific crime locations. I want to know everything about the company, especially Janko and that low-profile Anton guy. Stockbridge, what can you tell us about Richmond?"

Stockbridge stood. "Prameela reviewed the CCTV on the block in front of Harding's flat. The video isn't great, but it shows a man entering about an hour before the time they reckon she was killed. Medium height, slender build, the usual hoodie. It was dark, and the cameras are too far away to get any detail, other than that he appeared to be carrying something in his left hand and a large briefcase in his right. About two hours later, he leaves again in the direction he came from. Within a minute, a late-model Audi sports car turns the corner and passes in front of the flat."

Liz looked at the Richmond detectives. "Sheila told a witness that this Danny bloke drove a flash Audi." They nodded, and Stockbridge continued.

"We're canvassing the neighbors to see if anyone saw anything. The forensics on Harding came back negative for DNA, but that's not surprising because the bleach largely destroyed the outer layers of her entire body. We're also trying to track her movements after she arrived back here from Ibiza on Thursday. We'll keep you informed."

Elaine looked around the room. "Excellent. Let's get to it. Sniff for smoke, boys and girls."

TWENTY

"We've got cheese and tomato or . . ." Liz Barker squinted at the smeared label on the triangular plastic container she had pulled from a shopping bag. "I think it says 'tomato and cheese,' but I can't be sure. Which do you prefer?"

Bull rolled his eyes. "Prosciutto with gorgonzola, in a perfect world. Didn't they at least have roast beef or ham?"

"They did, but I've been around you long enough to know you shy away from anything remotely greenish." She handed Bull a sandwich container, peeled the plastic strip off the one she kept, and tucked in.

Bull squinted at the label on the plastic container. "I could have taken the lettuce off."

Liz's voice was muffled by the tomato and cheese. "It wasn't leafy green. It was fuzzy." She pointed with half her sandwich. "Ah! He's on the move."

Thirty meters up the street, Greene had emerged from his dingy office building and was walking purposefully into the neighboring parking garage. When his car appeared, Bull wheeled away from the curb and took up a position behind. Traffic was light, so he hung back a bit farther than usual.

Liz leaned forward. "He's in a bit of a hurry, isn't he? He must be late for a power lunch."

A few minutes later, Greene's car turned onto a run-down residential street. The rows of dismal houses on each side were pocked with gutted dwellings, boarded windows, and lewd graffiti. He parked and entered a dingy terraced house. Barker aimed her camera and took two shots of him entering. She noted the address. "I'll call it in and see if Vice has tagged it."

Bull took a bite of sandwich and grimaced. "It doesn't look exactly corporate, does it? I wonder if his client lives there or if he's the client. From what we've heard about him, I'd lay odds that he's both. Either way, we may be here long enough for me to choke down lunch. Pass me that bag of crisps and the bottle of water." He had no sooner opened the crisps than their quarry emerged yet again, this time carrying what looked like a partially full laundry bag. While Barker's camera clicked, Bull took a drink from the water bottle, clapped crumbs off his hands, and reached for the ignition to start the car.

Barker touched his arm. "Wait. He's not getting into his car." Greene had instead walked past two apparently abandoned dwellings and entered another ramshackle house. Five minutes later, he emerged again, still with the laundry bag. Click click click. "Now I ask you, my friend. What does that look like?"

"I know what it looks like, but he'll say he's collecting the weekly laundry from his dear ancient maiden aunties, so he can wash and iron it for them. After he feeds their cats too."

"I wonder if it's a regular Friday bag run."

Greene's only stop on the return to his office was at a burger chain restaurant. About an hour after they had resumed their surveillance, a silver Jaguar passed them, performed an illegal U-turn about half a block down the street, and swung into a yellow-line space at the front of the building.

Liz snorted in amusement. "My, he's cheeky. I wonder who he's visiting. Why don't we engrave him for posterity." Her camera clicked some frames as a young man with a briefcase uncoiled himself from the Jag and entered the building. "I got the number plate. Let's call it in. Time in is 13:33. I'm going in to see if he's visiting our Mr. Greene. Here's the camera." She got out of the car and ran across the street.

Bull called in the plate number and waited, intently watching the door of the building.

There he was. "Out at 13:41. Eight minutes." Click click. The young man threw the briefcase into the passenger seat, swung into the car, and pulled out into traffic. Liz ran to the passenger side and got in. Bull pulled away from the curb but wasn't able to turn around because of the traffic. By this time, the Jag had disappeared around a corner and was gone.

Liz slammed her palm against the dashboard. "Damn. No luck at all. I was watching the lift to see if I could catch the floor he went to, but he came down the stairs."

"We won't catch him now."

"No, we won't. But our assignment is Greene. We took snaps and called in the plate number. We don't know if he was seeing Greene or someone else. Let's sit tight."

For the rest of the afternoon, Bull and Barker sat in their car with nothing to do until it was time to go off duty. By then, they wished they had followed the Jag.

★ ★ ★

"All right, boys and girls. Bull and Liz have something to tell us."

Bull moved to the front of the room. "We watched Greene all day on Friday. He spent most of his day in the office, but he made one excursion in the early afternoon. He visited two houses. Hovels, more like. He was only in each house for a few minutes, and each time he left carrying a laundry bag with something in it. Liz took some snaps." He clicked a mouse and a picture of Greene leaving the first house displayed on the large TV. "We've asked Vice and Narcotics if they have any information about the addresses. As you can see, it's not exactly a high-rent area. We both doubt he was picking up laundry."

Liz took up the story. "After he got back to his building, he had a visitor we thought was interesting." She clicked the mouse. Another picture displayed the young man getting out of his car. "We aren't sure if this bloke was actually visiting Greene, but he's a young footballer type, so he got our attention. He got lost in traffic before we could turn around. The number plate is registered to a firm called Grampian Leasing. We passed that along to Evan. We were also wondering if we could split the shifts between us so we can cover more hours. Greene may make some nighttime expeditions."

"Excellent work. Blow up a picture of the Jag driver and get it to the super-recognizers to see if they're familiar with him. Also, check CCTV coverage in front of Greene's building. You might want to start with last Friday afternoon, about the same time. Then talk to Paula about a schedule."

Elaine scanned the room. "Evan, let's find out as quickly as possible if this Grampian-whatsit is another shell company. Do you have anything more to share?"

"We'll have Greene's bank accounts this afternoon or tomorrow morning. We've run our initial background checks on the Sreckos. On the Internet, Janko shows up clean as a whistle. Passport records show he arrived here twelve years ago from Belgium on a Polish passport. He doesn't have a police record here and no Interpol warrants. Anton has practically no Internet presence. There's nothing on the Internet about him besides his company profile, which is unusual for a businessman. Our immigration records show he arrived here ten years ago, again from Belgium on a Polish passport. No police record there, no Interpol warrants."

Elaine looked perplexed. "Have you made any progress on mapping the IRG properties?"

Cromarty looked at Bull, who spoke up. "IRG has several properties that are in the same cities as our crime clusters, but not in the same areas of the city. We looked at Internet street photos, and the properties that are listed all look like respectable places, prosperous office blocks and middle-class residential buildings. Nothing suspicious at all. Liz had a thought, though."

"Ummm, well. I thought we could check on that Cambrian shell company, and now possibly Grampian, for any connection nearer to the crime clusters. It might take some digging, but IRG would put any dodgy property under a different name, right? Like one of the shell companies?"

"That's a fair assumption. Good thinking. Why didn't you speak up sooner? Evan, give it a look. And I want more info on the Sreckos. Srecko doesn't sound very Polish to me. And how long were they in Belgium? Check with the Polish Embassy and see if they have any record for the Sreckos, criminal or otherwise.

"We're starting to see some connections, but there are too many gaps. I do not believe in coincidences, and I loathe gaps. We need to start drawing some solid lines on the board. Make real connections, not assumptions or conjecture. We have lots of smoke; we need fire. Get to it."

★ ★ ★

Evan Cromarty placed a cup of tea on Elaine's desk and took a seat. He'd been thinking and wanted to run some ideas past her.

"Thanks." Elaine took a sip of the tea and sat back. "Any results?"

"Not yet, but we're making progress. We've got the Leeds correlations done, but I don't think it's very illuminating. I'm wondering if there's something we're missing. Some question we haven't asked. Haven't thought of what it might be, though."

"Keep it in the back of your mind. What is it the computer boffins call it? Background processing or something like that? I'm looking for some kind of handle to grab hold of the Sreckos."

"Yeah. I've put the query in to the Polish Embassy about the Srecko cousins. We sent them the names and the passport numbers they used to enter the UK. We should hear back pretty soon. I'm sending their pictures and names to the Serbian Embassy as well."

"Why Serbia?"

"Only on the off chance they may have started their little pilgrimage because of something that happened there. It was what you said about the timing of their entry into the country, and that their name doesn't sound Polish. If it's not Serbia, then I'll check Slovenia and Bosnia. Oh, yeah. I looked it up. The name Srecko means 'lucky' in Serbian."

"Really? Put that on the whiteboard. I want as much information as we can get about them. When we talk to them, I want them to know we mean it and that we've done our homework. Can we do some kind of degree or enrollment verification or something to get their university records?"

"Sure we can. What about Greene?"

"For now, get as much as you can about him and his background."

TWENTY-ONE

Liz Barker slowed her car and watched Greene turn into the multi-story car park next to the building that housed the IRG offices. She entered a few seconds later, catching sight of the brake lights as his car turned at the top of the ramp. He parked on the second level, so she drove past and picked a slot next to several reserved spaces at the end of the row.

She made a show of fumbling in her purse as she trailed him under the covered walkway to the building. Once inside, he made directly for the lifts, so she stopped next to the building directory and rang Elaine.

"Guv, Greene's just arrived at the IRG offices. His lift stopped at their floor. I'm in the building lobby."

"Excellent. Wait right there. It's time we applied some pressure. I'll be there in ten."

Liz was on pins and needles with anticipation when Elaine arrived. "I suppose Greene's still there. I haven't seen the lift stop at their floor, and I haven't seen him come down through the lobby."

Elaine gave Liz a reproving look. "And I suppose there could be a back stairs. Don't you suppose that too?"

"Sorry, guv. It's a hard habit to break."

Elaine nodded and led the way to the lifts. "Right. I think an unannounced visit is in order."

The two detectives were standing at the reception desk when Greene emerged from a hallway, in conversation with a tall, elegant man whom Liz recognized as Janko from the photos in the incident room.

Elaine stepped into the men's path. "Mr. Greene. What a coincidence. We're here to speak with Mr. Srecko and his cousin, but I have a few additional questions for you about your relationship with Geri Harding. You've heard about her murder, haven't you?" Her normally quiet voice was raised several levels.

Greene looked stunned. He gawked at Elaine, then glanced nervously at Janko, whose attention had remained on the two detectives. Elaine's eyes locked with Janko's. Before Greene could answer, Liz broke the silence by producing her warrant card. "Mr. Srecko. I'm DC Liz Barker and this is DCI Elaine Hope. We're investigating the murders of Sheila Watson and Geri Harding. We would like to ask the two of you some questions." She glanced at Elaine, who remained quiet, refocusing her attention on Greene.

By now, Greene had somewhat regained his composure. "I saw the news about Miss Harding, Chief Inspector, but I know nothing about it. Tragic, isn't it? She was so full of life. I can't speak with you right now. I'm late for another appointment." He turned and scurried out the door.

Liz extracted her notebook and pen from her purse as Elaine spoke. "It's a shame that Mr. Greene had to rush. I was interested in how he would phrase his answers with you and your cousin present. We'll speak with him soon." A thin, immaculately dressed man approached them from the corridor, so Elaine took a guess and turned her attention to him. "I assume that you are Anton Srecko. Please join us. You surely have a conference room handy. Or would you prefer your office? It won't take long."

Janko smiled warmly and held out his hands. "Chief Inspector Hope. Constable . . . Barker, is that correct? As much as I would love to spend time conversing with two such lovely women, I'm afraid we are also busy this afternoon and cannot afford the time to speak. Please make an appointment with our receptionist and we will be happy to give you a few minutes as soon as our schedule allows."

Elaine continued in her steady tone. "I know you heard DC Barker say that this is a murder investigation, so I'm sure you understand that time is critical and we are very busy as well. In the interest of justice, we need to speak with you now. Once we have finished, you can resume your business."

"In the interest of justice." The hair on the back of Liz's neck rose as she heard Anton's quiet, emotionless voice. She turned and looked at the slightly built man who had taken a position at Janko's side. Whereas Greene was the definition of sloppiness and Janko was a perfectly marketable executive, Anton gave the impression of a ruthless, efficient predator. He continued in the same precise monotone. "Justice. And civil rights. You two women enter our offices unbidden and unannounced and demand our valuable time so you can ask us ridiculous questions about crimes we know nothing of. Such a hypocritical concept of justice. We have rights, and we will decide when it is convenient for us. Good day."

Elaine turned to face Anton directly. "A murder investigation takes precedence over your convenience. Your solicitor just scarpered; otherwise he would tell you that the only decision you need to make at this moment is whether the two of you speak with us in your offices or in separate interview rooms at our station. We find a place to talk or DC Barker here calls for uniformed officers. If she does, they will be here in roughly four minutes. That's the decision you need to make."

Janko again spread his hands. "Please, Chief Inspector. I assure you that we will cooperate with the Metropolitan Police to the best of our ability. This way please." He led the way to a conference room, in the center of which was a large oval table. He indicated chairs to Elaine and Liz. He and Anton took seats opposite them. "Now how can we . . ."

Elaine interrupted him. "Are you familiar with a company called Cambrian Estates?"

The two men looked at each other. Janko answered, "No. Should we be?"

"Do you have any connection with a company called Grampian Leasing?"

"What do they lease?" He turned to Anton. "Are they a client?"

"A vendor. We use them occasionally to lease equipment we don't want to capitalize."

Liz interjected. "Such as automobiles? Laptop computers?"

Anton shrugged. "Perhaps. Motors would fall into that category. I do not see what our business relationships have to do with any murder investigation."

Elaine ignored him. "Does the name Geri Harding mean anything to you?"

Janko again looked at Anton before he spoke. "I believe Greene hired her as a leasing agent for some of our properties."

"Such as an industrial park in Leaside?"

"I'm not aware of such a place. We own many small properties. They come and go. I would have to check."

Elaine nodded at Liz as she spoke. "Please do that, and contact DC Barker with a list as soon as possible." Liz slid her card across the table and resumed taking notes as Elaine continued. "What is your relationship with Jackson Greene? Surely a company as successful as yours could afford more than a second-rate solicitor. On your website, you list another firm as your legal contact."

"He was recommended by a friend. He's inexpensive and reliable for certain simple projects."

"Apparently there are quite a few 'certain simple projects.' He visits you quite regularly."

Janko shifted in his chair. "Does he? I personally see him only rarely."

At this point, Anton stood. "I reiterate. I do not see any connection between your questions and any murder investigation. You are fishing, and I consider this to be harassment. Get to the point. Otherwise, leave."

Out of the corner of her eye, Liz could see that Elaine did not look at Anton, so she remained focused on her notebook while Elaine continued.

"Do either of you know a young woman by the name of Sheila Watson?"

For the first time, Janko looked wary. "No. We do not. What is the name of your supervisor?"

Elaine answered, but her eyes stayed focused on Janko. "DCS Alec Cranwell. Here's a number you can call if you think we are overstepping." Elaine wrote the police community affairs number on the back of her card and slid it across the table. "Do you know a young man who goes by the name Danny?"

Janko stood and spoke. "How many young men named Danny do you expect there to be in London? We have endured enough of this, what would I call it, bobbing for apples. The interview is over. If you need to speak with us again, please arrange an appointment through our solicitors. Not Greene. The firm listed on our website."

Elaine stood. "I'll take that as a yes. That's my card. If you think of something you feel might be helpful, please contact me. I'm sure we'll be speaking again, though. Calling your solicitor will be entirely up to you." She motioned to Liz and they left.

★ ★ ★

Elaine pushed the buttons in the lift and turned to Liz. "I commandeered some uniforms to bring me here. I need a ride back with you."

Liz was happy to oblige. "Not a problem, guv. Wow. That was the first time I've been in an interview like that. Janko's just a typical smarmy businessman, but Anton reminded me of a Gestapo officer in an old movie. Those dead eyes and not an ounce of feeling."

"They were right. I was fishing. I mostly wanted to apply some pressure." Elaine pulled her coat tighter. "It's bloody cold out here in this wind. Let's hurry."

An engine roar caused them to turn, just as a blue Audi sports car whizzed by and squealed into one of the reserved parking spaces near Liz's car. A tall, athletic young man with spiked black hair emerged. He took a long drink from a plastic bottle and carelessly tossed it against the wall.

Liz grabbed Elaine's arm. "That's a blue . . ."

Elaine interrupted her. "Let's take our time. Why don't you look interested?"

As they walked past the young man, Liz spoke. "Nice car. I love the color. Is it fast?"

The young man ogled the two detectives. "Fast enough. Are you?"

Liz laughed. "Cheeky, aren't you? That all depends." She looked at Elaine, who frowned and disengaged from the pair. Liz stopped and flipped her hair from her face as Elaine walked ahead. "My aunt doesn't like you."

"I wonder why not. I like her. Older women are hot."

Liz feigned displeasure. "And I'm not?"

"I didn't say that. Not at all, luv. I much prefer redheads, especially ones like you. I'm Nilo."

"I'm Beth. That's my aunt. She doesn't like me flirting with strange men."

"But you do it anyway, don't you? And strange is as strange does, luv. I look at you and I want to be strange."

Liz laughed again. "I don't think my boyfriend would like me being strange with you."

"Then he's a tosser. Not the kind of bloke a woman like you should be with."

She glanced over his shoulder. Elaine was leaning against the wall in front of the car. She nodded at Liz, then looked away.

Nilo followed her glance to see Elaine staring in the other direction. He reached out and took Liz's arm. "Maybe you could ditch him this weekend. You and I could explore some strange new places."

Liz gave a small smile. "I absolutely love to dance. I get crazy."

Nilo sidled closer. "Do you ever go to raves? I personally know some fantastic DJs. We could party all night long."

"Oh, a rave? I don't know about that. What about dance clubs?"

"All the best ones." He named a few. "But later I go to raves. Why don't you give me your mobile number?"

"Not yet. Why don't you give me yours, then if I ditch Boris for the weekend, I might give you a call and we can get together. How does that sound?"

She entered his number into her mobile, and when she was prompted for the name, she remarked, "Nilo. That's an interesting name."

Nilo moved his face close to hers. "It's short for Danilo. Green eyes. I've seen your eyes in my dreams."

Liz gave another coy smile and playfully pushed him away. "Maybe this weekend you won't have to dream. If you're lucky."

He stroked her hair with his finger. "This weekend, then?"

"Perhaps." She kissed her finger, pressed it to his lips and walked toward Elaine and the car. After a few steps, she turned around. He was still standing where she had left him, watching her. "Hey, Nilo. How about a selfie? I want to show Boring the competition."

Nilo walked up to her and put his hand on her hip. "With such a beautiful girl? Sure. Maybe it will be the first of many photos. We'll start this weekend."

Liz raised her eyebrows and moved her face next to his. The phone flashed and clicked. She kissed her finger and placed it on his lips again. "Perhaps. But now I need to go. Auntie Dragon is getting restless." She raised her voice. "Okay, Auntie Dragon. I'm coming."

Liz blew Nilo another kiss as she got behind the wheel. He was still standing there watching as they drove out of the car park. As soon as they were out of sight, she shuddered. "Yech. I feel like such a slag."

Elaine chuckled. "I thought you were marvelous. He was gagging for you. But Auntie Dragon?"

"It was what came to mind. He thinks you're hot, by the way. Did you get it?"

"Oh, yes." Elaine held up a plastic bag containing Nilo's discarded drink bottle. "Did you find out anything useful?"

"His name. Nilo, short for Danilo. I think we may have found Danny."

"Good God! Anything else to share while you're showing off your detective skills?"

"He told me the clubs he likes. He's expecting me to meet him at a club this weekend and then go to a rave, if I can ditch my boyfriend. I got his mobile number, just in case. And a face shot."

"I saw the flash, but his mobile? No! You've got potential. I didn't know you had a boyfriend. And you will not meet him, Liz. You haven't had undercover training. Besides, I'm not sure what that would tell us. You don't seriously think he's so enamored that he'll confess simply to bed you, do you?"

Liz protested. "Chief, I may have just cracked Sheila's murder and maybe Geri's. Are you going to take it away from me?"

"Don't get carried away with a bit of success, Liz. You'll get credit for it, but let's move one step at a time. If his DNA comes back as a match for anything, we'll pull him in, and with luck, we won't need more."

"Well, okay, Chief. And I don't."

"Don't what?"

"Have a boyfriend. Not since I joined the Met."

Elaine had no response. She was familiar with that situation.

TWENTY-TWO

Nilo was high. The chase excited him as much as the catch, and, oh yes, the real victory afterward was the sweetest. That fair-skinned redheaded cunt would be extra special, like strawberries and cream. He banged open the office door and danced his way to the reception desk.

Joanna the receptionist flashed him her packaged smile. "Met someone?"

Nilo spun out another step. "You know me, sweetheart. I can't help it. I love redheads, especially if they like to dance. You can tell movers because they have such tight bums." He inspected his reflection in the window. "They're drawn to me like . . . like . . . whatever."

"It's probably your breadth of intellect and understated charm."

Nilo continued preening. "Could be, but I bet a tenner it's because I know exactly what to say. And I look hot, of course. She had a hot auntie too. Tall and lean. The auntie would be another challenge." He spun back to the desk. "Maybe I'll try for a threesome after I spend a bit of time with Beth. You older women usually do anything for attention."

Joanna's amused expression had disappeared. "We 'older women' can be dangerous. I think you need to tell Anton about your latest quarry."

"What does Uncle Anton have to do with it? He doesn't know fuck all about women. He doesn't even have one. I'm a man; I do what I like."

"Sure. But I think he knows something about those two that you will find interesting." She spoke into her headset. "Mr. Anton, Nilo has something to tell you about your two visitors. Yes, sir. Mr. Anton will see you now, Nilo."

He bristled. "You've spoiled it. I thought you were my friend."

"More than you realize, and my friendly advice is to talk with Mr. Anton straightaway."

Nilo glared at Joanna. The cow couldn't boss him around. He nodded at a picture on the window ledge.

"Your daughter is lovely. It's a shame I don't normally fuck blondes." He picked a candy from the bowl on her desk. "But I can make an exception."

Moments later, he stood quietly as Anton studied the papers laid out on his desk. *Every time*, Nilo thought. *Every time I'm here, I have to wait for him to give me permission to sit down, like some kind of third-rate servant, not even a member of the family. Like a fucking Bosnian.*

Anton didn't glance up. Nilo fidgeted, shifting his weight from foot to foot. This was bullshit. He wanted to blurt something, to get on with it, even if it meant a bollocking. Without looking up, Anton lifted his phone. "Please ask Mr. Janko if he would come to my office."

Nilo withered. Janko needed to hear it. Damn. What was so fucking important about two cunts? It wasn't the first time he'd chatted up a woman. Hell, he'd had half the pussy in the building. The decent ones from other companies, anyway. But not Joanna or any of the IRG slags. They were gagging for him, but IRG women were off-limits after what happened with that little whore in accounts. Shutting her mouth had been his first real assignment, and it had been fun. He smiled at the memory.

"Mrs. Christie said you have something to tell us." Anton's statement snapped Nilo back to the present. Janko had appeared in the chair next to him.

"I'm not sure what she meant. I told her about a girl I met in the multi and then right off she's on to you with it."

Anton's eyes never shifted. "There were two women in the multi. One young, red hair, and one older, taller, dark short hair."

How the hell did he know that? Nilo thought. *Oh, yeah, Joanna had said something about visitors. Am I going to have to clean this one up too?* He knew he needed to be careful with Uncle Anton. "Yes. That's them. The one I chatted up was maybe in her midtwenties. Red hair, green eyes, white skin. Name of Beth. The other was older, taller, with long legs. Beth called her Auntie Dragon. I didn't speak to her."

"You chatted up this Beth woman and you set a date with her?"

Nilo took a moment to consider his answer. "Not exactly. I asked her to a club, but she said she had a boyfriend. So I told her where I would be next Saturday night, and she said she might meet me there."

"Ah. So she will meet you some time, some place. And you did not speak with the older woman."

"No. She walked on ahead and waited."

Janko leaned toward him. "Did you give this Beth girl anything? Your IRG calling card, perhaps?"

Why did Janko always ask questions but Anton never needed to? He shifted his attention to Janko. "I didn't give her my card or hand her anything. I did touch her arm and cheek." He hesitated for a moment. Janko seemed amused at that, but he felt Anton's gaze boring into his head. "That's it."

Janko sat back and exchanged looks with Anton. Nilo couldn't contain himself. "What is this about? Were they in the office? Here?"

Janko ignored the questions. "Did they see your car?"

Nilo's voice was rising. "Of course they did! I drove right past them. What the hell is this about?"

Anton slid a business card across his desk toward Nilo. "You say her name is Beth. According to this card, she is actually Detective Constable Elizabeth Barker, so Beth makes sense as a name. The woman she called Auntie Dragon is Detective Chief Inspector Elaine Hope. They were here to investigate the murders of Sheila Watson and Geri Harding."

Nilo slumped back in his chair, stunned. "What do they know?"

Janko ignored him again. "When were you last at the Leaside property?"

"End of January. We were packing a shipment from Spain. Why do . . ."

"Did you take a young woman there about that time?"

Nilo hung his head. "Yes. It was only for a bit of fun. You know. Show her around."

Anton licked his lips. "The DCI was fishing, so it appears they don't know much at the moment. But they suspect. The Met murder detectives are efficient and thorough, and this one will certainly follow through. We need to learn some things and we need to act quickly. If you were not my nephew, I would consider eliminating you." Nilo felt his stomach knot as Anton continued. "But I will not. Right now, I think it is best if you stay low for a while. Use your house. Go there now. Do what the Americans say. Do not pass Go. Do not collect two hundred dollars. I would also add that you do not take the Audi. Go out the back entrance and take one of the Transit vans we use for maintenance. Leave your mobile with me. I will arrange for groceries and drink and a prepaid mobile and whatever entertainment is required to keep you there until we know what to do."

"Okay, Uncle Anton. Can I ask . . ."

"No, you may not. Go now. Use the stairs, not the lift. I will contact you when I need to know more."

Nilo picked up the Transit keys from the closet and stormed down the stairs. Thank God he had the sense not to say anything about giving her his number. Uncle Anton could be so bloody minded. Fucking detective bitches. That Beth or whatever her name was had played him like he usually played women. If he ever saw her again, she'd wish she'd never been born. Auntie Dragon my arse. Middle-aged bitch, more like. Standing by the wall putting on the act. What was her name? Elaine something-or-other. She wouldn't like meeting him again either.

He slammed open the back door to the building, startling two office workers outside smoking on their break. They glared at him with surprise and anger until he shouted, "What are you looking at? Fuck you!" and took two steps toward them. When they backed off at his belligerence, he sneered and swaggered to the first of two IRG maintenance vans parked at the back.

He started the small diesel and clattered toward Crouch End. Piece of crap transport. Entertainment, though. It might not be too bad if he could coke up a couple of tarts and party. Then he would have time to think about Detective Beth and Auntie Elaine. *That, Nilo my lad, would be a party to make even Uncle Anton smile.* He'd be sure to get some good fucking first. Not like with that other little tart. Then, afterward, it would be strawberries and cream. Sweet and slow. Strawberries and cream.

★ ★ ★

The boy was growing more out of control, which troubled Anton. It took extra energy to moderate Nilo's excesses and the unreliability that resulted from his increasing cocaine habit and his consuming taste for women. It would be so much easier if he hadn't made those promises to his brother Marko. The blood ties and the words that were spoken made it impossible to send Nilo back to face Serbian justice. Perhaps he could work something out with the Mexicans once the agreements were reached. Cabral would have no qualms about dealing with the boy if he got out of control, which would have to be *seriously* out of control given the Mexican cartel's disposition to using excessive violence. Nilo would either thrive or be found hanging from a bridge, relieving Anton of any responsibility in the matter. But the agreement hadn't been struck yet, and if Cabral got a hint that Met detectives were sniffing around, it could damage or seriously delay the alliances they had spent almost a decade forging. He would discuss alternatives with Janko, but first he dialed a number into the prepaid mobile he kept handy.

The answering voice spoke simply. "Yes?"

"Tell me about Elaine Hope."

Anton thought he heard a sharp intake of breath before the voice answered. "She's smart. A lateral thinker. She connects facts before anyone else even compares them. Doesn't back down."

Anton had thought as much from their brief meeting. "Weaknesses?"

"Too much loyalty to her team. She can be impatient and hot-tempered. She's got some enemies."

"Send me the names of her enemies. What about Elizabeth Barker?"

"Don't know much about her. Just out of uniform. Something of a protégé to Hope."

There it was. Nothing to it if you knew who to call. Anton closed the connection and walked up the hall to Janko's office. Janko was looking out the window and spoke as Anton entered. "This was not a pleasant afternoon. We need to handle this before we meet with Cabral's people."

"I'm taking steps. Have you spoken with Marko yet?"

"He's not happy, but he'll come around. I reminded him that if it weren't for us, his precious son Nilo would be fighting off rapists in Zenica prison. Or dead. What do you propose?"

"As long as he stays in his house, we don't need to arrange an accident. Let's keep him there until after the meeting. If it goes well, perhaps we can move him to Mexico to learn that end of the business. If not, we either arrange an accident or send him back and let Marko decide. Nilo's his son, after all."

Janko spun his chair around to face Anton. "We can't give him up. He's too unpredictable. Make sure he understands to stay out of sight. If he doesn't, we'll need to lock him down. Bring Goran over to deal with it."

"Did Marko say how things were going with our partners to the east?"

"On schedule. Waiting for us to close the loop."

Anton nodded. "We'll close it."

TWENTY-THREE

Cranwell stood at the side of his desk and indicated a chair. "Take a seat, Elaine. Care for tea?"

"No, thanks, sir." She sat and composed herself, notebook and pen at the ready on her lap. Cranwell invariably started unpleasant meetings with formality. He didn't appear to be in the best of moods.

He moved to his chair, primly adjusted his uniform trousers, and sat with his hands folded on the desk in front of him. "I've reviewed your progress up to now, as has Commander Hughes. He's uncertain about the direction you've taken, and frankly, so am I. How you could connect these two murders is quite beyond us. A teenager out on a surreptitious date, murdered and then dumped in a nearby ditch. A professional leasing agent murdered in her flat miles away from the teenager and left in her own bathtub. We both think you're putting entirely too much emphasis on what is a tenuous connection at best. Unconnected victims, dissimilar methods. Sheer coincidence."

Hughes, Elaine thought. *So that dinosaur was behind this.* Hughes could rarely remember his female detectives' names, so he always called them "Lassie" at social functions. She opened her mouth to speak, but he held up his hand. "Yes, there is the slash to consider, but that's the only consistent forensic evidence. Other than that, the methods are completely different. We don't see it. And now you start harassing a respectable businessman in his offices. It doesn't look promising."

Elaine knew the Sreckos hadn't lodged a complaint. For one thing, if they had, it would have been the first thing Cranwell mentioned. For another, she knew in her gut that they were dirty and thus didn't want any scrutiny from the Met. But she had to ask. "Have the Sreckos lodged a complaint?"

"No, they haven't. I heard of it through unofficial channels. But I suspect if you push them harder, they will. Given the weakness of your overall case, and the fact that there is absolutely no evidence that they have any involvement beyond your suspicions about that part-time solicitor, well, you're on thin ice."

Elaine took a moment to compose herself. "Sir, if I may, I know that the victims and methods are different, and I know that the connection isn't obvious. But it's stronger than it appears on the surface. I believe that Sheila and Geri were murdered by the same killer. The killer's motives and methods don't have to be the same for both victims. I believe he's simply a man who solves problems that way. Perhaps Sheila refused to have sex with him, so he beat her and slashed her to destroy her beauty. But he took her to the dump site through the industrial estate, so he knew about the wasteland and the shoddy fence. He'd been there before. We're convinced he had sex with Geri, but her death appeared premeditated. The sex was for fun or to get her to relax her guard. The common factor between the two is IRG, and it points to someone inside that firm. I'm convinced of that."

"You may be. We are not. Benford already made a hash of this investigation. He splattered egg all over our faces, haring off after that American doctor. The Directorate of Public Affairs has been wrestling with the press all week. Hughes wanted me to bring in a more experienced DCI after Marcus became ill, but in the end, we felt we needed a fresh approach. You certainly gave us that, didn't you? Are the tabloids going to splatter us again?"

So that's where this was going. Public relations. "With all due respect, sir, I've gotten a lot of damned fine results in my career.

Better than most of my colleagues. You made the right choice. And the tabloids never need an excuse to splatter whatever they want."

"You got a lot of those results working with Benford. But he's not here anymore, and it's beginning to look to us like we didn't make the right choice."

She started to grit her teeth but caught herself. "You did make the right choice, sir. We need a bit more time, and it will come together."

★ ★ ★

Elaine fumed. She stared at the situation board through the window that separated her office from the incident room, but Cranwell and Hughes dominated her thoughts. Bastards. Hughes was a consummate politician, but he wasn't incompetent.

Benford, the primary source of Elaine's knowledge about Hughes, had taken her to the commander's office several times to report on various cases and make sure she was noticed. She had also done some informal research on her own, mostly at the pub after work. According to the retired officers she had talked to, Hughes's early years as a detective were good but not brilliant. He achieved reasonable results, had cultivated the right mentors, and had taken advantage of his knack for being in the right place at the right time. After serving his time in the various divisions, he began a carefully planned move into the upper echelons of the Met. She had thought his office decor had been revealing. Oak desk, oak paneling, overstuffed leather chairs, one fake Turner, and three fake Wardles. He had a vanity wall with pictures of him receiving the awards for whatever rank he had achieved at the time.

On the opposite wall, nicely framed photos attested that he was a model family man (as he was, by all accounts), with a well-manicured, tweedy wife and three children, who, according to the photos, loved playing with large, hairy dogs on freshly mowed lawns. Hughes was the model of a modern, polished police executive who would have felt right at home in any large corporate executive suite. A model, except that he believed a woman's ordained role was as a supporting character.

According to Cranwell, Hughes believed that Elaine had built her hypothesis on nothing more than coincidence. Because Hughes believed that, Cranwell did too. Or said he did.

At least, Cranwell would never say he did not. He was in many ways the opposite of Hughes. He was older and had most likely topped out in his career, despite a good record with several high-profile results. Where Hughes was large, with a red nose that testified to his love of the grape, Cranwell was ascetically thin and teetotaling. Where Hughes liked luxury, Cranwell was almost Benedictine in his simplicity. Those differences aside, Cranwell was doggedly loyal, the perfect subordinate. As such, he would never challenge his superior officer.

Elaine decided there was no point hashing through the hierarchical politics of the Met for the millionth time. The only way to have her way was to be right and get a good result. She shoved Hughes and Cranwell out of her mind and refocused on the board, studying the lines connecting each bubble with other people, places, and times. The chart had plenty of bubbles, but it was woefully lacking in lines.

Sheila and Geri each possessed a photo and a bubble and had connecting lines to the Leaside industrial estate and "slash" bubbles. She felt that Danny—Nilo—was the other connection between the two, but they hadn't confirmed it.

She noted with some joy that Willend's information had been removed from the chart. She told herself that the joy was because her misgivings about his guilt were proven right, but she also realized it was because he was an interesting man. She wondered if he would call her. She wasn't sure if she wanted him to. There would be lots of tabloid fodder there.

Greene and Nilo had replaced Willend. There was little information about Nilo, but Evan was systematically checking his background. Greene was a common link, with lines to Geri, Nilo, and

Leaside. Other lines connected Sheila to the Leaside and slash bubbles, but she was unconnected to the others socially. Her connection to Leaside could be meaningless. But there was the slash.

They didn't have much. Like Hughes, any defense lawyer would chalk it all up to coincidence. Coincidences. She hated them. They really did not exist, at least not in the realm of criminal investigation. By the time an investigation was under way, there was usually a glimmer of connection. What decisions did the victim make? What decisions did the killer make? What is coincidence but the result of decisions taken by people who share some subtle nexus, some obscure impetus that, at some point, begins to forge a chain of events—a chain held at one end by the murderer's hand and at the other by the hand of the victim? Sometimes slowly, sometimes quickly, each party grasped the next link in the chain, driven by some personal need. With each decision, they made the chain shorter. Possibility crept toward probability. Whatever they wanted, whatever that desire was, they grew closer, until they reached a point at which only one link separated them. At that crux, a single decision either averted tragedy or made it inevitable.

Causality must exist, otherwise there would be no action, so Elaine gave short shrift to coincidence. But jurors could believe in coincidence, and that belief spawned reasonable doubt in their minds. Reasonable doubt led to acquittal.

She pictured the courtroom in her mind. The defense barrister, with his ill-fitting wig perched on a head filled with visions of silk, looked at each juror in turn as he succinctly pointed out that murders always occur near some property or other. Did that mean that the owners of the property were automatically involved in the crime? No. And what about the defendant? She pictured Nilo sitting in the dock, looking as benign as he could, while his barrister pointed out that, yes, he goes to dance clubs and raves. So do many young men in London. Young women go as well. The clubs are always crowded. Are we to suspect every young person who likes to dance?

"I hope wherever you were was lovely." Paula stood at the office door, smiling. "The lab says it can have the fingerprint results on the bottle tomorrow, but the DNA tests will take at least three days. Most likely a week."

Elaine shook her head to remove the thoughts from her mind. "I was strolling through the scrapyard of coincidence. It wasn't a pleasant place. So three days, eh?"

"Most likely a week. They're short-staffed and swamped."

"What else is new? That's sooner than it usually takes." Elaine pulled her jacket from the back of her chair. "I'm going home. I hear a hot bath, a bottle of Rioja, and an empty bed pleading for my company."

Paula laughed. "G'night, Chief. Too bad about the empty bed."

Elaine nodded, then glanced at the situation board once more as she left the office for her car. Greene was the common link between Geri, Nilo, and Leaside. Who was trailing Greene tonight?

★ ★ ★

No sooner had Elaine buckled her seatbelt than her mobile warbled. She answered without looking to see who was calling. "Hope."

An unfamiliar laugh floated from her earpiece. "I feel full of that this evening. Do you feel like a beer after you get off? If you have a favorite pub, I could meet you there." The voice was familiar.

"Ummm. This is DCI Hope. Who is speaking, please?"

"Oh. Sorry. This is Peter. Willend. Is this a bad time?"

Elaine hesitated. Funny how life can force a decision when you aren't ready to make one. She needed a moment. "I'll call you back. Two minutes." She rang off and sat quietly in her car, staring through her windshield at the brick wall of the station. The one time I don't check to see who the caller is, and it's him. Was it too soon? And what did "soon" mean? She wasn't involved with anyone or even getting over anyone. There was no solid reason not to meet Willend. Peter. It was only a beer, after all. The downside was that it would probably be awkward and uncomfortable for both of them. The upside was that it would most likely end with a vague "see you around" as they went their separate ways.

She dialed him back and he picked up on the second ring. Elaine got to the point before Peter could say anything. "I could use a drink. I assume you're at home. Got something to write with?" She gave him directions, ending with, "I'll be there in a half-hour."

TWENTY-FOUR

Elaine sat in a nook by the front window of Nelson's Glory, inhaling the comfortable yeasty fug and looking at the people around her. Two tables away, a young woman pecked at a laptop computer. Occasionally she would frown at its screen and take a sip from a pint of cider. From the pattern of her keystrokes, Elaine could tell she was backspacing as much as she was composing. She would clickety-clickety-clickety with both hands for a few seconds. Then she would scowl and clack-clack-clack using only her right hand. After alternating clicks and clacks for a minute or two, the woman sat back in her chair and crossed her arms, frowning.

As Elaine watched, a change came over the woman's face. She smiled, bent forward, and began a furious clickety with both hands, her attention riveted on the words flowing through her fingers. Elaine didn't know if the woman was writing a great British novel or a Dear John letter to her boyfriend; it didn't matter. A small triumph had occurred.

Most people want the big win, she reflected. They always try to hit it for six. Elaine knew that small victories add up and that it feels good to take one sure step in the right direction, even if it's a small one, and follow it up with another and another.

She scanned the pub again. A table over from the writer, nearer the door, a fashionably dressed couple sat with glasses of white wine in front of them. *Style and the money to buy it*, Elaine thought. Despite the wine, the couple seemed awkward. Fashionable Woman didn't face Fashionable Man directly. It appeared to Elaine that he was earnestly imploring the woman, but she wasn't buying it. She studied her wine, took a sip, and looked away.

Elaine looked closer and noticed the man wore a wedding band. Fashionable Woman did not. Aha. Was this a minor spat between lovers? *No*, Elaine decided, *it's a break-up*. The way the woman was scanning the men in the pub, she was considering an alternative. And judging from the interest sparking on her face, she had spotted an attractive option.

Elaine followed Fashionable Woman's gaze to the door, where Peter had just entered and was removing his coat. He waved at Elaine and started toward the nook. As he approached, Elaine watched Fashionable Woman assess Peter all the way across the pub, head to toe at first, then appraisingly at his back as he walked toward the nook. His pressed jeans fit well—not too tight but tight enough to give the impression of athletic thighs and a nice bum. His long hair was tousled and damp from the weather. He moved like an athlete, balanced and economical, very male. My goodness, he looked good. The high-class tart thought so as well and was clearly interested. Elaine felt a twinge of jealousy.

Wait a minute, Lainie, you . . . but Peter stopped in front of her before she could finish the warning. She filed her caveat away and greeted him.

"Hello, Doctor. Excuse me, I mean Peter."

"Good evening, Detective Inspector Hope. I can only assume another interrogation is in order. Does this place have a dungeon? It looks old enough for one."

Elaine went with it. "Oh, indeed, it does. There are stocks and a strappado in the cellar. You don't want to miss them. They haven't been used in two hundred years, but put a little oil on the hinges and they'll work fine."

"Doesn't the condemned get a last drink?" Peter indicated the empty table top. "It appears not. I'd hate to be strung up by my wrists and pretzeled with the thirst I have right now."

"I picked this pub because they have some very nice cask ales. The real stuff, not fizzy piss. I thought I'd let you have your choice. You know, in the spirit of the condemned man's last meal and such."

He laughed. "Why am I not surprised? Okay, then. What's good here? Gibbet Ale? Scaffold Stout? Flogger Lager? Didn't the condemned have to pay the executioner? You suggest, I'll pay."

"Such a treat. And it's Elaine, Peter." She suggested Navigation Stout and watched as he walked to the bar to order. Fashionable Woman's eyes followed Peter then switched back to Elaine, who smiled slightly. *Not tonight, strumpet.*

The detective in Elaine continued to characterize Peter. Differently than before, not as a suspect. *He seems in a good mood*, she thought, *so he must be getting back on his feet. No permanent damage, then.* She turned her face to the window and considered his candidacy. Smart, witty, musical. A bit better than decent looking, and there's that nice bum. All were clear positives.

He's a doctor. He knows all about long hours and professional imperatives, so either he's likely to be understanding about someone else having the same constraints or he wants a little Harriet Homemaker. No, he doesn't want a Harriet. Harriet would bore him.

He has deep emotions, judging from his responses to questions about his family. And that's what was bothering her. Peter carried baggage. Lots of it. She'd seen him lug it through the interviews. He's clearly still in love with his dead wife—Diana, that was her name. But then, he would always love her, wouldn't he? That's not a bad sign, unless he starts making comparisons. So perhaps it's a yellow flag, not a red one. And what about PTSD? What about his nightmare the custody sergeant had noted in the log book? She rolled her eyes at her reflection in the window. Speculations and analysis. Don't speculate ahead of the evidence, girl. Sort it out as it comes. If he gets too heavy or weird, there's always the kiss-off and the door.

She looked up when she heard him set the glasses on the table. They lifted their pints with a mutual "Cheers."

The ale did not disappoint. After a second taste, she set her glass down. "I can't talk to you about the case, you know. I have to be clear on that. Are you back to work yet?"

He didn't miss a beat. "You can't talk about your cases; I can't talk about mine. I start back next week. A&E shifts at first. After I've served my penance for helping the police with their enquiries, I may be able to go back to a normal case load and teaching, but no foundation kids. The director didn't want any rumors about me to upset the money cart."

Elaine studied her pint. "That's a shame. It has to be hard to take."

"Let's not talk about that. How did you ever find this pub? It hasn't been remodeled in what, fifty years?"

Elaine laughed. "Probably more like a hundred and fifty. It was a favorite of my father's. He'd drink here after he got back from Malaysia, back in the late fifties, I guess. Before we moved back to Glasgow. One of his army mates lived in the neighborhood and they would meet here for a pint."

"So your father was in the army, like mine? Wouldn't it be a coincidence if he married an English woman, like mine did?"

"He did! Imagine! And that's not all. He was a surgeon." She continued in response to his surprised look. "He fixed sick shoes. Took them apart, repaired what was wrong, sewed them up, and gave them back, good as new."

Peter grinned and leaned across the table. "I feel like Humphrey Bogart in Paris."

"How so? It was Sam who played the piano."

"And better than I do. I meant at that café, La Belle Aurore, or maybe it was in his apartment, when he asks Ingrid Bergman 'Who are you really? And what were you before?'" He shifted to face her directly. "I know what he was thinking. Tell me about yourself. Where did you grow up?"

"Can't you tell? I grew up above my father's shop in Drumchapel."

"He started it after the army?"

"It was his father's, and before that, his grandfather's. The family business. There wasn't much to do in Glasgow in the fifties. I think Dad joined the army to see what else there was out there for him, but I don't suppose he found anything. He was a craftsman at heart. Made bespoke shoes for people."

"It turned into his life's work, then."

"He had a steady clientele. Mum taught piano lessons and raised us girls. Between the shoes and the lessons, we got by. Not wealthy by a long shot, but we never wanted for what counted."

"There's a saying back in Texas: 'We was poor but didn't know it.' How many sisters do you have?"

"My oldest sister, Ailsa, emigrated to Australia when I was very young. Christine lives on a ranch in Alberta. They're both much older. Then there was Moira, but she died. I was the youngest by fifteen years. The Oops baby."

"Daddy's little girl, eh?"

Elaine studied the dark brown of the stout. "What about you?"

Peter appeared somewhat taken aback. "I would have bet you knew everything about me, what with the investigation."

Elaine's fingers turned her glass on the table. "Only on paper. And what you told us in the interviews."

They talked for another hour. About childhood and school, careers and bosses, travels. Shortly before closing time, Elaine placed both hands in her lap and looked down at the table. "This has been a nice evening, but I'm afraid I need to call it a night. I have an early start in the morning."

"Tell your boss you're taking the day off."

She laughed as they walked outside to the pavement. "Right. If you're good at dodging hurled objects, I'll let you tell him for me. If I'm extremely lucky, I'm off on Sunday, but it's really impossible to get away in the middle of an investigation. I want to take my mother to Brighton. She loves to watch the ocean and go to the Pavilion to have lunch and walk through the gardens for a while. She feeds the birds. Then we drive back. We usually stop in some village or other for tea. It's a full day."

"Did she come to London with you?"

"Dad passed away a couple of months after I joined the Met. She lived with me for a while, but one day she broke her hip. She got more and more frail, and it seemed like the dementia set in right afterward. It was too dangerous to leave her alone all day, so I had to find somewhere for her. It's a nice place in Surrey. I try to visit her every week or so, and we have an outing every couple of months. Usually we stay in London or go to Brighton. Sometimes we visit cousins in Exeter. It's been a while since we were able to get away, though."

"I hope you have a splendid time, then."

The conversation was starting to drag out. "We'll try."

"I've really enjoyed talking with you. Speaking of relatives, my sister, Kate, will be back from New York in a few weeks. I'd like you to meet her, if you want to. Maybe we'll have some dinner. It'll be me, Kate, and Nora, her partner." Peter's deep-set blue eyes looked down into hers.

Elaine hesitated. She wasn't ready for this, but he said it was a few weeks away. Who knew what would happen? "Perhaps. She sounds interesting. Whether I can be there depends on . . . you know. Work."

Now was the awkward moment. She certainly didn't want a kiss just yet and hoped he was perceptive and gentleman enough to know that. He didn't disappoint her.

He replied, "Then if it's all right, when the time comes, I'll ring you with the details and you can decide. How about that?" He took her hand in his. "Maybe we can get together for dinner again? Until then, take care."

She smiled and nodded. "Maybe. You too." She gave him a finger waggle, turned, and walked to her car, reflecting on the previous two hours. It hadn't been bad, not bad at all. He had let her choose the place, he was at ease and made good conversation, and he never once leered or made suggestive remarks. He'd listened to her and considered what she said before he replied. All in all, it was two adults making decent attempts at getting to know each other. The kiss-off could wait.

Elaine sat behind the wheel of her BMW, retrieved her mobile, and pressed Bull's speed-dial number. He answered on the fourth ring.

"Hi, Chief. What's up?" Bull's voice was partially distorted by the whoosh of wind and the rumble of the car. He was on the move.

"Where are you?"

"Headed west on Downham Road in De Beauvoir Town. He's been a right traveler tonight."

"That's a bit off his patch, isn't it?"

"It looks like errand night mixed with a bit of fun. He went to those knocking shops he visited last week. Came out with a blonde woman. They stopped at a couple of high-street shops and an off-license, then spent a half hour in a Tesco. Maybe they have a dinner party planned, but . . . *shit*!" Clattering burst from Elaine's mobile, followed by a thud. The whooshing rumble stopped.

"Bull? Bull! What happened? Are you there?" Silence. "Bull! Say something, make a noise!"

More clattering, followed by Bull's voice. "Sorry, Chief, I dropped my mobile. A lorry turned directly in front of me and I had to swerve. Ran partway on the pavement." Elaine heard a car door slamming. "Shit. No sight of Greene and his poppet."

"Any idea where they were going?" She wasn't hopeful.

"No. He's never been to this area since I've been watching him. It's not anywhere near his flat. He might have gone straight, but there are a lot of side streets along here. I suppose I could drive around and see if I spot his car."

Elaine considered. Had Greene spotted Bull's tail? Bull was relatively new to surveillance. There was no way to find out and no point bringing it up without sounding unfairly critical. She wished one of the older detectives had been with him. Maybe next time, if she could spare someone. This time she'd let him off lightly. "It's rotten luck. If you think there's a chance of finding him, give it a try. Otherwise, go home. I may have something else for you tomorrow."

"Right. I'll hunt for a while."

"One more thing. Invest in an earpiece for your mobile."

TWENTY-FIVE

Elaine listened to the noise building in the incident room. It was a few minutes until the status meeting scheduled for six thirty AM, and the team was engaging in the usual morning banter about football games, talking about who had gotten lucky the previous night or perhaps who had been luckless yet again. Technically, some of the humor crossed the line into what in these oh-so-correct times could be considered sexual harassment, but no one on her team had ever complained, and none of it was racial or hateful, so she ignored it. It had been different when Jenkins was on the team, but he was gone now.

A sudden lowering of the noise level caught her attention, so she leaned over and looked out the door. Paula, who was the team liaison with forensics, was rushing up the aisle between the desks toward her door. She didn't bother to knock or speak. She simply handed Elaine some papers across the desk.

Elaine scanned the forensic report, reading the first paragraph, then skipping down to the conclusions section. She felt her body tensing, and it was all she could do to keep her hands from shaking. "Halle-bloody-lujah! We needed this. Come with me." She stormed out into the suddenly silent squad room, Paula in tow. Faces turned as they passed, and a low susurrus of voices built in their wake as the two women took their place by the incident board.

"Right then, listen up! Everyone quiet!" The whispers faded away. "For those of you who may not recall, we got some DNA from the stray hairs SOCO found in Geri Harding's flat."

Elaine waved the new forensic report over her head. "Now we have this. Three days ago, Liz spoke with a man named Danilo Srecko in the car park outside the offices of IRG. She was able to get his mobile number as well as a photo."

Elaine allowed herself a slight smile as hoots and laughter erupted in the room. Progress was energizing. "Calm down everyone. I can vouch that everything Liz did was in the line of duty. But I think you had some fun with it, right, Liz?" Liz lifted her arms over her head and gave a happy dance, prompting more hoots.

Elaine let it run for a few seconds, then raised her hands for quiet. "We were also able to retrieve an empty sport drink bottle he discarded. This report states that the DNA retrieved from that drink bottle matches the DNA we found in Geri's flat."

Elaine scanned the now silent room, making eye contact with several of the detectives. Every face was grim and expectant, awaiting her next words. She pointed to the photograph of Nilo on the situation board. A sensitive technician had blurred Liz's face, leaving only Nilo mugging at the camera. "Him." She moved the photo of Danilo from the edge of the board to the center.

"We now have a prime suspect in the murder of Geri Harding. Danilo Srecko, passport says twenty-three years old, 1.8 meters tall, muscular build, dark hair, brown eyes, crooked nose. Small scar above his right eye. Goes by the name Nilo, and it's not too far-fetched that he could also use the name Danny. Does that sound familiar?

"My gut tells me he also killed Sheila Watson. If his conversation with Liz is any indication, he's always hunting, so we need to bring him in fast. Evan, have you made any progress tracking his background and phone records?"

Evan stood. "Two years ago, he entered the country from Belgium by the same route as his uncles Anton and Janko. He apparently uses a Slovenian passport instead of Polish. We're following that up. We've sent his fingerprints from the drink bottle to Europol to check against their databases, and we'll get the DNA profile to them right away. The only web presence under the name Danilo or Nilo Srecko we've been able to find is from a youth football team site in Serbia from four years ago. The lack of web presence is unusual given his age, so we're running the photo through some of MI5's new face recognition software to see if we get any hits from social media, but we're at the tail of the queue, and it could take days, if not weeks. We could use some help getting a higher priority."

Elaine nodded. "I'll do what I can. You know how MI5 can be. What else?"

Evan shook his head. "Nothing yet. No local address, no landline. He may be living in a flat registered to one of IRG's shell companies, so we'll check for those. His mobile number was issued from a small carrier in Slovenia, so it's complicated. I've made the formal requests through Europol to the Slovenian carrier and directly to British carriers for foreign number call reports, but that takes longer. And we've flagged his mobile number on our networks, so we'll be notified when he uses it. Again, if we were MI5, it would be a no-brainer. They don't worry so much about the niceties. But I think I can speed it up by going in the back door." He paused.

Elaine saw no choice but to take the bait. Evan was clearly doing a bit of grandstanding, but he deserved the spotlight. She gave him a wry smile. "I hope you aren't considering doing anything that could get us in trouble. Talk to me first."

Evan grinned. "Right, Chief. And no, it's nothing dodgy; we'll go at him from a different angle. We've already got Sheila's, Geri's, and Greene's call records for the last four months. We'll cross reference them for his number. I'd love to have Anton's and Janko's records, but I don't have enough justification yet to request them. With any luck, if he called them, he wasn't using a prepaid phone. Having a few more eyes to do that would speed it up."

"Paula, assign someone to help with the phone records and get his photo out to the uniforms. We need some eyes on the IRG offices. Find someone besides Liz to partner with Bull on the surveillance." She saw Bull and Liz exchange a look. "And Paula, come see me after you've done that."

There were more actions to consider. She looked at the sergeant who handled their liaison with other police units. "More to do. Get his picture and passport information to all rail, ferry, and airport officers with orders to be detained. Then contact regional police forces and get the word out that we want him. Make sure they all understand that even though we don't have a hard reason to think he has firearms, we do have reason to believe that he knows how to use a knife. So he is to be treated as dangerous."

Everyone in the room was grim-faced, silent, and focused. They lived to collar murderers. "Anything else? Right, then. We know our quarry. He's a killer, and the sooner we catch him, the sooner we can breathe easier. Let's hunt him down."

Some minutes later, Elaine called Paula to her office. "Who did you put on the phone records?"

"Barker. She didn't like it and put up a squawk about wanting to be on the surveillance team. I set her straight. Danilo knows her, and it wouldn't take him long to spot her red hair. I put Simon with Bull on building coverage. I'll go over it with them in a minute."

"She'll get over it. Tell Simon and Bull to be very discreet."

"Right. Chief? What about Liz? Do you think he might go after her?"

Elaine shook her head. "It's a possibility, but I can't assign someone to watch her 'round the clock. Sit her down and give her a talk about safety. Make sure she understands that she could be in danger. She's had the self-defense training?"

"Up to date on self-defense, and I heard she's taken some Krav Maga lessons. Bull is an ex-Royal Marine—Forty Commando—so I'll suggest that he keep an eye on her."

"He'll eat from your hand forever if you do that. Okay. It'll have to do. Verify the KM with her, and when you do, put some fear into her. Remind her that this is a murder and we're hunting a killer. We have to assume that he's had military training. Nearly all these Eastern European gangsters are ex-military or paramilitary. Suggest that she stay at a friend's place until we nick this guy."

"I'll have the talk. Maybe she and Bull will enjoy more time together. What do you want to do about Greene? More pressure?"

Elaine smiled to herself. Paula didn't miss anything. "No, we'll pull back from Greene for now. Give him some space. If he gets a notion he's being followed, he'll run to the Sreckos, and I don't want to tip them off. I want to be the first copper to see the look on their faces when we walk through their front door."

★ ★ ★

It required two sets of eyes to observe the office block that housed the IRG offices: one set to cover the main front entrance and the other set to watch the entrance to the multistory car park and the small service area in the rear, which was used mainly for deliveries and utility vehicles. If Danilo appeared, he would either enter the building through the car park or park in the service area in the rear. Simon had assigned Bull to watch the front entrance, with instructions to look for both Danilo and Greene. He stationed himself on the side street, where he could see the other two entrances. This was the afternoon of the second day, and their quarry had not entered or left the building. At least, he hadn't while they were on duty from six in the morning until six in the evening.

The boy could have been on holiday or on assignment. Perhaps he was coming and going outside of business hours. It did no good to speculate. He hadn't shown up, and Simon was concerned that they were wasting their time. The guv needed some kind of result. It was time to take action.

Simon had noticed that two office workers were in the habit of taking a smoke break on the back loading dock about every two hours. He checked his watch. It was almost four, so they were due. Sure enough, they appeared at a few minutes past the hour. He tore a sheet from his notebook, scribbled the IRG address on it, and walked toward them.

"Good afternoon, mates. I'm wondering if you could help me. I'm looking for a company called IRG. Is this the building? I have a job interview with them tomorrow, and I wanted to make sure I have the right place. No point in getting lost and being late, is there?" He pulled out the sheet of paper and showed it to them.

"Yeah, that's it, they're here. Take the lift."

"Right, then. Do either of you work for them?"

"Wouldn't work for those shites. They keep to themselves mostly. Always seem out of sorts. You know, not very friendly."

"Really? I ran into one of them in a pub the other day. He seemed nice enough. We got to talking, and I told him I was looking to change firms. I'm an estate agent, you know, and he said they may have something. You might know him. Young guy, footballer type, a few inches taller than me, short hair, sort of skinny. Seemed like a nice bloke."

The two men looked at each other and laughed. "Well, then you don't know him well, do you?"

Simon did his best to look taken aback. "Only met him the once. Like I said, we met in a pub, and he gave me this address. Is there something I ought to know about him?"

"He's one to steer clear of. Isn't he, Ben?" The speaker looked at his companion, who shook his head and took up the story.

"That's right. The way he came out of here last week, I thought he'd take on the both of us, right here. And we didn't do nothing."

Better and better. Simon moved a bit closer and raised his eyebrows. "Really? What happened?"

Ben was only too happy to tell him. "We were standing here, minding our business, enjoying a smoke, when he comes busting through that door there like he wanted to take the bloody building down." He pointed to a set of double steel doors. "Nearly knocked

Steve here on his arse. The way he acted, you would have thought we were the ones who knocked him about. He got all belligerent. Balled up his fists and shouted at us. Called us right fuckers, didn't he, Steve?"

"Did he start a fight?"

"Wish he had. We was ready, and we'd have taught him a good lesson if he pressed us. He made a fuss, then he got in one of those vans there and drove off." He pointed to two white Transits parked near the brick wall at the rear of the service area.

Simon put on a wide-eyed and impressed look. "What did you do when he came back?"

"Haven't seen him. Come to think of it, there's usually three of those vans parked there, but the one he took hasn't been there since then."

Yes, thought Simon. *Keep it going.* "How do you know? I mean, how do you know that one is missing?"

"It has a scraped wing on the off-side. You know, like it ran up against a wall or something. It's been like that a while and not been fixed. Typical of that lot."

"Maybe he was the one who mashed it and took it to the garage to get it mended."

"P'raps. Look, mate, we need to get back. Our break's over." The two men tossed the ends of their cigarettes in a nearby bucket.

"Right. Well, thanks for the help and the tip. I'll probably still show up tomorrow and do the interview. Maybe I'll see you around."

"Yeah." The two men nodded and went inside, leaving Simon alone.

He waited a few seconds to be sure they were gone, then walked across the tarmac to the two white Transits. A cursory inspection through the windscreen revealed clipboards and papers on the seats, tools, paint, and other builder's supplies in the back. There was nothing out of order with them. He jotted the number plate for each on his paper and pulled out his mobile as he walked to his car. Bull answered on the first ring.

"I did a little nosing with a couple of blokes who work in the building. It looks like our Danilo hasn't been here in a few days, and I don't think he'll be here any time soon. I think he's done a runner or gone to ground somewhere. I'm going to call the guv and report in. I suspect we'll be off this and back to the nick before long. I'll let you know."

He rang off. The guv never liked bad news, but at least he'd uncovered something concrete they could follow. How many white Transit vans are there in London? Eight or ten thousand? Probably twenty-five or thirty thousand in the country, at least. White Transits proliferated like rabbits. *Oh, well, Evan can sort that out. We have to find one with a scraped wing.* He punched the speed-dial button for Elaine.

TWENTY-SIX

As soon as Simon and Bull returned, Elaine gathered together the team members who were in the incident room.

"Good work, Simon. We need a break. Evan, find out who owns those vans. Everything you can about them. I bet it's that Cumbrian or Grampian or whatever company that IRG uses for its leased equipment. Then find out what other vehicles are registered in their name. Not just Transits, the full lot. Audis, Mercs, BMWs, all the way down to a G-Wiz or a motorbike if they have them. Also, when you find the other Transits, see if any have been involved in a minor shunt. When you find it, get the number plate and registration to Paula."

She looked at Paula. "Get this out to uniform. We're not only looking for Danilo; we're looking for a white Transit with a damaged left wing."

"Wait a minute, guv." It was Bull. "Suppose they have some kind of registry of cars for that building? You know, like we have to register our personal cars here at the nick, so they know which cars are allowed in? Would the building manager have something like that?"

"Simon, did either of those vans have a parking lot badge? Some kind of sticker on the windshield?"

"Didn't notice, guv, but we could go back and look."

Elaine considered. "We can't afford to have the Sreckos know we're snooping around. Let's let Evan see what he can find. If he comes up empty, we'll think about doing that. And let's pull away from the building for now. If Danilo's disappeared, it's because we spooked them last time. If they get a whiff that we're on to them, he'll be out of the country before we know it. First thing tomorrow morning, I want the two of you back on Greene. Evan, anything from the phone records yet?"

"Not yet, guv, but we should have all the permissions from Slovenia and the local carriers by tomorrow. Europol put some pressure on the Slovenians."

"Excellent. We'll get the team together at eight in the morning. Paula? Evan?" She nodded her head toward her office.

When they were all seated, Elaine opened the bottom drawer of her desk and pulled out a bottle of single malt whisky and three glasses. She poured each a shot of the whisky. "A perk of being a DCI. Nobody else noses around in your desk." Once they had all sampled the liquor, she asked, "How's Liz coming along? I didn't want to ask with the others around, especially Bull."

Paula gave a knowing smile. "So you noticed that too? I suggested that she find another place to stay, and a few minutes later I saw them talking." She laughed. "He looked a bit scared. More than she did."

Elaine placed her empty glass on the desk. "More power to both of them. I'd feel safe with him around. He's pretty intimidating. Find out for sure, eh? If she's nervous about admitting it, let her know that it's not a problem. Evan, how's Liz doing on the phone records?"

"Just fine. She grumped for the first hour, but now she's moving pretty fast."

"Good. Maybe she's trying to prove something."

TWENTY-SEVEN

It was quiet in the squad room at night, a good time to think. Elaine turned her chair away from her desk and gazed out the window. It had been dark for an hour, so she could see little but the reflection of herself and her office. She turned off the light and closed her door.

That was better. From her window on the twentieth floor of the Empress State Building, she could look north over much of London, past the dark pool of Hyde Park and the traffic moving along Bayswater Road, past the cosmopolitan hotels of Mayfair, and farther north past Regent's Park. To the right, almost out of her view, she could see the blazing lights of Emirates Stadium.

Beyond the stadium and to the west was Crouch End. Farther west was Highgate. What was Peter doing tonight? Perhaps he was on duty at the A&E. But if not, maybe he was sitting in that big chair she had seen in his bedroom, looking out his large window toward central London. Where she sat.

She leaned against the tall back of her chair. Peter was a strange duck, wasn't he? She had been his adversary at the moment they met. She had invaded his home, ripped him away from it, and locked him in a cell. She had said terrible things to him, tried to strip his soul to get at the truth. Her efforts had cost him his job and quite possibly destroyed whatever professional ambitions or dreams he had held. Then, when he proved fruitless to her goals, she had dumped him at his empty home and left him to try to rebuild the shambles of his life.

And after all that, with the exception of occasional anger and the nightmare, he had taken it in stride. Despite everything, he hadn't blamed her personally or seriously lashed out. When his purgatory was over, he had approached her and offered her a tentative fingerhold for friendship, if she wanted it. He clearly wasn't afraid of strong women. He was brave enough to take the first step and decent enough to give her space to decide.

Was it some misplaced sense of culpability, a bit of unwarranted guilt about how Benford—and she—had disrupted his life that made her indecisive?

She would have been attracted to him if they had met under better circumstances. As it was, she knew him deeper, sooner, than if they had met in some other way. Maybe she needed to take a chance at developing a relationship. He wasn't a murderer. That much she knew. She could wipe the slate clean of the unpleasant bits, couldn't she? It appeared that he had.

They had certainly clicked at the pub. She hadn't felt so comfortable, so natural, in a man's presence in years. She had felt immediately that, with him, she could be herself. She could open up and not fear being judged. She had felt free.

She needed to let him know whether or not she was going to his sister's birthday dinner. Kate, wasn't it? She'd be damned if she was going to weasel out of it, but it was a family gathering, and she wasn't ready for that. Perhaps he'd agree to meet sooner. She picked up her mobile from the desk and scrolled to his number in her contact list. Ha! She had added him after she had gotten home from their evening in the pub, so she had known then that she was going to call him. She tapped twice and, in a few seconds, heard the warble at the other end. Two, three, four times.

"How are you tonight?" His voice was quiet and soft. She could hear his breathing over the connection. She thought she could also hear his heart beating but then realized it was her own.

"Ready to leave the office. I'm calling about Kate's birthday." She paused. "That is, if you were serious about that."

She heard him exhale, and a second later, "Of course I was. It's only an informal family get-together. Nothing fancy." He paused. "No implications, either way."

"That's it, don't you see? It's family, and you and I don't have much of a track record yet. There are implications, like it or not."

"I see. Yes. I guess it's too soon to meet the mother and big sister." He was silent for three or four breaths, then spoke. "Are you wondering if I carry any hard feelings?"

"We've only met each other socially one time. Your mother and sister might be understanding, but they're going to have questions. I don't think they'd hold me in very high regard. Perhaps I need to be a bit more sure of myself." She hesitated. "And yes, I can't help but think you're carrying anger. I need to be sure of you."

"Okay. The birthday is still a month away. I'm off tomorrow and the next day. Maybe we can talk about how we feel over a curry and maybe a walk if the weather is clear?"

She exhaled in relief. "That would be nice. All right, then, tomorrow evening? You understand that I may get a call at any time. I'm never really off work, you know."

"I know. But we can think positive thoughts. I know I will. I'll ring you."

"Yes, talk to you then. Oh, tell me something. Where were you when I called? I mean exactly?"

"At home. In my bedroom. Sitting in my chair catching up on some journals. Why?"

"Just wondering." She rang off and took another look out the window toward Highgate as she retrieved her jacket from the back of her chair. She stopped and sat back down, digesting the insight that, in that moment, had risen to the surface of her brain. Then she walked to the map on the wall of the incident room. She wanted a visual aid to help think it through.

There was the red pin marking Peter's home. She removed it. An inch to the east and a bit south was another red pin, the Khoury's high street shop and the spot where Sheila had gotten off the bus. Her vision tracked to the right, east toward the yellow pin on Downham Road in De Beauvoir Town, where Bull had lost his tail on Greene. Farther east, in Newham, was a cluster of yellow pins marking the supermarket and shops where Greene had stopped to buy groceries, Greene's office, and the knocking shop where he had picked up the young woman.

She turned to the series of pictures that Bull had taken. In one, Greene and the woman stood in the parking lot of the supermarket, placing several full bags of groceries into the boot of Greene's car. In the next, they were getting into the car.

Then they had driven in the direction of the last place Sheila had been seen alive. If Danilo was in hiding, he was probably in a place he knew, a place where he felt secure and comfortable. A place owned by IRG. Even though Greene had slipped away from Bull, he had given them an idea of where that place was.

Elaine realized that Greene and the woman hadn't been going to a dinner party. The photo had shown too many bags for that. He was taking supplies and a prostitute to Danilo.

Elaine stepped back, unable to fully believe what her intuition was telling her. She went over it again, this time east-to-west, following the most likely path that Greene and the prostitute, which the young woman surely was, had taken. The route was as direct as it could have been. Bull hadn't relayed any evasion on Greene's part.

Granted, after Bull had lost the tail, Greene could have turned left on Southgate at the end of Downham Road. If he had, he could have crossed Regent's Canal to Hoxton.

But suppose he had taken a right turn when he reached the end of Downham Road? She tracked her finger up Southgate. He would have gone west on Saint Paul's Road. From there, it was only a couple of turns and he was within a half-mile of the Khoury's shop and, somewhere near there, Sheila's probable destination.

If her hunch was right, they could narrow the search for Danilo tremendously, focusing on a couple of square miles around Highgate and Muswell Hill instead of the entire sprawling city. If she was wrong, then Hughes would undoubtedly replace her and she would spend the rest of her career chasing taggers and finding lost dogs.

But she was right. In her gut, she knew it.

TWENTY-EIGHT

Bosko sat on the sofa, listening to the young woman's whimpers filter through the thin wall. *At least her yelping has stopped*, Bosko thought to himself. He certainly hadn't planned on this when he accepted Nilo's invitation for a spot of fun. Coke, lager, and a whore were what he had understood when Nilo had invited him to the house earlier in the day. But it had gone all crazy—crazier than anything he had experienced in his seventeen years.

He thought back to the time before he had left Serbia to come to London. Bosko had loved Nilo like the older brother he never had. He was also afraid of him. In their hometown, Nilo had been feared by almost everyone, and not only because he was a favored son of the most powerful family in town.

Nilo was utterly fearless, daring to do things that the other boys in town only dreamed about, urging them into risk, cheering them and clapping them on the back when they triumphed, berating and abusing them when they quailed at one of his challenges. Bosko had tagged along when Nilo had wanted to break into a house, steal a car, or go hunting for stray dogs. As a group, they had shared more than a few drunken girls. If the girl was quiet and cooperative, and lucky, she got a wad of Srecko money to show her what a whore she was and a warning to keep quiet. But most often, Nilo had slapped the girl around a bit afterward, leaving her with a bloody lip, bruises, and torn clothes as a reminder of what his family was capable of.

Then one day, Nilo hurt a girl so badly that she would never fully recover. And even though it was an accident and the Srecko family made reparations, the girl's family got the police involved, and Nilo had been forced to leave the country. Bosko hadn't seen Nilo again until he himself had come to London a year ago to do building maintenance work for Uncle Janko. He had expected to continue to have fun with Nilo, picking up where they had left off.

On occasion, they had some fun together, but Bosko soon realized that Nilo had changed. His older cousin had become more tyrannical, more volatile, more unpredictable. He constantly pushed the limits of what Bosko was prepared to do and experience. What was happening now was not like anything Bosko had seen Nilo do before.

Thumping noises from the bedroom startled Bosko back into the present. Nilo roared something incomprehensible and the squeals of pain began again. Bosko thought back to his days on the family farm. The sounds reminded him of a scared piglet. Then came a sudden crash, and the squeals stopped. He sat there, stunned, his blood pounding in his ears.

"Bosko! What the hell are you doing out there? Get in here!"

Bosko sat, afraid to move, afraid not to move. He heard footsteps in the short corridor, and Nilo appeared, naked, with smears of blood splattering his lower torso, a baseball bat in his hand.

"Bosko! Hey! Are you drunk?" He waited for Bosko to look at him. "You're not turning into some kind of poof, are you? Come in here." He turned and disappeared down the hallway.

Bosko waited a few heartbeats, then stood and shuffled numbly to the door of the bedroom. The woman was sprawled across the edge of the bed, her upper body hanging off onto the floor, her blonde hair matted with blood. Nilo stood over her.

"Stupid cow. Cunt!" Nilo bent and lifted one of her limp arms, then dropped it in disgust and threw the bat into a corner. He opened the drawer of a night table and extracted a large knife. Bosko gasped as Nilo bent down and poised the knife above the woman's face. "Naaah. She's used up. No fun now." He replaced the knife in the drawer. "Get over here and help me wrap her in the sheets."

Bosko couldn't make his feet move. He stood in the door, frozen. Nilo looked at him with clear disappointment. He spoke softly.

"Now, Bosko, don't lose your bottle when I truly need you."

Bosko's throat was so tight, he could only croak in reply. He shuffled to the woman and took her arm, lifting and turning her limp body onto the bed. He cleared his throat and looked blankly at the body but saw only the blood. "Why did you have to do this, Nilo? I wasn't ready for this. Her name was Katya. She was nice to me, at first. And now you've killed her."

"Nice to you, was she? She's a whore. She spread her legs for money. And I didn't mean to, did I? Ahh! Didn't want to, but it was all her fault. The crying bitch had it coming. Sooner or later, somebody would have got sick of her whingeing and topped her. Just happened to be me. Sooner, that's all."

They bundled Katya's limp body into the bed linens and dragged her into the sitting room.

Nilo tossed the keys to the Transit on the table. He opened a drawer, took out an FN Five-seveN pistol, and checked the magazine. Satisfied it was fully loaded, he stuffed it into his waistband. "Go get the Transit. Highgate isn't far from here. We'll dump it in the cemetery. Wait. Let's have a bit before. Nothing sets things right like whisky and a pile of Peruvian. And a Five-seveN."

The alcohol and cocaine steamrollered some courage into Bosko's brain. He snatched the keys and left to retrieve the Transit but returned within a minute. "It's been clamped."

Nilo's body jerked to attention. "What? Clamped? What the . . ." He rushed to the front window and pushed aside the curtain, straining to see the forlorn little van in the gathering darkness. "Fuck!"

"Yeah. It ain't going nowhere."

"Shit. Those goddamn pigs. It wasn't that far over the line." Nilo spun into a rage, shattering a chair with the baseball bat. Chips of plaster flew as he pounded the walls with the bat, cursing the police, Anton, the girl.

Finally Nilo calmed. "We'll have to use your motor. Bring it up to the door. I'll turn out all the lights."

Twenty minutes later, they clattered up the narrow lane to Highgate Cemetery in Bosko's clapped-out Fiesta. The gate was padlocked. A sign indicated that the cemetery had closed over three hours before their arrival. Nilo shook the bars, but the hinges and chain held firm. They navigated the streets around the cemetery, but the walls were either too high to climb or topped with iron spikes or wire. Each gate they tested was as sound as the first.

Bosko was growing nervous as the drugs and alcohol faded. "What do we do now?"

"Look there. I remember now." Nilo pointed to the fence running down the right side of the lane. "It's a park. Pull on the pavement, as close as you can."

Bosko complied and opened the hatch. They extracted the sheeted bundle and wrestled it to the roof of the car. From there it was an easy lift to the top of the fence. With a push they tipped the bundle over and were rewarded with a rustling noise, followed by a low splash.

"Excellent!" Nilo sounded relieved. "Your flat's not far, is it? I need to take a huge piss."

TWENTY-NINE

Liz parked her car and walked to Hassan Khoury's well-kept, modest home a block off Green Lanes in Harringay. The door was answered by a slightly built girl who looked to be early in her teen years. The scent of Middle Eastern cooking wafted through the opening.

"I hope I'm not interrupting your supper. I'm DC Barker. Is your father at home?"

The girl's eyes widened and she called back over her shoulder. "Mum, there's a lady at the door. She says she's a detective and she wants to talk to Dad."

Moments later, a stout middle-aged woman appeared in the hallway, wiping her hands on a kitchen towel. She glanced at the proffered warrant card. "I am Mariam Khoury. My husband is not here right now. He should be along soon. May I ask why you need to speak with him?" By this time, an older woman had joined them at the door.

"Some days ago, a colleague interviewed your husband about some customers at your shop. I have a couple more questions for him."

The older woman at once assumed a stern expression. Mariam glanced at her, then returned her attention to Liz. She smiled and stepped aside, giving a welcoming gesture with her hand. "Please come in. We are preparing supper. Would you care to join us?"

Liz entered. "No, but thank you so much for offering. Do you mind if I wait for Mr. Khoury?"

The older woman harrumphed. "Hassan mentioned that he had spoken to a detective. I am sure he told you all you needed to know then."

Liz assumed a businesslike expression. "We need to clarify something. And you are?"

The woman pulled herself erect. "I am Leyla Khoury, Hassan's mother. He will be home soon." She glanced again at Mariam. "Please wait in here with Sarah. We need to tend to supper." She turned and beckoned to Mariam, who gave Liz an apologetic glance before returning to the kitchen.

Liz took a seat on the sofa in the small sitting room. Sarah was perched on a chair across from her, an open notebook on her lap. From the appraising look Sarah was giving her, Liz knew a quiz was coming.

"I have a school project about what career we might want to have. I'm thinking about being a doctor. I mean, I really want to be one. But we have to write about at least three different choices. I'm wondering if you might help me."

"I'll try." Liz heard the sound of raised voices coming from the kitchen. An unexpected visit from a copper tended to raise the level of tension in any home. She looked back at Sarah, who clearly had heard the altercation. The girl made a show of shuffling her papers and making sure her pen was working. She looked intently at Liz.

"I think the first question is, why did you join the police?"

"Well, when I got out of school, I really didn't know what I wanted to do. I knew I didn't want to go to uni right away. I mean, I passed enough A levels, but I was tired of school. You must know how that is sometimes."

The argument in the kitchen was continuing, and Sarah spoke louder and more quickly. "I think so. I mean, I like it, but I'm really tired by the end of every term. So what did you do?"

"I got a job as a shop assistant, but it was so incredibly boring." Liz chuckled. "Same old stuff, day in day out. And I felt like I wasn't *doing* anything. Nothing that mattered, anyway. So I looked around. About that time, the Met was advertising for new officers, especially women, so I thought, why not? I like solving problems. I like feeling that what I do every day makes a difference. It certainly would have a lot of activity, and I couldn't imagine it being boring." She paused and listened. The voices from the kitchen were quiet. Apparently some sort of truce had been called until Hassan arrived home.

Sarah looked relieved at the silence. "Was it? Did it? All that, I mean."

Liz smiled. "Yes. I would do it all again. Same way, even."

Sarah appeared thoughtful. "I suppose. But it's dangerous, right? All those gangsters and druggies. If I'm a doctor, I can help people and not have to . . ."

The front door opened and Hassan Khoury entered. He noticed Liz, and Sarah and stepped into the sitting room.

Liz heard chairs scraping the floor and footsteps approaching from the kitchen. She stood and offered her hand.

"I'm DC Liz Barker, from the Met. Sarah was interviewing me about my choice of careers. She's such a bright girl. Are you Mr. Khoury?"

"Yes. Hassan Khoury. May I ask why you are here?" Mariam and Leyla had joined them in the sitting room, reinforcing Hassan. Sarah remained in her chair, her wide eyes flitting back and forth between her family and the lone detective.

"A few days ago, one of our detectives interviewed you about some customers who came to your store one night. Do you recall the conversation?"

"Yes, clearly. It was a woman, older than you, taller. A chief inspector. Hope, I think her name was. I told her everything I could recall."

"Yes, DCI Hope. And I'm sure you did. No problem there." She pulled an envelope from her purse and removed the picture of Nilo.

"Was this young man one of the customers you told DCI Hope about?" She held out the photo. He took it from her and moved closer to a lamp. The two women shuffled behind him, looking over his shoulder. Liz glanced at Sarah, who rolled her eyes.

Hassan scratched his head. "Perhaps. No, yes. I mean, he's the young Russian man who was in the store."

Liz was looking for a bit more clarity. "So are you sure that he was the young man in the store that Friday night? No question in your mind?"

"Yes, I'm sure. Do you think he's the man who killed that young girl? I read the news about how you arrested Dr. Willend, then let him go because he's innocent."

Sarah gasped. "Not Dr. Willend! He would never hurt anyone. He's our friend." Her eyes grew even wider as she looked plaintively at her father and took his arm. It was clear this was the first she had heard of the murder investigation. She regarded Liz with sudden anger.

Liz gave her a smile. "Dr. Willend was helping us with our enquiries. And no, he did not have anything to do with the girl's death. In fact, he is something of a hero. He saved the life of a detective who was having a heart attack."

She turned back to Hassan. "Let's say we would like to ask this young man some questions. We feel he can be of assistance to us."

Leyla Khoury reached around and took the photo from Hassan. "I have seen him also. He comes in from time to time. He usually buys cigarettes. But he's not Russian. He's from somewhere else over there. Bosnia? No, Serbia. His name is Daniel or something like that."

Liz saw an opportunity. "You have an excellent memory, Mrs. Khoury. Do you recall anything else about him? Where he lived, perhaps?"

"No, although he always came in and left in the same direction." She paused.

"And which way was that, Mrs. Khoury?"

"To the right. The south. Is there anything else you need to know? Our supper is getting cold, if it isn't already."

"No, that's all for now. Thank you for your help. We may contact you again if we have any more questions." She handed her card to Sarah. "And if you have any more questions about your school project, you can always contact me at that number."

She dialed Elaine before she reached her car. "Chief, Khoury ID'd the photo, and his mother recognized him too. Said she thought his name was Daniel. She remembered that he always comes and goes from the south side of the shop, so he probably lives in that direction."

"Good work. I'm still at the nick. Stop by and pick me up."

* * *

Elaine stood back as Liz pressed the button beside the brothel's door. The electric lock clicked, and the two detectives entered a dimly lit hallway. To the left was a bare-walled sitting room with a sagging sofa, a table, and two wooden chairs. Ahead of them, the hallway ended in a staircase.

A young blonde woman stood in the kitchen door beyond the sitting room, appraising them. She walked up to Liz and gazed into her eyes. "Threesomes usually cost extra, but I can give a discount in your case." Her voice was heavily accented.

"I'm flattered." Liz smiled back and showed her warrant card. "But that's not why we're here. I'm DC Barker. This is DCI Hope." The woman backed away and, with a look of disgust, thudded down on one of the chairs.

Elaine spoke calmly. "Don't worry. We're not with the Vice. We'd like to ask a few questions and show you a photograph. What's your name?"

The woman remained silent, staring at the floor. Liz walked to the kitchen door and looked in, expecting a punter or another girl. All she saw was a clean and tidy kitchen. At least one of the prostitutes had retained some domestic pride. She returned to the sitting room.

"DC Barker"—Elaine jerked her head in the direction of the staircase—"why don't you go find someone else we can talk to?"

The young woman looked up. "Don't go up there! It's private."

Elaine snorted. "I'd say we can go anywhere we want right now. You let us in. We weren't two steps in the door and you propositioned us for sex."

"You said you weren't with the Vice!"

"We're not. And as long as you cooperate, we're only interested in information. If you don't cooperate, we'll have to make sure you're here legally. And then we'll call the Vice. Did you hear that, Liz? It sounded like a woman cried out. Go check." Liz turned toward the stairs.

"Ximena." The young woman almost spit the name at Elaine.

"Ximena what?"

"Abaroa."

Elaine sat down in the chair opposite Ximena and leaned forward. "Thank you, Ximena. Cooperation is always more pleasant for everyone. Now. Is anyone else in the house with you?"

Ximena looked up. "Lana. She's with . . ." She stopped at the sound of a door closing, followed by heavy footsteps descending the stairs.

A large middle-aged man lumbered into view and stopped at the sight of Liz. "Well, now. What's this? New inventory? Where's your bed, luv?" He sidled up to her, putting his hand on her waist. His fingers began tracing a line toward her breast.

She smiled and extracted her warrant card. "Any farther and a custody officer will be giving you a bed in the nick." The man blanched, spun on his heel, and bolted out the front door.

Elaine turned back to Ximena. "I hope there are no more where he came from. Please call Lana down."

When Lana appeared, Elaine directed the two young women to sit on the sofa while she and Liz took the chairs.

"Now then. I assure you that we only want some information." She held the photo of Greene and the young woman outside the supermarket. "Do you recognize these two people?"

Ximena's eyes roamed over the photo. She nodded. "That's Gordo."

"Gordo? Is that what you call him?"

Ximena smirked. "He's a pig."

"Tell me. How do you know him?"

"He collects money. Puts it in a bag. If we don't give him a blow job when he wants, he says he will tell the boss that we stole the money, and the boss will beat us. Or maybe worse."

"I see. Who is the young woman? Do you know her?"

Lana spoke. "That's Katya. She works here too."

"Where is she now?"

"I don't know. She went with Gordo. He said the boss was having a party and asked for her."

Elaine held out the photo of Danilo. "Is this the boss?"

Ximena and Lana exchanged glances. Lana spoke again. "Yes."

"What's his name? Do you know where he lives?"

Lana shook her head. "Danilo. He's Serbian. He likes Katya. He takes her to his house sometimes for parties." She looked aside for a moment. "Katya knows how to please him."

"Do you know where his house is?"

The women looked at each other before Lana answered. "No. We've never gone with him, only Katya."

Elaine put the photo back in the envelope. "Right, then. Thank you both for your help. You see, we're investigating a much bigger crime than brothel keeping. Some young women have been murdered recently, and we have reason to believe that your boss is involved. We also believe that Katya is in danger and that the two of you may be as well. Here are our cards. Call us if you see or hear from Danilo. He's a very dangerous man."

"What about Katya? She's my cousin." Lana appeared worried. "I'm going to leave."

Liz pulled out her notebook. "Write her a note. We're looking for her too. When we find her, I'll see that she gets it. We're not interested in arresting her. We want the boss."

THIRTY

"Listen up, boys and girls." Elaine surveyed the faces gathered for the morning status meeting. "Uniform found a clamped Transit, not five blocks from the Khoury's store. The registration matches, so it looks like we may have been right about the area where he's gone to ground. Paula, organize a house-to-house. Liz, you're with me. Simon and Bull, we need to have a little talk with Greene. Bring him in and don't mess about. Arrest him for brothel keeping. Evan, request CCTV for the area, then get with Land Registry. We need to know the ownership of every property within a two-block radius. Look for anything that you suspect could be associated with IRG. I smell him, people."

She could tell from the intense faces of her team that each of them did too.

★ ★ ★

A soft pinging sound indicated a text message had arrived on Anton's off-the-books mobile phone. He read the single word and pressed a speed-dial key. As usual, there were no niceties.

"Greene's being arrested. Hope ordered it. He'll be in custody within the hour."

Anton rang off, replaced the mobile in the drawer, and turned his chair toward his window. He had seen it coming but hadn't realized how quickly Nilo would completely lose control. *Now, of all times, he runs off the tracks. Damn that irresponsible little shite.* There were definite benefits to running a family business, but there were drawbacks as well. It could make discipline difficult, especially when the miscreant was the boss's son. Something needed to be done about Greene and Nilo. Dealing with Greene was no problem. Dealing with Nilo would be. He walked to Janko's office and closed the door. Janko raised his eyebrows expectantly.

Anton got straight to the point. "Greene's arrested. Hope will have him in custody within the hour."

"Then we need to deal with him. Bail should be no problem. Make sure someone we know shows up as his brief. He knows where Nilo is. Do you think we need to move the brat?"

"I think we need an accident or two."

Janko nodded. "Goran is available. He can be here tomorrow. I'll talk to Marko."

★ ★ ★

The weather had turned blustery. Low, gray clouds had already begun to spit large drops of rain. It was getting colder. Elaine turned up the collar on her donkey jacket and took in the scene.

The white Transit looked forlorn, as if the big yellow boot engulfing its front wheel were a shark emerging from the tarmac, intent on dragging it into the abyss. The locksmith was there and had opened the door. Elaine and Liz watched as a gloved officer gave the van a cursory search prior to it being hauled away to forensics. Paula was nearby, organizing the house-to-house team.

Thank god the house-to-house on this street wouldn't take long. It was a short cul-de-sac, with eight fully detached red brick houses lining it on either side, each with the standard-issue small front garden and neatly trimmed hedge. Most of the houses appeared to have been built in the later years of Queen Victoria's reign, no doubt for bankers, solicitors, and merchants of the newly developing upper-middle class. The current residents were apparently in similar secure economic situations, as all the houses appeared well kept and in good condition.

As she scanned the street, she noticed an elderly woman peering around a curtain at the front of the house nearest the van. This was as good a place as any to start, so with Liz in tow, she strode up the walk and rang the bell. The door sprang open instantly. An ancient, tiny woman, with cataract glasses ballooning her blue eyes, stood before them. She began chirping as she motioned them to enter.

"Hello, luvs. Olivia Marston. Do come in. Harry and I were wondering what all the hubbub was about. We're so glad you're removing that awful van. It was such an eyesore. And it's not ours, in case you were wondering. We have no use for such a thing. Harry always had a nice British saloon. Our first motor was a Humber, and we had it for twenty years, but then I expect neither of you know what a Humber is. Far before your time. You young ladies probably drive around in one of those Triumph or Jaguar things that look like a fish. Now you make yourselves comfortable while I go get the tea. It's cold out, and you look like you could use something. I put the kettle on and arranged the tea cart as soon as I saw the officers sniffing around the van. Harry and I knew something was up." She looked at them expectantly.

Elaine couldn't help but smile. "I'm Detective Chief Inspector Hope. This is Detective Constable Barker. And tea would be lovely, Mrs. Marston."

"Call me Livvy, luv. I knew you were coppers. Detectives! It's so nice to see women coppers. Gives it a sense of caring, you know. Not as frightening, you see. I think I would have liked being a copper, but that kind of thing didn't happen in my day. And Harry would never have stood for it. Would you, Harry?"

Both Elaine and Liz started as two loud thumps came from the ceiling. Livvy cackled.

"One for yes, two for no. Always startles visitors the first time. My Harry doesn't ever come down anymore. Too dangerous, seeing as how he's blind now and I'm not as strong as I once was, so

I can't help him as much nowadays. Wrestling him up and down the stairs would be terribly difficult for me. He doesn't speak much either, but I know he appreciates everything I do, and he can hear just fine, which is a blessing. I suppose. Our grandson installed some kind of microphone that runs up to the upstairs room so Harry won't be left out. See? There on the wall. Nice boy. We're so proud. Cambridge. He got his degree in maths you know, and he works at one of those big companies in the City. Now which was it? Oh . . ." Three thumps reverberated from the ceiling. She looked up. "I'm sorry. I do prattle on sometimes. I'll go get the tea."

She had indeed arranged the tea earlier, because she returned in moments, pushing a small tea cart that groaned and squeaked under its load of a teapot in a cozy, the usual accoutrements, and a plate heaped with chocolate biscuits. Elaine began speaking while Livvy distributed the tea and biscuits. She spoke quickly, barely pausing between words.

"Thank you so much for your hospitality, Livvy. The biscuits are lovely. We were wondering if you happened to see the person who left the van in front of your home. I have a photo here I would like you to look at." She held out the picture of Nilo.

Livvy studied it closely, moving it up and down and side to side in front of her eyes. Finally, she nodded her head. "That could be him. My vision isn't what it once was. But it was a young hooligan. In such a hurry. They all are, it seems. He ran up on the pavement while he was parking it. Nearly frightened poor Emma Winthorpe out of her skin, he did. She was walking by, you see. Not that it's too difficult to do that, frighten her, if you get my meaning, but . . ."

"Thanks, Livvy. Do you happen to know if he lives on your street? We need to find him." Elaine knew the last statement was a mistake as soon as she spoke.

"In trouble, is he? Wanted for something he'll no doubt deny to the magistrate. Is he one of those vandals I read about? Or a burglar? A burglar on our street? We haven't had one of those since, oh . . ."

Three more thumps jarred Livvy back into the present. She sighed. "Let's see. No, I don't know, exactly. Maybe third house down, the other side? He went that way, though. Right after Emma gave him a piece of her mind for scaring her so." She pointed down the street. "He laughed at her, right in her face. You would think he had no sense of shame. Was there anything else, dear?"

Elaine realized that Nilo might be in the house right now. What would he do when an unarmed, unsuspecting officer knocked on his door? He was, after all, a violent killer and might be armed. She turned to Liz. "Go find Paula and have her immediately pull everyone back. Order up a watcher for the end of the street. Everyone needs to stand down, right now. Then get back here and let me know when you're done. I don't want a single copper to be seen in a two-block radius. Do you get my meaning?" Liz nodded and excused herself, pulling her mobile from her purse as she left. Elaine turned back to Livvy.

"I do apologize. Have you seen him since then? Coming or going?"

"No, I haven't. But Emma lives that direction. Third house down, this side. She may know. I know she's still all bumbies about it. We had tea yesterday, and she was going on about how she shook for hours, what with the fright and all. She was saying that the last time she felt that frightened was four, no, three months ago . . ." Three thumps. Livvy huffed at the microphone on the wall. "Now you listen, Harry. That's it from you. I'm just trying to help these nice detectives by giving them all the information they may need, telling them about that young lady who was attacked, and there you go interrupting me before the words even get past my tongue."

Elaine leaned toward Livvy, her eyes locked on her face. "Am I right that you said a young woman was attacked right here on your street? Did you know her? Did anyone notify the police?"

"We didn't know her from Adam. Or Eve, I suppose. The poor thing was running down the middle of the street, her clothes torn, crying to the heavens, and then she tripped herself up and fell in a heap. Jim Lewis was working in his front garden, so he screamed for Betty, his wife, and he went into the street and wrapped her in his jacket—it was a right cool November day, for that's when it was—and sat her down on his garden chair. She finally calmed down, didn't want to make a fuss. She said she didn't want any help and wouldn't say much. She only wanted to go home. So she thanked Jim and Betty and walked to the end of the street. I suppose she caught a bus. But she was running from that other direction. No doubt it was that same hooligan."

Elaine looked up from her notebook. "Do you remember anything about her? Her age? Did you get her name?"

"No, dear. I didn't speak with the poor thing. Or see her. It was my day to go to the center for my exercises and bridge. So it would have been a Wednesday. I heard all this from Betty. They live across." She pointed out the window. "You might ask her. More tea?"

The doorbell rang. Elaine stood, saying, "I'm sorry, Livvy, but that must be my colleague. I really must leave now. We do want to find this young man very quickly. You've been so gracious and helpful—more helpful than you could possibly know. I can't thank you enough."

She met Liz at the door, and together they returned to the car. Elaine knew it was close to over. The scent of her quarry was so strong, she was almost giddy. Her phone chirped before they got back to Liz's car. It was Bull telling her Greene was waiting at the station.

THIRTY-ONE

"His brief is on the way, Chief Inspector."

Elaine nodded at the young officer, who turned and left the observation room. Through the one-way window, she saw Greene sitting at the table. When he was taken into custody, he had acted indignant, asked for his solicitor, and refused to answer any questions. Like all lawyers, Greene had blustered and threatened legal action against the Met and against her personally. She had stood and listened quietly. When he had blustered himself breathless, she had quietly told him that really, she had much more experience at this sort of thing than he had, and as far as she could see, there was only one thing for him to do. They would all play their parts, but in the end he would listen to her. She had told him to wait and use the time to think about his situation and choose the route that he and his solicitor should take. Then she had left him alone with his thoughts.

As with anyone who wasn't truly hardened, his bravado disappeared as soon as there was no one to listen to it. First he paced, then he sat fuming, occasionally pounding his fist on the table. For the last five minutes, he had his hands over his face, talking to himself, mumbling and shaking his head. He was getting ripe. Moments later, the lawyer entered. Elaine walked up the corridor to the canteen. She wanted to enjoy a good cuppa before she ruined Greene's sorry existence.

Jack O'Rourke, the duty prosecutor, was sitting at a table with Simon and Bull. He smiled and waved some papers at her as she sat down. "I read the summary report. May I watch you have your way with him? I find it incredibly erotic, you know. Much better than porn." Simon sat back and rolled his eyes. Bull's jaw dropped.

Elaine looked down at her tea and grimaced. She really didn't have time for this, but the guy was a prosecutor and she needed him on her side. "You're a sick and twisted soul, Jacko. If the powerful in the CPS knew that, you'd be fast-tracking your way to stardom like that Olympic sprinter—Bolt or whatever his name is."

Jacko laughed. "I passed him long ago, luv. You know the dinner offer still stands, don't you?"

She didn't look up. "Oh, I'm sure it does. You just want to get me across the table so you can see what a good grilling feels like. Sounds too much like work to me."

"You figured me out, sweetheart. One thing. It's not a table I want to get you across."

"Oh, really? I had you pegged as a kitchen table kind of guy. A true romantic."

Paula was walking toward her with a sheaf of papers in her hand. *Thank God.*

"Guv? We found the house. Cambrian Estates is the owner, the same as the Leaside industrial estate. And guess what? One of the duty officers passed this along. Some kids were playing football in Waterlow Park this morning when a young woman staggered out of the woods. She was naked, covered in blood from a head wound, and she passed out before the ambulance arrived. She's in the hospital. It appears she was raped and beaten. The officers took photos at A&E. She looks a lot like the woman who was with Greene."

Elaine took the papers and scanned through them. Given the swelling and bandages, solid identification from the photo would have been difficult. But she felt it was enough. "Right, then. We'll take down the house. I'll call Cranwell to get authorization. You and Simon set it in motion with Specialist Firearms Command while I break down Mr. Greene. I shouldn't be long. Don't be afraid to interrupt me. Be sure to bring me anything you need me to sign. Bull, you're with me at the interview. Let's go." She pulled out her mobile and dialed.

★ ★ ★

Elaine removed several photographs from an envelope and looked at Greene, who sat across the table next to his solicitor. "I suppose you know why you were arrested?" Greene gave no response, so she continued.

"We've had some houses under surveillance. Vice is convinced they are brothels." She arranged several photos on the table. "These were taken some days ago. As you can see, you enter each of these houses, then emerge a few minutes later. The bag you are carrying appears to have gotten heavier with each visit. What was in the bag, Mr. Greene?" Again, Greene was silent.

"This next set of pictures was taken after you arrived back at your office. They show a young man arriving and leaving. Do you know him?" Silence.

"I assure you that we have enough evidence to make the brothel-keeping charge stick. Cooperation is your best option here, Mr. Greene. I'm sure your solicitor would agree. Here's a better photo of the young man." She slid the photo of Nilo's face across the table. "Do you recognize him now?"

Greene glanced at his solicitor and shifted in his chair. "I may have seen him once or twice. I'm not sure."

"I think you're lying. You've seen him at the offices of IRG, haven't you? What is your connection with IRG?"

"I handle various legal matters for them. I can't discuss it in any more detail than that. Privileged information."

"Do you know anyone who lives in Finsbury Park? Or perhaps Highgate? Crouch End?"

"I have friends and colleagues all over London."

"I have some more photos I would like you to see." She selected another photo from the stack. "In this one, you're collecting a young woman from one of the brothels. What's her name, Mr. Greene?"

"I don't know, something ending in 'ova.' I can't recall."

"Perhaps I can help you. Her name is Katya. Katya Demetrova."

Greene looked surprised. He glanced at his solicitor and cleared his throat. "Ah, yeah. That might be it. Sounds familiar."

"I wonder what she does in the UK. Where were you taking her?"

"We were going to a party, that's all."

Elaine slid another photo across the table. "That looks like a lot of groceries for a party. Where exactly was this party?"

"None of your business. Just someone's home."

"Do you normally take prostitutes to parties? As a date? Or for entertainment?" She didn't wait for a reply. Instead, she tapped the photo of Nilo with her finger. "Was this young man at the party?"

"I can't recall."

"What happened after you delivered Katya to the party? Did you and the other men there gang rape her? Beat her? What went on?"

"I didn't stay. I left after a few minutes."

"I see." Elaine gathered up the photos and replaced them in the envelope. "Are you familiar with the concept of being an accessory to a crime?"

"Of course I am. I'm a lawyer."

Elaine smiled and shook her head. "Not for much longer. You see, Mr. Greene, we have evidence that ties you to any number of crimes. Promoting prostitution, money laundering, various drug offenses, even human trafficking. Do you have anything to say about that?"

"No."

"Did you return Katya to her home after the party?"

"No comment."

"When you go to bed at night, and you're thinking of all those fun little vices you took part in during that day, the cocaine and the lap dances and free blow jobs, do you ever think about murder and attempted murder, Mr. Greene? You may recall I mentioned murder in our previous interview. First a young girl named Sheila Watson was found beaten and slashed. Her body was dumped in a wasteland. Then we found another woman. You knew this one—Geri Harding. Different place, different method, but we've tied her murder to Sheila's. Now there's another victim. The victim being, of course, Katya."

Greene blanched. Elaine leaned over the table.

"You see, you delivered her to"—she pushed a sheet of paper across the table—"this address." Greene's eyes bulged. He began to sweat.

Elaine sat back in her chair. It had been too easy. Might as well get it over with. "We believe we can tie you to a whole series of crimes. A real bouillabaisse of fishy connections. We've talked to the prostitutes, and they talked back to us, Mr. Greene. They shared lots of information. All about your regular visits and collection bags, your sleazy extortion for sex, all of it. So we can make those charges stick, and when we do, you can kiss all your fun good-bye." She collected the papers and envelope and made a show of placing them in a neat pile before she continued.

"And now we have Katya." She looked up and knew Greene was done.

"You see, she was supposed to be dead and dumped, same as young Sheila. But your Katya didn't die. She's in the hospital, and oh, we'll get the story from her. You can 'no comment' until you're hoarse, but it won't matter."

"I never killed anyone. Never even tried to. Not in my life."

"But you helped make it possible because someone asked you to. We know you're a small fry. Nearly insignificant when you consider the scope of what's happened. If it were only the brothel-keeping charges, and if you cooperated, perhaps the judge would take that into account at your sentencing. But now there's grievous bodily harm in the mix. And attempted murder's a different kettle of fish, isn't it? When we add accessory to that on top of the other charges, I don't expect a judge to be very lenient, do you? Especially if you don't cooperate."

His lawyer leaned over and whispered in Greene's ear. Greene nodded.

"I need to consult with my lawyer. And we would like to speak with the CPS."

"Right, then. You go ahead. You know that in these cases, everything comes out eventually. All the sordid little details. We find them. It's our job, and we're very good at it." She nodded at the door. "The prosecutor is available when you're ready. Constable Bull and I have some important business to take care of, but we'll be back soon. If you haven't made your statement before then, things could go much, much rougher for you." She rose to walk to the door but turned back. "By the way, you'll probably be interviewed by the financial crimes unit once we're finished." She left the room.

★ ★ ★

The cup smashed against the wall and shattered into hundreds of tiny, brittle slivers. Nilo cursed and kicked the coffee table halfway across the sitting room of the small flat. It was too small. There was no room to move, and he couldn't see more than eight feet in any direction. The view through the back window showed nothing more than the brick wall of the next block.

"What the hell? I just got that table two weeks ago." Bosko turned the table upright and carried it back to the sofa. When he tried to put it in its place in front of the sofa, Nilo stretched his legs out. Bosko stood there, holding the small table.

"Put it down there and I'll bloody well kick it to pieces. Plenty more flat packs at IKEA. Didn't want no goddam tea, did I? Don't you keep any blow in this fucking hole? No booze? How do you live here, anyway? No room to move. You never bring women here, do you? You never had a woman, unless it was me who found her for you. Right? Am I right?"

Bosko placed the table down and sat on it. "I've had girlfriends. More than you know about."

"We've been here for a night and a day with sod all to do and you're right out of all your *b*'s. No blow, no bitches, no booze." He cackled at his own wit. "That about sums you up. What do you spend your money on? You live in a crap flat, so it can't be that." He rose to his feet and looked out the grimy window.

"It's enough for me. Janko doesn't pay me all that much, you know."

Nilo snorted and began pacing the floor of the tiny sitting room. "Janko? Bloody good for you that it's Janko you work for. Janko's not much more than a salesman. Or maybe a politician. You fuck up with Janko and it's a slap and bed with no supper. Anton has higher standards. Demands more. You got to be willing to do what it takes to work for Anton. Christ, I need something. Gimme the keys."

"No. I won't. We need to stay put. What if someone saw us last night? And you're in no condition to drive. They might have found the girl by now. I don't want to go out."

Nilo was fed up. His voice rose to a shriek. "I know when I can drive and when I can't!" He turned and flung himself at Bosko, his momentum bowling them both against the wall. Bosko pushed away and swung his fist wildly, off balance, allowing Nilo to close and place a solid body blow under his ribs. Bosko crumpled with a grunt. He lay on the floor retching and gasping.

Nilo smirked and turned away. That felt good. Now he needed cash and a plan. He could get the first at a cash machine. The other would take some thought. Should he run or should he meet the enemy head on?

Right now, he couldn't run far. He could always run later, after he had settled the score. Two scores. Both bitches needed to learn they couldn't treat him the way they had. One at a time or together? One at a time would be better. That way he could focus his energy.

He could lay low back at his own house for a few more days while it all came together. He couldn't do it all on his own, though. He looked down at Bosko, who had struggled his way onto all fours and was still gasping for breath. Bosko would be good for errands, but once the fun started, he would only get in the way. Who could he depend on? Definitely not Anton. His uncle would not be pleased, which meant that it might—no, would—be too dangerous to contact him. But he had some friends back home who owed him favors, and they were solid blokes, so they might be able to come help him. He had enough cash in his account if he could get to it quickly. It could work.

Nilo felt the comforting pressure of the gun in his belt. Right. He'd get the cash and a prepaid phone. Go to his house for some blow and a shower. Make the calls and start the ball rolling. By now, Bosko was on his knees and his breathing had returned to normal.

Nilo couldn't take the chance on leaving Bosko alone. "Get up. We're going out."

THIRTY-TWO

"Have you seen anyone in the house?" Elaine asked Chief Inspector McIntosh, the burly Scot who commanded the specialist firearms team charged with taking down Nilo's house.

"No activity. Doesn't mean a lot, though. Our infrared sensors will only pick up body heat if a person is near a window or perhaps behind a door. The house could be empty or the suspect could be lying in wait. I've seen both scenarios in my time."

They were in the back of a large command-and-control van parked a block from the target house. The compartment was dark except for green and red lights on radio sets and six video screens that glowed from one wall. All the systems were monitored by three officers in headsets.

Elaine watched the black-and-white images on each screen. Two screens displayed images of the house, front and back. She assumed these were from fixed cameras, perhaps smuggled through the back doors of neighboring houses and positioned in windows. The other four screens appeared to be fed from body cameras mounted on the firearms officers' black helmets. These currently showed groups of black-clad officers clustered together talking. Elaine didn't have a headset, so she couldn't hear what they were saying.

McIntosh anticipated Elaine's question. "Each team is going over its role for the last time. Once they're done, the sergeants will gather in here for a final look and last-minute tactical questions. It gets crowded, so if you don't mind, DCI Hope, I'll kindly ask you to step outside until they disperse."

Elaine exited down the steps from the van door. Her team of detectives—Paula, Simon, Bull, and Liz—was waiting. She took a deep breath and looked at Paula. "Right, then. Anything I need to know before the show starts?"

Paula gave a quick nod. Elaine wondered if Paula ever did anything slowly; she probably slept quickly. "Traffic Control has detours in force. No vehicles within two blocks in any direction. All the neighbors have been evacuated, except the Marstons. Harry refused to leave, and Livvy wouldn't go without him, so they have an officer with them and orders to stay away from the front rooms in case shooting starts. We're ready here. We'll go in with you as soon as the assault team gives the all clear and the Srecko kid is collared."

Collared. Elaine wondered if it would be that easy. Either Danilo wasn't there or he'd put up a fight. She looked at the sergeants as they left the van to return to their teams. Would they all go home tonight?

Paradoxically, the fact the teams carried guns increased the possibility that someone might not go home. Elaine was a firm believer in an unarmed police force. From the beginning of their training, British police officers were taught to try to defuse a tense situation, not escalate it. Britain's concept of policing by consent was somewhat unique in the world. But unfortunately, there were times and situations where firearms were called for. This was one of them.

She scanned the faces of the other three detectives. Simon was his usual placid self. Elaine often wondered if he just couldn't be bothered to have a case of nerves. Liz was showing some strain, chewing on her lower lip and shifting from one foot to the other. Bull, the ex-Marine, looked eager and alert, as if he wanted to be on one of the firearms teams.

As Elaine watched, Bull placed his hand on Liz's shoulder, and when she looked at him, he gave her a sly wink, as if to say, "Now it's getting good. Just stick with me."

Elaine smiled to herself. Boys and girls. She climbed the steps and opened the door to the van. McIntosh waved her inside and handed her a headset.

"You'll hear everything I hear, but your microphone is off, so no one can hear you." He turned his attention to the screens. "The teams are moving into position."

Elaine put on her headset, and immediately a steady stream of quiet commands and responses flowed from her earpieces. One of the officers monitoring the video raised his hand. The radio became quiet.

On the screen fed by the stationary cameras, Elaine watched as the lines of black-clad armored police scuttled along the pavement, hugging the garden walls and hedges lining the street. At set intervals an officer in each line would stop, take up a position, and wait. Another screen displayed a similar line of officers behind the fence in the back of Nilo's house, squatting in place and waiting for the signal.

Once the tactical situation had been studied and a plan devised, it had all come together quickly. It amazed her how quietly and efficiently the armed teams moved into their positions. Training, training, and more training. She scanned the screens, her attention riveted by the herky-jerky motions of the helmet-mounted cameras. The cameras' perspectives shifted constantly as the officers looked left and right, up at the house, at other officers. Hand signals, inscrutable to Elaine, flashed on the edges of the screen. Only the sound of boots on pavement and the occasional muffled click and clink of equipment met her ears.

At once, most of the motion stopped. The radio became silent, except for the sound of twelve armed men breathing almost in unison. She thought she could hear their hearts pounding, but then she realized it was the sound of her own blood rushing in her ears.

Two officers crept silently past the front gate of the house, glided up to the front stoop, and positioned themselves on each side of the front door. One of them carefully grasped the front doorknob, but it didn't budge. He shook his head and gave a hand signal to an officer carrying what looked like a heavy four-inch-thick pipe with handles—a kinetic ram. The officer rushed up the steps and crashed the ram against the door, splintering it.

"GO! GO! GO!" At the shouted commands, black-clad lines of police flowed into the house. Elaine jerked her attention back to the other screens. Although it was daylight, the interior of the house was dim. Flashlights mounted on each gun whirled like a kaleidoscope over walls, lit the recesses behind furniture, probed into closets. Watching the screens, Elaine felt like she was looking over the sights of a semiautomatic rifle as the officer swept his vision and gun across each room. Over the radio link, she could hear pounding and crashing as boots rushed across wooden floors, up the narrow stairs, and into bedrooms on the upper floor. She felt dizzy from the images whirling across the screens and the tumult assaulting her ears.

At last, multiple shouts of "CLEAR!" arose over the communications channels. The house was empty. The raid had taken fifteen seconds.

Once the armed team had filed out, Elaine and her detectives pulled on their latex gloves and entered the house with the SOCO technicians. The place was in shambles. Discarded lager cans and pizza boxes lay strewn about the floor. She inspected the sitting room while Simon, Bull, and Liz split up to other rooms.

Within seconds, Simon's voice rang out from the bedroom upstairs. "Up here, guv!"

Upon entering the room, she saw Simon standing over a bloodstain next to the bed. Smears and spatters of blood marked the wall. Simon pointed to a corner, where a bloody baseball bat lay. There were no sheets covering the mattress.

"Looks like this is where he assaulted Katya. There's a pile of coke, I think, on the dressing table. It has blood spatters in it."

"Have SOCO start here. You stay and supervise the search. Take the place apart."

Paula's voice came up the stairs. "Found something, guv."

She was waiting for Elaine outside a pantry behind the kitchen. "Quite a collection."

Elaine looked into the small room. An AK-47 assault rifle was propped in one corner, next to a stack of its curved magazines. On the wall was a pegboard, from which hung four handguns and a collection of military knives. A semiautomatic pistol and a knife appeared to be missing.

"Well. We can assume that he's armed and should be considered extremely dangerous. Get that out to the uniforms as quickly as possible. If anyone sees him, they are to report but not approach. So when did he leave? And if he didn't take the Transit, he must have had another vehicle available. Bull said the blue Audi was still at the car park the other day when he was watching the offices. Ask the neighbors if they ever saw another car parked here. Let's go finish up with Greene."

* * *

Bosko saw the police detour from two blocks away. "Shit! What's up here?"

Nilo slid down as far as he could get below the level of the windscreen. "Take the next right. Then turn left at the next street." Bosko complied. As soon as they made the left turn, Nilo stuck his head up and pointed. "Turn in this drive."

The drive ran almost the full length of the block, providing access to the residences that lined each side. Bosko drove to the end and pulled into an empty space, shielded by a row of hedges. Nilo got out and slowly pushed apart some branches.

He could see the entire length of his street. A group of black-clad armed police were gathered around a large boxy van, helmets off, listening to an officer that Nilo assumed to be their commander. Uniformed police stood at intervals along the street, some solitary, some in pairs. White-suited forensic technicians hurried to and fro in and out of his house, along with what appeared to be a steady stream of police of all types. Then he saw them.

The dark-haired bitch was leading the way from his house, talking to the red-haired one. First they had deceived him in the car park. Humiliated him in front of Anton and Janko. Caused him to be exiled from his own family. Now these women had been in his house without his permission. He felt violated, invaded, degraded. No man should ever allow a woman to do that. But they had done it to him.

They were walking in his direction. Auntie Dragon was talking and gesturing normally, calmly, explaining and teaching. Teaching deceit and seduction. Teaching how to trick and tease and get inside a man's defenses. The rage started building inside again, stronger than before. As strong as anything he had ever felt.

There was only one answer for it. He would do something about the shame. He would do something about the humiliation. He would revenge himself on them, and he didn't give a damn what Uncle Anton thought. He'd clean it up later.

Nilo turned and motioned to Bosko to join him. He pointed them out, whispering, "That's them. Those are the ones we'll have. We'll have some fun with them. You're with me, right?"

Bosko watched the women. He bit his lip. "Man, that's some serious shit you're thinking about. They're police, aren't they? I dunno."

The women turned the corner without looking up, as if they were on an afternoon stroll down the pavement of their neighborhood.

Nilo motioned again and they returned to the car. "Maybe we'll have a little practice first. To rehearse it, you know? It will be sweet."

He looked at Bosko, who sat silently, gazing through the windscreen. It was clear to him that Bosko had lost it and wasn't to be trusted if it got dicey. Nilo needed to make him say that. "You're with me, right?"

Bosko took a deep breath and exhaled through his nose. He reversed the car into a space and rolled slowly down the drive. At the end of the drive, he turned left. "Look, Nilo. We're cousins. I'll let you stay at my place. I'll feed you. I'll run errands if you need me to. Take you where you need to go. But I'm not in for anything rough with either of those coppers. I came here to work. To get something better than that shithole of a village. I'm not spending the rest of my life in prison. It's not what I had in mind."

"So you're not with me."

"Not all the way, no."

Scummy little bastard. *Not all the way, no. What the hell is that?* He wanted to reach over and wring his fucking neck. What the fuck good is he? He felt the gun in his waistband, pressing against the small of his back. Two blocks to the next stoplight. He'd slide his hand behind his back, pull it out, and pop one in the fuck's earhole. He looked behind. A car about a block back, but no one right on their tail. There wasn't much traffic right now. He'd squeeze it off and be out and down the street in five seconds. The shitty little car would sit there idling until some poor loser walked over and took a look. By that time, he'd be gone.

Here it comes. A block. Half a block. Slowing down. Nilo slid his hand behind his back and felt the grip of the FN. He ticked off the safety with his thumb and scanned the street. Stopping. Wait. Bosko slid the gearshift into neutral.

A bright-blue BMW crossed the intersection in front of them. Wouldn't you know it? It looked like the Hope copper was driving. The flash of red hair in the passenger window confirmed it for him.

"There they are . . . follow them. See them? Don't lose them." He clicked the safety back on, scratched his lower back, and adjusted his jacket. Maybe some other time.

Bosko snicked the car into gear and turned to follow the BMW. "What are we going to do? Are you going to shoot them?"

"No, no. That might be fun, but not maximum fun. We'll follow them for now. I want to see where they go."

"Right. It's getting dark, though."

"I'll watch them. You do what I say. Do you know how to tail someone?"

Bosko snorted. "I'm not an idiot. Goran taught me as soon as I was able to drive." He settled behind the steering wheel, turning with Nilo's instructions. A few minutes later, he cleared his throat.

"Nilo. I've been thinking. You know, I'll do what I said I'd do. You're family. I won't stand in your way, and I won't grass you up. You know that. I've wanted to take a holiday for some time. Last week, Janko told me I'd earned time off. So here's what I'll do. I'll book a holiday. I know I can find something in the next couple of days. Maybe Majorca or the Canaries. Someplace warm and sunny. You can stay at my flat. Use my motor. Do what you need to do. What do you say to that?"

Nilo considered. He might not have to top the little shite if he could be useful for a couple of days, then be out of the way when the heavy lifting started. Plus, there would be a place to stay. It actually wasn't bad for his plan. He needed time to reconnoiter and prepare. He'd call Goran, and it would take a couple of days to set it all up. They'd stay at the flat and have a place for the fun. Goran would enjoy that.

So he wouldn't have to kill Bosko. Not now, anyway.

He smiled broadly. "That sounds like an excellent plan to me. I like it." He reached out and clipped Bosko on the shoulder. Bosko was smiling as broadly as he was, so he turned his attention back to the blue BMW.

* * *

Jenkins kept his eyes glued to the red Fiesta a half block ahead. He'd had years to hone the skill of tailing another car while avoiding collisions. He slowed, coasting so that he wouldn't run right up on the target's tail at the stoplight. The light changed, and he waited until it was ready to change again, then he zipped through and continued the tail, keeping his distance. It looked like the two boys were headed back to Bosko's flat.

Jenkins had identified Bosko early on and had quickly tagged him as the office gofer. The boy was no one to pay much attention to, but Jenkins had tailed him a few times while he was out running errands to get a feel for his daily rhythms and find out where he lived. He'd never seen him with Nilo, though. Nilo was another story, and at this moment, it was Nilo he was interested in.

Technically, Nilo was a distraction. But the kid had all the earmarks of a loose cannon—a budding psychopath. He sowed mayhem wherever he went, and mayhem could screw things up royally or it could create opportunities. You never knew, so you had to be ready either way it went down.

He had missed them when they left Nilo's house. One watcher can't watch everyone all day long, and he had other jobs to do. On a hunch, he had driven to the younger boy's flat. Sure enough, they had arrived there a few minutes later, looking worse for wear. He wondered what they had been up to.

The red car had been there in the morning and then after lunch. He picked them up again in the evening and followed them on the route back to Nilo's house. It had gotten good. Very good. Hope had arrested Greene, and the next thing you know, she calls an armed assault on the house. That wasn't going to sit well with the cousins, was it? Greene had better be happy he was in custody. With his binoculars, Jenkins had seen Nilo crouched behind the hedge and had watched him watching Hope and Lovely Liz. The rage on the kid's face was evident even from a distance. He chuckled. What happens when you push an unstable, violent kid too far? He would bet a tenner they were about to find out.

Hope and Liz. Elaine had unknowingly helped him, although he would probably never get the chance to thank her. She was a real danger to his goals, though it was still possible that they could both get what they wanted. Liz needed experience. She knew enough to get herself into trouble. He was sure he could teach her a thing or two, but he'd probably never get the chance with her either.

Where the hell were these two kids going? They were headed east. Bosko's flat was north. Something was up. A few minutes later, the red Fiesta slowed as a car in front of it turned. A blue BMW.

No shit. They were following Hope. The Fiesta drove past the turn and pulled to the curb a hundred feet down. Why were they stopping? Something had gotten their interest. He slowed to a crawl and looked as he passed the street. In the dimming light, he saw two figures getting out of a car. Hope and the ever lovelier Liz.

They were walking to the door of a rundown house. He cackled and accelerated past them, past Nilo and Bosko in the Fiesta. A hundred yards up the street, he turned around and headed back, pulling to the curb.

The women were in the house for only five minutes. Then the double tail began again, tracing back across town. The BMW stopped at a block of flats, where Liz got out and walked to the door. Jenkins noted the address and continued to follow as Elaine headed back toward the nick. He didn't want to break off yet. It might get exciting.

But it didn't get exciting. The red Fiesta with Bosko and Nilo inside drove past when Elaine entered the underground car park, and then it headed back in the direction of Bosko's flat. Jenkins decided to leave it for tonight. He needed to think. He thought about the story that had gone around the canteen at the station, how Liz had chatted up Nilo and they had gotten his DNA and a photo. Elaine had apparently been there too. How else had she gotten the "Auntie Dragon" moniker he had heard about? Nilo had something in his head about Elaine, or Liz, or both.

These eastern gangsters could be touchy. Nilo was planning something unpleasant. Well, it was none of his business. He had other things to think about, and it was all coming together. It had been an eventful day, and it was time to stand down. A bottle of Rioja was calling his name, and he didn't want to keep it waiting.

THIRTY-THREE

Elaine looked at Jacko across her desk. It had been a frustrating day. Tomorrow she would no doubt be called to explain herself to Cranwell, Hughes, the assistant commissioner, and whoever else was lining up to thrash her about budgets and waste of resources. She hadn't looked, but she was sure the line had begun to stretch around the block.

She was getting tired of Jacko. She had no stomach for listening to him try to wear her down, and she was having trouble concentrating. But a decision had to be made.

The prosecutor pressed on. "Right now, the only thing we can show cause to charge him with is brothel keeping. No matter what your suspicions are, that's all we have."

"And you want us to release him on police bail. I suspect him of being involved in at least one serious assault and possibly two murders. Not to mention a whole raft of devious financial schemes that likely fall under the Proceeds of Crime Act. The trafficking and prostitution unit want to talk with him. Other groups in Specialist Crimes are showing some interest. I need to be able to pressure him, Jacko." It was a bluff, but not a huge one. She had planned to call a briefing with the other groups who would be interested, but she hadn't gotten around to it.

Jacko persisted. "Look. It's not like he's violent. He's hardly likely to pose a threat to anyone. You may be the senior investigating officer, but you need to show a level of fairness in this."

What the hell did he mean by that? She studied his face. He usually didn't push an SIO this hard. Especially when he wanted into her knickers, which he would let her know, again, soon enough. All the more reason to keep up her guard.

"Fairness? We're not on a cricket pitch here. Besides, he might be in danger himself, from his clients. There's no telling what they'll do if we release him."

"Really? And what proof do you have beyond vague hunches that he's involved in any type of organized crime?"

"You didn't sit across a desk from those clients and study their faces. You wouldn't say that if you had. So what's up? You usually take your lead from the senior officer. Why is this one different?"

Jacko's eyes narrowed. "It's not. I don't think you have cause to deny bail. If you do, his lawyer made it clear to me that he would appeal."

Elaine looked out her window. She could refuse and sweat more information out of Greene, but she thought it likely that he truly didn't know where Nilo was at this point. And when the lawyer appealed, she'd have to appear in court and make the case to a magistrate, who would probably see no difference between this and other cases he had granted bail to. She believed in picking her battles, and this wasn't one she'd choose. Greene could be handled even if he wasn't in custody. She needed to devote all her effort to finding Nilo.

She shook her head. "All right. But I don't like it. I want a condition that he report here every day."

Jacko gave her a triumphant smile. She figured what was coming next, and he didn't surprise her. He stood, slicked his hair back with both hands, adjusted his jacket, and shot his cuffs. His tone was utterly smug.

"I can make that work. How about dinner? You've had a long day."

What a preening jackass. She looked up and gave a perfunctory smile. "No, thanks. I've got some things to do."

He leaned over the desk. "I'm sure my to-do list is much more fun. I've got steaks and a nice Montepulciano at home. I know how to cook too. Looks to me like you need to unwind."

Where was a garrote when a girl needed one? "I said no, Jacko. Not going to happen."

"Call me if you change your mind." He straightened up and walked out the door.

Elaine didn't answer. He had drained her reserves, and now she was distracted, wondering why she wasn't curled up at home with Scratch on her lap and a glass of something or other in her hand. Whatever was in the wine rack.

She waited two minutes to make sure Jacko was truly gone, then left for home.

★ ★ ★

Anton sat on a wooden kitchen chair in Bosko's sitting room. He had expected them both to be here, but the flat was empty when he and Goran had arrived, so he had decided to wait. Goran was watching the parking area. The boys would show up sooner or later. Meanwhile, Anton had three problems to mull over.

The first was Greene. He would be bailed out soon enough. Greene's solicitor would report what was said during the police interview, and Goran would arrange the rest.

What to do with Bosko was a straightforward decision. He had been insulated from most of the family's operations, and he was neither valuable nor a danger to their plans. Eliminating him would attract attention and complicate family relations. Sending him home was probably the best course of action. It would certainly cost less in time and resources. He would separate Bosko from Nilo and give him a good scare. His reaction would confirm which course Anton should take.

But what to do with Nilo? The boy was impossible to control unless he was watched around the clock by someone he feared. There was really no choice but to eliminate him. A shootout with armed police would be ideal. Marko could say nothing; even if he suspected Anton was the cause of Nilo's death, he would most likely understand. This was family business, after all.

Anton's mobile chirped. He swiped the green button on the screen and placed it to his ear. It was Goran telling him the boys had pulled into sight.

He closed his eyes and focused his mind. Two minutes later, he heard the door open and footsteps approaching up the flat's short entry corridor. When he opened his eyes, the two boys were standing in front of him. Goran handed him Nilo's gun, then moved to block the door.

Bosko was visibly shaking. He looked at Anton with huge, frightened eyes, then turned his head away.

Anton studied them both for a moment. Bosko was certainly better off as an errand runner and messenger. He then focused on Nilo. "Things are not going well for you. Your reckless activities are causing quite a lot of problems for your elders. You have attracted the attention of the Metropolitan Police. According to news I have received, they raided your house today." He paused. "On top of that, they arrested Greene for brothel keeping and have been questioning him most of the day."

He saw Nilo's jaw drop. Nilo was responsible for running the brothels.

"Those are very upsetting developments for all of us. Certainly for the two of you, but also me, Janko, and Marko. I had to ask myself what to do about all this. Before I can decide, I need information. I want to know what you have been doing and what your plans are. Nilo, please go outside with Goran. I want to talk with Bosko first."

Nilo opened his mouth to protest but stopped. He turned and walked outside with Goran behind him. As soon as Anton heard the door close, he spoke softly to Bosko.

"Now tell me what you have been doing the last couple of days."

"I . . . I . . . ," Bosko stammered. He was still shaking and shifting his weight from one foot to the other. It took him a few tries before he could begin. Once he started talking, the words flowed fast. He told how Nilo had asked him over for some fun with a whore and how Nilo had turned ugly. How they had dumped the girl's body and had then come to the flat and stayed until the beer and booze was gone. He spilled everything, right up to the moment they had seen Goran standing on the pavement outside the flat. By the time he had gotten to that point, tears had started to well in his eyes. He put his face in his hands.

Anton continued to speak softly. "Thank you, Bosko. Tell me. What are your plans?"

Bosko took another deep breath. "Janko told me I could have some holiday time. I want to go somewhere, maybe someplace warm, maybe back home. I told Nilo that I wanted to get away from this. Uncle Anton, I didn't expect it to be like this. I thought I would be working for Janko. And then I thought Nilo and I were just going to have some fun, you know? Then he hit that girl over and over and she died and we had to dump her body. And then we went back to his house and coppers were crawling all over it. Those two women coppers were there, and Nilo said he wants to top them, but I told him I won't help him with that and I want to leave. So that's what I want to do. Just go somewhere and not be here. Uncle Anton, I just . . ."

Anton held up his hand to stop him. Bosko would do as he was told. There was no reason to eliminate him. When Anton spoke, his voice was quiet and reassuring. "I think it best that you not go anywhere but home. I will arrange it with your parents. You will not return to the UK. Ever. That will be satisfactory for me, and it should be for you as well. Tell me if you agree."

"It is. I mean, I agree, Uncle Anton. Thank you. I'll never come back."

"Good. I thought you would see it that way. By the way, the girl was not dead. She was found wandering naked and is in the hospital. She is expected to live. So at least you will not be wanted for murder. You are very much out of your depth, Bosko. Please learn from this experience. Go ask Goran and Nilo to come inside. Then go to your room and close the door. Pack the minimum that you will need and wait there until I have finished speaking with Nilo. Don't worry. You will be away from here tonight and home in a day or two."

Once Nilo stood in front of him, Anton could see the gears turning in his head. The boy clearly did not know what to expect. That was good, so he began.

"I am faced with hard questions, Nilo. You have been extremely irresponsible since you came here to England. You have murdered two women and seriously injured a third. Yes, that's correct. The girl you and Bosko dumped is alive. She will no doubt talk when she awakes from her coma. Those are only the ones I know about. Granted, I may have been unspecific about what I wanted you to do with Geri Harding, but the fact remains, you are the one who killed her. You are wanted by the police, and I cannot allow you to fall into their hands. You may well be asking yourself what I will do with you. Before I decide, I want to know what you think we should do and what you had planned to do. Tell me."

Nilo stood still. He did not shift his weight or appear nervous. He gazed straight at Anton when he spoke.

"I didn't know that Greene had been arrested, so I think that as soon as possible, we need to deal with him and also make sure the police never find out what he knows. He's a threat. Then I want to deal with those detectives. The two women who came to your office. They are a threat as well."

"I agree with you about Greene. I am not sure that 'dealing with those detectives,' as you put it, is a wise thing to do. The police are very protective of their own."

"We are too. Here's how I see it. Greene knows a lot about our business. Too much. I think we take care of him and whatever records he kept. But you still have that older bitch to deal with, so we deal with her. *I* deal with her. I need to do it myself, and I think I know how to do it. Then while the police are putting it all back together, I can get out of the country."

Anton pursed his lips and studied the ceiling. It would take at least two operatives to deal with Greene properly. Disrupting the police investigation would be beneficial. He would partner Nilo with Goran. He could rely on Goran to do what needed to be done.

He decided. “I realize this is personal with you. I disapprove of the way you let your passions and eccentricities get in the way of your head, but there is something to what you say. I will consider it.” He looked at Goran. “Please bring Bosko in.”

Bosko shuffled into the room seconds later, carrying a small duffel bag. His eyes were red and swollen. He stood next to Nilo, looking at the floor.

Anton stood. “Right now we will leave here. Goran and I will take you to separate hotels. You are not to communicate with each other in any way. Bosko, tomorrow morning Goran will deliver you a new passport, some money, and a train ticket home. You had best be there when he arrives. He will take you to the station and see you on board the train.” Bosko forced a nod.

“Nilo, you are to stay in your hotel room until Goran collects you. If either of you get hungry tonight, order room service. No alcohol. Those instructions should be clear to both of you. It would be unhealthy to disobey them.”

THIRTY-FOUR

Elaine's mobile warbled as she arrived at her flat. Peter's voice was cheery.

"Hi. I'm getting ready to cook dinner and I'd like some company. Would you care to join me? It's nothing fancy, fried fish and a salad, but there's plenty for two. I can do a beer batter if you want, and there's a choice of wine or ale."

"No chips? I like chips. They're my favorite part. Pepper and vinegar only."

"I can do chips. I have malt vinegar, which is pretty good for a Yank. What do you say?"

I wonder how far he'll go. "Hmmm. No mushy peas?"

"No. I draw the line at peas soaked in sodium bicarbonate. Is it a deal breaker?"

She looked at the moo shu pork she had picked up on the way home. The pancakes were already soggy. It would keep—that's what fridges were for. "Give me a chance to change. I can be there in, say, an hour. Ish. Okay?"

"Perfect. I haven't started cooking yet."

Thirty minutes later, she was in her BMW, her mind racing, careening between thoughts in the same way she was slinging the car from lane to lane. *Well, Lainie, what have you started here? Where is it going?*

Keeping a relationship going hadn't been a big issue during her first couple of years in the force, while she'd been in uniform. In fact, it had been a nonissue. She had concentrated on establishing her career and had intentionally discouraged the rare men who had shown any interest in her. The days in uniform were long but fairly regular. After she was accepted into CID, with its chronic short-staffing and unpredictable schedule, her love life had almost ceased to exist. Men with regular jobs didn't understand her compulsion to work on a case all hours and weekends until she got a result. And starting something with another cop, well, from what she had seen, only compounded the problems.

You don't have to have a boyfriend, Lainie. It's not like you have to constantly lean on someone, and you sure as hell don't need someone who thinks he can tell you what to do all the time. She mentally laughed at herself. *Stick with Scratch. He only screams to be fed once a day, and he keeps your feet warm at night.*

Her last attempt at a relationship had ended with a drunken boyfriend barging into the flat late one night, announcing that he'd had enough waiting around, and he'd found someone who actually wanted to be with him instead of spending all her time God-knows-where, doing who-knows-what with who-knows-who. Now he wouldn't have to sit worrying about getting a call from the morgue. He wasn't going to live his life like that and blah blah blah. She had said, "Then don't," and had thrown his bag of dirty laundry down the stairs after him.

She couldn't imagine Peter doing that, though. Maybe she should take a chance on him. Maybe she needed to see what might develop.

And you know what they say about venturing nothing, Lainie. You'll never find out if you don't take the risk.

She swung her BMW into Peter's drive and gathered herself before she went to the door.

★ ★ ★

Elaine sat facing Peter over the kitchen table. "Thanks. The chips were lovely. But tell me—what prompted the invitation?"

Peter sat back in his chair, his hands folded in front of him. "I wanted to see your face." He tilted his head and looked straight into her eyes. "I think about you every day. I see something, or hear something, and I wonder what you'd think about it. I want to get to know you."

"Channeling Mister Bogart again? Do you think Rick and Ilsa ate fried fish with malt vinegar and washed it down with Sam Smith's ale?"

He laughed. "Maybe they did, sometime. Probably not in Paris."

It was her turn to laugh. "No, I can't imagine the Parisians putting up with the possibility of mushy peas." She paused. *Okay, girl, take the chance.* "I've thought about you too. That night I called you and I asked what you were doing exactly, I was looking out my office window. It came to me that you might have been sitting in that big chair I saw, looking out your window. And you were." She looked into his eyes.

He reached forward and took her hand in his. His touch was warm and dry and firm. His thumb traced a pattern on the back of her hand. "The first time I saw you, I thought you were someone special. I don't mean to me, not then. But when I saw you standing by the piano, silhouetted against the window, studying me, I knew you were someone who mattered, wherever you went. And every time I saw you, I got the same feeling."

He picked up the plates and cutlery and took them to the sink. "Yeah, I was angry about what I went through, what it did to me. I've never meditated so much in my life. If I believed that chakras really existed, mine would have been all out of line. But I couldn't be angry with you. Not personally. Each time I felt like screaming at you, I would look at you and realize that you didn't deserve to be treated like that."

"You didn't deserve the way you were treated either. By me or the system. You didn't deserve to lose your job and have your life wrecked. You had a right to be angry with me."

"I know that. But I couldn't bring myself to focus it on you. It was after you brought me home, after you released me. I had plenty of time to sit and think. I'm lonely. I've been playing it too safe." Peter kneeled next to her, his eyes and mouth only inches from hers. "I've been alone long enough. Starting a relationship is a huge gamble, but I want to take that chance with you."

He took her hand. "I'm hoping you can take that chance with me."

Wow. There it was. She looked at his deep-set blue eyes. She heard her blood rush in her ears, sensed her breath quicken, and felt the expectation deep in her body. His warm hand cradled her face. She pressed her cheek to his palm and sank into acceptance. His first soft kiss settled on her open lips, embracing each one in a delicate caress. She felt his breath move, warm on her throat, brushing a light path of kisses to her ear. *Oh, god.* His lips traced slowly back to her mouth. When he took her lip between his teeth, she gasped.

She had not been kissed like that in a very, very long time.

★ ★ ★

They embraced in the half-light of the large window in his bedroom. Peter took both of her hands in his, saying, "I'm not a pretty sight without the clothes."

She said nothing. After a few seconds, he lifted her hands to his lips and kissed them. He turned away and pulled the jersey over his head, baring his back to her.

The dim light through the window played over a patchwork of light and dark, shapes and shades and lines where his skin had been grafted. She remained silent, imagining the violence, trying to absorb what the flaying of his back must have done to him. Who was he before this happened? Did she need to know?

Elaine softly touched her finger to one of the raised lines that ran across his ribs and felt the taut muscle reflexively twitch under the skin. She traced along the line to where it joined with another, and on, until it crossed another. So many lines, so many tracks that had taken his life and loves from him.

Elaine realized she was trembling but was uncertain if it was sorrow or an acute desire that bordered on sorrow. To cease the shaking, she circled her arms around him and drew him to her, pressing his scars into her face, breathing his scent, kissing his back, at first lightly, then as she warmed and felt the tightening start within her, she opened her lips wider and kissed with more fervor.

Later she lay curled beside him, her leg wrapped over his, her head in the hollow of his shoulder. She stared at the window, seeing nothing, sensing only its pale light falling across them. *What happened*, she thought. *Who is he truly? Where will he go when he needs someone?* She turned and kissed his throat. He responded with a nuzzle and strokes on her cheek.

She looked up at his face, half-obscured by locks of his dark hair. *All that pain. He has to be able to share it with me.*

"Tell me. Tell me now," she whispered.

He looked down at her, his face in shadow over hers. "You want to know right now?"

She sat up in bed, draping the duvet around her shoulders. "Yes. If we're going any further than here and now, I need to know. Start at the beginning and tell me everything, and don't stop until there's no more to tell."

He leaned his back against the headboard and told her of Diana, how they had met in a university lecture room and had fallen instantly in love. They had never doubted each other, especially after Liza was born. Then came Iraq.

"What I saw in Iraq . . ." He paused and stared at the window. Seconds became a full minute.

To Elaine, it seemed he was holding his breath, waiting for a sign. She pulled the duvet tighter around her shoulders and slid closer to him. "Who were the people in the photos? You loved them, didn't you?"

He exhaled. "Carl and I were friends in medical school. He's the guy you saw in the photo on the piano. The one with me, him, and the woman, in Iraq. In those days, it was an almost endless stream of wounded kids. I mean, most of the troops were kids, and sometimes Iraqi women and children who'd been caught in the middle. I was the surgeon, and he was the anesthesiologist. We tried to help each other cope and do what good we could and think about home. We wanted to open a clinic after we got back. But they called us back again after the first tour."

Again he paused, so Elaine asked, "Who was the woman?"

"Laudy. Laudacia Miller. Our surgical nurse. Man, she could sing gospel. She was going to be in the clinic with us."

"You said she died too. When I asked, that first time in the house."

Peter's voice was hoarse and halting, words erupting from his mind to his lips and out into the half-light. "We were in the compound loading supplies on trucks for a hospital unit in Mosul when the mortars and rockets hit. We weren't wearing our flak vests. Carl was killed in the first salvo. An explosion and he was gone, vaporized, pink mist, just like that. We were looking for wounded when the second wave of rounds hit. A truck exploded and Laudy was lying on the ground, burning. I rolled her over and put her over my shoulders to carry her to the bunker."

Peter's voice stopped. He took deep breaths and pulled the bed sheet up around his shoulders. Elaine waited.

"It was heat and noise, then nothing. They told me that Laudy's body protected me from most of it. She saved me. The hospital in Baghdad gave me primary trauma care, sedated me, and put me on the next plane to Landstuhl in Germany. The army notified Diana, and she and Liza flew to London. Liza was going to stay with Kate. Diana and my mother were going to continue on to Germany. After they landed, Diana and Liza took a taxi into town from Gatwick."

He was the one shaking now, his arms wrapped across his chest. "There was fog and a huge chain collision on the M23. A truck plowed into the back of their taxi. The driver never slowed down or even touched his brakes. But you know about that, right?"

How did this not destroy him? Wordlessly, Elaine slid closer to him on the bed. *And now, his confession.* She took his hand and held it in both of hers. *Let him know you're here. There's no feeling lonelier than guilt.*

Peter continued, his voice tremulous. "When I came out from under the sedation a week later, Mom and Kate were there, but I knew something was very wrong. Finally, they had no choice but to tell me, and once I understood what they were saying, I wanted to die. I know it sounds trite, but their deaths were my fault. If I had simply died in Iraq, they would still be alive. I feel like I need to pay them back. Since then, I've existed on my work, Kate, and Mom.

"I've tried to start a few relationships since I came to London, but none have worked. Most of the women I've met either pitied me or couldn't handle the scarring and the dreams. The last time was a couple of years ago. Since then, I've avoided thinking it could ever happen again for me."

He looked at her. "Now you're in my life. And I cannot ignore you. I can't deny what I feel for you."

All those years of pity and rejection. He's reaching out to me. To Lainie. No man's ever bared his soul to me like this. And I know he's not done yet. It has to be all or nothing. "Is that it? Is that everything?"

"I still have PTSD. I probably always will. I don't have violent flashbacks or anything like that. Just a nightmare every once and a while, and it's always the same one. I wake up in a panic.

"Sometimes, if I'm really under stress, I see Diana and occasionally Liza too. While I'm awake. I've been told it's a grief hallucination, which is common, and it's supposed to go away at some point. They started when I was in the hospital. I didn't see them for a couple of years, but now I've seen them again a couple of times after you and Benford came that day."

He looked at her. "So that's it. I have some issues, but I'm not a raving madman."

Yes, that's all that matters. And I know what he means. "My mum never got over losing my dad. She still talks to him every now and then. Like he's right there. It's never easy, losing half your soul. It's not going to be easy for us either. You know that, right?"

Peter smiled and said, "I may hallucinate from time to time, but I'm not deluded."

She snuggled next to him again, pressing her breast against his chest, her nose and lips brushing his neck. After a few minutes, he kissed her and whispered, "I have to work the late shift tonight. See you tomorrow?"

"I have to work, early. But I'll call if I can." She kissed him and watched him pad silently across the floor to the bathroom. Damn. Work interruptions already. She lay back on the pillows and crooked her arm over her forehead.

I was right to take the chance. I owe him now, she thought. *He showed me his demons because I demanded to see them. I'm not sure if he would have done so on his own, so yeah, I had to ask. I need to show him mine. Maybe not right now, though. I'm not sure either of us could deal with any more drama tonight. I'll find the right time.*

When she heard the water running in the shower, she joined him.

THIRTY-FIVE

Elaine had a splitting headache. She sat at her desk and pressed her fingers against her temples, massaging them slowly. It was dusk, and she had spent most of the day being interrogated by three levels of her superiors. Her individual accountability had been reinforced to her by each level. They had all distanced themselves as far as possible from the decision to take down Nilo's house.

She thought back twelve years to her time as a Detective Constable. She had wanted advancement and had worked hard to get it. If you make enough decisions, eventually one will be wrong. *Move on, Lainie.*

There was a rap on the door frame and Liz entered. "Greene didn't show for his bail appearance today, and I couldn't contact him. I was getting ready to go find him when one of the DCs out of Plaistow called. Greene's office building went up in flames today. The fire brigade thought everyone was out, but they found a body. It looks like it might be Greene."

Elaine grabbed her jacket. "Let's go."

It was after dark when Elaine and Liz arrived at the fire scene. They showed their warrants to the officer at the barrier and went in search of the fire brigade's watch commander, picking their way around vehicles and over snaked fire hoses. The acrid reek of burnt wood and plastic and diesel assaulted their senses. Engines rumbled and electric generators rattled in a pulsing rhythm. Puddles reflected and amplified the flashing blue, red, and yellow lights of the emergency equipment. Firefighters scurried purposefully in and out of the building, which was brightly lit by portable flood lights. Through wisps of dissipating smoke and steam, Elaine could see dark figures moving behind the smashed windows on the upper two floors. She eventually found the watch commander giving instructions at the center of a small gaggle of firefighters. As soon as the group dispersed to carry out their tasks, Elaine introduced herself and asked about the body. The watch commander, who identified himself as John Harrison, was a burly man who stood a full head taller than Elaine. He looked preoccupied with his own responsibilities.

Harrison nodded at Elaine's question. "We're still searching the building, but yeah, we found the body of a man in the second-floor office, where the fire started. From the initial survey, it looks like there was an accelerant and some kind of fuse, so we're operating on the assumption that the fire was deliberate. The building directory shows that space is leased to a solicitor named Jackson Greene. We don't know if it's him or not, though. He's badly burned. If you're thinking suicide, I rather doubt it. There was a time delay on the igniter."

"I rather doubt it was suicide too. Is the forensic medical examiner here yet? Can we go in to see where the body is?"

From his frown, Elaine could tell Harrison wouldn't grant her request. "The medical examiner is here. The body will be out and off to autopsy in a few minutes. I don't want anyone but the doc and my investigators in there until we're as certain about the cause and chain of events as we can be. Besides, we're not sure the place is safe. We'll let you know when your people can enter the building."

Elaine tried again. "We're talking about a murder investigation, and Greene is—or was—an important witness. Seeing the crime scene early is critical to . . ." She stopped when the watch commander held up his hand.

"I understand, Chief Inspector, but this is the protocol. We'll make sure it's safe and work with your fire investigation team.

We'll fully inform you. We always do. Now, if you don't mind, I need to get on with it." From the way he raised his eyebrows, Elaine was sure that he wasn't going to budge.

She nodded and smiled at him. "I hope you understand that I had to try. One more thing. Do you know who owns the building?"

"It's a bank in Liverpool. We're still trying to get in touch with the right person. All that will be in the report you'll get."

"Right. I look forward to it. And please make me copies of the CCTV discs once you've got them. Thanks so much."

As she turned away, feeling a bit put off, she saw Kumar, the medical examiner, walking from the building. She motioned to Liz, and together they intercepted him before he reached the forensic van.

Kumar saw them coming. "Hi, Elaine. I had a feeling I might find you here. Call it pathologist's intuition. The same feeling tells me you don't think he died in the fire."

Elaine shook her head. "Did he?"

"His body was lying face up, so I doubt it. Perhaps he was unconscious. I'll know once I find out if there's smoke in his lungs."

"What about time of death?"

"The body is burned. The fire was called in at about five PM. So perhaps a bit before then. Beyond that, it's autopsy first. You know the drill."

"Certainly do. When do you think you'll know something?"

Kumar thought for a few seconds. "I can't get started until tomorrow morning. I'll give you a call."

"Do you think anything can be salvaged from his office?"

"Well, the SOCOs will know better, but it looked pretty bad. All the papers are burned. And there was a charred lump of plastic on the desk. It could have been a laptop, if that's what you're after."

"Right. Let me know when you start the autopsy. And thanks."

Liz spoke up once they were back at Elaine's car.

"You think he was murdered first, then they burned the office to destroy evidence?"

"I won't speculate about the murder. Kumar will tell us. They burned the office to slow us down and get rid of his files and laptop." Elaine reversed her car and slowly maneuvered around two emergency vehicles. "Maybe he kept some backup disks at his flat. We need to get there and seal it off, if Srecko's people haven't been there first. Call Bull. Tell him to meet us there with some uniforms. Then call forensics and get them on the way."

Elaine had barely pulled the car onto the street when Liz shouted, "Stop, Chief!"

Elaine slammed on the brakes. "What?"

Liz pointed to an ambulance parked at the side of the road. "Up there. I know it's dark, but I thought I saw him."

"Who? Nilo?" Elaine craned her neck forward and peered into the gloom. She briefly distinguished a familiar human form slipping behind a gaggle of spectators. *No. It can't be.*

She reached into a pocket of her jacket and retrieved a small flashlight. As they slowly cruised past the gawkers, she lowered the car window and shone the flashlight on the edges of the crowd. She reflected that there was nothing like a disaster to bring out the neighborhood. People of all ages were milling about. Several stood at the blue cordon, mutely watching the firefighters go about their business. Others gathered in small groups, talking and smoking cigarettes. A few shouted their annoyance when she played the light over them.

"I thought it was Jenkins," Liz said. "Maybe. It's dark. I can't be sure."

"If it was, he's not here now." Elaine was sure it had been Jenkins. She raised the window and accelerated up the street.

Twenty minutes later, Elaine stood in front of Greene's basement flat, staring at the half-open door with its splintered post. The strong, smoky smell of whisky wafted out to them. She and Liz pulled on their gloves and entered cautiously behind Bull, who insisted on taking the lead. Once inside, they saw the floor of the sitting room was covered with glass from broken bottles and smashed picture frames. Books had been pulled from shelves. Tables and chairs were turned over, their cushions slashed open. The two bedrooms and the bath showed the same chaotic disarray.

Would Jenkins have had time to do this? Elaine kept the thought to herself. Instead, she said, “Crap. Whoever the cousins used, they were pretty thorough. Let’s hope whoever did this left some prints. Maybe we’ll get lucky. Bull, call SOCO and have them get someone over here. Then get one of the night duty detectives over here to supervise. Make sure they call us if they find anything. Computer disks, records, and the like. Once you’ve briefed them, you can go home too. No point spending more overtime on this mess.”

THIRTY-SIX

The streets were surprisingly empty, so Elaine made good time on the way to her flat. The more she thought, the angrier she became. She had no doubt the cousins were behind Greene's death and the fire. Even if Nilo were smart enough to have planned the fire, he couldn't have done it by himself. Had Jenkins helped him, or was it some other Srecko muscle?

Greene's death was a setback. The sleazy lawyer's demise didn't cripple the case, but his testimony against Nilo about the assault on Katya would have made it easier. The good news was that the cousins were feeling threatened. Greene's death and the fire were signals that they were actively defending themselves. It made it more likely that they would make a mistake by doing something that she and her team could act on. Once she had found out what Kumar had to say, she would pay them a surprise visit and twist them a bit more. With any luck, they'd figure that Nilo wasn't worth the trouble and they would give him up. Elaine felt herself fading and realized she needed some food, so she stopped at a Pret A Manger and picked up a sandwich and fruit salad.

Later, she sat at her kitchen table, munching. Scratch purred contentedly at his bowl while she picked at the salad. She always ate the melon first and the strawberries last. Takeout had become a habit, as it usually did in the middle of an investigation. The population of containers in her fridge and rubbish bin was growing. Oh well, no one else would see them.

Unless she asked Peter to come to her flat. That would be nice. It had been too long since she had shared her bed. Especially with someone who had that much potential. She didn't think he was working tonight.

She should put that thought away. First things first. Once Nilo was in custody, she'd tidy the place and ask Peter to dinner.

And that didn't feel right either. She laughed to herself. *What the hell, Lainie? What do you want?*

Elaine put down her fork. *You want him. It's not breathless whirlwind lust. You're not a teenager. You are who you always wanted to be, and he knows it. Sooner or later, he'll find out you can be a slob. And what good is starting something with him if you don't give yourself a chance to work at it?*

She picked up her mobile and dialed Peter's number. There would be time to change the sheets before he arrived.

★ ★ ★

Kumar was weighing Greene's liver when Elaine arrived at the morgue the next day. He motioned her nearer to the table and began his usual dissertation about the corpse, explaining that it sometimes was difficult to ascertain the cause and time of death in a case where the body was burned, so generally the time of the fire was used. Elaine listened politely for a few minutes, as she usually did when Kumar was lecturing, then looked up at the clock on the wall as a sign that he needed to get to the point. He understood.

"My first indication that this gentleman did not die in the fire was this." Kumar lifted a flap of burned skin on Greene's throat and pointed to a small grayish bone.

Elaine had seen it before. "So the hyoid bone is broken? Manual strangulation?"

Kumar nodded. "He was strangled, probably with hands instead of a ligature. It would take a strong pair of hands to strangle a man this size, but a ligature wouldn't have broken it, and there's no trauma that makes me suspect it was broken in any other way. The flesh is too burned to show bruising, but I'll check some more.

There is no smoke in his lungs, so I can safely surmise that he was dead before the fire was set."

Elaine nodded. "Right, then. Thanks, Doc. Let me know if you find anything else."

The news that was waiting for her once she was back at her office wasn't helpful. The CCTV cameras in the lobby of the building, and their recordings, had been burned beyond retrieval. The closest street camera was too far away to give much detail, and no one they could recognize had entered the building earlier in the day. Certainly no one had entered carrying a large corpse. So Greene most likely had been killed at his office.

Most of the detectives on the team were out interviewing Greene's neighbors, associates, and the other tenants of the office building. She pressed the speed-dial key for Liz on her mobile.

"Liz, find Bull, and I'll meet the both of you in the car park at the Sreckos' office."

THIRTY-SEVEN

Low gray clouds were scudding in from the west by the time Elaine arrived at the multistory car park next to the IRG offices. Cold, wet weather was in the offing, and the wind was starting to gust through the open floors. Liz and Bull were already there, so Elaine briefed them on what she wanted them to do. Together the three marched across the drive and took the lift to the IRG offices. Bull waited by the door. Elaine and Liz flashed their warrant cards at the surprised receptionist.

Elaine spoke first. "We would like to see Anton and Janko Srecko. Right now."

Elaine could see the receptionist gathering herself before she answered. Her tone was chilly. "That's not possible. Mr. Janko is not in the office today, and Mr. Anton is busy."

Elaine hardened her expression. "Please tell Mr. Anton that unless he meets with us immediately, I shall proceed with my plans to obtain a search warrant for these offices. No one—no employees, clients, or visitors—shall be allowed in or out until we have questioned them."

The receptionist's eyes stayed fixed on Elaine as she spoke softly into her headset. After a moment, she tilted her head toward the corridor leading to Anton's office.

The door to Anton's office was open and Elaine marched through it with Liz behind her. Liz did not shut the door. Anton sat behind the desk with a cold-blooded look on his face. He didn't speak.

Liz sat in one of the office chairs and took out her notebook. Elaine remained standing and began speaking at Anton in a loud voice. "We are investigating the murder of Jackson Greene, and we have strong evidence that someone from your firm was directly involved and was instructed to kill him and burn his office."

Anton's voice was even and softly pitched. "I deny that. Keep your voice down when you speak to me. You are fishing again, Inspector Hope, and it is clear that you are harassing me. No magistrate in Britain would give you a search warrant for these offices. I shall strongly protest this behavior to the Independent Police Complaints Commission and your Professional Standards department, or directorate, as you call it. I shall also contact the press. If I see or hear anything in the media about these outrageous allegations, I will file a slander suit against both you and the Metropolitan Police Service. I trust I am being clear. Now I want you to leave. Do not come back."

Elaine placed her hands on the desk and leaned across, her eyes locked on his. She spoke barely above a whisper. "I am not fishing. You think that your people—Nilo and someone else we haven't identified yet—destroyed everything with the fire. You think they swept Greene's apartment clean. But you didn't think about the cloud, did you? You didn't think that Greene had stored his backups and all that incriminating information out in Neverland somewhere? As we speak, our forensic people are hunting those files down. They will find them, be assured of that—everything leaves a trace—and when they do, you will be in very serious trouble, Mr. Srecko."

Anton stared back at her. "I told you I did not want you in here. I will not answer any of your insinuations or accusations."

Elaine allowed her voice to rise until she was sure it could be heard up and down the corridor. "You also realize that we are still searching for your nephew. He is a violent murderer, and we need to catch him before he kills again. If we discover that you or anyone in this company has been hiding him, you can be held accountable as an accessory."

Anton was impassive. "For the last time, get out of my offices."

Elaine motioned to Liz, and together they walked back to the foyer, where Bull stood by the door. On their way past the reception desk, Elaine noticed the picture of the blonde girl on the window sill. She stopped and indicated the picture with a nod of her head. "Lovely daughter. University?"

The woman's hesitant voice betrayed her uncertainty. "She is lovely, thank you. Uni is next year."

Elaine leaned over the desk. "I apologize for having spoken so loudly. I hope I didn't disturb you. I know from personal experience that uni can be expensive, even with a scholarship. Here's something to think about. What do you think would happen to your daughter's future prospects if her mother were charged with profiting from brothel keeping, being an accessory to serious financial crimes, and possibly being an accessory to murder? I suggest you think seriously about your situation."

The woman looked shocked. "That's outrageous! How dare you say something like that?"

Elaine shrugged. "Easily. Based on what you do and what you must know, it's a no-brainer. I would be happy to say it again." She turned away and led the other two detectives out of the office.

★ ★ ★

Outside, the weather had turned and the wind was strong, cold, and damp, buffeting them and driving occasional raindrops into their faces. They hurried to the car park without speaking.

Once under shelter, Elaine turned to Bull. "Did anyone try to leave while we were in there?"

Bull nodded. "One fellow, not quite my size. Trained muscle, from the way he moved and carried himself. I stood in front of the door and told him he couldn't leave until he told me his name and what business he had here. He stared at me for a bit and then went back down a corridor. Not the one where you were, the other one. The woman at the desk looked like she was about to bolt out of the room. Extremely frightened, I'd say."

"Did he talk? Say anything?"

Bull shook his head. "No. Just glared at me."

"I'd wager he may not speak much English. Let's get back to the nick and you can talk to an artist so we can build an electronic composite for him."

Liz spoke up. "What you said in there, about Greene's backup files being out in the cloud. Is that true?"

"Not exactly. I did tell Cromarty to have the digital forensics boffins do some hunting, but as far as any hard evidence that they exist, there's nothing right now."

"It didn't seem to faze him when you said that."

Elaine shrugged. "I was closer to him than you, and I think it did. I hope so. It's what I intended."

"What do you think he'll do? Will he go to Professional Standards and the Complaints Commission?"

"Probably not. Right now, he needs to keep our investigation confined to the murder case. He's sure we have the goods on Nilo, and it's only a matter of time." Elaine indicated her car. "Let's get inside. It's too bloody cold and windy out here."

Once Bull had squeezed into the back seat, Elaine resumed. "So, my chicks, what will he do? Anton's biggest concern is to protect the family business. He has some options. He could give Nilo up anonymously or try to get him out of the country. I don't think he'll give the boy up. Anton most likely can get him out of the country with a few phone calls and some planning. It's what I would have done. Maybe he's already tried but couldn't for some reason."

Bull interjected. "He can't afford for the kid to get caught. Too risky."

"Exactly. Nilo knows too much. Maybe he won't talk when we first question him, but he could let something slip out of bravado or anger or plain stupidity. The kid doesn't seem to make good decisions. I'd bet a week's pay that Anton didn't want Nilo to kill Geri Harding, just scare her, and that Sheila's murder was Nilo's doing, all alone. Maybe she told him no and it pissed him off. I doubt we'll ever know."

Liz looked thoughtful. "Are those all of his options?"

Elaine chuckled. "Oh, no. Another option for Anton would be to kill Nilo and make sure someone finds him in a week or so. Case closed, the police move on to other things, the family gets back to business. They would certainly use foreign muscle that could be in and out of Britain in a day or two at most, without a trace. That fellow that Bull confronted is probably one of them. I'd bet another week's pay that he killed Greene. Anyway, if Nilo's murdered, you can be sure it would never be traced back to Anton."

"He'd kill his own nephew?"

Liz looked and sounded nervous, but Elaine continued with the lesson. "If he thought it was best. In the end, it's about the survival of the family, not individuals. It's almost like having God on their side. Anything can be justified." Elaine stopped and considered. Liz and Bull were both looking away, out the side windows of the car, not speaking. They were probably only just now realizing the depth of the evil they faced and what it was capable of doing.

Bull spoke, "What if that Anton bastard hurts someone? I mean one of us. That's what you're saying, isn't it, boss?" He turned back to face Elaine. "We have to get that bastard."

Elaine shook her head. "We need to stay focused on the case. It's Sheila's murder we're investigating. Our first priority is Nilo. Anton needs to get us off his back, so I think he'll bring this to a close pretty soon. He'll see to it that Nilo gets out of the country or that we never find him. One way or another."

Neither Liz nor Bull looked completely convinced, but Elaine decided to press on. They could sort through it all later. "Now let's talk about citizen complaints and Professional Standards. What do you think Anton will do?"

Liz spoke first. "He sounded really serious, guv. His eyes told me he'd go through with it. Maybe he'll do it just to distract us? But Jesus, I've barely started here."

Bull extended his arm and placed his hand on Liz's shoulder, then spoke more to her than to Elaine. "I don't think he'd file a complaint, swee—" His eyes shifted to Elaine, and he withdrew his hand before he continued. "He'd have to give evidence, and we'd have to talk about why we were there, then he'll get questioned again, and who knows where that will lead. I don't think you have to worry about that. I'm not going to."

Elaine smiled to herself. *Time goes by, but nothing changes, does it?* She picked up where Bull left off. "You know how thorough and relentless the Professional Standards officers are. So you don't have to worry. Even if Anton fools me and files the complaint, when it gets ugly, I'll cover you. I didn't tell you what I was going to do before we went in. You were only there because I took you there with me. They won't do anything more than speak sternly to either of you, if that. They'll be after me."

Liz turned and looked at Elaine askance. "What should I do? I won't say anything about it on my own, but what if they call me to give evidence?"

Elaine sighed. "If you're witnesses, you do what you should always do. You tell the truth about what you saw and did and what I said and did. No embroidery, no suppositions, no whining. It's what I'll do." Liz gave a small nod.

There was no response from either of the young detectives, only silence. It was time to let them think about it. She gave a short laugh. "Thus endeth today's lesson. Both of you take the rest of the day off. Get yourself home or to Bull's place. Wherever."

Liz opened the door of the car, but before she got out, she looked at Bull, then turned to face Elaine. "You know, we realized from the start of this that you were giving us a huge opportunity.

Me and Bull, both. Thanks, guv. We've appreciated it, and we've tried hard not to blow it."

Elaine shrugged. Bull was waiting patiently for Liz. "You haven't blown anything." Liz closed the car door, and Elaine drove out of the multistory car park, wishing she was as confident about the case as she tried to appear.

★ ★ ★

Anton's hands trembled and his blood pounded in his ears. The bitch had threatened him. She had marched into his office and challenged him face-to-face. It had taken every ounce of his restraint to remain calm and seated. If he had been back in his village, he would have picked up a stick and beaten the impudent sow until she could no longer squeal for mercy.

He took a deep breath. He needed to calm down, so he turned in his chair and faced the window. The sun was setting. Its final light was not much more than a red line below the heavy layer of winter clouds. He closed his eyes. What should he do?

Hope had put on a brave bluff about finding Greene's backups and the cloud server, but he knew her threats were empty. Nilo and Goran had reported back promptly after setting the fire in Greene's office. At first that stupid pig thought they had bailed him out of jail because they needed him. When he realized he was in danger, he thought he could save himself by cooperating, so he showed them how to access his remote backup files on the cloud. After they had written it all down, he had begged for mercy until Nilo restrained his arms and Goran's hand clamped on his throat like a vise. The fire afterward was routine housekeeping.

By the time the fire brigade had found Greene's charred body, Anton had already downloaded all of Greene's backup files to a disc. Afterward, he had deleted everything in Greene's directories. He knew deletion wasn't foolproof, and he knew that perhaps Greene had another backup location he didn't tell them about, but Anton had done all he could do with the information he had. He very much doubted that the police would find the correct server, much less be able to recover anything. So that was taken care of.

But this Hope bitch. She was bold. She took chances. She had more balls than most of her male counterparts he'd run across, at least more than the high-ranking coppers who went to the corporate and charity affairs and who ate and drank at the same posh restaurants as he and Janko. They all seemed so smooth, so concerned with what the public thought. They took great care about appearances and perceptions, more like politicians than police. Hope didn't seem to give much of a damn about appearances. Not the way she had trespassed in his office—not once, but twice—and had threatened him across his own desk. She had cast herself as his nemesis, and her investigation was a huge risk to his plans. She had as much as told them she knew there was more to IRG than showed on the surface. There was really no way to know what she would discover if she had enough time. As far as he was concerned, she was a loose cannon.

So was Nilo. Anton had already called Marko and laid out how the family's plans were jeopardized by the murder investigation. One of their options was to give up Nilo to the bitch. He could arrange for an informant to tell the detectives where to find him. But once he was in custody, the boy would be too unpredictable. He was always feeding his ego and his insatiable appetite. He would probably try to match his cunning against the police interrogators, which anyone with brains knew was always a losing game. He would begin to crack after he'd been shuffled between a cell and the interrogation room for two days without any cocaine or cigarettes or alcohol. He'd shatter like a dropped crock, and there was no telling how many beans he would spill.

Enough of that. Simply put, he needed for the murder investigation to go away, and he needed to remove any reason the police and the CPS would have for investigating further. There must be no trial.

After sitting and thinking another half hour, ideas that had been amorphous and obscure solidified. A plan emerged that reached far enough to succeed, even if it was risky. Anton was satisfied. It never took long to work out what to do once he clarified his goals. He felt calm, more like himself, now that he had a plan of action.

Still, it was such a shame. Nilo had shown promise early on, but he was resistant and didn't listen. There hadn't been enough time for Anton to train him to control himself. Like so many young people, he constantly confused gratification with power. Anton hadn't been able to teach the younger man to harness his ego and give direction to the relentless drive that flowed from within, a drive that was fueled by needs that few people could comprehend. Nilo had not learned to let his desires work for him. If he had, he would understand how exhilarating it could be to crush your opposition. It was better than drugs or women. It was like galloping on the back of a huge and powerful stallion, sitting up high, looking down on other, lesser people. Anton knew how to be the man on horseback.

THIRTY-EIGHT

Elaine had just wrapped up the morning status meeting when the constable protecting Katya called to say she had awakened from her coma. Elaine and Liz left immediately for the hospital.

Katya's doctor wasn't keen about allowing Elaine to question her patient, but after many assurances, she agreed to a compromise. "She's off the respirator, but she is still quite fragile. I'll be in there with you. You have a maximum of five minutes, but if she shows signs of strain, I'll end the interview right then."

Elaine nodded and moved to the side of Katya's bed. Liz and the doctor stayed back. Katya's head was swathed in a bandage that also covered her right eye. Bruises surrounded her left eye and covered her left arm, which lay across her body.

"Hello, Katya. My name is DCI Hope. I'm so glad you're back with us and on the mend. DC Barker and I have spoken with your friends Ximena and Lana, and they were very worried about you. I'd like to ask you a few questions about the people who did this to you. Is that all right?"

Katya tried to speak, but no sound would come out, so she nodded her head. Elaine took a picture from a folder she was carrying.

"This is a photo of you and a man called Greene. It appears that you are putting some groceries in a car. Do you remember the night you did that?"

Katya nodded.

"Good. You're being very helpful." Elaine took out another picture, this time of Nilo's house. "Did he take you to this house?" A nod.

"And there were men there?" Another nod.

"Excellent." Elaine took out the picture of Nilo. "This man is called Nilo. Was he there?"

Katya's left eye widened and she tried to turn her head away. It was clearly painful for her to move. The doctor took a step forward but stopped when Katya nodded yet again.

Elaine continued. "You are doing remarkably well, Katya. Just a few more questions, then we'll be finished. Is Nilo the man who did this to you? Who beat you and hit you in the head?"

Tears ran from Katya's left eye. Elaine pulled a tissue from a box and dabbed it gently to her face. "I know this is painful for you. Take your time. Again, is this the man who hurt you?"

Katya nodded.

"Was there another man with him?" At Katya's nod, Elaine took out the electronic composite picture. "Is this the man who was with him?"

Katya shook her head slowly. The man Bull had seen wasn't Nilo's accomplice.

Elaine reached out and took her hand. "Thank you. You've helped us a great deal. When you're feeling better, perhaps you can give us a description of the other man. We're going to catch these monsters, and your testimony will be very important for putting them in prison. I don't want you to worry about being safe. We're keeping this location a secret so no one will know where you are, and you'll have a constable here to protect you at all times. We may need to ask you some more questions later, but now you can rest." She smiled and gave Katya's hand a small squeeze.

Elaine didn't speak until they were in the lift. "We'll make a public appeal for information, showing Nilo's picture along with a warning that he's dangerous and most likely armed. He is not to be approached. Call Paula and tell her to get it rolling with public affairs. You can help her with it."

The appeal was broadcast that evening. Elaine took the lead, flanked by Cranwell, with the core of her team—Paula, Simon, Liz, and Bull—behind her. She described the crimes as brutal murders, stressing the brutality of the assaults along with displayed portraits of Sheila and Geri. She described Nilo's assault on Katya as attempted murder. The photo of Nilo was displayed on the screen for much of the rest of the broadcast. The video of the appeal was added to the main Met website as well as the various social media sites where the Met had a presence.

The telephones on the phone bank started ringing immediately afterward. Earnest eyewitnesses, hundreds of miles apart, reported seeing Nilo in Truro and Newcastle. Many scores of other callers claimed that he looked like their sponging brother-in-law, annoying neighbor, or ex-husband. None of this was unusual for the experienced officers answering the telephones. In the end, every call—including the cranks, weirdos, and wild hares—would be sorted, categorized, and considered. It was detailed police work that needed to be done, despite the expense in equipment and staff.

Elaine monitored the responses for a while. Once she was satisfied that everything was running smoothly, she went home, having left instructions to be notified of any likely leads.

★ ★ ★

Liz poured coffee from the cafetière into her cup, added milk and two cubes of sugar, and looked out the kitchen window of the flat. It was still cold, but the fluffy clouds and blue sky promised a sunny day. She needed a break from the rain.

Bull had gone in to the station already to get started on the follow-ups from the appeal. Elaine had felt Liz might be in danger, so she had scheduled Liz for a refresher class on using her baton—the "asp" as many called it. She would go to class, then report to the incident room. She hoped she got there before Elaine left for wherever she was going today. She valued her time with Elaine as much as, or truth be told, probably more than, the time she was able to spend with Bull.

It was for different reasons, of course. She wanted to take her time with Bull, getting to know him and letting him get to know her. How else would either of them know if it was right or not? He was such a mystery. He was normally kind and soft spoken, gentle, and she knew he could even be tender. But she also saw the tethered violence that lurked under his outward persona. It revealed itself in the way he moved, the way his eyes immediately developed an alertness whenever he sensed any kind of threat. She had only seen him unleash it in Krav Maga class, but even then it was restrained. She was always amazed when he transformed from good-natured DC Philip Bull into a lethal Royal Marine. She trusted him completely as a partner because she knew he would give his life for her if necessary, as she would for him. That was much more than many married couples could ever expect from each other.

With Elaine, it was different. Liz wanted to watch and listen and learn from her all day, every day. To learn how to conduct an interview and evaluate evidence, how to bring a woman's perspective to what was still a predominantly male occupation, and how to be dominant when a dirtbag tried to intimidate you. Elaine taught how to be a detective and how to be a cop.

Her hand went to her belt where her asp hung in its small holster. She jerked it out and flicked it hard. The steel segments slid out to their full length with a loud click—and the hardened tip struck the cafetière, shattering it and sending oozy coffee grounds flowing over the top of the counter. Crap. She obviously needed the refresher course.

Glass and coffee cleaned up, Liz hurried to her car. Was that an envelope under her windscreen wiper? Had Bull left her a note? Brilliant! He had a habit of leaving little teases and cute sayings, sometimes quite naughty ones, folded up and stashed in places where he was sure she would find them. She grinned as she opened it.

It was not from Bull. She'd handled it with her bare hands, but that couldn't be helped now. She pulled a plastic evidence bag out of her purse. Holding the letter by its corner, she slid it and its envelope into the bag. Baton class would have to wait.

⋆ ⋆ ⋆

Upon arrival at the station, she immediately went to Elaine's office. Liz rapped on the doorpost and entered but stopped short when she saw a square of paper in a plastic bag, lying on the desk in front of Elaine.

Elaine saw the recognition in Liz's face. "Come in and shut the door. You got one too, didn't you? What did yours say?"

Liz handed her the plastic bag. Elaine turned it to see the printing, smoothed the plastic, and read it in a low voice.

"*Hi Little Red Dragon Bitch I saw the TV last night and what a Sad Show that was. Not Funny!!! NOT AT ALL SO SAD because you just stood there you little WHORE and you let your Auntie SLAG do all the talking well I'm ready to show you how I deal with dragons. You don't have me now and you won't ever because I'm going to have you first and when I'm finished with you it will be Strawberries And Cream for you but NOT ME! Be ready for Strawberries And Cream.*"

Elaine picked up the evidence bag containing the note she'd received. "Very much like mine, except mine was more graphically detailed. Was it on your windscreen?"

Liz nodded again. "Under the wiper. The envelope is in the bag too. Did he say the strawberries and cream thing to you? What did he mean by that?"

Elaine hesitated before answering. "Yes, he used it with me. Told me that I deserve it, and I'll get what I deserve. He could mean that he thinks it's sweet to brutalize women, that he loves it. I think it's more likely, though, that to him 'strawberries and cream' means red blood on fair skin. Notice how he says 'for you but not me.' He said something similar in his note to me. That's my best guess right now."

She picked up the evidence bags and headed for the door. "Let's do something about this."

Liz followed Elaine to Cranwell's office. He was turned toward the window, reading a thick report. Elaine rapped on the doorpost.

"May we have a word, sir." It was a statement, not a question. She led the way into the office.

Cranwell looked up and raised his eyebrows in a query, first at Elaine, then Liz, and finally back to Elaine. He motioned to the chairs. "Of course. What's happened?"

Elaine pushed the two notes in their plastic bags across the desk. Liz saw his face change from interest to horror to angry resolve in a matter of seconds. His hand was shaking when he put the bags down.

"That's . . ." He hesitated, then got himself under control. "Outrageous is the most polite term I can think of! How dare he threaten you! Get the letters to forensics immediately. You'll need to be moved to a safe house. Is your self-defense training up to date?"

Elaine answered. "I'm up to date. Liz may need a refresher. However, she's being watched over closely by a constable who's a former Royal Marine."

"Ah, yes. Bull." He picked up his telephone. "I'll get the rehousing approved. You each should find somewhere to stay tonight besides home. Be sure to stay in touch. I'll arrange to have an ARV pass by each of your flats every half-hour or so. Meanwhile, see what you can do to catch this monster."

THIRTY-NINE

It was a good thing the traffic was light and there weren't many people out in this weather. Elaine flogged her car through the streets, driving wildly and unrelentingly. She arrived at Nelson's Glory a few minutes early. The evening rush hadn't begun, so the pub was sparsely populated and quiet. Thank God for that. She ordered two pints of stout and found a small nook in the back where the other patrons wouldn't notice her fuming.

Cranwell was right. Being threatened by that punk was outrageous. She'd see to him, though—once and for all. He'd pay for a very long time, but not before she reduced him to jelly. And that cold slab of evil, Anton. He'd put Nilo up to this, so he'd fall too. *Nobody disdains me or my team. Nobody threatens us. In the end, I hold the power of justice over those kinds of scum. Before I'm done, they will know it.*

She needed to calm down before Peter arrived. How should she tell him about the threats and the rehousing? In theory, he would be supportive and recognize that she was the expert and she could take care of herself. In practice, however, he would probably revert to his male instincts and get protective and proprietary. She wouldn't push him away, because it showed he appreciated her, and it was natural behavior for a man. But she would have to have a chat with him about life with a Met detective. This Met detective, anyway.

Elaine snapped herself into the present. Her hands shook as she picked up her pint. *Calm down and focus, Lainie. Being distracted isn't safe.* She took a deep breath and a small sip of stout before she began scanning the pub, careful to not let her eyes settle on one person for too long. Two businessmen stood at the bar, talking animatedly, which meant the conversation was about either money or football. A middle-aged couple, American tourists by the look of their "I Heart London" hats and inadequate coats, sat staring out the window at the rain, their barely touched pub meals cooling in front of them. The bargain trip to London in winter wasn't turning out as they had hoped. An elderly man with a gentle smile sat in a nook across from Elaine, glancing at her. He nodded when her eyes scanned past him. She had no idea who he was.

And here she sat again, in Nelson's Glory, dissecting the people around her. Being the detective. The detective who couldn't put down the job.

Now her dedication to that job had set forces in motion that threatened her. She couldn't remember all the threats she had received throughout her career from criminals she had nicked and who were spending much, if not the rest, of their lives at Her Majesty's pleasure. They deserved what they got. Most of their threats were hollow.

This was different. She directed the action now that she was a DCI. Professional needs aside, her decisions had placed someone she cared about in harm's way. It didn't matter that Liz had willingly shouldered the dangers of being a police officer. Elaine knew that, but she was still a woman who cared about people and their welfare. It was one reason she became a copper. Liz wasn't ready . . .

"Hi, there." Peter's voice brought her into the present. He leaned over and kissed her on the cheek and sat across from her. "You looked absorbed in something. I must have been standing there for ten seconds or so. I didn't want to disturb you."

Damn, she had been daydreaming again. Elaine smiled in greeting and lifted her glass in a toast. "Sorry. You should have."

"You looked like you were second-guessing yourself. Was it anything you can share?"

How did he know that? Elaine trailed her finger around the rim of her pint glass. "I was thinking about the fact that I'm never really off work because I'm in the middle of my perfect career." She looked up at him. "I know you are too."

He tilted his head in thought. His blue eyes never left her brown ones. "We both spend enough time at them." He took a sip of his pint.

She shook her head. "It's not the hours. It's the way our brains work. Or rather the way mine works. It worked this way even when I was a kid. I think being a detective was inevitable."

His eyes fixed on hers. "You've never struck me as fatalistic. I can't imagine you saying 'it is what it is' about something you think is wrong and then leaving it at that. I ought to know." He placed his hand over hers. He had warm, dry, strong hands. His touch was always gentle, never tentative, and when he touched her, she felt safe. He moved around the nook to sit next to her.

She smiled. "That sounds like someone I've come to know too."

Peter wrapped his arm over her shoulders, pulling her closer. Her head fit perfectly into the little hollow between his arm and his throat. He said, "As long as we understand each other," and kissed her hair.

She lifted her face and kissed his chin in return. His five-o'clock shadow scratched her lips. Quite nicely, in fact. "Can we go?" she asked.

They left their unfinished pints on the table.

★ ★ ★

This time with Peter it was more urgent, more necessary. Elaine knew what she needed and where she wanted to go and took charge immediately. Each time the wave rolled through her, she cried out, whimpered, then cried out at the next crest, as if she had glimpsed some missing, vital part of herself, lost sight of it, and then glimpsed it again. Finally the waves stopped and she lay shattered in his arms. Peter embraced her, kissed her, and held her until her shaking ceased.

He pulled the duvet up over them, asking, "Are you cold?"

She was still breathless. "No. God no. It's just . . ."

He whispered. "I can't describe what just happened."

"Don't try."

She lay next to him in the moonlight that streamed through the large window.

"Where to from here?" she murmured.

"The here and now. I've been trying to find my way to a moment like this for years, so I want to stay in it."

She snuggled closer. "I feel like this has happened so quickly. At first, I thought you might be having me on. You know, revenge."

"Never. I'm not a vengeful person. I try to put things behind me. I think I truly realized it when you visited me that night. Did you really have questions for me?"

She poked him. "Of course I did. Clarifications. And you told me something important."

"Really, now. What was it?"

"Can't say. Police confidential. But that was one of the strangest first moves anyone has ever laid on me."

He laughed. "I meant every hint of it. I needed to get something going with you."

"Why was that?"

"I had to find out if what I was feeling was real."

"Was it?"

He wrapped his fingers in her hair and pulled her face to his until their eyes were inches apart. Then he kissed her. Deep and hard.

Later in the shower, he took her again, with her face and hands pressed against the tile and the steamy heat swirling around them. Afterward she sat curled on his lap in the big chair, her arms around his neck, the duvet covering them.

He stroked her hair. "I have to go in to work, but you're welcome to stay here tonight."

"Thank you. I will." She unwrapped herself and stood by the big window, looking out at the lights of the Docklands sparkling in the distance. "I need to tell you something first, though."

⋆ ⋆ ⋆

"So you weren't Daddy's little girl, then." They were sitting at the kitchen table. Peter spooned some jam onto a piece of toast and slid the jar across the table to Elaine, who scooped some out for herself. *We both need some calorie replacement*, he thought.

She smiled across at him. "Good jam. That workout made me hungry." Her face took on a serious cast. "No. That was Moira. Like I told you before, I was the Oops baby. Oops really meant Oops to him. He tended to blame things on me. He wasn't violent; he never touched me. But he knew when to yell and when to give the silent treatment long enough to make me feel wretched. He might have been a good interrogator."

"Maybe you got it from him."

"Could be. Mum stood up for me when he yelled, and she paid attention to me during the silent times. Ailsa and Christine were already married and gone. I hardly knew them. Moira was still at home, mostly, when she wasn't God-knows-where with one boyfriend or another. I knew he worried a lot about her. She had a drug problem, but I didn't understand it then."

"You must have been just a child."

For a half minute or so, Elaine appeared to weigh something in her mind. "She, that's Moira, was supposed to be watching me while Mum and Dad were off visiting his sister in Exeter. I was seven. She did watch me too. It was going okay until one of her boyfriends rang. I remember several. This one was named Jake, and I didn't like him."

Elaine paused while Peter poured tea. "I didn't want to go. She told me I had to come with her, cursed me for being a whingeing little shite. She scooped me up and off we went."

"You were a child." Peter sat back in his chair, his arms extended on the table, his head cocked to one side.

"She was such a sweet woman until it came to drugs. Heroin was the drug of choice in the Drum in those days. She couldn't afford it on her own, but her boyfriends could get it at times, and they always called her when they did. No telling what it was cut with."

"The Drum?"

"Drumchapel, where I grew up."

"Was it an overdose?"

"I wish it had been as peaceful as that. No. Jake had a filthy little council flat. Filthy. She left me in the sitting room and they went in the bedroom. I don't know what happened, but I heard him shouting, and then thumps, and Moira started screaming. I wanted to run away, but I was too scared to even move." She was silent. Peter didn't speak, so she continued.

"Then it got quiet, and after a few minutes, I went to the bedroom door. He was sitting on the floor next to the bed. She was lying on the bed with a pillow over her face. I ran out of the flat. A woman on the landing stopped me and called the police. Jake got fifteen years, but he died in prison."

"And you've paid for it since then." Peter offered the teapot.

Elaine covered her cup with her hand. "My dad said I had let it happen. He said I was supposed to scream and run for help. That if I had, Moira wouldn't have died. A few years later, he said that he forgave me, but I don't think he ever did. For the rest of his life, I could see that look in his eyes, usually at holidays. He died sixteen years ago, after I became a cop."

"He stayed bitter, then?"

"Right. I don't think he ever let go of it."

"And you?"

She swirled the tea leaves in her cup. "I'm okay."

FORTY

Liz had stuffed the last pair of jeans into a suitcase when her mobile rang. She pulled it from her purse and answered without looking, thinking it was Bull. It wasn't.

A shaky female voice asked for her by name. "Detective Constable Liz Barker?"

The voice sounded familiar, but Liz couldn't place it. "Who is speaking?"

"This is Ximena Abaroa. You left me your card, remember?" The young prostitute almost whispered. "You asked me to call you if the boss came here. He did."

"Is he there now?"

"No. He was here and he hit me. He left, but he said he was coming back. I'm alone. I don't know where to go. Can you help?"

Liz thought for a moment. The woman sounded fearful. "It will take me about half an hour to get there. Leave the house and wait for me on the street. Try to stay out of sight. Either I or another police officer will be there to pick you up. If you see a police car, stand in the street and wave it down. Do you understand?"

"Yes. Leave the house and look for a police car."

"Right. I'll be there as soon as I can. I promise." Liz punched a speed-dial button.

Elaine answered on the second ring. "This is Hope. Liz? Where are you? Are you at your hotel yet?"

"No. Bull will take me as soon as he gets here. I got a call from Ximena, from the brothel. She said that Nilo had been there and had beaten her. He left, but he'll be back later. She wants us to pick her up."

"Right. You and Bull meet me there. I'm on my way."

Liz rang off. *Where the hell was Bull?* She glanced at the time on her mobile. He should be here, unless he had been delayed for some reason. To save time, she could meet him next to the street. She grabbed her coat and purse and headed for the door. As she turned the lock, the door slammed against her with a force that drove her into the sitting room and tumbled her over the back of the sofa. Before she could regain her feet, a fist slammed into her midsection, forcing her breath from her. She bent in agony, and a blow to her back crumpled her to her knees. A third blow to the side of her head stunned her, and she collapsed sideways on the floor.

Inside her brain, the world was turning over. A roaring sound filled her ears. She waited for another blow, but it didn't come. She struggled to all fours, but a weight on her hips drove her facedown to the floor. She felt her arms being forced behind her back. She tried to rise, but a huge hand slammed her head into the floor and her world went black.

Sounds filtered through her ears, growing closer, louder—crashing, banging, grunts, breaking glass. She couldn't move her arms, so she wriggled to a sitting position in time to see Bull throw a large man across the room into the wall. Instead of retaliating, the man spun around and rushed out the open door. She heard Bull's voice and felt his huge, strong arms around her.

"Sweetheart! Can you hear me?"

Liz nodded. "I . . . can't move." She felt him tugging at her arms and then her wrists were free. Bull's face was in front of her. Blood ran from his nose and from a cut over his right eye. She tried to speak but could not form sentences.

"Elaine . . . the women . . . go . . ."

"Elaine? The women? What do you mean?" He said more, but his voice was distant and distorted. Liz told him to stop mumbling, but her voice didn't sound right either. Someone said an ambulance would take too long. Now he was carrying her, placing her in a car. She didn't feel this was right. She needed to tell Bull. They had to help Elaine.

Liz felt as if she couldn't breathe. She needed time to think. She found the switch that opened the window and gulped in the cold air. Finally she could speak.

"Stop the car and let me think." Liz scrabbled to find the seat-belt release. She pushed the button and she was free.

"No!" Bull shouted. "We're going to the hospital! What are you doing?" He pulled the car to the curb and reached over to fasten her seatbelt.

Now or never. She reached up and shoved him back, then held her hands out to make him stay away. The cold air and urgency helped her thoughts clear.

"No! Listen to me!" She took a deep breath, then another. "Nilo is at the brothel. Elaine's on her way there. She was calling for backup. We have to go."

"I need to get you to a doctor. She knows to wait for backup."

"No! She's our guv. My friend. Your friend! I said I would meet her there. If you won't take me, I'll get out! Let me out!" She felt like her head would split open.

Bull's voice was calmer. "All right. Please. All right. Put your hands down and let me fasten your seatbelt. We'll go make sure Elaine's all right. Then it's to the hospital with you. No arguments." He put the car into gear. "Do you have your phone? We need to call in."

Her fury had passed. She felt the pockets of her jeans. "No. It's still at the flat. Give me yours."

He pulled his phone from his pocket. It was bent, and the screen had been shattered in the fight.

★ ★ ★

Jenkins followed Nilo aimlessly through East London for much of the evening. Finally the kid turned onto a sleazy street lined with what appeared to be crack houses or twenty-pound knocking shops. It was hard to tell which was which, but it looked familiar.

Ah, Jenkins thought, *why is the kid back here? What's he doing that I can use against him?*

Nilo parked, got out of the crappy Fiesta, and entered one of the less derelict houses. Jenkins found a vantage point about a hundred meters away and parked. From the athletic bag on the seat next to him, he pulled out his night vision binoculars, a cello-wrapped sandwich, an apple, and a water bottle. He ate and watched. Five minutes passed and another car cruised by the house. Jenkins slid lower in the seat and watched it pull onto the opposite pavement. A thug got out of the car, *a real goon*. Over six feet, probably fifteen stone of muscle. No one would complain to him about parking on the pavement. Lights flashed and an alarm bleeped as Goon locked the car and strolled to the same house Nilo had entered. *They must have some dollies in there.* He settled down to wait.

Fifteen minutes later, a familiar blue BMW turned the corner at the end of the street. What the fuck was Hope doing here? He watched as she cruised by and parked on the pavement near Goon's car.

FORTY-ONE

Elaine sat in her car and assessed her situation. She had dialed 9-9-9 on her way, but the dispatcher told her that a gang fight had erupted, shots had been fired, and every armed response vehicle and authorized firearms officer in the district was busy. They would route the next closest ARV to her location, but it wouldn't arrive for at least twenty minutes.

From the driver's seat, she could see clearly only in one direction. She would rather see what was around her and be able to move than be ambushed in her car. There was no point taking chances. She got out, found a deep shadow against a wall, and pushed the speed dial for Liz. She let the phone ring until it went to voice mail.

"It's Elaine. Call me." Maybe Liz was on a call.

She dialed Bull. His phone went to voice mail immediately, as if it were turned off. That was odd. Met detectives didn't turn off their mobiles.

Had Liz and Bull already arrived? If they had, one of them would have remained outside to wait for her—unless something had happened inside the house. This wasn't good. Nilo may have returned early, and he was most likely armed. As she slid into a shadow closer to the house, she heard a high-pitched noise, like the cry of a bird. She heard it again, only this time louder. It was a woman's scream. That could be Liz. Damn.

She dialed 9-9-9 and identified herself as she moved to the house. "I'm entering a house to investigate two female screams. I suspect an officer has been attacked." She gave the address. "I need backup immediately. Anyone you can send." She put her mobile in her pocket, flicked her asp to its full length, and pushed open the front door.

Elaine darted inside and pressed herself to the wall away from the door. She waited a moment, listening, picturing the interior from her previous visit. Stairs straight ahead, up one flight to a landing, then a second flight to the upper floor. Sitting room door three steps on the left, kitchen door two steps after. *Check the sitting room first.*

Remember the layout. Sofa against the back wall, two wooden chairs facing it across a low table. Probably scattered magazines and newspapers, so take care with the footing. By now, her eyes had adjusted to the even dimmer light inside the house. She moved slowly forward along the wall to her left, asp in ready position, until she was nearly at the sitting room door.

"Police! Bull? Liz?"

Scuffling sounds and a muted woman's cry came from the sitting room. Had Liz come here alone?

"Nilo! Let her go and come out unarmed. Backup is on the way. You don't have a chance."

No response. She waited, but the only reply was the same muted sounds. She knew he was probably armed, but there was no choice now. Elaine took a quick glance around the doorpost. A dim figure stood against the back wall. She moved to the door and through it. Yes, a woman was standing there, but the room was too dim for any detail.

Nilo's voice came from the darkness. "Stupid cow. I knew you'd come."

Elaine could vaguely discern a figure behind the woman. "My backup is on the way, Danilo. Let her go."

"Your backup? Who? Liz the Little Red Dragon? You think she'll be here?" Nilo laughed. "We've got her in the boot of a car by now. I'll be done with you in a few minutes. Then after we deal with her, we're off to Mexico. Goran."

A lamp snicked on to her left, revealing a large man watching her. Across the room, she recognized Ximena standing in front of Nilo looking at Elaine with huge dark eyes. His hand was across her mouth, and he held a pistol to her head. She wasn't struggling.

"Mexico? You'll never get . . ." Elaine didn't have a chance to finish. With a sudden movement, Nilo slammed Ximena against the wall. The pistol cracked and Elaine felt a searing hot pain tear through her right leg. She cried out and grabbed her thigh, dropping the asp and toppling to the floor as her leg collapsed.

★ ★ ★

Jenkins watched as Elaine entered the house. The woman had more bollocks than sense, but he wasn't surprised. She had flicked an asp, but she wouldn't be armed otherwise. The Met didn't like its detectives to carry weapons, even asps, but only an idiot would enter that house without more than a baton to rely on.

It didn't look good. Jenkins pulled on latex gloves and slid his balaclava over his face. A half-minute later, a light appeared in the front window, followed by the distinctive flat crack of an FN FiveseveN. Damn! The situation and his job were turning to shit fast. He jumped from the car and dialed 9-9-9 as he moved along the pavement. He needed to get help on the way as fast as possible.

"Code zero. Gunshots fired. Officer down. Ambulance is required." The operator asked him to identify himself, but he ignored her and rattled off the street name. "Did you hear me? Officer down! DCI Hope has been shot. Officer down!"

He ended the call and slid his Glock 26 from its holster under his arm.

★ ★ ★

Elaine tried to rise from the floor, but her right leg wouldn't support her. As she pushed herself up, a force like the blunt end of a log struck her in the stomach, driving the breath from her. She collapsed on her back, her knees curled almost to her chest.

Nilo grabbed her jacket, pulling her upright. She tried to punch, her fist glancing off his arm and scraping his ear, eliciting a curse. She gasped for breath.

Get away from him. But she couldn't. Her leg would not hold. He held her by the collar of her jacket. A fist smashed her mouth twice in rapid succession.

Try to breathe. Stay up. Up. Can't. A smash to her right eye. Another. Blood ran into her eyes. Whatever was holding her up let go and she collapsed on the floor.

Try to get up. Move away. A boot in her stomach. She retched. Her world narrowed to a point of red light.

Don't pass out, dammit. Stay awake. A loud crack. Elaine jerked in surprise, but there was no more pain.

He missed. She felt tugging at her waist, her feet.

He's stripped me. No. No. Nilo's voice sounded far away, his words muffled and faint.

"This one's all mine. Get your car. I won't be long."

Elaine felt a hand grab her hair and something slid down the side of her face. Her brain reeled with burning pain. She tasted the blood rolling into her mouth. Smashed teeth felt like gravel under her tongue.

"Strawberries and cream, Auntie. Enjoy." A face hovered over hers, separated only by the needle point of a large knife.

She needed one more chance. Her eyes squinted of their own accord, blinking away the blood. A fit of coughing seized her as she struggled for breath, expelling blood and teeth into the face in front of her. She gasped.

"Damn you whore!" The knife clattered to the floor as his hands grabbed her waist and flipped her facedown across the low coffee table. "Here's what you deserve, bitch. Ready? The last thing you feel will be me. The last fucking thing."

Nilo grasped her hair in his hands and pulled her head back. A flare lit in her consciousness. Her mind screamed as Nilo's weight shifted forward, his head next to hers.

"Here it is, cunt." He pressed into her.

She kicked her legs and tried to lever her body upright, but her hand slipped in the blood, sliding off the edge of the table.

Nilo grunted and pounded her ribs with his fist. "That's good. Fight me. It's so much better."

Elaine writhed under him. His head was next to hers; she felt him press deeper, his breath against her skin. She extended her arm, again trying to find some purchase to hold, to push against. Her hand touched something heavy, a hilt. The knife. She gripped it and curled her arm back over her shoulder, striking with all the strength she had left. It pierced something, and she pushed the blade until she could push it no more.

Nilo's heavy breathing became a gurgling howl.

★ ★ ★

The second shot cracked as Jenkins moved toward the low stoop. Moments later, the front door began to open, and he dodged into shadow just as Goon emerged. Jenkins let him take a step, then swung the Glock squarely into the big man's face. Goon toppled over, cracking his head against the brick. He lay stunned, unconscious. Jenkins kicked him once in the head, pulled a zip tie from his pocket, and secured Goon's hands behind his back.

Jenkins had tightened a second zip tie around Goon's ankles when a high-pitched scream came from the house. Goon lay still. No more worries from him, but who—or what—screamed like that?

He moved carefully up the steps and into the house, his Glock in ready position. Light shone through a doorway on the left, and his training took over. Back against the wall. Weapon in low ready. Thumb the safety. Keep your breathing even. Take short, soft steps now. Two meters. One meter. At the door. Weapon up. Quick. Move in and across. *Jesus Christ.*

The sensory shock broke his trained rhythm. Blood spattered across the walls and puddled on the floor. Its perverse metallic incense saturated the air. He swept the room with the Glock and his eyes.

To his right, a young woman with only half of her head lay crumpled on the floor, her brains and blood staining the wall behind her. Across from her, Nilo sat on the floor against the sofa, his trousers around his ankles, his head skewed to the side. A Fairbairn-Sykes combat knife protruded from the base of his throat. Blood pumped weakly past the blade and pulsed down his chest in wide, soft waves. Nilo blinked and moved his hand. As Jenkins watched, the hand twitched, the blood stopped flowing, and Nilo's eyes glassed over.

Good work, Elaine. You saved me the trouble. Let's see about you.

Elaine was stretched facedown across the low table, her legs and arms hanging over the edges. She was naked below the waist. A jagged exit wound glared from the back of her right thigh. Her body was covered in sticky redness from her hair to her knees.

Please don't let it be hers, he thought. *Not all of it.*

Jenkins pressed his gloved fingers against Elaine's throat. He felt a pulse, not a strong one, but it was steady. Her breathing was shallow but regular. He adjusted her head to the side to prevent blood from pooling in her throat.

A police siren screamed as flashing blue lights strobed past the window. *Time to get out*, Jenkins thought. His arrest would mean he would have to get his superiors involved, and his superiors did not like explaining themselves to mere police. Being caught would jeopardize three years of rotten, scummy work. Jenkins slipped through the kitchen and out the back door as officers rushed in through the front. He needed to make it to his car before they had a chance to set up a perimeter.

As he ran down the alley, a cacophony of sirens wailed from every direction. More blue lights flashed and spun, around and around. The sound and glare ricocheted off the walls of the broken houses, filling the night.

FORTY-TWO

"How many fingers can you wiggle?" Peter watched as the young boy dutifully wiggled all five fingers poking out of the plastic brace on his lower arm. Peter smiled and scruffed the boy's hair.

"Looks good, champ. Next time, make sure the drain pipe is sturdy before you try to climb it. Even better, don't try to climb it at all. Tottenham or Arsenal?"

The boy sat up straighter. "I'm a Spur."

"Loud and proud, mate. Excellent." Peter pulled a Tottenham sticker from a pocket and placed it prominently on the brace. "Now everyone will know." He kept the Arsenal and West Ham stickers in different pockets.

He turned to the boy's mother. "The swelling should go down in about twenty-four hours, and we'll be able to give him his cast. Make an appointment for the day after tomorrow. Be sure he keeps the brace on." He looked at the beaming boy. "No climbing." Peter strolled to the nursing station to complete the boy's medical chart. He never made it.

Sally Springfield hurried down the corridor, speaking quietly but intently. "Peter. We need you in the trauma room. Stat."

He dropped the chart on the counter and hustled up the corridor with her, listening to her summary of the case.

"Female, approximately forty. Unconscious. Gunshot upper right leg. Pressure bandaged, appears to have missed the femoral artery but possibly clipped her femur. Laceration on face. Severely beaten about her head and torso. Multiple contusions. Probable broken ribs. Breath shallow but regular. Pulse 140 and rising, BP 90 over 50 and falling. O_2 90. Saline drip begun in ambulance."

Hell, Peter thought. A gunshot wound didn't sound right for a domestic. When they turned the corner, he saw a large man with his arm around a crying young woman standing in the corridor outside the trauma room.

"What are they doing here?" Peter asked. "Have them wait out front." Then he recognized the man as Bull. The woman's face was buried in Bull's huge chest, but the bright-red hair told Peter it was the female detective he had seen with Elaine in the interview room. He pulled up short.

Bull croaked. "It's you. Jesus and Mary, it's you! You've got to help her, Doc." He looked at Liz, then back at Peter. "I know you can. I was there, when you saved Benford. For God's sake, help her."

No. Oh God, no. Peter entered the trauma room, pulling on gloves as he went. The sight froze him. They'd made love not four hours earlier and had agreed to make a go of it. Now Elaine was lying on the trolley, bloody and beaten. He wanted to scream out and rush to her. What had happened?

He sensed the young house officer and nurses watching him, waiting for instructions. He needed to get a grip on his emotions. It didn't matter what had happened earlier in the evening; he was the A&E surgeon, and the patient's injuries would not wait. But he would need help.

Peter asked Sally to call in a thoracic surgeon and then snapped into the protocols. Elaine already had an IV, so he called for vital signs and instructed the house officer to insert a tracheal tube and connect a respirator. Her right leg was wrapped in a fairly clean pressure bandage with no sign of heavy bleeding. It looked to be through and through. It could wait. Good paramedics.

The contusions on her chest and abdomen suggested that broken ribs were likely. The racing pulse and dropping blood pressure indicated serious internal bleeding. He checked her pupils and decided to focus first on her abdomen. She would need blood, maybe a lot of it. He told Sally to reserve it. It would be a long night.

★ ★ ★

Six hours later, Peter was out of the operating theater. He and another surgeon had repaired Elaine's lacerated liver but had removed her spleen. They had cleaned the bullet wound, closed the slash on her face, and stabilized her mouth and jaw. Sally had performed the rape protocols.

Peter washed and changed out of his bloody scrubs. Despite the ungodly hour, he called two friends—one who could fix the slash on her face and another who specialized in maxillofacial reconstruction. He went upstairs for one more check on her, then ventured out to give a status.

The waiting room was filled with police officers talking among themselves. Voices trailed off and faces turned as he entered. Bull and Liz sat to the side. Her face was badly bruised.

"Has anyone seen to your injuries?" he asked Liz.

"Yes, thanks." She didn't look up.

Peter recognized the thin, middle-aged man as DCS Cranwell. He was probably the person to speak to for the sake of protocol.

"Things are still a bit touch-and-go, but the outlook is much better than it was a few hours ago," Peter said. "DCI Hope's out of surgery and stable. She'll be under sedation for three or four days. We'll bring her out of it slowly. That's the best way for trauma this serious. Has anyone notified her mother and sisters?"

Cranwell stood. "That's excellent, Dr. Willend. We will notify them as soon as possible. But we need to talk with DCI Hope to find out what happened. How soon . . ."

Peter held up his hand. "I realize you need to interview her, but like I just said, we can't rush it. Even if she were conscious, which she is not, her jaw is broken, so I doubt she could answer you. She's strong and healthy. I have every reason to believe that she'll recover, given time and rest. But it will be at least several days before you can speak with her." He looked from face to face. God, he was tired.

Cranwell cleared his throat. "Yes, I understand, of course." He looked around the room as if he wanted another officer to speak. None did, so he turned back to Peter. "I want to say thank you from all of us who work with Elaine. You saved her life. You have allowed us to keep two people who are dear to us. First DCI Benford and now Elaine. The Metropolitan Police Service owes you a debt of gratitude, Dr. Willend."

Peter wondered if that little speech was spontaneous or if Cranwell had rehearsed it. Either way, it must have been difficult for the officer to say. He didn't respond.

Liz started to speak, but her voice cracked. Bull put his arm around her shoulders and gave her a squeeze. He whispered something in her ear that Peter didn't catch, and she nodded. She finally gathered herself. "What about her face? How will the . . . the cut heal?"

"It's a clean slice, so we were able to close it nicely. Two of my friends will contact the Met about performing the reconstructive surgery to her face and mouth. Is there anything else you need to know right now? If not, I suggest you go home. If there's any change to her condition, we'll let Mr. Cranwell know."

Within a minute, all the officers had filed out except for Bull and Liz, who sat quietly on the sofa, holding hands.

Peter pulled up a chair in front of them. "Elaine will be under sedation for quite some time. Why don't you both go rest?" He looked at Liz. "Do you want me to have another look at your face? No? Okay. Leave me a number, and I'll be sure to call you first if I have any news."

Liz asked, "Did you talk to her? Before, I mean. Did you know?"

"We were together until I came to work. What was I to know?"

Liz shook her head. "Police stuff. I was wondering if she'd talked to you about something that happened today. Yesterday."

"Ah. She told me she had received threats. She was going to stay at my house for a while. It's as secure a place as any. Now why don't you go home."

Halfway down the corridor, she turned back to face him. "I'm glad it was you who took care of her."

Peter looked at his feet. "Yeah. I . . . me too."

A shower and another set of fresh scrubs later, he lay down on a sofa in the staff lounge, wondering what the night's tragedy meant. Elaine had brought change to his life. Since he had given himself permission to need her, he started each morning with her in his life. His emotional numbness, his need to be alone with his past, had been dissipating. Now she was the one who needed him. He would certainly be there for her. He loved her.

They had started building their relationship as equal partners. Now he had undoubtedly saved her life. They were no longer simply man and woman; they were savior and saved. A balance had been tipped. Any focus on the debt of a life owed and gratitude for a life given could topple what they had begun to build. It was a paradox. How each of them solved it would define their relationship or destroy it.

He closed his eyes. God, he was tired. Elaine started calling his name. Diana joined her. They were right in front of him, but for every step he took toward them, they backed farther away. *If only they would wait. Please, just wait for me.* Another voice called his name and he woke.

Sally stood over him. "Are you all right?" He nodded and sat up. Damn dreams.

Peter splashed some water on his face and took the lift to the intensive care suite. Elaine lay in the dim light, covered by white hospital linens, swathed in bandages, sprouting IV tubes and drainage tubes and sensor wires. The rhythmic hiss of the respirator and the soft, regular beep of the monitor were the only sounds. He watched the screen for a minute, then checked the charts. Her vital signs had been steady for the last three hours. Good. Three hours? Had he been asleep that long? He leaned over the bed and stroked the strands of her hair that weren't covered by gauze.

"Hi, sweetheart. You're going to be fine. I have to say, you coppers stick together. Bull, that young detective—Liz, I think—Cranwell, and a bunch of other cops I didn't recognize. They were all here, crammed into the waiting room. There's a constable stationed outside your door. I wouldn't be surprised if Bull hijacked the guy and sat out there around the clock to protect you."

He took her hand. "I didn't tell you last night before I had to go. I e-mailed Kate and Mom about you the other day. I didn't tell everything, of course, but I told them I wanted to make a go of it with you. Mom thinks it's wonderful. Kate is sort of wait-and-see about it, but I could tell she's positive. She's always been territorial about her little brother, but she comes around, eventually. They'll be home soon, and we can have that dinner party we talked about."

"And I do love you." He kissed her forehead and sat by the bed, holding her hand.

FORTY-THREE

"If I'd had my mobile, I could have told her. She must have thought Ximena was me!" Liz broke down sobbing and curled closer on the bed. "I know that's what happened." She was exhausted and scared, reacting to shock and guilt. Bull held her and didn't say anything.

He had told himself much the same thing. If he hadn't stopped for petrol and to clean the fast food rubbish from the car, he would have been with Liz and she wouldn't have a concussion, bruised ribs, and a black eye. It seemed such a little thing at the time. And why hadn't he checked his phone before they left? It was damned hard not to blame himself. Liz and the guv were the two most important women in his life, and he had let both of them down. He needed a lot of forgiveness.

No, they would certainly forgive him. What he needed was atonement.

He remembered what his sergeant in Afghanistan had said when one of his squaddies didn't make it. He held Liz close. "Listen to me, sweetheart. You didn't do this, the Sreckos did—that Nilo bastard and that Anton guy. Get angry at them. Rage against them. But don't blame yourself. They're the bastards who hurt Elaine."

Liz looked up at him and kissed him on the cheek. "It's hard to accept that. I keep asking 'what if,' and it's always down to me."

"Exactly. I think the same thing. But it's not all down to you or me. This maybe could have been prevented weeks ago if someone had done something just a little different. Who knows? But you and me, we can't control the past. The Sreckos planned it and did it. Nilo is dead. The others aren't, though."

He held her face softly between his hands and smiled at her. She didn't look convinced, so he went on. "Cromarty said that Srecko means 'lucky' in Serbian, right?" She nodded and he continued. "It doesn't anymore. Not if Bull and Barker have anything to do with it."

She smiled at him. "Thanks for that. We'll make damn sure we have a say. When do we start?"

That was more like the Liz he knew. He kissed her and wrapped his arms around her. "When we're ready. Right now, I think you need a hot bath and a long sleep."

As soon as he heard the bath water start, Bull slumped back against the sofa. *What the hell had happened in that hole?* He and Liz had arrived at the same time as the ambulance. They had run inside to find blood-spattered walls and Elaine lying unconscious across a table, half-naked. The room reeked of blood. A dead woman was lying on the floor across the room from Elaine. Nilo was sitting against the sofa with a stupid, shocked expression on his face, a Fairbairn dagger sticking out of his neck like some kind of weird second head.

"Wherever you are, you bastard," Bull said to himself, "you need to know that Auntie Dragon got you. She put paid to your bill. I hope you realized that before you died."

Now Elaine lay in the intensive care unit. Doc Willend had said things looked positive. Bull got up from the sofa. Liz would need help and recovery time too. He would deal with the Sreckos later.

★ ★ ★

It was obvious to Peter that the nurse was upset and afraid to talk. She was almost shaking as she spoke. "They came this afternoon. Five or six coppers and some paramedics. Scooped up her medical records and rolled her right out. Matron tried to stop them, find out what they were doing, but they just flashed a paper at her and swept her aside."

Peter was dumbfounded. He had visited Elaine's room before every shift to check on her progress. After his shift, he would sit with her into the early morning hours, reading or playing music to her from his iPod. It had been four days, and today they had begun withdrawing the sedative. He had been looking forward to her being aware of him tonight, but her room was empty.

"Did they say where they were taking her?" he asked.

"No. We tried to find out. One of them said it was for her safety, so they couldn't tell us. Then they were gone with her."

He thanked the nurse and walked back to the lift. So they had her under protection. Until now, there had been a female constable in her room, one large male constable at her door, and another where the corridors crossed. To Peter, that seemed to be plenty of protection. He had never dreamed the Met would spirit her away.

His next thought stunned him like a blow between his eyes. If they were scared enough, they could make it permanent and he may never find her. She could be here in London or on a beach in Virgin Gorda, and he'd never know.

He knew he couldn't let that happen. He had lost Diana forever, and he vowed not to lose Elaine. He wouldn't abandon her.

Elaine still needed medical care, follow-up surgeries, recovery, and rehabilitation. He could try the other surgeons. He didn't think the Met would change surgeons at this point. Even if they did, most of the British medical community was no more than two degrees of separation apart. He could listen to rumors and cajole hints from people who owed him. It would take some prying, maybe some bribing, but someone had to know where she was. Liz and Bull might help, of course, although he couldn't ask them to do something that would damage their careers. He'd start with her reconstructive surgeon.

Besides, Elaine wouldn't tolerate being shut away forever. Even if he couldn't find her, eventually she would find him.

He picked up his mobile and dialed.

FORTY-FOUR

Elaine stood at the window of her seaside cottage, watching a squall move in from the Atlantic. Waves rolled, crested, and crashed the rocks of the headland across the small Devon bay below her. Clouds gathered, as thick and gray as the frothy ocean. Rain obscured the horizon.

She pulled her thick cardigan and her thoughts tighter. Why had Cranwell warned her away from the Sreckos? He had heard of their complaints through "unofficial channels." Why had Jacko granted bail to Greene? Had they been pressured by someone higher up? Had Nilo known her backup wouldn't arrive in time? It made no sense for Jenkins to have had any part in Greene's murder, but why had he been there? Who had sent him?

The longer she thought, the more certain she became that someone in power had a reason to protect the Sreckos. She had been betrayed.

The ormolu clock from her London flat ticked into the surrounding silence. Time to put the tea on. *Coffee. Peter drinks coffee, and he'll be here in a few minutes.*

Her cane clacked on the wooden floor as she hobbled to the kitchen. Three weeks ago, when she first arrived at the cottage, it had taken twenty-five agonizing steps, and as many seconds, to walk fifteen feet to the kitchen door. Now she could make it in ten seconds, using only twelve steps. According to her therapists, that was progress. Maybe in another eight weeks, she could run to the kitchen, they chirped.

She knew that wouldn't happen. Her femur was too weak, even with the plate and its screws. The chunk of quadriceps and biceps femoris muscles that the bullet had carried with it on its way through her leg would never grow back. She'd looked it up and told them she understood the situation, but they continued with the peppy encouragement. It was part of their job.

Scratch hopped up on the kitchen counter as she leaned on it for support. She gave him a stroke under the chin and shook a few kibbles onto a plate to occupy him. When she reached for the coffee, she almost toppled to the floor. Once she had steadied herself, she began to reach again, but the doorbell rang. It was Peter, right on time, damn the man.

"Give me a minute!" she shouted, and she began her shuffle back to the front room.

⋆ ⋆ ⋆

Elaine watched the rain approach and sensed him standing solid, quiet, behind her. He granted her silence for her thoughts, as if he understood that although he had fixed her once, she could not allow him to fix everything.

Liz had told her that when she was unconscious in those first days, Peter would sit next to her bed at all hours, talking, reading, playing music softly to her, or merely sitting in the dark. He had done what people do when they love.

She was under protection in the weeks after they moved her from London, secure and alone. During that time, Peter had given Liz letters enclosed in funny greeting cards, which she forwarded to Elaine at first, then brought with her when she was allowed to visit the cottage. One day a letter from Peter arrived directly. He had finally found her. He asked if she would see him. He would not reveal how he discovered where she was.

Elaine remembered his cathartic revelations during their first pillow talk and how they had talked about doubts, about their careers, and what the stress and uncertainty could do to them. Peter had listened quietly and accepted her concerns without interrupting or making facile denials. His response had been simple and direct, as always. He had said to her, "I'd rather deal with all that than not have you."

She had known then that the passion they shared would last, because she felt the same. She had allowed herself to be more intimate, sooner, with Peter than she had with any man in her life. It didn't take long for her to know he was hers for the asking. That hadn't happened for her before. She had always seen reservation in men, a wariness of her independence and strength. Most men didn't realize that even the strongest woman sometimes needs a soft place to fall.

She owed him her life. What could she say beyond thank you? What will happen here, now, she asked herself.

"Look at me," she said, turning to face him. He already had looked at her, of course. From the moment she opened the door to him, he did not once cast his eyes away nor flinch at what her face had become. He did not react to the cane or her hesitant hobble. She knew that to him, she would never be "poor, damaged Elaine." She would always be the woman he loved.

His palm cupped her cheek. There was no pity in his manner. "I want to be here for you. With you." His love felt as natural as breath, as warm as his hand brushing her skin.

"Oh, Peter." Raindrops rattled against the window. "I don't know where *here* is or where I'm going. Do you understand that?"

"Possibly better than you imagine."

She watched the drops merge on the glass and wander downward, beginning their journey back to the ocean. "Perhaps you do." She did not know how to tell him that she was not ready to make her journey his.

How could he comprehend rape? Every morning she woke in isolation. She shuffled through her day with silent toleration for her therapists, the nurses, the maids who cooked and cleaned for her. Then, when they had gone at the end of the day, she sat in darkness and raged against the helplessness. The unceasing rage turned into acid in her gut, threatening to slowly dissolve the old Elaine and everything she had felt or held dear. She hated much now but not him. She needed vengeance, and she could not ask him to help with that.

"There are things I have to do, and I simply don't care what happens to me when I do them. Did you feel that? When you were in the hospital?"

Peter moved closer. She felt the strength in his arms as he wrapped them around her.

"It's lonely, rebuilding. It's a lot of work. I'll be there for you." His whispers caressed her ear.

If only I could let go of everything and accept his care, she thought. But she could not let go of the questions that constantly whirled in her brain, questions about terror, disfigurement, betrayal.

He stood next to her, looking out the window. "Have the nightmares started?"

"Yes. They warned me about that. I'm in a maze, then I look down at the floor and it's red. I feel something hot against my cheek, and I scream and wake up." She couldn't bring herself to tell him how the helpless anguish of the invasion twisted her mind into knots or how she feared the heat of her own hatred.

"You feel probably the most intense anger you've ever felt in your life, right?"

"It's deeper than that. And I think I never want to let go of it."

"It takes a long time to rebuild. Friends help."

She knew her journey was not one of rebuilding. With every step she took, wrong would feel more right. She did not want to begin that journey without him. Would a man like him even join her on such a quest?

"A long while may be too long." She turned to him and gathered his hands into hers. "I have things to do, things that I can't explain right now. I have to find the right people, and then I have to use them. I must ask them to do things that I could never ask you to do."

His face was quizzical, as if he could not imagine what she was saying, as if he could not comprehend the decision she had made. She needed to finish this.

"When you were desolate and grieving, could you have asked your mother or Kate to do something that you knew went against everything they thought they were? To betray themselves? I mean, you know they would agree if you had asked, but would you have asked them?"

He didn't answer. His normally brilliant-blue eyes had gone gray.

"There are burdens I can't share, darling. If I do, I'll either come to depend on you too much or . . ." She couldn't admit to him that his love might diminish her hatred. She was not ready for that. She held his hands to her breast.

"I'll come to you when I'm free of all this."

He wrapped his arms around her and kissed her as he did the first time. His lips traced the path she would always cherish, brushing softly over her mouth, to her eyes, to her throat, and back to her mouth.

Elaine pressed herself to him, burrowing into his safe, warm place. *How good it feels,* she thought. *Hold on to this.* She closed her eyes, breathed in his scent, and vowed to herself that she would keep the love of this man in her heart. She soaked him in until she could absorb no more.

Then she kissed him softly on his lips, placed her hands on his chest, and gently pushed him away.

ACKNOWLEDGMENTS

I couldn't have written this account of Elaine's journey without the help of many generous and talented friends and teammates. Thanks go to my critique partners—K. P. Gresham, Anna Castle, Connie Newton, Dan Roessler, Clint Whitaker, Gogi Hale, Jan Rider Newman, Michelle Escudier, and Amber Gunst—who kept me focused and learning. I also thank Nona Farris, Linda Ritzen, and Martin Barkley for their astute comments and suggestions.

Many thanks to Bill Woodburn, a remarkable writer, critique partner, and professional counselor. Besides his nuanced critiques, his keen insight into how damaged souls cope with trauma and posttraumatic stress disorder was invaluable.

Retired Detective Chief Superintendent Sue Hill, of the Metropolitan Police Service, gave instrumental guidance on police culture, regulations, and procedure. I promise I listened, Sue, but I write fiction, so any procedural errors in the book are mine alone.

The incredible Deb Rhodes of BetterBetaReads showed me how a reader would look at my story. I cannot recommend her service highly enough.

My deep appreciation goes out to my agent, Elizabeth Trupin-Pulli, for her humor, guidance, and wisdom while beginning my education in the ways of the publishing business. Thank you, Liz! And to Anne Brewer, my editor at Crooked Lane Books, I give my sincere thanks for making Elaine's story better. I cannot thank both of you enough.